The Russian Boomerang

JEAN MILLS

First published in Great Britain by the author in 2019
Copyright © Jean Mills, 2016
First edition, second printing.

The moral right of the author has been asserted.

This is a work of fiction. References to real events and people are only used for historical context or relate to opinions or views of the fictitious character speaking. Names, characters, places and incidents are either the product of the author's imagination or are used factiously, and any resemblance to actual persons, living or dead, business establishments, companies, events or places is entirely coincidental.

All rights reserved. No part of this publication may be reproduced or transmitted in any form or by any means, electronic or mechanical, including photocopy, recording, or any information storage and retrieval system without permission in writing from the author.

Cover design by John S.

Set in 12 pt Tinos Regular
Printed and bound by Ingram Content Group

ISBN: 978-3-00-064012-4
www.russianboomerang.com

This novel is dedicated to Werner,
for his unwavering faith, and to
Gordon Mills who never doubted

"Russia is a riddle wrapped in a
mystery inside an enigma."
Winston Churchill

1

Thursday, 10th February 2011, Moscow, 11.00 a.m.

The black Mercedes ML 500 sped through the busy Moscow traffic with ease. Vanya was a good driver. From the back seat Armen watched the Kremlin disappear out of sight over Vanya's right shoulder. Vanya was not only a good driver; he was a top bodyguard, trained by the elite in close combat at Abel's camp on the outskirts of Moscow. Abel was Armen's trusted friend, business partner and security advisor. Abel had chosen the car Armen was sitting in, had it fitted out with all the necessary extras which included, of course, bullet-proofing. And Vanya was one of Abel's best graduates.

Armen shouted into his Blackberry in Russian. He spent most of his day on the phone and a lot of hours in his car. They would need another thirty minutes to get to Khimki just twenty kilometres north of the centre of Moscow up the Leningradskoe Chaussé, the main road running from the centre of Moscow northwards. Main roads were often called "Chaussé" in Russia, a left-over from the nineteenth century when the upper class in Moscow spoke French rather than Russian. Khimki was built on the main railway line from Moscow to St. Petersburg in 1939 during the Stalin era. St. Petersburg was called Leningrad in those days. Today no-one wanted to talk about Lenin and used names of the past, names that existed before the communist revolution and had less emotional effect on the generations still alive. After the Second Wold War, Khimki's proximity to Moscow city centre, its large population of 200,000 people and good rail and road connections were ideal for aerospace defence development projects. Khimki was situated just outside the Moscow city boundary, not in the jurisdiction of the powerful mayor of Moscow who needed support from the Khimki city council to build the new Moscow-St. Petersburg motorway which was planned to go straight through the forest surrounding Khimki. Building roads was a federal issue but making sure federal projects went ahead was a matter for political lobby at the highest level. Until October 2010, Yury Luzhkov had been the Mayor of Moscow. Luzhkov, one of Putin's men, fell out of favour when he was unable to defend Moscow against the smog from the wildfires in the summer of 2010. So President Medvedev fired him and replaced him with his own political ally, Sergei Sobyanin. That was the day Armen knew he had to double his precautions. Doing business in Moscow was like a continuous game of chess and he had just lost one of his main pieces on the board, one of his knights. And now this ridiculous statement that Sobyanin had made at a breakfast meeting in Davos in Switzerland. Armen had cursed as he had seen Sobyanin's statement repeated on

Ren-TV this morning by some foreign correspondent. Armen's voice was loud and high-pitched as he shouted into his cell phone:

"Who on earth does Sergei think he is? What did he say? 'We are removing everything that hinders business.' Did I hear correctly? Everything that hinders business? Has the Swiss air gone to his head?"

There was a short silence as Armen tried to listen to Abel's voice but he couldn't concentrate on what he was saying. His blood pressure had soared, his red face fixed in anger and his eyes as cold as ever.

"I don't care, Abel. We need to ensure that all our business activities can carry on without interference, and I mean all of them. Your production licence for vodka doesn't run out till the end of next year. My import licence for wine will expire at the end of February. I know that import licences are a federal matter but Sergei's comments just prove openly what's going on everywhere. We were the ones who built the economy, gave people jobs. And now they want to investigate our businesses, cancel our licences, even put some of us in jail. Abel, we have to meet to discuss how the Conseil should react."

The Conseil was a group of seven business partners with multi-million empires and a mutual interest in certain activities. This was no longer the nineteen nineties with its mafia clans. This was the twenty-first century and business interests were at stake. Abel was the primary contact for all the members of the Conseil.

It was interesting how the heads of these multi-million

empires referred to themselves as the Conseil, not a Russian word but a French word. Throughout the last three hundred years, ever since the Age of Enlightenment, the Russian upper classes embraced French culture and French became their language of preference for polite conversation and intellectual discussion. Russian was for the masses, the romantics, the poor. The resurgence of the Russian language at the beginning of the twentieth century became an ideological principal after the Revolution and pride in all things Russian had increased even more over the last twenty years, after the end of the communist era in Russia. However, some habits are emotional and die hard. Armen may have been driving a German car but that was a decision based on security and functionality. He spoke good English because he needed to converse with international business partners. When it came to culture, he spoke French, drank red wine from Bordeaux, ate foie gras and took his favourite girlfriends to Paris on holiday.

Abel agreed reluctantly with Armen's suggestion and said he would arrange a meeting for that evening. He put down the phone and sighed. Armen really was extremely headstrong and very irritable. He wasn't sure that the Conseil really did need to meet this evening to discuss Armen's problems with the licensing authorities. This was Russia and such problems were a day to day reality. They all had to cope with the way business was done in Russia and if Armen couldn't cope any more, then he was on his own. The Conseil had more important things to do and the most important task of all was to ensure that each member abided by the rules they had laid down almost thirteen years ago, in September 1998 after the bank crisis in Russia.

Abel looked out the window of his office at the beautiful gardens within the walls of his industrial compound just sixty kilometres from the traffic jams in the centre of Moscow. He was powerful, rich but isolated, living behind walls and followed everywhere by bodyguards. He was respected not only by the business world but also by the Russian army. He had connections in high places and was a weapons and armoured vehicle expert. He had help develop the Boomerang armoured personnel carrier. The first model had just been replaced by a more advanced vehicle. His work as a consultant for the Russian army had won him a lot of friends and allies including the head of the Liberal Democratic Party, Valdimir Zhironovsky. Zhironvsky was often viewed as a right-wing opposition leader but for insiders he was a Kremlin servant used to float populist and radical ideas to test public reaction. Abel sighed again and walked over to his desk to phone the other members of the Conseil.

Half an hour later Abel put the phone down for the fifth time and mentally ticked off one more name on the list. He had just invited the last member of the Conseil to dinner that evening, in one of the private rooms of his favourite restaurant, Nostalgie, at eight-thirty. All the members of the Conseil knew what it meant when Abel invited them for dinner. They would all be there with no questions asked. Nothing could be more important to this elite group of businessmen. An invitation from Abel overruled all other prior commitments. Abel had given instructions to his assistant and head of security, Volodya, to ring the restaurant immediately to book their room and check it out at seven thirty before he and his guests arrived. The manager of Nostalgie was on their payroll and a good friend and trusted ally.

Armen's car reached the end of Leningradskoe Chaussé and the main road emerged from the city with its blocks of flats on either side to become the M10 motorway, just before they reached the signpost to Khimki. They passed a huge shopping complex with illuminated signs for IKEA and Auchan, the French hypermarket chain which the Russians spelt Ashan. To pronounce "au" in Russian they would have had to use a curious combination of letters which would look unnatural, foreign, not Russian, which, of course, Auchan was. The French hypermarket chain was doing well in Russia with its large assortment, fresh produce, wide aisles and underground car parks. Khimki was a typical target community for foreign investment. The population of Khimki had above average disposable income. The city wasn't far from Sheremetyevo airport which was the home of the Russian airline Aeroflot and where most of their planes were based. The airport had been renovated in 2005 and was now a very modern and efficient airport. Its concourses had been renamed into Terminal A, B, V and D, the first four letters of the Russian alphabet. Armen looked out of the car window. The forest was beautiful and very Russian. He always felt quite moved by the mystic beauty of Russian forests. Passengers landing at Sheremetyevo could see miles and miles of coniferous trees enveloping the city like a protective medieval wall when approaching the airport from the west. The forest was part of Russian tradition and the plans to build a motorway from Moscow to St. Petersburg meant cutting through this beautiful landscape. It was a great shame but he knew that the new motorway was an absolute necessity for Russia's and Moscow's infrastructure. Even if Armen was Armenian by birth, not Russian, he knew the Russian soul better than most. However, he was pragmatic about such decisions. He wasn't an environmentalist. He was a businessman. It was his aim to make money, lots of money, which he used not only for himself and his family but also to enhance the Armenian cause throughout the world and to sponsor projects in Armenia to build hospitals, schools and housing for those less fortunate than himself. His money subsidised one of the chairs at Yerevan State University and helped buy equipment for the famous medical school. As a boy he had grown up in Armenia which was then part of the Soviet Union. His grandmother had told him stories of the former glory of Armenia, the very first state to adopt Christianity as a state religion in AD 301. In those days Armenia was such a large country. Parts of present-day Turkey, Iran and Iraq were within Armenia's borders in the medieval tales of brave warriors and happy families that his grandmother had learnt from her grandmother. Mount Ararat, the symbol of Armenia and the mountain where Noah's Ark is said to have come to rest after the Great Flood, was geographically within the borders of the Kingdom of Armenia in those days. Today it was in Turkey but it could be seen from Armenia and the psychological bond between Armenians and Mount Ararat, their national symbol, was as strong as it had ever been.

Armen straightened his tie as his Mercedes passed the main gate of RusAeroSpace, the largest aerospace concern not only in Khimki but in the whole of Russia. Armen was proud to be on the board of such a strategically important company. All the other members of the board were Russians, born and bred. But after the bank crisis in 1998 the Chairman of the Board had recognised the need to harness all the elements of power, both financial and political, in the top echelons of the company and had approached Armen with an offer that he not only couldn't refuse but which also fulfilled some of his burning ambitions. The barrier to the long drive that led to RusAeroSpace Headquarters had already been raised and the guard saluted as Vanya drove past. He pulled up at the front door and jumped out to open the door for his boss, looking around quickly, lifting his head to take a glimpse at the office windows and taking in the whole surroundings in a couple of seconds. This was a routine he never neglected wherever he was. He may be on friendly territory but his job was to make sure that his boss got around quickly and safely, not only on the road but also in and out of buildings securely. Danger could be looming anywhere. Power always bred enemies and money created envy. And in Russia the top five per cent of the population made a lot of money, billions. Business partners Armen knew of or some he even knew personally still disappeared mysteriously or drowned while yachting in the Caribbean.

Being a high-flyer in Moscow was a dangerous occupation and he spent a lot of money on security.

Vanya handed Armen his black leather attaché case and both men walked with long strides towards the entrance to the huge glass building, Vanya towering over his boss. They walked through the automatic doors and across the shining black tiles of the hallway towards the polished wood reception desk where Armen was met by the Chairman of the Board, Evgeni Shopkin. Evgeni walked forward with open arms as he saw Armen.

"My dear Armen, Privyet, welcome" he said as they embraced, first the left cheek, then the right. The skin of the cheeks touched lightly in greeting. "How wonderful to see you and you look so well. Kak dyelá? How's business?"

"Privyet, Zhenya, " Armen replied, using the familiar diminutive of Evgeni's first name. "Khorosho, fine, just fine," he added as they walked towards the lift. "Has everyone arrived?" Armen asked, hoping that some of the other members of the board who were notorious for their lack of punctuality had been called to order by the Chairman due to the seriousness of the topic. Armen had been brought up in a culture which didn't consider discipline an essential virtue. However, most Armenians had an acute sense of business and wasting his time was wasting his money. Punctuality was therefore not a courtesy as far as he was concerned but an integral part of business ethics.

"Yes, surprisingly all on time," retorted Evgeni with a mischievous wink in Armen's direction. They walked to the lift that the bell-boy had kept open. The young man in a pristine uniform with polished gold buttons and accurate creases in his trouser legs pressed the button for the fifth floor, walked back out of the lift and touched his cap as the doors closed.

Armen closed his eyes for a split second, a silent protest at the long meeting ahead of them, the long-winded arguments from some who would, at the end of the day, accept the decision in the interests of reason and increased wealth. Not only the country's wealth, but their own individual fortunes. The meeting would be inevitably long and he would have to control his impatience. After all, the lobbying he and his closest allies had done over the last few weeks was about to pay off and it was of the utmost importance that everyone agreed to the resolution which had been put forward. Armen took a long deep breath and braced himself. This was going to be a day to remember.

*

Thursday, 10th February 2011, Moscow, 2.00 p.m.

In the FSB headquarters in Moscow Inspector Vladimir Antipov listened to a voice clip from their monitoring unit. The word that had been picked up by the voice monitor was "Conseil". Inspector Antipov had been observing the Conseil for some months now. He was part of the URPO, a specialist department within the FSB, the Russian secret service which dealt with matters inside Russia. The URPO had been founded in 1996 and had about a hundred and fifty specialists fighting organised crime, some of them undercover agents within criminal organisations working under very dangerous conditions. Inspector Antipov listened to the voice clip again. He knew that Abel Plemyannikov was the head of this organised group of oligarchs and that Armen Makaryan was a member. He sat back in his chair and thought about the information he had just received. He could make out a few words and the fact that they were to meet that evening. He knew that the Conseil usually met over dinner in an expensive restaurant called "Nostalgie". Attempts to gather information from the restaurant had proven impossible and the URPO had decided to send an undercover agent to seek employment at the restaurant with a reference from a high class hotel. But the agent wasn't in place yet. Photos of the people going in to the restaurant and coming out again could at least demonstrate that his evidence up to now was correct. He picked up the phone and rang his boss. He needed a surveillance team and photos of Nostalgie's main entrance with all the guests entering and leaving in the next twenty four hours. He needed car registration numbers, make of car and colour. His boss listened to his request and granted it. Vladimir Antipov put the phone down. That's what he liked about the URPO and the FSB. No unnecessary bureaucracy. Short lines of communication, a good argument and done. He looked at his watch and picked up his mobile. He wouldn't receive the transcript of any snippets of conversation the monitoring unit had managed to pick up until later that afternoon. As the phone rang on the other end he walked to the coffee machine and pressed "Americano". A young female voice answered the phone with the usual nonchalant "Allo".

"Hi, Natasha, it's Volodya," he answered. "Is everything OK with Katya?"

"Sure, everything's fine. We went to the park this morning and she really enjoyed ice-skating with a group of kids. She ate all her dinner and had a rest after lunch. She's drawing a picture for you in her bedroom. Would you like to speak to her?"

"Yes, put her on."

"But don't tell her you know about the picture. It's a secret."

"I won't. Look, I don't think it'll be too late tonight but have your supper without me just in case."

"OK. No problem," the friendly, up-beat voice said. "Here's Daddy to speak to you," Natasha said. There was a little scream of pleasure in the background and his daughter, Katya, grabbed the handset.

"Daddy, Daddy! Are you coming home soon?"

"Not yet, sweetheart. I've got to do a bit more work. But I'll be home to kiss you goodnight and on the weekend we'll be able to spend a lot of time together."

"Can we watch a DVD?"

"Sure. Be a good girl for Natasha and I'll see you later."

"OK." She gave the phone back to Natasha.

"Thanks, Natasha. I'll see you later."

OK," she said and hung up.

He looked out of the window. Katya was just seven

years old. Since his wife died a year ago in a car accident his daughter had had a difficult time. With no grandparents nearby to help, no relatives at all in Moscow, he had hired a full-time nanny, Natasha, who worked 24/7 if necessary. He loved his daughter and still missed his wife bitterly. He blamed himself for her death. She was driving his car when the accident happened because her car was in for a service. It was never proven but all the evidence indicated that the four-wheel drive that rammed the car she was driving had actually expected him to be at the wheel. The driver had got out, gone to the driver's seat and drawn a gun. An eye-witness said that he looked quite shocked at the sight of the driver through the dark windows, put the gun back in its holster and drove away. One of his really reliable informants, high up in the right circles, had confirmed that a hit-man had been hired to remove him. They never caught the driver. In the file it was just another unsolved hit and run case, one of hundreds in Russia's busy capital. At her funeral he had thought that he should never have joined the FSB and definitely not the UPRO with a wife and daughter. But now his wife was gone it was too late to make amends. He loved his daughter and would do anything to protect her and make sure that she was happy. Tatiana's death had reinforced his will to destroy organised crime in Moscow and the Conseil was a big part of it. He wasn't going to hide from them, however many hit-men they hired. But he had become more cautious. He didn't want his daughter to grow up an orphan.

2

Thursday, 10th February 2011, Germany, 12.00 p.m.

There was a February chill in the air but the vineyard was bathed in sunshine. The sky was a brilliant blue and there wasn't a cloud in sight. Thomas looked up, stretched his back, wiped a bead of sweat from his forehead then carried on pruning his vines. The electric cutter clicked as he chose the place to cut the vine. He left two canes from last year's growth, one to bend to the right of the vine, one to the left. He had learnt how to cut and trellis Riesling vines from his grandfather. As a trained viticulturist he also knew that this way of trellising wasn't only traditional, it had been proven to be the best method for Riesling vines in the south-west of Germany. He snipped the canes and left the wood to hang loosely in the wires. Svetlana's eldest son, Misha, would collect all the dead wood in the next few days. At the age of fourteen, Misha always looked forward to doubling his pocket money by helping in the vineyards. Ever since Svetlana had moved in with Thomas seven years ago, he had treated her sons, Misha and his younger brother Alex, as if they were his own flesh and blood, the family he had never had.

Thomas examined the next vine and decided which canes to cut off and which to leave. His forty acres of vineyards in the Alsenz valley were all on steep sandstone slopes. A blessing for the vines, well-drained soil and vineyards at an acute angle to the sun, but it meant quite a lot of manual work. He didn't mind that at all. For him, being able to work outside was a welcome break from the other tasks he had as owner of a wine estate and wine broker business. At the age of thirty-nine Thomas had re-built the wine estate his father and grandfather had loved so much. His father would have been proud, he thought, as he moved on to the next row of vines.

The winter had been quite hard. In December the south-westerly winds had brought snow. Misha and Alex had pleaded with Thomas for days and in the end he had succumbed and bought the boys a toboggan. They had been so excited about a white Christmas at long last, a rare treat in this part of Germany. The snow had melted in the New Year with the rivers swelling as the water drained off the hills into the river and moved downstream. The first two weeks of January had been quite mild and dry. Then suddenly the wind turned and the temperature dropped. The high pressure zone over Russia had brought in the usual light easterly winds with freezing but dry air. No rain and snow, thank goodness. As long as the ground was dry and the vines couldn't suck up too much moisture, they were extremely resilient to very low temperatures. The end of January had been very cold with temperatures dropping at night to twenty degrees centigrade below zero. If the vines had been full of moisture, the water would have frozen and split the wood, killing them. As he walked along the row he was pleased to see that all of the vines were healthy and had survived the hard winter.

The alarm on his watch started ringing and broke his concentration. It was ten past twelve and time to pack up his cutter and drive back home to lunch and the office. He walked down the steep slope listening to the sound of his boots on the gravelly soil. It reminded him of his childhood, helping his father and grandfather as they pruned the vines in exactly the same way. He smiled. "Schön," he thought with satisfaction "good that some things don't change."

As a schoolboy there had been absolutely no doubt in his mind that he would follow in his father's footsteps. Good vineyards, a hundred-year-old farmhouse with enough room for all the family, three maybe even four generations, a business that was worth working for and that would be his own one day. He had worked hard at school. His grandmother used to say that he was industrious and diligent - two words which were typical for her generation. Such a compliment expressed for her the best possible characteristics anyone could and should possess. Omi Nate, as he used to call her when he was a toddler and couldn't pronounce her name, grew up during the Weimar Republic in the nineteen twenties. As a teenager in the nineteen thirties she joined the Hitler Youth movement. In those days a bike-ride to Kirn with a picnic and a campfire was the highlight of her summer holidays. And the Hitler Youth

Club organised everything, even leant bikes to the poorer children who didn't have one. All the teenagers looked forward to these outings and in their naivety thought that the outings were organised to please them, not to indoctrinate them. He smiled at the thought of how his clued-on step sons with their multi-media talents would react if he suggested a similar outing. No way, he thought. Omi Nate was strict, hard-working and never questioned any form of authority, be it the family doctor, a policeman or the government. Authority instilled respect and she had been brought up to accept the will of authority. It had taken her a long time to accept that the authorities in Nazi Germany in the thirties and early forties had abused their power and a fact she rarely dwelled upon for any length of time. That was over and done with and she had got on with surviving in post-war Germany. In German they were called Trümmerfrauen, Women of the Ruins, women who had often lost their husbands and helped to clear the ruins of bombed sites with their bare hands and re-construct buildings.

He laid his thermos flask on the passenger seat of his blue Ford Ranger and put his cutter on the floor in front of the seat. He didn't bother to take his jacket off for the short ride home. He got in, started the engine and drove slowly along the grass track then turned left on to the country lane. He drove down the steep winding lane until he reached the T-junction at the bottom. As he stopped, one of the farmers in the village, Sven, turned to look to see who was passing by. In this farming area with its small villages and hamlets, everyone knew everyone else. Thomas opened his window and greeted Sven with a congenial smile.

"Hi, Sven, how's the winter barley doing?" he asked.

"Not too bad," Sven replied. "And your vines?"

"No frost damage so far. See you at the ball on Rose Monday," he said, closing his window and looking at the traffic left and right on the main road. He waved to Ulrike who was looking out of her kitchen window across the road and turned left on to the main road which ran through the Alsenz valley. He drove through Hochfeld with its smart new housing estate on the right, the little church with its pretty little spire on the left. He passed the village pond that was very quiet at this time of year, just a few wild ducks. The geese wouldn't be back until March or April when the weather became milder.

The Alsenz was quite a fast flowing river and flanked on both sides by tall, slim poplar trees which marked its course through the village. On both sides of the river the fields were only used for grazing horses and sheep, not for arable crops, as spring and summer floods were quite frequent. A small stream ran into the village pond not far from the church and the pond fed another stream which flowed into the river, just before the white water splashed over a weir. He drove past the old mill and the last farmhouse at the end of the village and admired the view as he emerged from the patchwork of cottages, houses, outbuildings and barns. The sun was behind him and was shining on the south-facing slopes of the hill just a mile in front of him with its neat rows of vines. At the bottom of the hill lay his little village, Unterbach, with its large stone church built over six hundred years ago. The church was far too big for the village, out of all proportion. It hadn't been built for the villagers. Originally it had been built as a church for the lords of Randfels castle at the top of Schlossberg hill and a secure defence in the troubled times of the Middle Ages. The ruined castle of Randfels was one of many medieval castles built in the twelfth century which were destroyed by the French army as it retreated in 1690 after the War of Succession between France and Germany, or rather one of the German princedoms of the south. The castle had never been completely rebuilt and in the middle of the nineteenth century most of the villagers had used the empty ruin as a source of precious sandstones to build their houses and barns. In fact, one of the cornerstones of Thomas' barn had the date 1174 etched into the soft yellow sandstone surface.

At the next junction he turned right on to the country road that meandered into the village of Unterbach. He passed the yellow sign with the village name on it and reduced his speed to a sauntering thirty kilometres an hour. The main street was narrow and the old farmhouses and cottages bordered the road and there was no footpath. Most of them had no driveway and he was always wary of children, dogs and cats suddenly emerging from the darkness of a porch or from behind a half-open farmyard gate.

Thomas arrived at his farmhouse in Unterbach, drove through the open wrought iron gate and stopped on the cobble stones of the front yard. He looked at the sandstone facade of the house with a feeling of satisfaction. He had spent a very large sum of money on the house in the last five years and it showed. New wooden windows with wooden shutters, all freshly painted in his favourite colour, Bordeaux red. The colour was a stunningly effective contrast to the yellow sandstone. It had taken three stonemasons from Lithuania two months to clean and re-joint all the stonework. It had been expensive but worth it. The house had never looked more beautiful. The carpenter in the next village had done a great job making new doors for the barn, the stables and all the various outbuildings. The large oak cellar door was his pride and joy. It led to the barrel cellar, tasting-room, re-corking clinic and wine storage rooms beyond. The heavy door opened slowly and Svetlana stepped into the yard with a bottle basket in her hand which contained six wine bottles. Her long blonde hair was tightly pulled back in a ponytail and she was warmly wrapped in a sheepskin jacket. Her blue eyes lit up and she smiled as she saw Thomas' car, although she could only see his outline through the dark windows. He smiled back fondly, admiring her beautiful face that looked as if it had been lifted from a Russian icon. He opened his window and called out to her.

"What's for lunch," he said. "I'm starving."

"You always are," she replied. "I was just getting a bottle of wine to open for lunch. I've cooked Misha's favourite, slow-cooked beef with horseradish sauce and steamed potatoes."

"You spoil that lad," he said shaking his head in complicity and reaching for his cutter under the glove compartment and his empty thermos flask on the passenger seat.

"Alex likes it, too, and I can't remember you ever leaving it on your plate!"

There was an excited bark and Blackie, the family dog, leapt through the cellar door, bounded over the yard in a feigned gallop and jumped up at Thomas, reaching his chest with his paws and almost licking his face.

"Down," Thomas said, and the dog sat in front of him with his head cocked to one side. Blackie looked like a mixture between a German shepherd and a Labrador. He was the friendliest dog Thomas had ever had, rescued as a puppy by a dogs' home and forever grateful to his new owners for all the care and attention they gave him. He was "old faithful" to Svetlana and at the age of six a clever companion and watchdog. Thomas walked through the front door of the house with the dog at his heels. He took his shoes off by the door and put on the sandals he wore around the house. He hung up his thick jacket and laid the cutter on the dresser.

"It needs sharpening", he said. "I'll take it into Frank this afternoon when I pick up the corks."

He walked into the large farmhouse kitchen. The kitchen was warm and cosy, the kind of warmth you only get from a wood fire. Last year he and Svetlana had bought a Wamsler oven. It was split into two halves – the one half was fired by wood to heat the room and you could cook on the top of the stove; the other half had an electric oven and hob, ideal for cooking, baking and roasting. Svetlana had found it in one of the numerous kitchen shops she had visited, looking for an oven that would allow her to cook all the modern recipes she collected but give the kitchen that farmhouse romance she felt it deserved. The wooden fire was a pile of red-hot cinders and on top of the stove there was a pot of potatoes and a huge pot of beef. Alex and Misha were sitting at the large wooden table, each with a glass of milk.

Thomas looked in their direction and walked to the sink.

"Hi, boys, how was school?"

Alex groaned as Thomas washed his hands at the sink. "Terrible," he said. "Mrs. Hartmann has gone on maternity leave and we've got this stupid new teacher, Mr. Studert. More like Mr. Stupid, if you ask me. He looks as if he's come straight from the army or the police force."

"You just don't like maths, that's all" said his elder brother, Misha. "He doesn't look that bad."

"How would you know?" Alex scorned. "You haven't had him yet. And he's given us half an hour's homework to hand in tomorrow before nine."

"Sounds OK to me," said Thomas suppressing a smile. "Maybe he actually wants to teach you something about maths. Could it be he's actually an enthusiastic teacher? They do exist, I'm told."

Thomas wasn't a great fan of the German school system and couldn't resist a little dig at a profession he felt mainly contempt for. He still held on to his romantic vision that teaching was a calling. For him teaching meant total dedication to giving youngsters the right tools to cope with the vagaries of life. Most of the teachers he'd met since the boys had started at the local school were more interested in making sure their pupils got high scores in exams to secure their own status and, the most important topic, when the summer holidays would start. Svetlana walked into the kitchen with the wine basket and a small bunch of snowdrops and put them in a tiny crystal vase.

"Did you pick them in the garden?" Thomas asked.

"Yes, next to the barn where they get a lot of sun. It's a wonder that Blackie had left the bulbs unturned." she said with a laugh in her voice. "I think he's been looking for bones again:"

She washed her hands and looked at Misha and Alex.

"OK, boys, time for lunch. Misha, you put the meat and potatoes on the table. Alex, you take the plates and I'll bring the sauce. Tommy, can you tell Conrad that lunch is ready, please."

To an outsider she may have sounded like the commander of an army but Thomas knew she ran their household in a very efficient manner. And he loved her for it.

Thomas ran up the stairs two at a time and knocked at his brother's bedroom door. Conrad, his elder brother, answered with a loud, deep "Come in" and Thomas stepped into Conrad's world.

"Hi, Conrad, what are you doing?" Thomas asked.

Conrad turned round and smiled as only he could smile. "It's a secret," he said turning to his desk and covering up a small radio with his huge hands.

"Lunch is ready," Thomas announced, feigning disinterest.

Conrad looked a little disappointed. He had been working on his radio ever since he got back from work and had been waiting for someone to discover it.

"I'll show it to you if you want," he said, revealing a small radio with half of its innards hanging out.

"Where did you get that?" Thomas asked with a frown, anticipating the answer he was going to receive.

"I bought it at the flea market. The man said it only needed a new battery but I think it's more than that. I'm going to repair it," Conrad announced as if this was the easiest task in the world.

"How much did it cost you," Thomas asked and his brother turned his back on him and looked down at the bundle of wires hanging out of the back of the radio.

"Not much," Conrad said evasively and added, "I'm hungry," as he got up to go downstairs.

Thomas turned to go and Conrad followed him. Thomas knew instinctively that Conrad had probably spent all his pocket money on his new radio. It was a source of constant sadness that other people abused Conrad's simple mindedness. His brother had a form of autism and needed continuous guidance. But it wasn't possible to look over his shoulder twenty-four hours a day. Thomas had felt responsible for his brother ever since their mother had died almost seven years ago, just before Svetlana moved in. Thomas and Conrad walked into the kitchen to a slightly reproachful look from Svetlana.

"Well, you two took your time," she said and started serving lunch. Thomas kissed her on her neck and whispered in her ear. "Sorry, I was admiring Conrad's new radio."

She turned her head to look at Thomas and gave him an indulgent smile. Svetlana had got used to Conrad's habit of buying everything he could from silver forks to electric razors.

Thomas smiled back and sat down at the table. He watched Svetlana and thought she looked just as young and beautiful as the day he had met her in 1993. He remembered as if it were yesterday, how she had walked into his life at university. What a fool he had been to neglect her and let her walk out of his life again after just six months. That was seventeen years ago. He had been so busy trying to cope with his degree course and keep the wine estate going after his father's death just four years before. Thomas just didn't have any spare time at all to spend on a rather demanding girlfriend. She may have a German passport but there was no denying her Russian origins. She had lived in Novosibirsk until she was eighteen when she matriculated in 1991. Her father died that year and her mother decided to move back to Moscow with Svetlana and her younger sister Olesya, to the throbbing capital of Russia, where she as a girl had grown up. Svetlana loved Moscow and was thrilled when she was accepted at the Faculty of Languages and Area Studies to continue her study of German Language and Literature at the world famous Moscow State University, still known to most Muscovites as Lomonosov University. She spent twelve months in Germany in the third year of her language studies, to perfect her knowledge of the language. After she graduated in 1995, she returned to Mainz where she had spent her year abroad. Svetlana was highly strung and in those days she believed, as many of her Russian girlfriends did, that the male sex was born to be the provider and that his main task in life was to spoil her. That was one of the reasons, no doubt, why her marriage to Klaus had failed. She had only known Klaus for a few months when she discovered she was pregnant and they got married in April 1996, just five months before Misha was born. Alex was born three years later. The responsibility of bringing up her family had changed Svetlana. She had matured but was still as extravagant as she used to be. She seemed to be happy living with him and the boys, caring for Conrad, helping Thomas with his work and managing the house. He loved her dearly and she loved him but he sometimes wondered if she missed the attraction of a big city with its shopping malls, theatres, discotheques and lots of friends. He knew that having a bank account in Russia, a flat in Moscow and enough money to spend as she liked also helped their relationship along. It financed Svetlana`s frequent trips to Moscow to visit and help her mother. Their patchwork family seemed to be working and who was he to philosophise about her motivation and her character. After all, he wasn't a saint either and, as Omi Nate always said, no-one's perfect, only a perfect fool.

3

Thursday, 10th February 2011, Podolsk, 3.00 p.m.

At three o'clock in the afternoon a forty-foot truck approached the fortified steel gate of Vodalko on the outskirts of Podolsk, forty kilometres south of Moscow, not far from Domodedovo airport. The sun was gradually sinking behind the forest to the west in the clear blue sky. The temperature had dropped in the night to minus twenty degrees centigrade. The roads had been clear, thank goodness, but the driver of the truck, Pavel, was pleased to have arrived with no long traffic jams or unnecessary hold-ups at Customs or elsewhere. The temperature regulator in his refrigerated truck would keep the temperature of the wine inside at around ten degrees centigrade but you never could rely on these reefers to work for the whole journey. He had switched the system off when he reached the signpost that said "Moscow 150 km" to save diesel. The goods would cool down a bit due to the freezing temperature outside but that wasn't such a bad thing. It meant the polythene wrapping around the pallets wouldn't sweat when the cold February air hit it when he unloaded at the warehouse. It had taken him almost four days from Bad Kreuznach in the south-west of Germany to Podolsk on the Berlin route through the south of Poland and then the south of Lithuania and Latvia to join the M9 motorway in Russia. It was a longer route than driving as the crow flies west-northwest but it meant he didn't have to drive through Belarus. Pavel wasn't the only Lithuanian truck driver who preferred driving through familiar territory on his way to Russia from Germany rather than put themselves at risk in Belarus. The government in Minsk was just too unpredictable and the police eager to cash in on a few bribes knowing that the truck drivers were always on a tight schedule and had a wallet full of foreign currency.

He had crossed the border into Russia with no problem at all. The Russian customs agents had insisted on his truck being weighed but the weights in his documents were correct and they didn't bother to check his load. His final destination was Podolsk and his load would be checked again by Russian Customs when he arrived. Once he was in Russia he kept on the M9 highway until he reached "The Road of Death", the outer ring-road around Moscow officially known as the MKAD but nicknamed the road of death by all who used it because of its poor lighting and notorious reputation for fatal accidents. Fortunately he only had thirty kilometres to drive along the MKAD, from the west to the south. A couple of months ago he had had to drive almost all the way round the five-lane highway to drop off three loads, all one hundred and ten kilometres of it. Terrible! He sighed with relief as he drew up at the gate to Vodalko and touched his cap in a friendly greeting to the two guards at the top of their towers on each side of the gate. The brakes of his truck hissed loudly in the crisp, February air. He reached over for his transport documents and his ID. He had stopped a couple of kilometres back in a lay-by to put on his fur-lined windcheater which he now zipped right up to his chin. He grabbed his fur yshanka with ear flaps to keep out the cold and his heavy duty gloves. He opened the door of his cabin and jumped down to greet the guard who had waited for him to get out before venturing out of his hut. It wasn't warm inside the hut but it was a lot warmer in the hut than outside on a winter day in the middle of Russia.

The guard recognised the face of the driver who had been to Podolsk many times before. He greeted him and took his ID and transport documents. He checked the seal on the back of the truck and walked all the way round the truck just to make sure that there was no visible damage or signs of a break-in or sabotage. Although Lithuania was now part of the European Union and had been independent since the early nineties, most Lithuanians spoke Russian which they had learnt at school during the Soviet era. And about a quarter of Lithuania's population spoke Russian as their mother tongue. Nevertheless, there was no love lost between Russians and Lithuanians. Their history of ruler and ruled went back hundreds of years. It wasn't only in Soviet times that Lithuania had been annexed by the Russian bear. The history of oppression dated back to the eighteenth century and had bred mistrust and a deep dislike of each other.

Pavel was looking forward to his lunch. There was a canteen at Vodalko with good coffee, warm porridge and maybe some meat and potatoes for good measure. Sonya, the canteen manager, was always good to him and he never forgot to bring some little present from Germany or elsewhere which she could show her friends and brag about. The guard went into his hut, stamped the documents, signed with his initials and handed the documents back to Pavel. The heavy steel gate started to open slowly, like an ancient drawbridge to a medieval castle. As the gate opened the guard checked that all the CCTV cameras were activated in the whole complex, observing the trucks, their drivers, the loads being unloaded, checked and stored in the warehouse. Vodalko was a thoroughly modern factory and storage facility. The guard had given him a ticket with Gate 12 printed on it. Pavel backed up his truck to the shutters with number twelve printed on them and waited for the shutters to open. He jumped out as they were raised and greeted the young man in a similar windcheater and yshanka as his own. The only difference was the orange sleeveless reflective vest with "Vodalko" printed on the back in black which he wore over his windcheater. He broke the seal on the handle of the truck doors at the back, checked the number against the documents and ticked the seal number as correct and intact. Pavel knew the routine and watched carefully. The doors of his truck were opened, the restraining bars which held the load in place removed and the twenty-nine pallets inside were taken out one by one by a fork lift truck and the label on the side scanned and taken to a pre-arranged numbered spot in the warehouse. The fork lift driver scanned the sign above the warehouse bay and then scanned the pallet again. The system was fully automatic. Once the pallets had been stored, every movement was tracked by the warehouse computer. The pallet codes contained all the information the warehouse needed – supplier, wine, the date of arrival and the number of the shipment. Vodalko had a system which left no room for manipulation, fraud, loss or damage, or so it seemed. Pavel waited until all the pallets had been safely transported to their designated resting place without any damage or breakage. The young man in the orange vest signed the documents – all pallets received – no external damage. Pavel thanked him, stored the restraining bars, closed the rear doors of his truck and then jumped into the cabin again. He drove to the parking lot and parked his truck alongside three others, all of them Russian. He jumped out, rubbed his gloved hands and smiled at the thought of a warm, satisfying meal.

As soon as the truck had arrived, Yuri, the warehouse manager, had rung Transmir to confirm its arrival. Transmir had already handed duplicates of the customs documents to the Customs Officer at Podolsk and customs clearance was now a mere formality. The customs officer was on the payroll at Transmir, a friendly official, and wouldn't search for any discrepancy which he could turn into a lucrative problem. Transmir had given instructions to the driver not to arrive before three. Transmir always waited until the morning shift had left the Customs house and "their man" was in charge for the rest of the day. They then arranged for the papers to be stamped and cleared without the truck even appearing at the Customs warehouse. Yuri knew that it was better to wait until he had received a copy of the customs clearance before he stripped the ten pallets with a green label on the top and extracted the wooden cases of Bordeaux from the inside of the pallets. All in good time, he thought. No need to rush.

At four thirty Pavel had finished his lunch and exchanged a few jokes with the other drivers, given Sonya her present and discussed with the other drivers the best and the safest place to park his truck overnight. There had been a lot of burglaries in the last few months and Pavel always kept himself up to date on where not to spend the night. He was to pick up his load back to Lithuania the next morning in Khimki and wanted to drive there tonight and be first in the queue before the gates opened on Friday morning. With a bit of luck he would be back home in Vilnius on Sunday morning, with his wife and children, a warm meal, a good beer and a soft mattress.

*

Thursday, 10th February 2011, Moscow, 5.00pm

Inspector Antipov looked at his watch and started packing up his files. He put several files into his top drawer and locked it. He put three files in his old-fashioned leather satchel. It was so old, so retro that is was almost back in fashion. He looked up as the door opened and his assistant came in.

"You'll love this," he said pushing a wad of papers in his hand.

"What is it?" Vladimir Antipov looked questioningly at his smiling assistant.

"It's a transcript of the whole conversation between Armen Makaryan and Abel Plemyannikov, not just a voice clip."

"You're joking," he said starting to read as he walked over to his desk.

"Would I joke about those two?" his assistant said sitting down across from his boss.

"How on earth did we get hold of it?"

"It seems that Mr. Makaryan was a little too cocky and used an insecure phone for this conversation. He must have been really furious to make a mistake like that."

"Wow!" Vladimir exclaimed looking at his assistant as if someone had just answered his prayers. "This is incredible! So now we know why the Conseil is meeting tonight and that our anti-corruption measures are beginning to get to them. Great!"

Vladimir leant back in his chair with his arms crossed behind his head looking at the ceiling. He felt as if Christmas and Easter had fallen on the same day. "Bloody marvellous!"

Armen stood in the luxurious board room on the fifth floor of the RusAeroSpace building with its leather chairs and polished mahogany table. He looked out of the tall windows and sighed inwardly as he watched the sun disappear behind the fir trees of the never-ending forest. He had spent the whole afternoon discussing the Moscow-St. Petersburg Highway project with the eleven other board members but at least they had reached a consensus. The board would support it and the resolution was carried unanimously. The company needed good road communications to St. Petersburg and the west for the expansion of their space projects, to connect their headquarters to test sites, sub-sites and sub-contractors. It was a pity that the forest would become a victim to progress but they would deal with the environmental protests in their own way, quietly and efficiently. After all, they had a huge influence in Khimki, not just in industrial circles, but also an unfailing political lobby and influence with the different forces who maintained law and order. Armen walked back over the plush red carpet and shook the hand of each member of the Board. When he reached the chairman, Zhenya took his hand in both of his and thanked him for his patience and support. He put his hand underneath Armen's elbow and moved him towards the window away from the other members of the board.

"It is not always easy to consider everybody's interests, particular in such an important issue," said Zhenya. "I think we reached a positive conclusion and a lot was thanks to your successful lobbying behind the scenes, Armen. I am most grateful for your support. Most grateful," he repeated with a smile which spoke a thousand words. Armen had worked hard to ensure the outcome of today's meeting and he knew he would be rewarded well for it. He nodded and added "always at your service, dear Zhenya." Zhenya smiled back and they parted company. Armen walked towards the double doors which were opened by two invisible doormen who were watching every movement on CCTV. Armen walked towards the lift and the bell-boy pressed the button for the ground floor, nodded and walked out of the lift, leaving Armen alone with his thoughts on the way down. As he walked through the hall, he was acknowledged by the staff at the front desk. They had already seen his imminent departure on their CCTV monitors and had rung Armen's chauffeur, Vanya, who was now waiting in front of the revolving doors. Vanya walked out in front of his boss, checking the driveway and the surrounding area in a sweeping movement of his eyes and head. Armen followed a few steps behind. Vanya opened the rear door of the black Mercedes ML500, on the passenger side, and Armen sank into the leather upholstery of the interior. Vanya walked round to the driver's seat, sat down behind the wheel and waited for his instructions.

"Straight to Nostalgie, Vanya!" Armen said in a rather tired voice.

"Yes sir," Vanya replied and drove off slowly on the salted driveway. There was no time to go back to the office or visit one of his lady friends. He would have a drink at the bar before the others arrived and review the events of the day. It had been a good day, one that justified a small celebration.

Armen was relaxing in the back seat of his Mercedes on the drive back from Khimki to Moscow when his mobile phone rang. It was his secure mobile phone and the name in the display was Alex, his import manager. Alex reported that the truck from Germany had arrived and all the Customs documentation had been stamped. Everything was "in order". Armen grunted his approval. "Khorosho, good," he said, "see to it that Yuri strips the pallets and brings me the Bordeaux tomorrow afternoon, but not before three" he added. Tonight he had to meet Abel and the other members of the Conseil for dinner. And then he would chill out in the discotheque upstairs. Maybe he would invite one or two women back, for a drink and a few other pleasures. He had enough wine in his cellars to host an army and enough speed to supply the whole of Moscow's yuppies!

At seven thirty Armen was safely perched on a bar stool at the private members bar in the cellar of his favourite restaurant, Nostalgie, not far from Novy Arbat, one of the main roads in Moscow which runs west to a bend in the Moscow river where the famous luxury hotel Ukraina towers over its banks . He ordered an Armenian brandy and drank it as if it were water. "Another", he growled at the barman, and turned round as he sensed someone walking up behind him. It was Andrey, the restaurant manager. Andrey walked towards him with open arms. "My dear Armen," he said, and gave him a delicate bear hug as only those with humble roots but important positions can feign. "It is such a pleasure to see you. Your next brandy is on the house."

"Join me," provoked Armen and watched Andrey flinch. He didn't like spirits but his customers were his living. "Of course," retorted Andrey and clicked his fingers at the barman who re-appeared with another glass of brandy. "Who are we drinking to," Andrey asked. "To you," Armen replied, "the man who is going to introduce me to two wonderful ladies tonight who will take away all the cares of this world."

Andrey smiled. He knew exactly which kind of ladies Armen liked. He raised his brandy glass and smiled at Armen. "At your service," he said. "Chin, chin". Their crystal brandy glasses touched lightly, ringing like a tiny silver bell and the deal was done. As Andrey swallowed the last sip, Armen looked up and said: "Ah, I've brought you a little something from my home town." Armen smiled and gave Andrey a small pink envelope with a ribbon. "Thank you, Armen, most attentive of you," Andrey replied. "If you please, I'll unwrap it in my office. Thank you." Armen nodded and Andrey bowed his head very slightly, turned and went up the stairs to the restaurant. He walked straight to his office, opened the safe in the corner and placed the pink envelope carefully inside. He would check the contents later. Hopefully the amount would cover his gambling debts.

At eight o'clock two more members of the Conseil walked into the restaurant, took off their coats, scarves, hats and gloves and handed them to the concierge who came scuttling back with a numbered coin for each of them. They dropped the coins nonchalantly into their jacket pockets as they walked down the stairs to the bar. They could see Armen sitting at the bar and Dmitri called over.

"You've beaten us to the Armenian brandy," he called mockingly in a loud voice. Armen stood up and turned round with a mischievous grin on his face. Armen knew they only drank vodka. He gave them both a bear hug, just touching cheeks lightly on both sides. Both of the new arrivals ordered vodka, Moskovskaya vodka, and swallowed the first slug without it even touching their taste buds. Dmitri and Cyril had both had a challenging day and they needed a little alcohol to chill out, begin to enjoy the power they wielded. As they chatted with Armen it was all about power, money and influence, reminiscent of a peacock display without the colours and feathered tails. You had to know the language and watch their facial expressions change slightly to understand the code and what was actually happening. Ten minutes later Abel walked through the main door and threw his overcoat literally at the concierge. Abel headed straight towards Vladimir and Boris who were standing talking in the entrance hall. Vladimir, who insisted on everyone calling him Volodya, the more familiar diminutive form of his name, was wearing a sheepskin coat and hat. He could have been mistaken for a normal Moscow yuppie and his friendly, discerning manner set him apart from the rest. Those who knew him well, though, weren't deceived by his appearance and affable manner. Inside the playboy exterior was a trained mind and body, discipline to the very core. That's how he ran his business and had built an empire second to none. Volodya and Boris took off their coats and gave them to the concierge who took them with a slight bow of his head. The poor man tried at the same time to give Abel a numbered coin, to no avail. He gave up and slipped it in his pocket. The three men walked downstairs to the bar and greeted the others with booming voices. The whole group was just about to move through into their private dining room when Sasha walked into the bar. He was always the last to arrive. Now they were all present, the proceedings could begin.

The large round table was beautifully laid out with silverware, silver chandeliers, porcelain and crystal glasses from the Imperial Porcelain Manufactory of St. Petersburg, the very best you could find in Mother Russia. The polished wood of the table shone like a mirror and the comfortable upholstered chairs were a very good imitation of the chairs which Empress Catherine the Great had sat on in her palace. Only the finest was good enough for such important guests. It was important that the table was round. No one sat at the head of the table, even if Abel coordinated proceedings. They all took a seat as if they had received seating instructions. There were none. They weren't needed. Two waiters came in and flicked open the smoothly ironed linen serviettes and laid them gently on the lap of each gentleman. Another waiter came in with a bottle of Staraya Moskva vodka in an ice bucket. He put the bucket on a side table, opened the bottle for all to see and poured some into each small glass. Behind him a fourth waiter wheeled in a trolley with fine Beluga caviar, blinis and sour cream.

One waiter took the silver platter of warm and fluffy blinis, small, thick pancakes, and the other the silver bowl of black caviar on ice. They served as the gentlemen chatted among themselves. When they had all been served, Abel rose his glass, looked at each one of them in turn and said:

"Thank you, gentlemen, for responding so reliably to my invitation. I raise my glass to you all. Na zdorovya!"

"Na zdorovya!" they all replied in unison and drank the clear liquid as if it were water. The waiter replenished their glasses and they ate the delicious caviar, gently placing it on the small blinis and adding a generous teaspoonful of sour cream to the top. They talked among themselves in animated voices. The vodka continued to flow. The waiters collected the used plates and silver cutlery and as if on some secret command left the dining room, the last one shutting the double doors quietly behind him.

"Before we continue with our main course," Abel said in a measured voice, gently tapping his wine glass with a fork to call for silence, "I would ask Armen to explain the latest developments concerning the licencing authorities and national customs."

"Thank you, Abel," Armen replied with a nod in his direction. "As you all know, the situation has become more and more difficult in the last eight weeks. Now I am afraid that events have taken a dramatic turn. This morning I was informed that the licencing authorities have refused to renew the import licence of two of my companies, including our alcohol importing company which operates out of Podolsk. This means that we will have to set up a new importing company and apply for a new licence which will probably take two to three months. We can't, however, afford to interrupt our imports and distribution of wine and imported and Russian spirits. Until we are ready to import again ourselves, I am asking you, gentlemen, if one of your importing companies will be able to register our products with customs without using the official channels which would take too long and make me a reasonable offer to support me in this awkward situation."

Armen paused to let his news sink in and to watch any reactions he could see in their faces. There was little reaction. This meant that the news had not come as a surprise.

"I presume that this is not a personal vendetta against the companies I own so I would be interested to know if all of us are facing a similar situation, with more frequent document checks, balance sheet inspection, customs documentation examination, not to mention the sudden replacement of certain officials who have been transferred out of Moscow to "the regions" and replaced by officials we do not know and therefore cannot control."

When any Russian businessman talked about the physical distribution of his domestic affairs he talked about Moscow, St. Petersburg and "the regions" meaning around eighty regions and large districts spread around this enormous country, the largest country in the world with over seventeen million square kilometres. As far as wines and spirits were concerned, forty per cent of their turnover was done in Moscow.

The first to speak was Volodya. "The situation you are

describing, dear friend, has been apparent in several of my enterprises for the last two to three months. Up to now we seem to have averted any delicate questions and the inspectors who have called have not yet been able to find anything which would arouse their suspicion. However, I too am being faced with officials who are not on the payroll and therefore loose cannons. I have started enquiries as to the root of my troubles, as I'm sure you have, too, Armen, but so far I've drawn a blank. It is most unusual, in fact unprecedented, that no-one seems to know where the paper chain leads back to and who is responsible for our woes."

"We may not be able to prove who is responsible, Volodya, "interjected Armen, "but we all know that our troubles began in November. I know you and Sobyanin are close, but I have come to the conclusion that he is not on our side. This means that the Kremlin isn't on our side either. We built the economy in Moscow, we survived the crisis of 1998 and continued to pay taxes, employ voters and increase the influence of Russia in international business. And the thanks for all that is what? We have to react, as a group, to this change of policy. We have to use the political and financial influence we have in order to stop this madness which is crippling our businesses and will eventually cripple the economy."

Sasha waited until Armen put down his glass. "I agree with Armen," Sasha said. "We all know where the trouble is coming from and we must react. It may cost us money, big money, but allowing the present conditions to continue will only cost more."

"I couldn't agree more," said Boris. "My troubles only started in the New Year when my workers were stopped from entering one of my factories when they returned to work after the holidays on the tenth of January. It took three days of negotiations to persuade the district authorities to re-open the gates and one of the conditions was a pledge to support the officials in their investigations who arrived the following day and crawled all over our internal affairs. I was treated like a criminal although I employ thousands of Muscovites. It's unbelievable and it's now gone too far."

"Well," interjected Abel, "Armen and Sasha are for consolidated action. "Volodya?"

"Yes," he said, nodding his head and frowning slightly. "Yes, but it will cost us dearly. However, we can't afford our influence to be undermined and weakened, in particular in the run-up to the Presidential elections in 2012. I'll support a group action and I'll make Armen an offer for him to import his wines and spirits through one of my companies."

"Thank you, Volodya, your assistance is much appreciated," Armen replied and raising his glass he made a gesture of a toast in Volodya's direction. "

"What about you, Boris," Abel asked turning his head towards the shrewd businessman on his left.

"I'll support a group action," he said. "We can't afford not to act. Toleration would indicate weakness to the wrong people and the situation may well deteriorate."

"And you, Cyril," Abel questioned looking through the chandelier to the thin, bearded gentleman across the table.

"What's your valued opinion, dear Professor?" he asked.

"I agree with the others and I'll support any group action we unanimously agree to," Cyril declared. Abel smiled as Cyril pronounced the word "unanimously". The "Professor" as he was affectionately nicknamed had indeed been a professor of philosophy and law at Moscow State University before he went into business some twenty years ago. They were all grateful for his insights and the calming influence he had on the group. His words were a quiet reminder that any decisions the Conseil made had to be carried unanimously if they were to be put into practice.

Dmitri looked up, aware that he was the only one who had not spoken so far. "I'll support a group action," he said. "Several of my companies are under investigation, too, and it really must be stopped or at least controlled."

"Good," said Abel. "Then we are all in agreement. The motion is carried unanimously," he added, with a nod towards the Professor. I will start to put a plan together tomorrow and inform you all through the usual channels."

Abel pressed a button under the table next to his right knee and a few seconds later the heavy doors opened. Two wine waiters walked in silently, one carrying a Jeroboam of expensive Bordeaux in their hands, five litres of pure red gold, the other with a silver tray of large Bordeaux glasses, hand blown by Riedel. Armen knew that the wine would taste better in a thin, crystal glass with the right shape and these Austrian glasses were the best one could buy. Armen checked the label, Chateau Margaux 1er cru classé 1996, and the wine waiter with the precious bottle moved to the side table where he was joined by the head sommelier with one of the simple, elegant glasses in his hand. The head sommelier took the waiter's knife and carefully removed the top of the capsule. Then he removed the cork with the cork screw. As it was gently pulled out of the bottle neck, all eyes were on this amazingly expensive bottle of wine which was worth around eight hundred thousand roubles at a reputable dealer and probably three times that amount in a restaurant. The sommelier smelt the cork to ensure that it hadn't influenced the wine in any way and put the cork on a silver plate which he placed in front of Armen who smelt it and nodded his consent. The head sommelier poured a litre of the ruby red liquid very gently into a decanter and then poured a small amount from the decanter into the eighth glass. He sniffed the wine then swilled the wine around the glass to increase the oxygen intake and sniffed the wine again. The intense aromas started to develop and he couldn't help but smile at the expectation of tasting this extraordinary wine. After a few minutes he took a small amount into his mouth and with his lips and tongue increased again the oxygen in the wine with a delicate slurping noise. The wine enveloped his taste buds, bursting into life, a perfect example of one of Chateau Margaux's best wines, one that Robert Parker, the famous wine journalist in the USA had given 99 out of 100 points to. This was a once in a lifetime experience, to be savoured and never to be forgotten. He swallowed the wine, memorising all the different flavours in his mouth and throat as he did so. Fantastic! To die for!

"This bottle is from my private collection," Armen said, "to thank you all for your support. Chateau Margaux is one of my favourite wines and I particularly like the 1996 vintage as a Jeroboam. Just right for drinking now, wouldn't you agree, Pyetr?" The head sommelier nodded in agreement and moved with the decanter in his hand to the table, pouring just a little in each glass to try. The wine would need a little more time to open up but he knew his guests were eager to tantalize their taste buds with this rarity.

The main course was wheeled into the dining room and Armen raised his glass.

"A toast to you, gentlemen, to the Conseil and to our friendship," he said. "To the Conseil," they all reiterated and sipped the liquid gold in their glasses, feeling its warmth, its luxury and uniqueness as these connoisseurs of all things expensive let the wine envelop their palates and enchant their taste buds. Armen's eyes lit up with pleasure and he received admiring and approving looks from around the table. This is what it's all about, he thought. Being able to savour precious and expensive things others can only dream of.

His thoughts were interrupted by a waiter who gently placed a plate of the best Australian beef in front of him. Another waiter silently placed some potatoes Dauphinoise on his plate and some French green beans wrapped in slices of bacon thinner than the human skin.

"Priyatnovo apetita," Abel said, "enjoy your meal."

"Yes, enjoy," they all said, taking up their steak knives and forks and cutting into the meat with virtually no effort at all.

It was around eleven fifteen when the members of the Conseil had finished their deserts and were enjoying a Cognac to round off their superb meal. Abel summoned one of the waiters who disappeared to call Andrey to the private dining room. Andrey arrived and listened to the group's praise. The meal had been of the highest standard, prepared to perfection and served as usual extremely professionally. Andrey confirmed that all their drivers had been informed of the imminent departure of the gentlemen and their cars would be waiting for them outside in ten minutes. As the group stood up and said their goodbyes, each hugging the other and wishing him well, Armen felt excited at the prospect of plunging himself into the nightlife of the club on the second floor and meeting the ladies that Andrey had no doubt primed for his most esteemed customer.

In the apartment block across the road the FSB agent watching the entrance to Nostalgie was looking through a long-range telescope. He kicked the agent on the armchair next to him.

"Something's moving," he said. "One of the cars is in front of the entrance, some others down the street. "

His partner jumped up and knelt in front of one of the cameras with a long-range lens. The other agent took the wide-angle camera to get a good view of the scene. They started taking continuous high-speed photos of each person leaving the restaurant. They had pictures of people going in but quite often their backs were turned or their faces only partially visible. They had all the cars and their number plates but now they wanted really good photos of the faces of Moscow's rich and powerful.

"Here we go," the agent with the bald head said and pressed the "burst" button.

After half an hour six of the cars had drawn up, taken their cargo on board and driven off.

"There's still one missing," the agent with the long-range camera said.

"It looks as if that's all for now," his partner continued, looking through the telescope. "The manager has gone back inside. We're in for a long night, mate. You take over and I'll close my eyes for a while."

The agent got up and stretched his body, walked round the small room which was sparsely furnished and then flopped into the armchair next to the window. His partner took up his position in front of the telescope on a wooden chair and made himself as comfortable as possible.

4

Friday, 11th February 2011, Sydney, Australia, 6.30 a.m.

As Moscow's night owls were just beginning to get ready for play in one of the most vibrant cities in the world, fifteen thousand kilometres and seven time zones away, people in Sydney, Australia, were just beginning to wake up and get ready for work on Friday. The morning sun rose on the horizon to herald yet another sunny, late summer morning. The sun's radiant colours seemed to light up the calm ocean as if setting fire to the bright blue water in explosions of amber and red. Sam had just returned to his condo, a mere stone's throw away from the harbour with an amazing view of the bridge and the opera house from the thirteenth floor of his penthouse, one of the few tall buildings near Sydney harbour, built before building permission was denied for high-rise blocks. He took in the breath-taking view as he sipped a glass of fresh orange juice on the deck and wiped the sweat from his brow with a towel. He just loved going out for a run in the early morning, before the heat of the day took a grip on the city. The cool morning breeze from the ocean, the smell of the sea, the spectacular sunrise – he savoured every single element of this precious moment. It gave him the strength he needed to cope with an ailing business, a demanding wife, a daughter in her teens and a lifestyle which vastly exceeded his net income. Thank goodness his father had had the foresight to buy a condo in the harbour when this building was first built. It was the one asset which Sam really appreciated. When his parents were tragically killed in a plane crash some ten years ago, Sam had inherited the family business and his parents' fortune. It hadn't taken him long to spend a lot of that money. His largest expense was "Billy Jo" – his sixty foot luxury Azimut 62 Evolution Flybridge motor yacht. He'd bought it through Five Star Motors in Sydney a couple of years ago. The equipment and furnishings were state-of-the art, as was the Italian interior decoration and design. He spent most weekends with his wife on the yacht and entertained a lot of his friends and business acquaintances on board. Billy Jo had cost him well over two million dollars but it had been worth it. It combined the spirit of yachting with the lifestyle he chose to live. It was part of his life just as much as this view, his family and his business were.

Sam walked through the lounge and put his glass down in the marble and white wood kitchen. The condo was immaculate. The lounge had large picture windows to show off the fantastic view. With its light-coloured leather and oak furnishings, designer lamps and vases, it looked as if it had just been lifted out of a glossy magazine. Karen really knew how to choose expensive furniture and furnishings.

He had to hand it to her though, she had style. He quietly opened the door to the master bedroom where his wife was sleeping, her long blond hair strewn across the pillow. She stirred as he went into the bathroom to shower and shave. He had a gruelling day ahead.

It was seven thirty when Sam drove his seven series BMW out of the underground garage and on to the street. The light blinded him even at this early hour and he put his sunglasses on. He listened to the news on the radio and then the traffic news. Most of the traffic was coming into Sydney and the rush hour hadn't really started yet so he should have an easy drive out to Frenchs Forest to see Pete Owen. His business with Pete was quite lucrative but he still needed a joint venture partner with enough capital to help expand the business into more profitable areas.

Sam's main business was manufacturing anti-venom for snake bites, a very important part of life in Australia which is home to five of the world's deadliest snakes. Sam's father had built a processing plant in Hawkes Lift in Queensland just an hour's drive west of Brisbane. Manufacturing anti-venoms which are purified antibodies is a highly specialised business. His company manufactured anti-venoms for the Tiger snake, Brown snake, Taipan, Black snake, Death adder and the Sea snake. To manufacture anti-venom, small doses of venom are injected into a host animal to produce antibodies. For all the anti-venoms Sam's company produced, the host animal was the horse. Sam's father had loved horses and had bought two hundred hectares of prime grazing land in Queensland in the Lockyer Valley.

At first, it was just a hobby. Then he started to breed horses for the specific task of producing anti-venom. The small doses of venom are injected into the highly sophisticated blood circulation system of the host horse. The venom dose is gradually increased as the host animal builds up resistance to the toxins in the venom. In response to the introduced venom the horse produces antibodies. Samples of the horse's blood are then taken and the antibodies are separated out. At the processing plant in Hawkes Lift the antibodies were fragmented and purified by a series of digestion and processing steps. At the end of the processing procedure, the anti-venom contains antibody fragments which bind the venom in the patient's body. This binding neutralizes the activity of the venom and prevents further complications for the patient. Anti-venoms have been made in Australia since the eighteen nineties and Australia was one of the first countries in the world to experiment with snake anti-venoms.

Hawkes Lift had survived the horrific floods in Queensland which started just two months ago. 2010 had seen the wettest spring since 1900 and Queensland had seen torrential rains throughout December brought by the notorious La Niña weather pattern. Six rivers in Queensland had flooded an area larger than France and Germany put together. Over two hundred thousand people had lost their homes, a lot of them had lost their livelihood and forty people had lost their lives. Hawkes Lift had survived the flash flood in the Lockyer Valley as it was on higher ground. But his pastures were a mess. In fact, his pastures were a disaster. And he had lost half of his herd to the floods. There just hadn't been enough time to get all the horses out. The water came so quickly. Even though the staff all rushed to round up the herds and most of the locals who worked at the factory in Hawkes Lift drove out as far as they could to help, the loss of livestock was still huge. The helpers used rowing boats to swim the horses to dry land, attaching floats to the horses halter under the heavy head to keep the horses' nostrils above water as they swam the horses distances of up to a thousand meters to dry land, towing them behind the boats. His risk insurance was not based on the cost of replacement but the cost of the loss. So basically the financial loss was going to be horrific. Replacing the horses and a three month production gap would cost a lot of cash he didn't have. Thank goodness the forests hadn't been damaged. He could still harvest his Quaker Butterworth trees and the Macadamia nut plantation. But the floods had caused a drain on his liquidity and the banks were becoming a little bit nervous. In the aftermath of GFC, the rather quaint abbreviation for the most devastating global financial crisis of the century, Australian banks had started to review their customers' businesses and in most instances reduce lending thresholds. A lot of his friends had gone through the same problems in the last couple of years. Lending limits were being slashed and many companies were even taking secured loans from some of their owners using the invoiced amounts on their books as on-going financial security. Factoring was a sign of the times and times weren't easy. To make matters worse, the mining industry in Australia was still booming and taking all the qualified labour into the mines where people could earn a small fortune in a short while. That meant that qualified labour was in short supply and darned expensive. His labour bill had increased over the last five years by twenty five per cent. In the same period his exports revenue had declined by fifteen percent as the Australian dollar continued to rise. His products were exported and invoiced in local currency which meant less revenue when the dollar increased in value. As they say, it never rains but it pours!

As he drove along the highway he thought about Billy Jo and taking the motor yacht out on Saturday. He had invited the part-owner of a risk insurance business who was looking for an interesting area to invest his money in. That could be an alternative to the side-line he had set up with Pete Owen out at Frenchs Forest. Pete's company, Long Life, processed some of the plants, fruits and trees in the sub-tropical north of Queensland to sell to pharmaceutical companies making homeopathic medicines. Nux Vomica was one of the fruits that Long Life processed, not just for homeopathic medicine which was just a niche market, but as the raw material for strychnine. As a lethal poison, strychnine was strictly controlled. However, it had always been sold on the black market and used all over Australia. Sam was supplying Pete with Nux Vomica from his Quaker Butterworth trees. He was only declaring fifty per cent of the deliveries. Pete paid him in cash for the rest. The deliveries which were paid for through the bank and invoiced legally were really made into the raw material for homeopathic medicines. The rest was made into strychnine which Long Life was selling on the black market to sheep farmers who even used it in wild dog traps to make sure that the animals died quickly when snared.

Pete Owen lived in Frenchs Forest and flew up to Queensland a couple of days a week. He had his own four seater Cesna and was a qualified pilot. It helped him to get around quickly without drawing attention to his itinerary, his business partners or his banking arrangements. Pete had just returned the night before from Brisbane when Sam's seven-series BMW cruised into the oval drive-way which was surrounded by small trees and countless azalea bushes. The colours were just breath-taking. Pete loved his garden and made sure it was tended with the utmost care. Pete's office was at the front of the two storey house shaded from the heat and the midday sun. He could also admire the garden and observe the comings and goings at the house. Pete raised his eyes as the sunlight danced off the car's bonnet and waved his right hand in greeting. Pete shut down his lap top, got up from behind his desk and walked into the hall to the front door. Sam reached the front door just as Pete opened it and was greeted first and foremost by Pete's sandy-coloured Golden Retriever, Pebble. Sam patted the dog on its head, careful not to get hairs all over his dark grey suit trousers. His next appointment today would require a suit and there was no time to change.

"Pebble, down boy," said Pete holding out his hand. Sam shook it and smiled.

"Hi, Pete. How was your trip?" Sam asked.

"Not bad, not bad at all. Things are picking up nicely. Come on in." He stood back to let Sam through the porch and into the hall-way.

"Jean's out," Pete added. "She's gone shopping with Regan. Fancy a coffee? "

"Love one," said Sam.

"An expresso or a cappuccino?"

"A cappuccino would be great," Sam said as they walked into the spacious kitchen.

Pete opened the fridge and took out the full cream milk.

"None of this skinny cap stuff," he smiled. "One a day and it's got to taste good!"

Pete went over to his Harvey Norman coffee-maker, foamed the milk and then pressed the button to ground and make the coffee. Pete had the beans specially roasted at his favourite coffee-shop near the Hilton. He liked them not too dark, extremely aromatic and not too acidic.

Pete handed Sam a mug.

"Let's go talk in my office. There are a couple of things I want to show you," he said.

It was just after ten in the morning when Sam picked up the metallic briefcase Pete had given him, shook hands with his business partner and putting on his sunglasses, walked to his car. The temperature had risen to a warm twenty-five degrees centigrade. Pete watched Sam open the trunk of his car as he walked towards it and place the briefcase inside. He closed the trunk gently, letting the hydraulics slide the door into place and snap shut. He walked to the driver's side and opened the rear door. He took his suit jacket off, folded it and placed in on the back seat. He got in behind the steering wheel, closed the door and drove round the oval island with its exotic colours to exit the drive and gave Pete a short wave as he did so. He got back on to the highway and drove back towards the city centre. It only took him half an hour to get back home. He parked his BMW on his allotted spot in the underground car-park and took the metallic briefcase Pete had given him out of the trunk. He locked the car and took the lift to the thirteenth floor. He turned his key in the lock and walked into the hall. Karen was on the deck reading a magazine. He slipped into his office unnoticed and walked towards his Yale safe. Karen kept her jewellery and some cash in the bedroom safe but he deposited confidential documents and large amounts of cash in his office safe. He was the only one who knew the combination and it was very secure. He emptied the contents of the metallic briefcase in stacks of one hundred thousand Australian dollars. There were five stacks, half a million dollars. That should keep the family going for a while, until he could sort out the business. He took some accounts out of his leather briefcase and put the folder on one of the shelves of the safe. The folder was marked Long Life 2010 and was a complete record of his transactions with Pete. It was safer to keep a hard copy even if it was a bit tedious. It would be easier to destroy paper evidence than wipe his computer clean if he were ever investigated. Electronic data could be reconstructed much more easily.

He opened the door to the deck and kissed his wife.

"Just come in for a juice", he said with a smile and

walked back into the kitchen. Karen grabbed a t-shirt and slipped it on over her bikini to follow him in.

"You seem pleased with yourself," she said. "You obviously had a good meeting with Pete."

"Yep," he replied, putting a couple of oranges in his Breville juice fountain. "It seems 2010 was a better year than I thought it was going to be."

"Well that's good" she said and smiled. Sam never discussed the details of his business with Karen. She wasn't interested. She just spent their money without really caring where it came from. She had no idea of the debts he had and the financial difficulties his business was in. So he didn't need to reassure her as she had no doubts whatsoever.

"Fred rang to say he'd got some really good fish down at the market this morning for dinner tomorrow. He'll be stocking up the fridges on Billy Jo at six tomorrow morning. He put the wine and champagne on board yesterday. So everything's ready for Tom and Nancy."

"That's great," Sam replied. He knew his wife would have organised a splendid gourmet evening for Saturday night and have everything their guests could desire. She really thought of everything, every single detail. She would put a bottle of champagne in the fridge of the VIP stateroom, fresh flowers, fresh fruit and enough nibbles to ensure their guests got off to a good start. John, their infallible steward, would bring salmon and caviar to the VIP stateroom at five in the afternoon as their guests were getting ready for dinner. He could smell the sea as he thought about their outing tomorrow - the sights in Sydney Harbour in the early morning and then south towards Jervis Bay. They'd watch the dolphins as they ate their lunch and then turn back after a snooze in the afternoon to see Sydney Harbour in all the glory of a splendid sunset over dinner. And on Sunday an exciting sail out to the summer feeding grounds where they could watch humpback whales. Everything would be perfect, it had to be perfect. Sam needed Tom, needed Tom's money and connections. Tom was part of his plan to rebuild his business.

Sam drank his juice, went to the bathroom to freshen up, picked up his leather briefcase in his office and walked back into the kitchen. It was eleven thirty and he had an appointment with the bank at twelve noon. He knew they would all be polite, all smiles and warm handshakes, but their knives would be sharpened. He kissed Karen goodbye.

"See you later," he said and managed a smile.

"Don't forget to bring some cash back with you," she said softly. "You wanted to pay the crew in cash."

"I won't forget," he said. In fact, he was going to pay everything in cash for the next few months, but she didn't need to know.

Sam walked around the harbour to take in the view of the Harbour Bridge and the Opera House. How he loved this city. He walked down George Street for ten minutes looking at the shop windows, bistros and name plates on office doors to take his mind off the meeting ahead. Eventually he turned right into the ABD Bank through the glass revolving doors and into the air-conditioned entrance hall with its smart tiled floor and polished wood and brass. He walked up to the desk where three tall, slender women in blue suits with white blouses busied themselves with phone calls and computers. As he approached the desk, one of the uniformed receptionists smiled a broad hello and asked him how she could help.

"Sam MacPherson to see John MacDonald," he said, returning her smile. She looked up the appointment on her screen and entered in a message for the General Manager's secretary.

"Follow me, please." The tall, slender figure walked towards the lifts behind the two security guards posted to the right and left of the entrance to the inner workings of the bank. She walked into the lift with him in her extremely high heels. They made her legs look even longer and accentuated her smooth calf muscles. He often wondered how on earth his wife could walk in such shoes. They reached the third floor. He followed Samantha - that was the name on her badge - to a corner where brown leather armchairs awaited him.

"Please take a seat," she said with a gesture of her right arm towards the armchairs. Mr MacDonald's secretary, Amy, will be with you in a few minutes." She turned on her high heels and walked back to the lift as if she had practised the slight movement of her hips to achieve the perfect combination of sexy yet efficient. Samantha disappeared into the lift, conscious of his eyes fixed on her as she went.

Sam picked up the Sydney Herald on the coffee table and glanced over the headlines. He couldn't read the articles. He was a little nervous and found concentrating on another topic just too difficult. He felt like a schoolboy who had been summoned to the headmaster. No, he felt like a lamb being brought to slaughter. Amy walked towards him in her grey skirt and tailored jacket. Her auburn hair bounced as she walked. Her shoes were a little more sensible than Samantha's and her whole demeanour oozed an air of extreme competence and efficiency.

"Gooday, Mr. MacPherson," she said in a friendly voice with a welcoming smile which helped settle his stomach. "Mr MacDonald will receive you in the board room. Please follow me."

He sprang to his feet and straightened his suit. He took a quick look in one of the mirrors on the wall to check that his collar, tie and hair were just as they should be. He was dressed in a dark grey suit with a red and grey striped tie and a white shirt. He approved of his mirror image, the serious businessman with a sporty look in a well-tailored expensive suit. He took long strides behind Amy and forced his whole body to relax. He could do this. He had to do it. It would be just fine.

*

The cold night air had frozen the last puddles and melting snow on the streets of Moscow and the night owls were heading for home. The FSB agent kicked his partner who was sleeping in an armchair. He awoke with a snort and a jolt.

"The last one's car has just drawn up to the side entrance. He must have been upstairs in the club." He looked at his watch. It was one-thirty in the morning.

"Jeez, what a life," the agent said as he moved himself in front of the camera with the long-range lens.

"His or ours?" the second agent said and took up his position in front of the camera with the wide-angle lens.

"Good question! No answer!" his partner laughed. The agent with the bald head whistled.

"Wow, got a pretty lady with him," he said.

"Yep, and I've got both of them. Number six in the bag," he said. The driver opened the door for the lady. Number six said something and got in first moving over to the other side of the rear passenger seat.

"Doesn't want to get his nicely polished shoes wet," the agent with the bald head said. The lady got in carefully and was a little unsteady on her feet. It could have been her high heeled shoes but it was probably the effect of too much alcohol, the fresh air and maybe drugs as well. The chauffeur shut the car door. He opened the front door on the driver's side, sat on the seat and rubbed his shoes together to clean them before he put his legs into the car. He shut the door and the car drove off. The agents relaxed. The lights went off in the hallway of the restaurant. The rest of the staff started leaving by the side entrance. The last one to leave was Andrey, the restaurant manager. The agent took a last photo, just in case. Then they waited half an hour, packed up their gear and walked down the stairs and out into the alley at the back.

5

Friday, 11th February 2011, Germany, 7.30 a.m.

It was seven thirty in the morning and the air chilly. Thomas walked to his blue Ford Ranger with a wad of documents in his left hand and his car keys. He opened the door and sat behind the wheel. He placed the papers on the passenger seat, took off his gloves and started the engine. His truck of wine had arrived from France at seven this morning in Bingen and Horst, his friend who worked at the Customs Office had rung him so that he could be present at the routine inspection of the documents. Thomas didn't expect any difficulties but it was always better to be present, just in case. There were thirty two pallets altogether, a total of nineteen thousand two hundred bottles and a total of almost one hundred thousand Euros worth of wine. That alone would warrant him being there but when he considered that in Russia half this wine would bring him an annual profit of almost four hundred Euros and the other half sold off on the German market for a small profit of around ten thousand Euros to keep his books looking balanced, then he most certainly didn't mind going to the Customs Office once a year to make sure that everything was in good order! It was a lot of money and he knew that he had been lucky to earn this kind of money over the last six years and he had spent at least a million renovating the winery buildings and farmhouse. Most of the work had been done by Lithuanians working in Germany on a three-month visa and being paid in cash. No invoice, no questions asked. The rest, a modest part, had been invoiced and the work given to local craftsmen so that he had some invoices on his books for the fiscal authorities. He had opened a trust fund for his brother, Conrad, so that there was a total of five hundred thousand Euros he could use for his brother or if Thomas died first then his account executors could use the money for Conrad. The bank was convinced that Thomas had received this money from insurance policies which had paid out after his mother's tragic road accident. Thomas had supported this view with a few comments and made sure that the right gossipers in the village knew it and passed it on to others so that it became an accepted "fact" within the community. He also dropped a few hints about how successful his brokerage business was, particularly with Bordeaux wines. That stopped his rather envious neighbours speculate about where his sudden wealth had come from.

An hour after his phone call, Horst looked out of the window as a blue Ford Ranger drew up into the forecourt in front of his office. Thomas grabbed the documents on the passenger seat and jumped out of the car. Horst got up and went to the front door of the reception area to greet him. He liked Thomas. They played cards together in one of the local pubs in Bingen and jogged once a month along the Rhine River on the cycle path. Thomas was an affable person and he didn't show how successful he was. Horst liked that. Not a trait that was to be found very often in successful businessmen! And Thomas looked after his handicapped brother, his partner's two sons and his partner. He had re-instated the reputation of his family's winery and Horst knew he was a philanthropist, helping a lot of people along his way.

Horst opened the door and shook Thomas' hand.

"Good to see you," he said and Thomas walked into the reception area for truck drivers. "We have the papers. Your driver only speaks French and has gone off to shower while we process the load."

Horst was the Department Head for Imports and Exports and being in the middle of four wine-growing regions, there was quite a lot of traffic coming through his relatively small station. One of his favourite members of staff was a large, bear-like man called Kurt who watched them out of the corner of his eye. Kurt was forty-one, had a wife and two kids, loved his beer and his football, was never sick and made sure that everything ran smoothly. Horst turned to Kurt and motioned him towards them. Kurt shook Thomas' hand. They had met before and Kurt knew that this was a "preferred" customer.

"Can you deal with Herr Becker's truck of wine just come in from France?" he asked, knowing fully that Kurt had already processed most of the documentation.

"Sure," he said and smiled at Thomas. "I've had a look at the paperwork. It seems fairly straightforward. You have a good forwarding agent looking after your logistics. They haven't made any of the usual mistakes!" Kurt added.

"They aren't the cheapest but over the last few years they have been very reliable," replied Thomas, trying to feign the routine which other wine importers inevitably have when receiving truckloads from all parts of Europe and overseas.

"I've put all the data into the machine," said Kurt "and I should be finished in the next half hour."

"Come and have a cup of coffee with me," Horst said.

"Much appreciated," said Thomas who knew that these valuable thirty minutes would increase his relationship to this very important friend.

Horst opened the door to his office and walked to his espresso machine. If you have to work, he always said, there's no point in drinking bad coffee! He had a Nivona – the best on the German market – and chose the coffee beans himself.

"What would you like?" he asked, turning back to look at Thomas. "Espresso, café latte or cappuccino?"

"I think I'll have a cappuccino this morning. I missed breakfast!" Thomas replied.

"Then I've got just the thing for you in my cupboard."

Horst went to the cupboard and took out two pieces of cake. Thomas' eyes lit up.

"I hope this suits," Horst said with a smile, putting the cherry cake with crumble on the top on the small table near the window.

"Looks great to me," Thomas said taking a seat at the table. "Anything sweet and filling at this time of the day!"

Horst made a cappuccino for Thomas and an espresso for himself. He brought the coffee mugs over to the table and sat opposite Thomas.

"So how's life," Thomas asked.

"At the moment a little difficult since Anne was diagnosed with breast cancer." Thomas flinched. He didn't know that Horst's wife was sick.

"I'm sorry to hear that, Horst," he replied, obviously saddened by the news. "I didn't know she was ill."

"No, none of us did. She is quite young for breast cancer, just forty two, and discovered a lump four weeks ago. She went straight to her gynaecologist and he sent her for a mammogram. Within two weeks she was in hospital and they removed the tumour. Unfortunately it seems to have spread so she'll now have to go through chemotherapy and radiotherapy."

"Goodness," said Thomas, quite shocked. "I'm really sorry to hear that. It's obviously going to be tough over the next six months. If there's anything I can do, anything at all, please let me know," Thomas added with a genuine desire to help his friend. He knew what terrible things illness could do to families. His father had died at the aged of forty four of a massive heart attack after all the trials and tribulations of the glycol scandal in the German and Austrian wine industry which had stripped him of his reputation and the means of his living overnight. His widow, Thomas' mother, had battled on until she had died in a tragic road accident, leaving him to cope with the ruined wine estate and a handicapped brother. He knew that life could be cruel and you just had to make the best out of it.

"Thanks," Horst replied. "I really appreciate how supportive everyone I know has been. We are trying to be really positive about the whole thing. My two sons, Max and Johannes, are only twelve and fourteen and for them it really is quite distressing but they'll cope in their own way. Max talks about it to his Mum but Johannes has closed up, doesn't want to know about it or so it appears. He needs a bit more time to come to terms with it. Anne is going for a check-up next week and then we'll know a bit more. I'll keep you posted," said Horst.

Kurt popped his head round the door, looked at his boss who nodded and walked up to Thomas.

"Everything's fine," he said. "Here are your copies. I know I don't have to tell you they need to be kept for ten years!"

"Thanks," said Thomas with a smile. He finished his cappuccino.

Thomas got up and so did Horst who held his hand out to shake hands with Thomas.

"Give Anne my best regards" Thomas said, "and I hope she makes a speedy recovery," Thomas replied shaking hands and then turning on his heels to walk over to his car. He looked at his watch. It was eight-thirty. The boys will have left for school, he thought, and Conrad catches the bus to Felsenhausen at eight-fifteen to go to the handicapped workshop. So he could go home and chat to Svetlana and have a cup of coffee before he got on with his work. On his way home he'd ring the warehouse in Gensingen and let the manager know that the truck would be arriving shortly.

*

Friday, 11th February, Khimki, 10.30 a.m.

In Moscow it was ten thirty in the morning and Pavel was still waiting for his documents at the drivers' office at RusAeroSpace warehouse. The parts he had loaded needed to be taken to Vilnius and the export documents had to be stamped by customs. It had taken him almost two hours to get round the MKAD, the notorious ring road, and on to the motorway. He'd left Podolsk at five in the morning to avoid the traffic on the ring road but there had been an accident which held him up. It had taken him half an hour to get past the accident. Stupid drunken fools, he thought as he saw two mangled SUVs with parts spread all over the road. By the time the highway patrol had cleared one lane, there was a tail-back of trucks waiting to get past. He had heaved a sigh of relief as he left the ring road and saw the big IKEA sign which meant he was almost there. At the RusAeroSpace warehouse in Khimki security was taken very seriously. It had taken him another half an hour just to get through the gates. The guard scanned in his passport and some unknown ghost up in the control room would have checked on-line if the passport was genuine and if he had any fines pending or had done anything remotely wrong. Big Brother is watching you, he thought, as he tapped his fingers on his steering wheel to a tune on his cab radio in the car park near the warehouse main gate. He had put the cab heating on and zipped up his fur-lined windcheater. His yshanka was tucked into a pocket, ready to be pulled down over his ears against the cold as soon as the guard gave him permission to drive through the gates. He chewed on his sandwich which Sonya in the canteen at Vodalko had slipped into his pocket, wrapped in a paper bag, as he kissed her goodbye. He was looking forward to a hearty breakfast with a large helping of porridge followed by sausages and potatoes, swilled down with a mug of black tea but he'd have to wait until he had left Moscow behind him. He finished chewing and opened up his thermos flask, a gift from his wife Laima at Christmas, and poured some of the black tea into the plastic lid. He'd filled his thermos to the brim at the tiny kiosk in front of the HGV park in Podolsk this morning and he was grateful for the hot liquid. He warmed his hands around the cup, drank his tea and screwed the small cup which served as a lid back on to the flask. The door to the guard's house opened and Pavel saw a small cloud of cigarette smoke followed by the guard. Thank goodness, he thought, he's coming over to me, at last. As the guard approached Pavel switched the ignition on and opened his window. He put his yshanka on and gave the guard a friendly smile. The guard was a surly man in his late thirties definitely in no mood for small talk.

"You're OK to go to gate twenty-three," the guard boomed at Pavel and pushed his passport and documents through the window with a receipt showing the time he had arrived, the time he was allowed through the gates and the gate he had to go to. Russian bureaucracy, thought Pavel. I bet no-one actually keeps these and does anything with them.

"Thanks mate," he replied with a feigned salute to his yshanka. The guard turned and walked back to his little hut and Pavel switched on his engine. He backed up and then rolled slowly to the main gate. As he got there, the guard flicked a switch and the huge metal gates opened. The black and yellow striped road blocker disappeared into its hole in the ground and the light jumped from red to green. His brakes hissed as he released them and moved forward into the inner sanctuary of AeroRusSpace.

Just five hundred metres away, the Chairman of the Board of AeroRusSpace, Zhenya Shipkin, was having a telephone conversation with the mayor of Moscow's office.

"Yes, we have agreed to back the project and you can tell Mr. Sobyanin that we will ensure that any protests are kept to a minimum and will be, let me say, low-profile."

"Thank you, Mr. Shipkin," an efficient voice on the other end replied. It was the Mayor's Assistant, a man who got up at four in the morning, kept his figure trim and his body fit, didn't drink alcohol, had studied law and politics in Moscow and in the USA and was now one of his most powerful allies in the Moscow City Government. "I will tell Mr. Sobyanin as soon as he returns from his meeting. Good day, sir." The voice on the other end put down the receiver. This man really must have done a course in efficient use of time, Zhenya mused and the thought brought a smile to his lips. He knew the message would be passed on and that was the most important thing, He looked at this watch. It was almost eleven. He pushed the button on his intercom.

"Tanya, I'll just have some salad and potatoes for lunch at twelve thirty," he said.

"Yes, sir, I'll organise it," came the familiar reply and he turned his attention back to the report he was reading. He wished the author of this report had been as succinct and efficient as Mr. Sobyanin's assistant. He sighed and continued reading.

At the Vodalko warehouse in Podolsk the twenty nine pallets of wine which had just arrived from Germany the day before had been put into bay twenty six. The supervisor, Oleg, and two of his staff were sorting through the pallets one by one. In the warehouse everything was automated so the pallets had been scanned in. Now they had to strip ten of the pallets, take out the expensive Bordeaux for one of the boss' special customers, rebuild the ten pallets with a space in the middle so they still looked identical to the others and mark them with a special label for Las Vegas, a wine bar in Moscow which belonged to Abel Plemyannikov. When they arrived at Las Vegas the delivery note would say one hundred cases of six bottles per pallet but the manager at Las Vegas knew there would be only ninety cases per pallet. He didn't ask why. He just acted on Mr. Plemyannikov's instructions. So as far as the warehouse was concerned, the ten pallets came in and went out with one hundred cases each on the delivery note. Their books balanced and everyone was happy. Just in case there was a customs check or the fiscal authorities came to visit, the pallets in the warehouse had to look alike. It was just European red table wine bottled in Germany with a ridiculous name on the label, Red Lady, and a picture of a Hispanic looking beauty in a low cut dress. It didn't really matter what the wine tasted like. At Las Vegas people came to drink, play the machines and the tables. The drinks had to be reasonable in price so the customers ordered enough to encourage them to gamble. A lot of young women liked Red Lady. It was light, just 9% in alcohol, and had around thirty grams of residual sugar meaning it was pretty sweet. Most of these young beauties with slim hips and long, slim legs sat around in their cocktail dresses sipping Red Lady while their boyfriends ordered vodka and played the tables.

Oleg checked the pallets of Red Lady and all the labels on the pallets a second time and nodded his head in approval. Everything was OK and the pallet with one hundred wooden boxes of Chateau Malvaux could now be shrink-wrapped and driven to the special customer. The warehouse staff put metal edge protectors on all four corners of the pallet and shrink-wrapped the pallet four times, taking in the bottom of the pallet to make sure the cases wouldn't slip if the delivery truck had to brake. Oleg watched the fork-lift truck take the pallet to one of the smaller ramps on the left of the warehouse where the delivery trucks waited for their loads. Vodalko had their own trucks and delivering wine was part of their logistic service. The pallet was loaded and Oleg gave the driver, Yury, the papers which needed to accompany the load. The police in Moscow, the Militsiya, were very, very active with road checks at the moment. The new police reform was about to come into force on 1st March and a total review of all police officers had to be carried out by the end of May. The reform which Dmitry Medvedev, the President of the Russian Federation, had signed was to increase efficiency, cut costs and, most important, combat corruption. The reform stated that the Militsiya, re-named the Politsiya, would lose twenty percent of their staff and that meant that one in five officers would lose their jobs. Since the publication of the reform, every police officer in Moscow was determined to prove his worth. They increased their road checks, identity checks and the sickness rate suddenly dropped. Oleg knew that every truck which left the warehouse must have transportation papers which were absolutely correct. If there was one little mistake, it would give the police reason to check the load and even impound the truck. Last year drivers just gave the officer in question a packet of cigarettes which had money in it. Now, with corruption high on Medvedev's list of priorities, bribes were out of the question. Only at higher echelons of the police force could money still be an incentive. So Oleg had checked the papers for this truck himself, picked his best driver, Yury, a reliable, soft-spoken man who was persuasive and polite, a rare combination in a rough Slavic world. Oleg gave Vitaly the papers and looked at him seriously.

"I know that there are a lot of checkpoints on the ring road, Vitaly," he said, "and I know you'll get past every one of them with no delay. Mr. Makaryan is expecting his wine this afternoon but not before three. Make sure you get the full name of the person who signs for it and if you don't know the person, check his identity. The wine is valuable."

"Understood, panyatno," Vitaly replied with a smile. Underneath the pile of papers was a small envelope. Oleg appreciated Vitaly's way of dealing with important clients and always showed his gratitude. That would help the family out until the end of month, Vitaly thought. Times were tough and money just seemed to fly out the window these days. He jumped into the driver's seat and closed the door. The sign on the door was for a company called "Podolskiy Logistics". The word "Vodalko" always attracted the police like moths to a light so Abel Plemyannikov had created a logistics company with a name which didn't attract attention. Oleg hoped that this would be the case this time as any intensive investigation would show that they had no import papers for the wine. That would cost a lot of money, not just for the fine but to get the customs officials off their back and the thought of all that paperwork sent shivers down his spine.

6

Saturday, 12th February 2011, Sydney, 7.00 a.m.

The sun had risen over the Pacific Ocean and the view from North Head was spectacular. Pete Owen and his daughter Regan had driven out to North Head just to see one of nature's most splendid moments. They had watched the sun rise slowly on the horizon way out over the ocean. They had sat in silence as they always did for twenty minutes or so. When the sky lost its radiant orange and red colours and started to turn blue, they'd head back towards Frenchs Forest and stop at their favourite coffee shop for a cappuccino and pancakes. Pete really enjoyed these moments with Regan. His wife, Jean, wasn't an early riser but Regan relished the early morning hours unlike most of her peers. She had inherited her father's sense of adventure and enormous respect for nature's beauty.

"Isn't this just awesome," Regan said, turning to her father and stroking her long, dark hair back from her eyes. Pete nodded in agreement and whispered "too beautiful to describe" and smiled at his daughter. They were on a bench in the viewers' area on the top of the sandstone promontory. They'd preferred to have been sitting on the edge of the steep cliff in the grass among the scrubs but there were quite a lot of snakes around, even up here in the Sydney Harbour National Park. After ten minutes or so Regan turned back to Pete again and quizzed his face. "Hungry?" she asked. "Sure," he said. "Let's go! I was just thinking about all the people that were quarantined here in the nineteenth century. And even until the late twentieth century. I remember my grandfather, your great grandfather Joe, telling me stories of smallpox and whooping cough epidemics particularly among the immigrants who came to Australia for a better life."

"Hmm," Regan mused. "A good job that people can be vaccinated against diseases like smallpox now. And have anti-dotes for snake venom," she said with a smile. Regan was twenty and studying pharmacology at the University of Sydney. She had known since she was fourteen that she wanted to take over her father's business but first she needed all the scientific knowledge she could gather and five years' work experience in another company. Her father had insisted on that when they finalised her career plans before she went to university. Regan untied Pebble whose lead was attached to the leg of the bench they were sitting on. A pity they couldn't let her run free but it really was too dangerous, what with the craggy promontory, snakes and poisonous ticks. Their last golden retriever had died as a puppy from a poisonous tick and Regan was adamant that it wasn't going to happen to Pebble.

They walked back at a quick pace to the car park along

the gravel path. Quite a few tourists walked past them, eager to see the fantastic view over the Pacific Ocean. Regan and Pete said hello to each group. He had taught her to be polite at all times and to all people but especially to make sure that all tourists took back a positive impression of Sydney and Australia. Pete was Australian through and through; six generations of Owens. Their forefathers came from South Wales and emigrated to New South Wales in Australia in 1852. They weren't fleeing from disease and starvation as almost a million Irish people did during the Irish Potato Famine when potato blight caused the potato crop to fail. The Owens came from sheep farming country and had heard from relatives and friends that there was gold to be found in New South Wales. So the first young pioneers in the Owen family sailed to Sydney and moved to Bathurst where they searched for gold and made enough money to buy land for a small homestead in Orange.

A few more tourists walked past them. "They've missed the best bit," Regan whispered to her father and smiled. Pete smiled back. Indeed, the moment the sun seemed to rise out of the water on the horizon was the most dramatic moment, the sky ablaze with colour, sometimes orange, red and yellow, sometimes with purple hues. Every time he saw the sun rise at North Head, he thought, the colours were different. It was always a slightly different experience every time which literally took his breath away.

*

Saturday, 12th February 2011, Sydney harbour, 7.00 a.m.

Captain "Lucky" Jack Gilbert was on the fly bridge of Billy Jo with his checklist in his hand. Billy Jo was berthed at Balmain Marine Centre just west of Sydney harbour. It was just after seven in the morning, the weather forecast was perfect – not too hot, blue skies, very little wind and a calm sea. Sam, who the Captain called Mac, a nickname only close friends and family used, had given him instructions for both Saturday and Sunday. "Must be really important guests", Jack had said when he had finished reading the instructions and took a quick look at Sam's face to catch the answer. Sam looked a little tense. "Very important, VIPs," Sam replied and then he smiled. Jack understood. Some deal was going on which was really important to his friend Mac and Jack would make sure that everything went smoothly on the trip. Fred and John were already on board, loading the fish, fruit and vegetables into the galley. Jerry, the Michelin star chef, would arrive as usual just before they weighed anchor, the star walking on to the stage in front of a full house. Jerry may be a bit full of himself but he sure could cook! The meals he had orchestrated on Billy Jo so far were out of this world. Jack would eat in his stateroom allowing Sam the privacy he needed with his guests.

Jack went to his stateroom and left his holdall on the floor. He looked at his watch. It was ten past seven and time he went down to check the fuel tanks and the water tanks. Billy Jo carried almost four thousand litres of fuel and a thousand litres of water. Then he'd have a look at the two Caterpillar C18 Engines. They were overhauled regularly so there was nothing to check but he enjoyed just the sight of these twin diesel engines and revelled at the thought of the two thousand horse power they generated. He walked back up to the helm station and started the engines. He couldn't suppress a smile as they purred into life. As he had such important visitors on board, his checks would be even more thorough this morning, although it was difficult to imagine that his checks could be any more thorough than they always were. Jack was lucky but his luck also came from his methodical attention to detail. He checked all the gauges – all ship-shape and ready to go. He spread out his maps and weather forecasts on the table on the fly bridge so he could show the guests where they would be going and what wonderful weather they would have. Jack really knew how to do everything in style which Sam appreciated and paid well for. Jack contacted harbour control and then at seven-forty-five he saw Sam and Karen about to board. Their guests, Tom and Nancy Wyatt, had just arrived by taxi, Nancy in white jeans and a white t-shirt with a white peaked cap with "Sydney to Hobart 2011" written on the curved visor. He knew Nancy was Tasmanian and her cap made the lines under his eyes crease in a friendly way. Jack liked people who came from islands and had been brought up with the sea. The Sydney to Hobart Yacht Race known as the Blue Classic started in Sydney every year on Boxing Day and ended in Hobart, Tasmania after six hundred and thirty nautical miles of battle. Jack had stood crew a couple of times and knew why it was considered one of the most difficult yacht races in the world. He would have loved to have been aboard Wild Oats XI when they crossed the line in Hobart after just one day eighteen hours twenty three minutes and twelve seconds. Amazing! He had used "Hobart1182312" as his password on several occasions. Jack forced himself to turn his attention away from the attractive forty-five-year old and to her husband, the mighty Tom Wyatt. Everyone in Sydney knew about Tom who had worked in risk insurance all his life. Now at the age of fifty eight he owned a huge business empire in Australia, having invested his money wisely in several medium sized companies looking for an investor and partner. Tom was a shrewd businessman and success hadn't turned his head. His lifestyle was luxurious but not exorbitant. He wore white shorts and sailing shoes, a white tailored polo shirt with a blue stitched motto on the left breast: Macquarie Links. Tom was a golfer, a very good golfer whose handicap had long gone into single digits. He was a member of two golf clubs in the Sydney area but Macquarie was his favourite – a links course with spectacular views of the ocean, designed by the famous golf course architect Robin Nelson who had transformed so many courses around the world, particularly in south-east Asia. Tom had been a member of Macquarie since it opened in 2002. He liked the undulating challenging course and the privacy of a members-only club. Tom spent a lot of time on the golf course which accounted for his well-tanned face, arms and legs. He was a tall man, over six feet, with a well-trained body and an athletic walk. Jack immediately felt a wave of empathy as Tom greeted Karen and Sam with a wide, genuine smile.

"Got your sea-legs on?" Sam asked them. "Billy Jo weighs anchor at nine and then we're off to Jervis Bay and out to see the dolphins."

"It looks like a great boat," Tom said with an admiring sweep of his hand. He knew it was a great boat! He'd read all about it before coming along. As a top businessman he knew that preparation was the be all and end all of success. *"Amat Victoria curam"* – Victory loves preparation - was one of his favourite sayings.

"Come on board and we'll show you around," said Sam, holding out his arm to invite Nancy and Tom to board. John had seen the guests and owners arriving and had placed himself to one side to take their bags. He now walked up the walkway behind them at a respectable distance and went to put the luggage in the staterooms. All this luggage just for one night, he thought and made his way as instructed to the VIP stateroom first.

Sam had just finished showing Tom and Nancy the boat when they heard a whistle outside. Jerry, the star chef, saluted to Sam and boomed: "Permission to come aboard, sir!"

"Granted," said Sam and smiled at him indulgently. "It's a good job you're such a damned good chef otherwise I might have said no!" he teased.

Jerry had two bags – one with his cooking utensils which he would not do without even on a motor yacht and one small overnight bag. John walked down the walkway and took his bag.

"Jerry, let me introduce you to Nancy and Tom Wyatt. Nancy, Tom, this is Jerry Carey, the best chef in town and he even has sea-legs as well!" They all shook hands with a "pleased to meet you". Now they were all on first-name terms. Tom smiled at Jerry. Tom enjoyed good food and good wine and Sam knew it.

Half an hour later Tom and Sam were on the fly bridge with Jack poring over sea charts and weather forecasts. The ladies, who had changed into shorts and thin t-shirts over their bikinis, were sipping a glass of champagne on the aft exterior deck where Sam had a beige leather padded bar. While the men talked about the sea and all things brave, the ladies discussed family. Sam had briefed Karen to stay away from topics like expensive handbags, jewellery and designer clothes. Nancy was an attractive woman and like her husband enjoyed a discreet, luxurious private life but not an exorbitant one. When Sam had told Karen who he'd invited aboard Billy Jo for the weekend her mind just boggled. All that money, what she could do with all that money. But he had briefed her well – no showing-off, no bragging, just plain small talk, family, friends, golfing, her charities, Tasmania and horses. Nancy was a keen rider and had some really impressive show-horses. Tom shared her passion but from the ground, and not for show-horses but for racehorses. He had two young stallions stabled up in New South Wales and spent as much time as he could watching them race.

Jack switched on the intercom so that Karen and Nancy could hear him as well.

"All eyes right," he said. "We're just about to go under the Harbour Bridge and then emerge to a breath-taking view of Sydney Opera House and the skyline of Sydney in the background bathed in sunshine before we set sail for the Ditch and Jervis Bay."

The Tasman Sea was commonly known in Australia as the Ditch as it separated Australia from New Zealand and bordered to the north on the South Pacific Ocean. It could be quite choppy but today it was as smooth as a mill pond with just a very light breeze. They all sat back to enjoy the day ahead.

7

Saturday, 12th February 2011, Germany, 6.30 a.m.

Svetlana's alarm on her iPhone rang at six thirty. She switched it off and rolled over to kiss Thomas on his cheek.

"Time to get up," she said.

He put his arms round her and held her tight.

"I'll miss you," he said kissing her neck.

"I'll be back on Monday evening. Thomas, we have to leave at eight or I'll miss my train."

On Friday evening she just hadn't felt like packing. Thomas had taken her to her favourite restaurant in Bad Kreuznach, Viva Italia, and they had spent a romantic evening with good Italian food and wine. Thomas had ordered a bottle of Gavi from a good producer because he knew it would go really well with their rocket salad and seared scallops in a tantalizing orange sauce. He also ordered a fantastic Chianti by Antinori to follow to accompany their main course, rack of lamb with rosemary. They didn't drink all of the wine and Svetlana felt embarrassed that they had left some in each bottle. Thomas had told her that the sommelier would be pleased because he didn't always get a chance to try expensive wines. They had arrived home at half past ten. Misha and Alex were alone in the house with Conrad and although Alex was now fourteen and very responsible, they didn't like leaving him alone late at night. They checked on the boys and Thomas popped his head round the door of Conrad's room. Conrad was immersed in some undefinable electric equipment which he had taken apart as usual and would definitely not be able to put back together again. They had gone upstairs to shower and get ready for bed. Svetlana had put on a stunning nightdress which Thomas had bought for her at Christmas. She was a beautiful woman with a beautiful figure and Thomas watched her as she gracefully moved around the bedroom hanging up her clothes so they didn't get creased. She felt his gaze and turned round smiling. She slipped under the duvet and moved over to his side. She put her hand up his pyjama shirt and kissed his belly button. They had spent a long time enjoying just touching and kissing before Thomas could wait no longer. He undid her nightdress and she slipped it over her head. He had long discarded his pyjamas and now rolled over on top of her. Thomas was a good lover and she adored his strong shoulders and arms around her and the gentle way he penetrated her, strong but gentle. He was her gentle protector and lover and their relationship had grown into a full-blown love affair in the seven years they had worked and lived together. And tonight he had finally asked her to marry him. She was overjoyed and their lovemaking that night was very special, very special.

A sexual thrill hit her stomach as she remembered the

night before. She kissed him and said, "I must get up and pack". He sighed and she jumped out of bed. She didn't need much for just three days and put her clothes into a small blue Titan suitcase. She went and showered and Thomas followed her into the bathroom. At seven thirty she was downstairs making them porridge, a very Russian winter breakfast which Thomas appreciated on such cold February mornings even if it was considered a little old-fashioned in Germany. She had made some coffee and Thomas relished the smell as he walked downstairs. While they had breakfast, Svetlana went through all the things that the boys had to do while she was away. Thomas nodded. She had already given him lots of instructions but as her nervousness increased with her departure now very close, her need to repeat everything and make absolutely sure she hadn't forgotten to tell him anything grew to a point that was so tense she couldn't stop herself from going through it all again. Before they left, she went and kissed her sons who were fast asleep and they rolled over without waking up. Thomas had gone to the garage to warm the car for her and put on the seat heating. He put her small blue suitcase in the boot of the car and closed it with a sigh. He felt lost without her. He knew that everything would be alright but there was still a slight risk, a slight risk that she may be searched. He dreaded the thought and forced himself to concentrate on the car, pushing the gear lever into reverse. As he backed out of the garage, Svetlana put on her winter coat, picked up her handbag, gloves, scarf and hat and closed the front door behind her. She went to the car, threw her handbag on to the back seat with her gloves, scarf and hat. She took off her coat and laid it over her handbag and quickly sat down in the passenger seat. It was very cold outside. The warm seat was certainly welcome. She looked at the house one more time and Thomas put his hand on her knee.

"The house will miss you too," he said and smiled.

"Just three days," she said.

"And when you get back, we'll go and find the most beautiful engagement ring you can imagine!"

It only took them an hour to drive to Frankfurt International Airport as there was very little traffic early on a Saturday morning. They had listened to music on the radio, the news, traffic news and found it difficult to make small talk. Thomas drove quite fast but kept to the speed limits along the highways. He left the A3 at the exit for the airport and braked before taking the sharp bend on the slip road. Five minutes later they had parked in the short-stay multi-storey car park and were walking to the long distance railway station at the airport. Svetlana's intercity express ICE 103 was leaving at 9:53 from platform 5. They walked over the station concourse with its huge glass dome to check the departures board and saw that her train was on time. It was nine fifteen and they moved towards the Starbucks on the west side of the concourse. The trains came in underground and the concourse was a shopping mall. They sat and drank their cappuccinos and talked about Thomas' plans for the next week. At nine forty-five Thomas picked up her case and they walked arm in arm to the escalator.

On the platform it was cold and there was an unpleasant breeze from the west. The large grey concrete pillars supporting the underground tunnel made it feel even colder. Thank goodness the sides were glass letting in the ethereal grey light of a mid-February morning. There were quite a few people milling around on the platform waiting for the intercity express. They checked the board to see which section of the platform coach 32 would stop at and walked to section D. As the arrival of the train was announced Thomas hugged Svetlana and whispered in her ear. "Be careful," he said.

"Don't worry," she replied. "I'll be back on Monday evening."

The train screeched to a halt and they walked a few yards to the door which opened automatically and disgorged the travellers who had come from Dortmund or even further north from Hanover. Svetlana climbed up the steps and Thomas handed her the small blue suitcase. She moved along the coach and he moved with her on the platform. She found her seat and put her suitcase in the rack above her head. She turned round and waved, forcing a smile. He smiled back. A whistle blew followed by a loud, high-pitched peeping noise. The doors closed and the train pulled slowly out of the station. Thomas carried on waving until Svetlana was out of sight.

*

Saturday, 12th February 2011, Sydney harbour, 7.30 p.m.

The evening in Sydney harbour was just perfect. Lucky Jack had given them a short cruise around the harbour. They had all seen Sydney Opera House and Harbour Bridge hundreds of times before, but it was still a magnificent sight which thrilled each and every visitor time and time again. They had moored on one of the temporary moorings on the other side of the harbour to have dinner with this breath-taking view through the Azimut's picture windows in the main salon. The table was laid for four with solid silver cutlery and white square porcelain plates. The Riedl glasses sparkled in the sunlight which shone into the salon throwing various tones of orange and red onto the highly polished cherry wood table and cream leather chairs. John was behind the bar mixing cocktails. Nancy and Karen were sipping colourful non-alcoholic cocktails perched on two cream leather bar stools. Tom and Sam were talking business. Both had a Bombay Sapphire and tonic with lots of ice and lemon in their hand. They drank slowly. Both men were aware that they needed to keep a clear head for the first two hours while they did their talking. At five John had knocked on their stateroom door with an ice bucket in his right arm containing a bottle of Röderer Cristal 2002 cooled down to 10°C and two champagne glasses in his left hand.

"With the compliments of the Captain," he said with a smile and spread the white linen table cloth on the small cherry wood table and put down the glasses and the ice bucket gently. "I'll be back in a jiffy with a few nibbles and I'll open the champagne for you," he added as he left the stateroom to pick up a silver tray of delicious "snacks" as Jerry irreverently called them. Jerry sure knew how to cook, John thought and his mouth watered at the thought of the fresh oysters with a twist of lemon and lobster in a silver aperitif spoon with a creamy foam around it which smelt of fine cognac. John had knocked at the stateroom door again and on hearing a "come on in, John" he opened it wide to give Sam's guests a full view of the fantastic array of "snacks".

"Wow," Nancy exclaimed. "If that tastes as good as it looks then I've blown my diet in just twelve hours," she said with a laugh. The gentlemen laughed politely with her but with a knowing look which told her that her figure was fine as it was!

Sam continued his explanations of the anti-venom business for Tom who concentrated on every single word.

"Last year we lost about a half of our equine stock in the Queensland floods," he said matter-of-factly. "We managed to save the other half by swimming them out behind rowing boats. We couldn't use motor boats because of the noise which would have scared them and the danger of injury to the horses from an outboard motor or just panic. It was a mammoth rescue operation. It cost a pretty fortune to replace half the herd to ensure that our production of anti-venom didn't lag behind the orders on our books. In the last few years the demand for anti-venom has increased by fifteen to twenty per cent annually." Sam paused to let this last fact sink in. Tom had made a mental note of it.

"I understand that you can't use other animals for anti-venom production. Is that right?" Tom asked politely knowing the answer already as he had researched the topic on the internet. Sam nodded with a sense of pleasure. Tom's reputation as a man who was always well-prepared was obviously very true. He had done all his homework. "That's right. The horse is one of the oldest animals alive, around two million years old if you count it's rather odd looking ancestors. They have survived for several reasons, one of them being their ability to flee at the first sign of danger at high speed. In order to support the physical effort this needs, horses have an extremely complex blood circulation system which allows them to withstand high ambient temperatures of up to 43°C with no shade and low ambient temperatures as low as minus 25°C with no shelter. It's this blood circulation system that makes them unique and gives them the ability to produce anti-venom when small doses of venom are administered into their blood. All we do is take the anti-venom out of the horse's blood and use it to make anti-dote. It sounds pretty simple but of course it is a very delicate high tech business which requires extremely rare skills and knowledge. That makes our business quite unique," he added and paused again to let this last seed be planted in Tom's mind.

"So how do your business prospects look at present?" Tom asked. Now we were getting to the nitty gritty, Sam thought.

"The banks haven't been very helpful lending us the amount required to replace the horses we lost and increase our cash-flow to produce the increased demand in our export volume. The GFC has a lot to answer for," he said, taking a few nuts from the glass bowl in front of him. Tom nodded sympathetically. Every business in Australia seemed to be complaining about the way banks were handling company loans and credit lines. "And of course the strength of the Australian dollar has reduced income as most of our export deals are done in foreign currency. To reduce the impact of currency fluctuations, we have several foreign currency accounts. We only cash in different currencies when we either see a risk in the currency held or a slight drop in the dollar's value. It means though that you need extra cash flow to be able to afford to choose when you activate the different currencies."

"So if the banks aren't playing ball, are you looking for capital on the private sector?" Tom asked.

"Not openly. This is a family business which is dear to my heart. We need more cash but I don't want to just accept an investor who may not have the future of our business and the best interests of our staff in mind but just his profit. But we are open to discussion with the right person or business to form a partnership. Are you interested, Tom?"

"Maybe," Tom replied. "Being in the risk insurance business, I like the idea of supporting dynamic businesses with good potential and solid business foundations but with a risk element that makes them difficult to insure and prone to large fluctuations which stock markets and insurers don't like. The benefit is, of course, that the returns are high in high-risk companies for private investors and that's what interests me. I sold a large amount of mining shares eight months ago as the strength of the dollar had increased the price of raw materials and the demand for metals and ore in China was slowing down somewhat. I reckon BGF are going to go through a couple of rough years and I'm looking for alternative investments. Interest rates are just too low to consider the normal channels so it has to be high risk."

Bingo, thought Sam. My sources were spot on. He really is interested. What did Jack always say: Luck is being in the right place at the right time.

"If you like I'll send you over some figures and balance sheets on Monday and if you like what you see, give me a ring and we can meet to discuss options," Sam said trying to suppress the overwhelming sense of relief that this expensive little trip might just pay off.

"That's fine with me," Tom replied. "Now we can turn our attention to these two lovely ladies," he added in a loud voice turning his head to Nancy and Karen on their stools. Both ladies understood the cue. Business was over and they could now join their husbands to start the small talk and fun. Karen asked John to make her one of his Daiquiri specials and Nancy decided to join her. The men continued drinking their gin tonics slowly. They both knew that there were some really special wines for dinner.

The sun had set in a glorious blaze of colour lighting up the Opera House and the Harbour Bridge and making the blue water dance in red, orange and purple hews. The party aboard the Azimut Evolution 62 was in full swing. The first course which Jerry had nicknamed "lobster on a bed of roses" had been washed down with a fantastic Chardonnay made by Philip Shaw, one of the most renowned winemakers in Australia with a string of prestigious awards under his belt. Then Jerry came in with a Sauvignon Blanc sorbet to refresh their palates for the fish platter with three different foams – lemon and lime, mango and passion fruit and Sauvignon Blanc and gooseberry. Jerry described this dish as "exotic culinary explosions". John proudly presented a Pouilly Fumée to accompany the fish platter and poured a little into Sam's glass. Sam nodded and John poured a little into each glass starting with Nancy, then Karen, Tom and Sam last. John put the bottle on ice and left the party to enjoy their fish. Jerry had started work on the main course, a perfectly marbled piece of Wagyu beef which he had prepared into four steaks, two large, two medium, and which he intended to flame in brandy and serve with braised artichoke hearts lightly sautéed in his special herbal butter. He waited for John to decant the bottle of Penfolds Grange vintage 2003 before he grilled the steaks. John hurried back to the galley to take the plates, the two medium steaks first, so that they were still piping hot when they were delicately placed on the table. Jerry followed with the two large steaks for Tom and Sam. The beef was exquisite. It cut like butter and tasted out of this world. Sam asked John to fetch Jerry who was still working on his new creation – a Merlot and Chocolate mousse. Jerry walked in and they all clapped. Nancy was first to speak. "Jerry, every course has been a very special experience. Absolutely delicious and amazingly creative."

"I think Nancy has said it all," Sam said, raising his glass to her. "Jerry, we toast you and your very special culinary skills," Sam said. They all raised their glasses and said in chorus, "to Jerry" and sipped the red liquid gold in their glasses. Jerry beamed. All artists like an appreciative audience. He made a funny little bow and disappeared back into the galley.

After dessert Tom turned to Sam and complimented him on his choice of food and wines.

"That Bagnuls with the Merlot and Chocolate mousse was stunning," he said. "I really must try that combination again. An excellent dinner and a wonderful day. Thank you Karen and Sam. We salute you," he said. Nancy and Tom raised their glasses and smiled at their hosts.

It was midnight when the ladies finished off their last glass of champagne and the men an XLO cognac. John held up the bottle of champagne but Nancy put her hand over her glass. "No more for me, thanks John. Otherwise I won't sleep," she said and smiled at her husband. Tom stood up perfectly on cue and said:

"Well, all good things have to come to an end and I think we probably all need some beauty sleep. We loved watching the dolphins today and exploring the coastline from the sea. And we certainly look forward to seeing some whales tomorrow."

"Lucky Jack has promised us that he'll find their current

feeding grounds," Sam said. "And he hasn't disappointed me yet."

They all walked towards the salon door. Tom and Sam shook hands, the ladies just touched the men's cheeks with theirs and Nancy gave Karen a friendly hug. They all said goodnight and Tom and Nancy disappeared.

"We'll have breakfast at nine John. Jack said he wants to lift anchor at nine thirty at the latest."

"Right you are, sir," John replied and disappeared.

Karen looked at Sam. He kissed her on her left cheek and said "Tom is definitely interested in a share in our business, darling. It was a splendid evening. Thank you for everything."

They walked into the master stateroom still holding hands. "What an evening," Sam said. Karen unzipped her evening gown, looked at him over her shoulder and said, "And the best is still to come."

*

Saturday, 12th February 2011, Zurich, 2.30 p.m.

Svetlana got off the train in Zurich with her small blue suitcase and looked up and down the platform. Her brother Victor was never on time. He was over six feet tall and had a bald head which made him stand out in a crowd. She sighed in frustration. It had been a long journey. She had had to change trains in Basle. The train had been late and she had to run to catch her connection. The platforms were crowded. Where did all these people want to go on a Saturday afternoon, she asked herself? When she finally reached Zurich she had hoped that Victor would be there to greet her, give her a hug and carry her case. She should have known better! Victor was her eldest brother, forty-six years old and very Russian. Punctuality was not his best trait. Svetlana on the other hand had lived in Germany for so many years that she had adjusted to German way of life where punctuality was a question of respect and good manners. All of a sudden she heard her name being called from the far end of the platform.

"Svetka, Svetka, I'm over here," Victor's baritone rang out above the noise of passengers being greeted and a train coming to a halt on the next platform. Svetlana could see a fur hat and a hand waving in the distance. With a sigh of relief she moved towards the waving hand. Finally, as the crowd on the platform thinned out, she could see her brother plainly in a thick winter coat and a broad smile on his face. Victor, the engineer of the family, who worked in Switzerland as a foreigner for six months of the year. Even if he did only earn sixty per cent of what a Swiss engineer would earn for the same job, he earnt enough in six months to ensure that his family had a spacious flat in Moscow, a minimum of comfort and a good education. He spent the rest of the year working as a consultant in Moscow, keeping his know-how up to date and earning extra cash that didn't have to be declared to the fiscal authorities.

Victor hugged his younger sister in a bear-like hug. He

could have crushed her but he didn't. He was a gentle giant and genuinely pleased to see her. They only saw each other once a year in Switzerland and once a year in Moscow when she visited their mother in summer.

"How are Masha and the children," she asked as he picked up her suitcase. "Fine," he said. "Everyone is fine. Except for Mama, of course. But Olesya has told you all about that. A maximum of three years isn't a long time," he mused. "Grigoriy is going to see her at Easter," he said. Grigoriy was his younger brother, four years younger than Victor and almost five years older than Svetlana. Olesya was the youngest. Grigoriy lived in St. Petersburg and was the artist of the family. He had no money but lots of talent. He worked at the Mikhailovsky Theatre and lived for his work. He wasn't married and most of the family was convinced that he was homosexual. Victor and Svetlana adored Grigoriy. He had inherited the creative spirit of their father. Victor and Svetlana took after their mother – business-like, pragmatic, and ambitious.

"Mama will be delighted," she replied. "I'm planning to go over for a week at the beginning of March. I need to sort some finances out. Mama and Olesya can carry on living in the apartment and we'll send Olesya five hundred Euros a month to help pay for bills and any medication Mama might need."

"That's very generous of you and Thomas," Victor said sincerely. "I won't be able to give the same amount but I was thinking of giving her five thousand roubles a month."

"But Victor, that's a lot of money and soon you'll be

paying university fees for not just one but two children."

"Big children," he said with a smile. "Don't worry, sis, I have a bit of money on the side which I can use for Mama."

Svetlana felt guilty. Her brother had two grown-up kids, could only work six months of the year on a reasonable salary and wanted to give their mother money. Whereby she was here to pick up forty thousand Euros from their bank account in Switzerland and he had no idea how wealthy they were. Sure, they would need the money later for Conrad and Thomas had set up a trust for him which amounted to five hundred thousand Euros. Armen had "donated" the money, a legal donation for a friend's sick brother. "Peanuts," is how the Russian fiscal authorities described the amount when the German Finanzamt launched an official enquiry. They knew how much Armen was worth. And that was his official worth. Most of his money was in bank accounts abroad! The great Russian businessmen, milking the state and then not even investing the proceeds in the Mother Country they were so proud of! The rest of the revenue from Thomas' business transactions with Armen was paid in yearly amounts – two million roubles amounting to fifty thousand Euros to Svetlana's sister and twice that sum to a Swiss bank account from an account on the Cayman Islands. Olesya kept eight hundred thousand roubles in two accounts. One account was to pay for everything for their mother. She only needed half the amount Armen gave her and the rest was in a savings account at the Sperbank earning twenty percent interest. That was Olesya's reward for looking after their mother. And rumour had it that Armen had an expensive lady friend in the city. Svetlana had bought the apartment that Olesya and her mother lived in for just under eighteen million roubles six years ago with Armen's help. That help usually meant ensuring that the occupier no longer wanted to live in the apartment and no other buyer appeared with a serious offer. Svetlana knew that the methods Armen and his so-called associates used to buy desirable properties were not legal but no-one was interested. And those who should have been interested such as the FSK turned a blind eye and carried on being paid for their blindness. For the last six years Olesya had sent Svetlana one hundred thousand roubles a month in Euros, around two thousand five hundred Euros a month or thirty thousand Euros a year as "rent". Now that the payments from Armen were going to stop, Svetlana would no longer need any more "rent" from Olesya and Olesya could continue to live rent-free with her mother as long as her mother needed her. That was the arrangement. Five hundred Euros a month for her mother would allow them to live comfortably plus five thousand roubles a month from Victor. That should be enough. And when her mother was no longer there, a thought she dreaded but she had forced herself to discuss it with Olesya, then Olesya wanted to move out of Moscow to Ekaterinburg where her partner lived. So Svetlana would lease the apartment and that would help pay for Misha and Alex to go to university if they both made the grade.

"You've gone quiet, sis," Victor said.

"I was just going through all the expenses Mama will

have in the next few years. I think we should have enough and if not, Victor, then I'll find some more, Thomas is adamant about that. You know how he feels about family and he considers our family his own. His father dying so young and having a handicapped brother really have influenced his whole way of thinking."

"I still think it's very generous of him," Victor said. "And he looks after your boys as if they were his own."

"Soon they will be," Svetlana said and looked Victor in the eyes to catch his expression of surprise.

"His?" he queried.

"Yes, Thomas and I are going to get married and I'm going to ask Klaus to let him adopt Misha and Alex so Thomas really will be their father on paper as well as in practice."

Victor overcame his surprise and beamed.

"After all these years, my goodness, seven years, I really am pleased for you, Svetlana. That's wonderful news. And Thomas will be a wonderful husband and father…and brother in law come to think of it." Victor laughed out loud and his laughter was so infectious that Svetlana had to join in. Her guilty thoughts vanished.

8

Sunday, 13th February 2011, Frankfurt, Germany, 1.15 p.m.

The Emirates Boeing 777 from Dubai landed At Frankfurt Main International Airport on time at 1.15 p.m. The handsome, well-spoken man in first class had just returned from Sydney where he'd spent two weeks' holiday, mainly surfing, diving and biking. He looked like a body builder and his tanned, well-trained body was always welcome in the trendy, high-class discotheques of Moscow. As the plane taxied towards Terminal 2 he switched on his smartphone and checked for messages. The plane came to a complete stop after five minutes, time enough to check the most important messages. He could see the jet bridge approaching the doors. All doors were now in park and the cabin crew gratefully swung the doors open to let in the fresh air. The man was travelling on a Russian passport under the name of Andrey Ivanov. He answered to quite a few different names but his passport, whatever nationality, was always genuine. Andrey had worked for the FSB, the Russian Federal Security Service, until 2008 when the then head of the service, Nikolai Patrushev, left to become Secretary of the Security Council of Russia. The new Director, Alexander Bortnikov, had barely had time to put his feet under the desk when Andrey resigned. He was then 32 years old and had all the necessary business knowledge and business connections in Moscow to run his own business and work for the great and mighty in the business world of Moscow under cover using the special skills he had acquired during his six years at the FSB. Officially he was a businessman with a Masters degree from the ESCE International Business School in Paris and fluent in four languages.

Andrey's father had been a high-ranking officer in the KGB, the Committee of State Security in the former Soviet Union. Andrey was born in 1976 in East Berlin where his father was stationed. He was thirteen when the Berlin Wall came down in 1989 and attending an international school where everything was taught in German, Russian and English. In 1990 his father was ordered back to Moscow and Andrey was sent to an international boarding school in England to perfect his English. After leaving school top of his year, he was sent to Paris to learn French for a year. He then applied for a five years Masters course at the ESCE International Business School in Paris where he perfected his fluency in French. In 1999 he went to work in Mannheim for John Deere who were making in-roads into Europe in general and Eastern Europe in particular. After three years in Mannheim he had travelled Germany extensively and lost any hint of an East German accent. He was a talented linguist with a musical ear. He could pass for a German from Hanover or even Bavaria and notably as someone born in the Palatinate region. His grasp of regional accents was second to none. In 2002 he returned to Moscow where he was recruited by the FSB, having been groomed for the service over the past decade.

The man he had come to meet was called Norbert Mayer. It would be a quick visit and everything would be arranged without emails or phone calls. Andrey was in Frankfurt as a stopover before flying back to Moscow the next day and would introduce himself to Norbert Mayer as Thomas Becker. He grabbed the warm winter coat he'd taken out of his cabin luggage and threw it over his arm. In Sydney the temperature had been in the thirties and now he was back to European winter with temperatures around freezing in Frankfurt. He grabbed his cabin bag, smiled at the cabin crew as he strode pass them on to the walkway. He'd been to Frankfurt many times "on business" and had a business visa courtesy of a friend of a friend. Money talked and Andrey had lots of cash in different bank accounts around the world. He had arranged for a transfer of a tidy sum from the Cayman Islands to the bank account of a friend who lived in Australia. His friend had withdrawn a large sum in cash and changed fourteen thousand dollars into Euros. The bank knew that this valued customer went abroad on business regularly so no eyebrows were raised. Andrey had spent most of his Australian dollars in the two weeks he had been on holiday. He had put nine thousand eight hundred Euros into his cabin bag, partly to spend on the prettiest woman in Frankfurt he could find and partly to pay Norbert

Mayer for his services. He could bring under ten thousand Euros in cash to Germany with no questions asked.

It took him ten minutes to walk to passport control where his passport was checked with a scrutinizing efficiency. That didn't worry Andrey at all. His passport was genuine. The border policeman checked his screen with all the photos of undesirable and wanted aliens, looked at the man in front of him, swiped the data page of his biometric passport and watched the screen.

"Vielen Dank," said the polite border policeman.

"Bitte schön," Andrey replied with a smile, took his passport and put it in his inside jacket pocket. He walked to concourse E to collect his luggage and waited for a few minutes at the carousel. His hard-shell black Samsonite arrived quickly and he was nodded through customs as he walked through the "nothing to declare" green zone. He stopped at the lifts and put on his coat. As he stepped outside the cold air was refreshing, almost exhilarating. He strode quickly to the taxi rank pushing his case and carrying his briefcase in his right hand. He got in the first taxi in the line and the driver looked at him in his mirror. Turkish, thought Andrey. Born here most probably.

"Zum Hotel Steigenberger Frankfurter Hof", he said.

"Jawohl", the driver answered as he eased the cream-coloured Mercedes out of its parking space and on to the set-down road in front of the terminal. It wasn't every day that a guest wanted to go to the most famous hotel in Frankfurt, one of the best hundred hotels in the world. It was just a short ride to this world of luxury just twelve kilometres from one of the busiest airports in Europe. Fifteen minutes later the driver stopped in front of the main entrance and turned towards his guest with a smile.

"Fünfundzwanzig Euro siebzig," he said. Twenty five Euros and seventy cents, cheaper than in Moscow Andrey mused. Germany was an expensive country but taxis and eating out still remained extremely good value for money. He gave the driver a twenty and a ten Euro note and told him to keep the change.

"Das stimmt so," he said.

The driver thanked him and asked him if he wanted a receipt. As Andrey put the receipt in his wallet, the driver jumped out the driver's seat and opened the rear door. He had opened the boot of the car automatically from the driver's seat before getting out. He walked to the back of the car, took out his guest's case and handed it to the bell-boy waiting next to the taxi with a luggage trolley.

At reception Andrey Ivanov booked into the Executive Suite he had reserved from Sydney. The receptionist eyed him from head to foot. Rich, handsome guests with no wedding ring were always welcome, she thought and smiled at the German-speaking guest with a Russian passport. He was paying by credit card and she swiped his card to reserve the appropriate amount. She gave him his card back and gave the key to his room to the bell-boy. The bell-boy walked ahead of him to the lift. The wood everywhere was highly polished and the brass fittings gleamed. That's what Andrey liked about Germany. You got what you paid for and it was efficient and clean. The lift stopped at the third floor. "Links, bitte," the bell-boy said indicating that the gentleman should walk to the left. The bell-boy opened the door to Andrey's suite and said: "Bitte, mein Herr," letting Andrey walk into the elegant room with a polished parquet floor. Andrey gave the bell-boy a five Euro note and the young fair-haired teenager with greyish-blue eyes thanked him and walked out closing the door softly. Andrey took in the doors and windows, noted the next fire exit and looked out of the windows to see where they looked out on to. A habit he would never lose. He walked into the marbled bathroom and washed his hands. He looked at his watch. It was just after three in the afternoon. Time for a refreshing bath after the long flight from Sydney and time to log in to his email account before he went out on the town.

*

It was six o'clock on Monday morning in Sydney and the sun was beginning to light up the sky in the east. Pete Owen had woken up his daughter Regan and was now packing his holdall. They would be back on Wednesday evening and only needed a small overnight bag. Pete owned and operated a Cessna 172 Skyhawk SP, a small aircraft with a range of just over seven hundred miles and a cruising speed of one hundred and forty five miles an hour. It would take them about four hours to Brisbane. It would have been quicker to take a domestic flight but as flying was a hobby, he preferred to use his own plane unless the weather was really bad. He looked around the master bedroom where his wife, Jean, lay in bed with her blond hair strewn across the pillow. She was fast asleep and Pete decided not to wake her until he and Regan were ready to go. The bedroom was furnished in a pseudo-colonial style with wood and cane furniture. He had opened the window which had a mosquito net to keep the tiresome mosquitos out but also the poisonous spiders that crawled in even in Frenchs Forest, a north-western suburb of Sydney. True to the Australian spirit he never worried about poisonous spiders and snakes but life had taught him to be careful. He put his anti-venom kit in his holdall. He put on his merino wool socks and walked quietly out of the bedroom and down the stairs. He had agreed to show Regan round the factory in Hawkes Lift and Sam MacPherson's plantation of strychnine trees, otherwise known as poison nut or Quaker Buttons. The Quaker Buttons plantation was only about ten miles from Hawkes Lift and Regan had asked if they could ride there. It was only about an hour's ride on horseback and Pete had four horses stabled near the factory. He stroked Pebble, their golden retriever, as he went past the bathroom. Pebble was waiting for Regan to come out after her shower and even the thought of the kitchen and breakfast wouldn't make her leave her spot. He smiled and went into the kitchen to make some coffee and scrambled eggs. It would be a long day and they wouldn't get lunch until they got back to the factory. Pete was thrilled at the idea of showing Regan round the factory and just give her a few insights into the workings of his business. Don't push her, he thought. She has to make up her own mind when she's ready. And finish university and work in another firm first. But he was bursting to share some of his business life with her and she was eager to learn and to know about it all. The sun started to appear above the horizon and shone into the modern kitchen with its white wood doors and marble surfaces. Jean had insisted on having the bedroom and the kitchen in the east. She said she needed the sun to wake her up in the morning and entice her out of bed. And she needed the sun in the kitchen where she spent a large part of the morning. The kitchen was large and stretched over the width of the house. In the west there was a white dining table and four chairs where the family ate their informal meals every day. The dining room was much more formal, in the north of the house and opened out on to a large patio with a swimming pool beyond. The whole area was paved and furnished with wicker chairs and sofas with soft cushions depicting tropical birds and flowers. In summer it was great to have breakfast out on the patio and dinner with guests in the dining room on the long wooden table with the patio doors open. On Australia Day on 26th January he had invited Sam and Karen to join them and a few other good friends. Jean had prepared a wonderful spread of cold salmon, salads and vegetables and Pete had barbecued some fantastic Queensland beef that he brought back from his trips to the factory. There were three times as many cows in Queensland than people and the grazing land for beef was some of the best. Pete made himself a cup of coffee and a piece of toast. He scrambled four eggs and cooked them in the microwave. When he heard Regan come out of the bathroom he made her a cappuccino and put a couple of slices of toast in the toaster.

"Dad, you're awesome. I really don't know how you do it. You're ready to take the world on as soon as you get out of bed."

"Well, gorgeous, I think you may take after me in looks but you have your mother's morning muffle syndrome," he said with a smile. "Try just a little of my special scrambled egg. Here's your cappuccino to get you going."

"Thanks," she said sitting down at the table with him.

Pebble walked up to Pete and wagged his tail.

"OK, boy," he said. "Your breakfast will be coming along straight after I've finished mine."

Pebble sighed and lay down next to Pete's chair.

"Joe said he wants to take off around nine so we need to leave here around half past seven, in just twenty minutes," he said. Normally Pete would have flown his four-seater Cesna himself but Joe had offered to fly them and it would allow Pete to concentrate one hundred percent on Regan. "Have you packed?" he asked.

"All ready to go," she said. "Just got to put my sweatshirt on and find my riding boots."

"They're outside with mine. I gave them a once-over last night."

"Dad, you're impossible," she said and put her empty plate and cutlery into the dishwasher.

"Have you put your riding hat in your bag?" he asked.

"Yes, even if I am the only twenty-year old who has to wear a riding hat." She knew this topic would stir him up and he turned on his heels. "Maybe other twenty year olds don't have a brain to protect," he said and turned to pick up their boots. "I've even put my hat in my bag."

"Maybe I'll take a picture of you and put it on Facebook," she goaded.

"Don't you dare. I know it's not the essence of your Australian pioneering spirit but I have a responsibility to you, Mum and all our workers so even if my brain isn't as good as yours, it still needs protecting."

He walked into the porch and grabbed their boots. They always wore ankle-high leather riding booties, even when they were just walking the dog. A small protection against snake bites as well as comfortable footwear. Pete put them next to the front door then ran up the stairs two at a time and into the bedroom. He zipped up his holdall and Jean stirred. She opened her eyes and looked at him.

"Are you ready to leave?" she asked.

"Yep. We want to get away at seven thirty to make sure we get to the airport at a quarter to nine."

"I'll come down then," she said, turning over to get out of bed and slip on her dressing gown. She put her fingers through her hair and threw her hair back over her shoulders. He kissed her and asked

"Did you sleep well?"

"Not bad," she said. "When do you and Regan expect to be back?"

"Tomorrow evening around ten," he replied.

They walked down the wooden stairs into the spacious hall where Regan had put her holdall and was just putting on her boots.

"Hi, Mum," she said.

"Hello, darling," Jean replied. "Are you looking forward to the trip?" she asked.

Regan smiled at her father and then replied: "Yep, sure am. It'll be awesome," she said and it was obvious that she really meant it, a sentiment Jean couldn't really share as she wasn't very interested in Pete's business, particularly not the manufacturing side.

"I hope you both enjoy your day," Jean said, kissing her daughter goodbye.

"We will," Regan replied.

Pete had put on his boots and then kissed his wife goodbye. Pebble was wagging his tail next to Regan hoping that they were going for a walk.

"No, Pebble, tomorrow," Regan said. The dog understood from the tone of her voice that the reason for an early start this morning was not a long walk along North Head and sat down with short whine, his eyes almost pleading to change Regan's mind. Regan stroked his head and with both hands and said "I'll be back tomorrow, Pebble."

Regan and Pete walked towards the black four wheel drive and threw their holdalls into the boot. Pete started the car. Jean stood in the hall framed by the open door and waved. Pete and Regan waved back and Pete drove slowly round the beautiful flowering island in the middle of the drive checking right and left to enjoy the bright colours of his azaleas.

They arrived at Bankstown airport at half past eight.

Bankstown airport is a small but busy airport around twenty kilometres west of Sydney. Most of the planes operating out of Bankstown are light aircraft under seven tons with a large proportion of private owner-operated planes. The formalities for regular traffic were pretty basic. Pete drove his car into the car park, went through the main entrance, said good morning to the clerk at the departures desk and showed him his pass and signed Regan in as a visitor.

"Morning, Pete," replied the clerk taking a quick look at Pete's pass just to make sure the expiry date was OK.

"This is my daughter, Regan, Phil."

"Pleased to meet you," the clerk said and signed the book next to Pete's entry. "When do you expect to be back," he asked.

"We should be in around nine tomorrow evening," he replied. "Joe's done all the paperwork. My day off today," he said with a smile. "Joe's flying us out to Archerfield today."

"Aren't you the lucky one," Phil said. "Have a good flight. The weather looks good."

"Thanks," said Pete and he and Regan walked towards the door. On the tarmac the morning air was still quite fresh but the sun was shining and it was going to be a beautiful late summer day. Perfect, Pete thought. Couldn't be better.

They arrived at Archerfield just outside Brisbane at one o'clock. Joe had flown as low as possible to give Regan a good view of the countryside as they travelled. Pete gave her a running commentary. After all, he had flown this route in the Cessna at least a hundred times. He knew every town, every road, and every bay along the coast. Quite often the weather wasn't as kind as it was today and for Pete it really was a thrill to show his daughter the part of his life his family hadn't really shared up to now. They taxied along the runway and the small Cessna Skyhawk came to a halt about five hundred yards from the small terminal building. Pete and Regan both thanked Joe for a great ride and jumped out on to the tarmac. Bill, Pete's second in command, was waiting to pick them up with sandwiches for lunch. In the car on the way to Hawkes Lift Bill and Pete caught up on a few pressing topics and Regan listened in. It was around three o'clock when they arrived at the stables. Sam MacPherson had offered Pete four of his horses a couple of years back – two seven-year old mares, a five-year old gelding and a twelve-year old gelding. Pete had picked them from a group of twenty horses Sam had selected. Pete was delighted. They were great little horses for the outback. Pete had been an extremely good rider in his younger days, winning competitions in dressage and show-jumping. It was a fantastic hobby for a young man. There weren't many young men around the horses, mainly young women, and any decent young male rider had the pick of the harem. That's were Pete had met Jean and ever since they had been married Jean and Pete kept four horses in Frenchs Forest just to hack out. Regan had learnt to ride at the age of seven and was a proficient rider but not interested in competing like her girlfriends. She preferred hacking out with her parents, discovering nature, plants, trees, animals. Pete was looking forward to a really good ride out to the plantation. Bill had arranged for Mike to ride with them. Mike had grown up in Queensland and been around horses all his life. He was their supervisor out in the southern part of the Temple Forrest and he knew Sam MacPherson's plantation like the back of his hand. Pete always insisted on grooming and saddling his horse himself. He called it good social behaviour and one of the ways to ensure that the horse and rider had the correct bond and the horse knew who the boss was. Regan was grooming one of the mares, Mike had already saddled the seven-year old for himself and Pete was grooming the twelve-year old gelding, Tucker. He loved Tucker. He always managed at least one ride with Tucker when he was up in Queensland. He said it kept him fit and sane. They finished saddling the horses and walked them to the front of the stables and mounted. They walked their horses along the road and then turned off into the forest along the main forest track. The main tracks were man-made and prepared for big wood-cutting machinery. They were made of compacted gravel overgrown with short-cropped grass. The grass helped to stop erosion and was cut by the transporters going to and from the plantations to keep it short. It was ideal for riding – no snakes, solid ground with a soft surface. Mike turned to the others and said "ready to put into second gear?" Pete and Regan nodded and Mike's horse Sunny Boy started to jog along the track. After about a mile of "warming up" Mike put his left leg back, gave Sunny Boy more right rein and clicked with his tongue. The horse obediently sprang into a lope, a lazy kind of canter. After five minutes they arrived at a long straight stretch and Mike looked back to see that everything was OK. He then moved into fourth gear and Sunny Boy let loose with Regan and Pete each at a safe distance behind him and each other. The horses galloped along the track for fifteen minutes before the track became narrower and started to climb. Mike reined Sunny Boy back to a jog with a soft "Easy, easy boy" and then with another "Easy" back to a walk. He patted his horse affectionately on the neck and the horse responded with a nod.

"Good work, boy," he said and the horse seemed to appreciate his praise, tossing his mane to fight off the flies.

"Wow, that was fun," Regan said.

"It sure was," said Pete.

"The track is a little trickier after the hill so we'll keep the pace nice and easy," Mike said. "We should be there in about twenty minutes."

When they arrived at the out-station on the edge of the planation of Quaker Buttons the horses were still sweating even though they had walked the last couple of miles to cool them down. They all dismounted and Pete and Regan took off their riding hats. Two youths took the three horses from them. Pete looked at Mike with a raised eyebrow. "Students doing a bit of work experience," Mike said answering Pete's quizzical look. He turned to the youths and added: "Put the saddlebags in the office and make sure you wash the horses down before they go out to graze. We don't want any sunburn."

Pete put his arm round Regan and they walked behind Mike to the "office" which was basically a small container with a couple of windows. In the office Mike introduced them to the plantation manager, Sean, and showed Regan and Pete which sector of the plantation they would have a look at the next day and gave them both a cup of coffee.

"All ready to go" Mike said after he had finished showing Regan the different maps and pictures of the plantation and the data they had on each lot of trees. "Sean and Judith will be waiting for you."

Regan and Pete grabbed their hats which they had tied to their saddles during the ride and their saddlebags. They had packed their overnight gear in the saddlebags and given Bill their holdalls with the rest of their belongings for the following day. The sun was gradually sinking in the sky as they walked to the buggy for the ride to sector BZ23 and Regan was as excited as a five year old on Christmas Day.

9

It was nine thirty in the evening and Andrey was sitting in Jules bar in a chic part of Frankfurt. The concierge had recommended this expensive night club and his taxi driver had agreed that it was the place to see and be seen. He had eaten a light meal in his room at the Frankfurter Hof and dressed in a smart Italian suit which he particularly liked because of its slim line fit and silky material. He had checked all his mails and answered the ones that were important. He didn't use an encrypted system. He knew that every secret service in the world, not just the FSB and the NSA, could read any emails they wanted to. So he wrote what appeared to be normal emails to a normal account but the message in the email was always a matter of interpretation for the recipient. Andrey wasn't a beer drinker. He preferred good wine and he had ordered a bottle of Müller Catoir Riesling, one of his favourite producers of Riesling in Germany. The lady on the other side of the bar had been watching him for at least twenty minutes. He asked the barman for a second Riedl wine glass and walked over to the long-legged blonde in a tight-fitting black cocktail dress with the bottle of wine in his hand.

"The wine's just too good to drink alone," he said with

a smile and the lady smiled back.

"I like a man with expensive taste," she replied and nodded to the plush leather bar stool next to her, inviting him to sit down.

"Let's go over there," he said, pointing to a low table with leather chairs. "More comfortable, quieter, easier to talk," he said. She grabbed her silver clutch bag and slid off her stool. Her long blonde hair hung quite wild around her sculptured features and her eyes were full of questions.

It was six thirty when Andrey woke up. His alarm hadn't gone off yet – he only put it on out of routine. His body woke up when he told it to and this morning he had several things to do. The night had been better than expected. Nicole turned out to be not only intelligent but a pleasure to sleep with. His thoughts went back to her smooth skin, the delicate fragrance of her hair and the tenderness of her touch. They had left the bar around eleven thirty and took a taxi to his hotel. Andrey had stroked her bare shoulder with his hand as he helped her into her stole. In the taxi her sculptured profile shone against a background of passing lights and her long, Swarovski earrings glittered as they caught a beam of light from an on-coming car. When they arrived at the hotel, he paid the driver from the back seat and just said: "Keep the change". He opened the door and jumped out. He could feel her eyes on him as his athletic body stood up and walked round the car. He opened the door and offered her his hand to lean on as she stepped out of the car. Her black high heels appeared first with her tanned skin showing through her sheer stockings. She swung her body up and out of the car like a gymnast. Yes, he thought, closing the car door and put his right arm around the lower part of her back, just touching very lightly. The concierge said "Good evening" in a polite way, discreetly turning his head away from the couple walking to the lift. They stood in the lift in silence and walked down the corridor to his suite as if they did this every night. As he opened the door to his suite, Andrey stood back and smiled. "After you," he said, extending his left arm to invite her in. She walked to the window and looked out at the city lights.

"Would you like something to drink?" he asked, taking her stole from her shoulders. She turned round and smiled. "No, thank you. I think I've had enough for tonight. I'll just have a glass of still water."

He walked towards the door and put her stole on a series of designer hooks on the wall. He walked towards the fridge, stopping at the chair behind the desk to put his jacket over it. He took a bottle of Evian out of the fridge and poured them both a glass of cold still water. He handed her a glass and stood at the window next to her. He could hear her breathing. They drank in silence for a moment. He looked at her and his whole body suddenly seemed to be enveloped in a longing he rarely felt. He put his glass on the window ledge, took hers and put it next to his. He took hold of her hand gently and she followed him into the bedroom. He kissed the top of her bare arm and stroked the underside of her lower arm, taking in her delicate fragrance. He gently pulled her body towards him and undid the zip at the back of her dress. She really was beautiful.

She laid her hands on the knot of his tie, undid it and unbuttoned his shirt. She stroked his strong muscular chest, the body of a well-trained man. She kicked off her shoes and took a step towards the bed where she lifted her right foot on to the covers, put her hands on the lace top of her thigh high stocking and slowly unrolled it down her leg. Andrey took off his trousers and laid them on the armchair. He could feel her eyes on him as he laid his Prada silk shirt and Calvin Klein boxer briefs on top of his trousers. She was taking in every inch of his tanned muscular body, the body of a surfer and swimmer. She hadn't asked many questions about him. She didn't want to know but he said he'd just arrived back from a holiday in Australia to attend a trade fair in Frankfurt and it was obvious that he hadn't been lying. She lay on the bed displaying her beautiful body and watched him come over to her in an obvious state of excitement. He slipped on to the bed and rolled his body next to hers so that their skin touched from her perfectly formed breasts to the tip of her long, slender toes. He caressed her and she reacted by kissing and feeling every part of this man's body, as if checking his trigger points. After several minutes he couldn't wait any longer and rolled on top of her. Their bodies entwined and he moved slowly and gently over her, caressing her breasts. He kissed her and their lips expressed what their tongues were not allowed to say. As he penetrated her a sexual thrill shook her body and it increased as he moved inside her. After several minutes he took hold of her upper body and turned over. She sat on him watching the expression on his face as she moved backwards and forwards, contracting her muscles to give him as much pleasure as possible before he reached his climax. His breathing became heavier and her movements stronger and shorter. They were both perspiring and enjoying pure sexual pleasure. Andrey could wait no longer and as his whole body was engulfed in extreme sexual pleasure, his groan and spasm triggered an orgasm in Nicole's groin which she had never felt before with a paying client. It surprised her so much that it took a few seconds before she caught her breath and came back to her senses. After all, this was just paid sex, nothing more. She slid next to Andrey's warm body and put her left arm over his chest. He stroked her skin in a way which said "Just give me a moment," and she knew the night held a few more sexual pleasures in the wings. She wanted him to remember her.

She had slipped out of his bed at three in the morning, put on her clothes, took the money he had discreetly laid out on the table with a little note saying "thank you". He had pretended to be asleep as she closed the door to his suite. He immediately got out of bed and checked for any foreign objects in his room. You couldn't be too careful in his line of business and no-one was exactly as they appeared to be. Especially ladies who worked for escort agencies who could be bought. Satisfied that everything was alright, he went back to bed and slept for another three hours.

Andrey had eaten fruit and yoghurt for breakfast and ordered an omelette with mushrooms and ham and slices of tomato. The coffee was very German, strong, aromatic and just a little too acidic for his taste. But with cream it was delicious. He wiped his mouth with the white linen serviette and pushed his chair back. The waiter who had served him wished him a good day and held the door open for his guest. Back in his suite, Andrey went to the bathroom and took the pale blue contact lenses out of his Samsonite toiletry bag. He put the lenses into his eyes carefully, blinked a few times and looked at himself in the mirror.

"Good morning, Herr Becker," he thought.

He had shaved attentively that morning and rubbed in a special make-up which would stop his dark stubble from appearing until late afternoon. The pale brown wig he had bought in Sydney matched the hairstyle of the picture he had received with his holiday photos by email of a middle-aged German he had never met but was now about to become. He put the wig into his empty cabin case along with one of his Moscow Armani suits and changed into the clothes laid out on his bed – casual clothes any businessman would wear, nothing flashy, nothing to say where he or the clothes came from. He had chosen a grey suit, black winter shoes, a light blue shirt and a striped tie – much more conservative than he would normally wear. He put on his coat which covered up his new look, closed his case and rang for the bell-boy who appeared so quickly that Andrey wondered if they weren't standing outside the doors of all the guests who were leaving that day. He asked the bell-boy to put his suitcase in the baggage room and the young man came back with a ticket. Andrey gave him a five Euro note and the young man thanked him profusely. Andrey walked round the suite checking that he had left nothing. He had rinsed the glasses from the night before and wiped the fridge door and the bottle of Evian. He went into the bathroom and gave the taps one last wipe with a towel. He put his tight-fitting leather gloves on in the hall and grabbed his cabin bag. He opened the door and walked to the lift. He moved swiftly to the smart-looking man at reception whom he hadn't seen the day before when he checked in.

"I'd like to check out," Andrey said, passing his key card to the young man.

"I hope you enjoyed your stay with us, Mr. Ivanov," he said, checking the name in his computer at the speed of light. "Your bill, sir."

Andrey saw the total but didn't examine it closely. He just put his credit card on top of the bill and waited until the reception clerk handed him back the card and then the bill with his credit card receipt in an envelope with an embossed crest.

"We look forward to welcoming you again at the Frankfurter Hof," the clerk said and Andrey replied "Ganz gewiß," – most certainly – smiled and walked towards the door with the bell-boy in tow with his cabin bag. He took the first cream-coloured Mercedes taxi parked in front of the hotel on the right-hand side and the bell-boy opened the door. The driver got out and the bell-boy gave him the small suitcase.

"Zur Messe," Andrey said before he got in the car. He wanted the bell-boy to know that he was going to the trade fair.

At seven thirty in the morning the traffic in downtown Frankfurt was beginning to build-up. Most people started work between seven and eight thirty. The permanent trade fair building was right in the middle of the city. Its tower looked like an old-fashioned pencil case from afar. With its sixty-three storeys it was a city landmark. The tower was only used for offices and the actual trade fair buildings were just a stone's throw from the tower. The taxi ride was only twenty minutes. The driver pulled up outside the main visitors' entrance to the fair. Andrey paid the taxi driver and asked him to write out a receipt with "from Frankfurter Hof to the Trade Fair". Andrey pocketed the receipt, took his small cabin bag and walked towards the entrance. To the right he saw a sign marked WC and walked into the gents' toilet. There wasn't a soul in the washroom – too early. It was only just before eight and the fair didn't start until nine. He went into one of the toilets, closed the door, took off his coat, hung it up and then he opened his cabin bag. He took out the wig and put it on. He walked out of the toilet and adjusted his wig in front of the mirror. He was about the same height as Thomas Becker and now he had the same colour eyes, the same hair and clothes which a wine broker in Frankfurt on business may well have worn. Satisfied with his appearance, Andrey left the toilets and walked towards the registration desk. A young lady asked him if he had already reserved an entrance ticket on-line. He showed her the reservation and she printed out his badge: Andrey Ivanov, Managing Director, The Sportshouse, Moscow.

"I'm afraid that visitors can't enter the fair until nine

o'clock, Mr. Ivanov" she said.

"Then I'll check my emails first. It's already eleven o'clock in Moscow," he replied. "Can you tell me where I can get the best cappuccino in the building?"

"On your way to hall six there's a coffee bar on your right, Alfredo's. He definitely has the best coffee in the whole building," she said with a radiant smile that said, "Aren't I good!"

Andrey thanked her and walked off towards hall six and to Alfredo's where he sat for half an hour over his cappuccino and his Blackberry. At nine o'clock he walked towards the entrance to hall six. He put his badge on the scanner and the barrier opened its gate. Now he was registered as a visitor to the fair. The German system was very efficient – it registered how many people came, who they were, where they came from. A visitor's badge was validated when he scanned it at the entrance to one of the halls. And when he left, it would scan again and register one person leaving at nine forty-five but not which person. Just that one person had left.

At ten minutes to ten Andrey came out of the main trade fair building and hopped into another cream-coloured taxi at the taxi rank outside the trade fair building. He showed the driver an address on the Zeil in the most expensive shopping precinct in Frankfurt, in fact one of the most expensive in the whole of Germany. Norbert Mayer was a jeweller and owned a jeweller's shop on this exclusive street. According to Andrey's source in Sydney Norbert Mayer lived in one of the most exclusive areas of Frankfurt, on the Nobelring in Lerchesberg on the south bank of the river. It was quite convenient for his business, a good address and only fifteen minutes by car from his shop. Since planning permission for the new north-west runway at Frankfurt international airport had been granted and the construction of the new runway just months away from being put into operation, the prices for real estate on the Lerchesberg had started to fall and his house had lost thirty per cent of its value. His mortgage wasn't his only problem. His addiction to poker was an even bigger burden and had forced him into certain activities on the black market with precious stones and, through a contact in Sydney, with illegal substances.

Andrey alias Thomas Becker paid for his taxi and put the receipt in his wallet. The taxi driver opened the door for him and took his small cabin bag from the boot of the car. It was just after ten and the Zeil was already beginning to buzz with customers along both sides of the street as the shops on both sides of the street opened their doors. Andrey looked at the sign above the jeweller's shop: "Mayer & Mayer GmbH". He walked through the entrance doors which had warm air blowing from the sides against the cold air outside. The inside of the shop was pleasantly warm and inviting, alive with light, mirrors, gold and diamonds. A young lady asked him if she could help.

"I have an appointment with Mr. Norbert Mayer," he replied taking off his coat.

"May I have your name," she asked.

"Becker, Thomas Becker."

The lady disappeared as she said "just a moment, sir" and left him alone in this world of luxury.

A few minutes later Norbert Mayer appeared from his office and workroom. He was in his early fifties, his hair was somewhat unkempt. He was wearing a suit which had seen better days and a red bow tie. He came to the middle of the shop and held out his hand.

"I'm very pleased to meet you, Herr Becker. I have everything you need. Please follow me. Let me hang up your coat." Norbert Mayer took the client's coat and hung it up on an old-fashioned apple-wood hat stand in the corner of the shop. Andrey followed the jeweller into his office. Norbert Mayer pointed to a leather chair at a desk with a velvet cover on it and said:

"Please, take a seat. I'll go and get the diamond."

The jeweller turned to his talented young trainee and said. "Nina, could you please look after the shop while I show Mr. Becker his diamond. Thank you."

She turned on her heels with a slight air of disappointment at not having satisfied her curiosity and the jeweller disappeared into an ante-room. He came back with a small velvet bag and a box which contained six tubes. He opened the bag and emptied its contents on to the velvet cover. The diamond sparkled in the bright light. It weighed just over a carat which was equivalent to 200 milligrams and was perfectly cut. Normally it would have cost around seven thousand Euros but Norbert Mayer was selling it for cash, for just four thousand Euros and the small box with six tubes of strychnine for one thousand more. No receipt, no questions asked.

Norbert offered Mr. Becker his tweezers and Andrey picked the diamond up, held it against the light and nodded. The jeweller checked to make sure that his nosey trainee was in the shop and then opened the lid of the box. There were six small tubes of colourless small crystals, each tube containing 50 milligrams. The tubes were accurately positioned in foam padding and the box closed with a high security, tamper-evident seal.

"Please be careful with the box," the jeweller said. "One of my customers had an accident last month and just breathing in the substance almost killed him. Fortunately he got to hospital in time. You must have a lot of rats," he said with a questioning look.

"An awful lot," Andrey said. He took an envelope out of his small cabin bag. The jeweller took the money out and counted it. Andrey waited until he had finished counting then put the small box into his cabin bag. He took the diamond with the jeweller's tweezers and slipped it into the empty coin compartment of his wallet.

"Thank you," he said to the jeweller as he pushed his chair back and stood up.

"My pleasure," Norbert replied. The jeweller went to the coat stand and helped Mr. Becker into his thick winter coat. Then he escorted his customer into the shop where they shook hands and said goodbye. Mr. Becker disappeared into the growing throng of shoppers along the Zeil and walked towards the Hauptwache, the old main police station of the city which was completely destroyed in the

Second World War and rebuilt in 1958 above one of Frankfurt's underground train stations. Here he walked over to the taxi rank. The driver opened the boot from inside the car. Andrey put his small cabin bag safely inside and closed the boot. He looked at his watch. It was eleven o'clock and he was still on-time. He got into the taxi and gave the driver an address in Kelsterbach on the south bank just west of the international airport.

10

In Hawkes Lift the sun was setting with a blaze of colour. Sean was at the barbecue on his wooden deck where four large steaks were sizzling and spitting. His wife, Judith, had put cushions on the chairs and a bowl of fried potatoes on the table. Judith came out with an oil lamp, lit it and placed it in the middle of the table. Pete and Regan were both enjoying a cool beer and watching the sky turn red and purple.

"It looks as if you're going to have a nice day tomorrow," Sean said.

"Sure does," Pete replied.

"So how was your day?" Judith asked Regan.

Regan smiled and in the last rays of an orange sun and the flickering light of the oil lamp on the table her face seemed radiant, almost ethereal. "My day was awesome," she said and chuckled as she looked at Pete. "I've learnt so much about poison nut trees that I think I could write a thesis on it! And the horse ride to the plantation and back was out of this world. Dad and I don't often get a chance to ride together these days."

"Sean, thanks again for all your help today," Pete added. "We really appreciate it. And thanks to you and Judith for putting us up."

"Judith's pleased to have the company," he said. "During the week nothing much happens in Hawkes Lift and now the days are drawing in she enjoys having a few guests, don't you Judith."

"I sure do. I hope your rooms are OK," she said, looking at their faces to catch any hints of something not quite right.

"Our rooms are just fine," Pete said, "and I'm sure I'm going to sleep like a log!"

Sean cut one of the steaks to see if it was done enough, piled them high and put them on the table.

"Tuck in," he said.

"And help yourselves to potatoes," Judith added.

"Your beef is as good as ever," Pete said with a smile. "Or should I congratulate the barbecue chef?"

"No, I just watched it. The grazing land up here and the cattle we have is a good reason to stay put, despite the flooding last year. We were lucky at Hawkes Lift. Being on a hill we didn't get washed out like the thousands of others in Queensland who lost everything. It was pretty scary, though. You just weren't sure which river was going to burst its banks next and you only drove around if you really had to. Judith had enough food and water in to keep us going for a couple of months just in case things got worse. I reckon she could have fed an army."

"Dad said that Sam lost half his herd of horses," Regan said. Judith and Sean glanced at each other.

"Yes, that was a real catastrophe," Sean said. Most of us

drove out to Stags Leap where his horses were grazing on pasture near the river. The water rose so fast that the horses couldn't get to higher ground quickly enough. Anyone with a boat got it out there somehow and we towed the horses behind the boats to higher ground. We had to row the boats to avoid injuring the horses. Their heads were just too heavy and they found it difficult to swim a long way and keep their nostrils above water. So we took the life jackets out of the boats and tied them around the horses' heads. That did the trick. We managed to save about half of them. I hope we don't have to go through anything like that again," he said looking at Judith.

"Judith lost her brother in the floods," Sean said. "His house collapsed in the flash flood that hit Toowoomba," Sean said.

"I'm sorry to hear that," Pete said. "You hear about a couple of hundred thousand people being affected and are thankful that there weren't more deaths but you really don't capture the personal tragedy behind each person lost. I'm really sorry," he said and touched Judith's hand.

Judith looked up with a sad smile. "Thanks, Pete. We're all trying to cope as best we can and there are lots of folks worse off. Warren, my brother, had gone back to his house on the morning of the tenth of January, goodness knows why. No-one really knows what he went back for. Jenny, his wife, and their two small boys were in Brisbane. It had rained more than sixty inches in the thirty-six hours before the creeks burst their banks pushing a huge wall of water through the city centre. Warren's house collapsed and trapped him under a beam." Judith called her dog, Sandy, and patted him on his head to distract her thoughts.

"So Regan, what's on the order of the day for tomorrow?" Sean asked, breaking the silence.

"Tomorrow I go into the lion's den," she said, trying to bring a bit of light-heartedness into the conversation. "Dad's going to show me round the factory."

"But you've been a couple of times before," Sean said.

"Yes, but now with some pharmacology under my belt and a vested interest, I'll be looking at the whole operation with a different mind-set," she said.

"Aha, I see method in your madness," he said with a smile.

"Yep," said Pete. "It's no secret that Regan is interested in following in my footsteps. Probably not the right expression as she'll most likely do everything different to what I've done which was more learning by doing. But first she wants to get her degree under her belt and some experience in another company. Being the boss's daughter is not the best way to learn the ropes."

"Sounds like a good plan," Judith said handing her the bowl of potatoes. "Then you'll need a few more of these for stamina," she said and they all laughed.

*

Victor had told his department head that he would be coming in at eleven which was an hour outside their flexitime. His boss knew that Victor's sister was visiting from

Germany and had said that wouldn't be a problem. So Svetlana and Victor walked to a café not far from Victor's apartment which Victor frequented regularly. Living on his own in Zurich, he enjoyed his breakfast among other guests on a Saturday and Sunday. The waitress was surprised to see him on a Monday morning. He had smiled and explained that his sister was visiting him. He had ordered coffee, rolls with ham and cheese and pastries. They sat huddled at a table and spoke quietly in Russian so the other guests couldn't hear. Svetlana had told him that she wanted to catch the ten o'clock Intercity to Frankfurt so that she would arrive before the rush hour started. At a quarter past nine Victor had paid the bill, helped his sister into her winter coat and they walked back to his apartment to pick up her case. His silver grey BMW 318d was parked in the garage. The rush hour had finished and it only took them twenty minutes to drive down town. Victor pulled up in the set-down area in front of Zurich's main railway station. He got out, opened the boot of his car and handed his sister her small blue suitcase. Victor hugged his sister as if it were for the very last time and said: "Look after yourself, sis. And give my best to my brother-in-law to be," he added with a wink. Svetlana smiled. "And tell Alex and Misha to be good otherwise there'll be no Easter eggs from Switzerland this year." Svetlana kissed him on both cheeks. "Poká," she said holding back her tears, "see you soon." She always tried to make their parting casual, as if she were just going to the shops, but she never really managed it. She loved her big brother, her Russian bear as she called him. And he doted on his sister. He was so proud of her, how she had brought up her boys almost single-handedly, finally got together again with Thomas and how they had worked so hard to renovate the wine estate and grow their business. He called her "the German of the family". That was a half-truth anyway. Their roots were German. She had studied German and lived there for fifteen years so it was quite normal that she had adopted a lot of German habits which set her apart from other Russian women of her age. But her soul was Russian, he was sure of that! And her heart was made of pure gold. She walked towards the main doors looking back over her shoulder several times to wave at Victor who was standing by his car. She waved a last goodbye and fighting back the tears walked into the busy forecourt of Zurich main station. She walked over to the ticket machine and bought a day ticket for all public transport. Then she went down the escalator to the S-Bahn, a system of rapid rail-connections in the region around Zurich. She only had to wait a couple of minutes before the number six arrived. It took her just ten minutes to get to Tiefenbrunnen. She got off the train and could smell the humid cool air coming from the lake. Seefeld was an upmarket area on the east side of Lake Zurich with a beautiful view across the lake and a backdrop of snow-capped mountains. It was only a short walk from Tiefenbrunnen station to Seefeldstraße where the Helvetic International Bank had its main office. It would have been much quicker by taxi but she always felt safer on public transport. No-one could trace where she went and what she did.

She entered the bank at twenty past ten. The hall wasn't luxurious but pragmatic and tasteful. The lady at reception greeted her in Swiss German. Svetlana explained that she wished to make a withdrawal from her account. In Germany where she lived she would have to phone in advance if she wanted to withdraw forty thousand Euros because of the time lock on the safe which didn't allow large sums of money to be withdrawn. For a Swiss bank a withdrawal of fifty thousand francs was a small amount and the transaction only took around ten minutes. Svetlana went to the service desk and took a seat. A young man in an immaculate grey suit with a light blue tie took all the details and asked for her passport. It only took him five minutes to check her identity and request the money. She then went over to the cashier and collected the money which the cashier had counted while she stood there and discreetly placed the bundles into a large brown envelope. She put the envelope into her small blue suitcase, thanked the cashier and walked slowly out of the bank, her heart thumping in her breast. She knew that the banks CCTV would have her on film but she was just another customer picking up some funds from her account. It was just after half past ten when she left the bank and walked back to the S-Bahn train station. The streets were fairly empty and she would have noticed anyone taking too much interest in her. She tried to relax. She reached the station at five to eleven and walked quickly to platform twelve to get the Eurocity Express to Basel. The train was of course on time, as punctual as a Swiss made watch, she thought. She got into a second class carriage and checked where her seat number was. The compartment was fairly empty. She didn't sit down but went straight to the toilet. She locked the door and opened her suitcase. She took out the brown envelope and tore it open. She pulled up her blue pullover to reveal a money belt wrapped around her just above her waist. She put the money, one bundle at a time, into her money belt and closed her case. In the corridor she threw the envelope into a waste paper bin and walked back to her seat. With her slender figure and a loosely fitting pullover, no-one would ever imagine that she was carrying all that money. She sat and looked out the window, thinking of Thomas, her boys and Conrad. She had to keep reminding herself why she took the risk of smuggling money from Switzerland to Germany, even if it was her, no, their money. She got off the train almost an hour later, and looked for the exit to the busy platform at Basel station. Some passengers were rushing to catch connecting trains; others were rushing to get out of the station. Some were even wheeling their bikes which they loaded on to regional trains. Svetlana walked from platform ten to platform twelve and got on to the ICE 278 to Mannheim where she would have to change again to get to Frankfurt. She didn't mind changing trains if it meant she could get home earlier. She would reach Frankfurt just after three in the afternoon where Thomas would be waiting for her. If there were no big traffic jams, they'd be home by half past four. Home, she thought and sighed. She couldn't wait although she'd only been away for two days. She had missed Thomas and the boys and thought of them as the train approached the

Swiss-German border. A Swiss customs official accompanied by a German policeman walked through the carriage. The policemen checked each passport or identity card and the customs official asked politely if the passenger had anything to declare. Svetlana smiled politely, said no and put her passport back into her bag. They moved on to the next row and a few minutes later they had left the carriage. Svetlana tried not to show the relief she felt.

*

Just before noon Andrey got out of the taxi and walked into the main reception of an international freight forwarding company in Kelsterbach near Frankfurt International Airport. He walked up to the desk and asked for Hubert Walter.

"Do you have an appointment," the young lady asked.

"Yes," he said. "My name is Becker, Thomas Becker."

The receptionist rang through to the head of logistics, put the name of the visitor into her computer, printed out a badge, put it in a plastic holder and handed it to Andrey.

"Here's your badge, Mr. Becker," she said with a smile. "Mr. Walter will be with you shortly. Please take a seat over there and you can hang your coat up in the coat rack over here," she said indicating a few comfortable chairs at the back of the entrance hall and a row of coat hangers on a chrome rack. A few minutes later Hubert Walter walked in and held out his hand to greet his visitor. "Walter," he said as he shook hands in the very formal German way of just announcing his surname.

"Becker, Thomas Becker," Andrey replied. "I'm pleased to meet you."

"Just follow me," Hubert Walter said. He turned on his heels and strode up to the main glass doors. He swiped his company ID. The doors opened and the sudden noise of twenty or so logistic clerks, most of them talking quite loudly on the phone, was quite a shock after the quiet reception. The Head of Logistics had an office with glass walls at the back of this large open plan office. He walked into his office and offered Thomas Becker a chair at the small conference table. Hubert Walter switched his telephone on to mute and sat opposite him. He was a large man in his early fifties who obviously slept badly, ate and drank too much and didn't get enough exercise.

"Our mutual friend told me you have a small parcel which needs to be taken to Moscow discreetly with one of our truck drivers," Hubert Walter said matter-of-factly and looked at his guest waiting for confirmation.

"That's correct," Andrey said. "I'll need to know the number of the truck, the name of the driver, the date it is due to cross the border from the EU into Russia and where the truck will pass customs. The information should be emailed to this email address." Andrey alias Thomas Becker handed the logistics manager a handwritten card with the name Thomas Becker and a German email address. The handwriting was typical for a well-educated German businessman.

"This is the box," Andrey said. The jeweller had carefully sealed it with sticky tape which read "fragile". Underneath the box was an envelope with one thousand Euros in it. The logistics manager looked inside the envelope. He wouldn't count it with so many prying eyes on the other side of the glass. Without removing the money, he closed the envelope and put it with the box in his small office safe. "Please make sure whoever sends the email writes the following subject line in English: "URGENT Truck left with goods for Moscow." Andrey spoke this English sentence with a slight German accent and Hubert Walter wrote it down on the back of the card. "Will do," he said. It was a pleasure doing business with you, Mr. Becker."

Andrey pushed his chair back and followed Hubert Walter back through the noisy logistics office to the double glass doors which opened automatically this time. The two men shook hands. Andrey walked over to the receptionist and handed back his badge.

"Could you please call me a taxi," he said. "Of course," she replied. "Where are you going?"

"Back into the city," he replied without hesitation.

The receptionist rang the taxi company and put down the phone. "Your taxi will be here in five minutes, Mr. Becker," she said.

"Thank you," he replied. "I'll wait outside." He walked to the coat rack, put on his coat and carried his small suitcase to the main doors. The cold winter air was quite a shock as he walked through the doors but at the same time quite refreshing. He put on his gloves and took a scarf out of his suitcase. The taxi pulled up a few minutes later. The driver put the suitcase in the boot. Andrey looked at his Rolex. A quarter to one. Time for lunch.

"I'm going to the trade fair," he told the driver and sat back to relax.

After twenty five minutes Andrey got out of the taxi and used his visitor's badge to walk past the electronic gates and into the fair. He put his gloves and scarf in his suitcase and slung his coat over his arm. He followed the signs for the restaurant where he then spent an hour enjoying a light lunch. It was just before two o'clock when he walked out of the fair and headed towards the gents. He wasn't alone. He slung his coat over his suitcase, washed his hands and then went into one of the cubicles. He took out his blue contact lenses and placed then in a small container. He took off his pale brown wig and put it with the container into his small suitcase. He took the Armani suit which had a slight shimmer and a blue tie out of the suitcase. It wasn't very comfortable to change in the cubicle but he wanted to come out looking like Andrey Ivanov. He put the suit he had worn all morning into the suitcase with the striped tie. He took out a comb and combed his hair. He waited for a few minutes then left the cubicle and washed his hands again and combed his hair in front of the mirror and adjusted his tie. Welcome back, Andrey Ivanov, he mused. His dark stubble was just beginning to appear on his chin and above his lips. He put on his coat and walked out of the gents towards the exit. He took a taxi to the Frankfurter Hof and asked the taxi driver to fill in the receipt "from the trade fair to Frankfurter Hof". Andrey walked to reception where the young lady who was on duty when he had checked in the day before greeted him with a smile. He walked past her to the concierge and gave him the ticket stub for his suitcase. The concierge gave it to the bell-boy who disappeared into the luggage room and quickly re-appeared with his Samsonite. The bell-boy followed him to the taxi rank and Andrey gave him five Euros. The boy beamed. "Thank you, sir," he said. The driver got out and helped him with his luggage as Andrey said within earshot of the young bell-boy "To the airport, please. Terminal 2."

*

At six minutes past three, on time, the Intercity ICE518 from Mannheim pulled up alongside platform 6 at Frankfurt International Airport long distance railway station. Svetlana could see Thomas. She had sent the number of her carriage to his mobile and he was waiting apprehensively. Then he saw her face and his eyes lit up. The train stopped and the door opened. She walked down the steps and Thomas held out his hand to take her case. They kissed each other and she held him just a little bit longer in her arms, letting the warmth flow through her body and a glow of security and happiness enter every single cell.

"I'm so happy to be back," she said.

"And I'm so pleased to see you," he replied with a smile. "Everything OK?"

"Yes, everything's fine. Victor sends his love, to his brother-in-law to be," she said with a smile. Thomas beamed back. "He's as happy as a sand boy. Just a bit worried about our mother and missing his family. Otherwise fine."

They walked arm in arm to the escalator. It took them fifteen minutes to walk to car park 1 where Thomas had parked their car and another five minutes to get to the car.

"I'll be really pleased when the new Squaire car park is finally opened," he said. "That'll save a lot of time."

"When is it due to open," Svetlana asked.

"Sometime next year. The Squaire, or New Work City as it's going to be called, is finally going to be officially opened this year. They say it's cost over one point two billion Euros!"

"Wow," Svetlana whistled. "And I get nervous just handling forty thousand!" They laughed as they got to the car.

*

At seven in the evening Andrey Ivanov was sitting in the business class cabin of one of Aeroflot's new Airbus A320-214 enjoying a glass of champagne on his way back to Moscow. The flight was only three hours but with the time difference of two hours he wouldn't arrive in Moscow until almost midnight local time. He smiled at the thought that there would be no more winter and summer time when the clocks went forward in March. President Medvedev had suddenly decided to do away with winter time. He had decided to use daylight saving all year round. From now on the difference to Europe would only be two hours in summer but then three hours next winter until someone decided to change it all over again. A car would be waiting for him at Sheremetyevo airport and would have him home in no time. At least there would be no traffic on a Monday evening at midnight. Andrey moved the back of his seat into a more relaxed position and enjoyed the refreshing sparkle of a very good glass of French champagne, not its less famous Russian namesake.

11

It was just before eleven on Tuesday morning when Armen arrived at Vodalko in Podolsk. As usual he had spent most of the morning on the phone and was interested to hear why Abel had asked him to pay him a visit. He hadn't said why and Armen hadn't asked. Armen disliked being summoned but Abel was the head of the Conseil. So he went, sullenly, but he went, no questions asked. His driver Vanya waved at the gate security guard. He didn't have to sign in as other guests did. Vanya drove up to the office building, looked around out of habit when he got out of the car. Not that anyone would take a pot-shot at his boss here, in this almost para-military compound. Unless they had a death wish, he thought. He opened the back door and Armen stepped out. He walked up the rather pompous neo-romantic steps to the front door which a concierge opened from the inside. Vanya walked behind him. Armen entered the entrance hall to Vodalko's offices which sparkled with large gold chandeliers and was decorated like an Armenian presidential palace. A tall man with deep-set eyes, bushy black eyebrows and a large hooked nose came towards him.

"I am Emin Simonian, Mr. Plemyannikov's new assistant," he said. He didn't hold out his hand but lowered his head a little in a gesture of deference. A good name for an assistant, Armen thought. Emin in Armenian meant faithful. It obviously wasn't only his name which was Armenian. The assistant's looks were Armenian through and through. It was unusual for a Russian to have an Armenian assistant but his thoughts were interrupted by Emin's deep voice: "Please follow me, Mr. Makaryan."

Emin knocked on the dark oak double-winged door and opened the wing on the right-hand side. Abel was sitting at his desk, smiled at Armen and stood up. They greeted each other in the middle of the room like old friends. Abel gestured to a low polished wood table and three leather arm chairs around it. "Do take a seat, my dear Armen."

"Thank you," Armen replied as he lowered himself into one of the chairs.

"I hope you and your family are well," Abel added. He knew that Armenians were family people and it was polite to ask this question before moving on to any business.

"Yes, very well," he said. Armen wasn't married but the word family included anyone you felt was part of it.

"I hope that is true of yours," he said.

"Yes, thank you," Abel smiled. "My granddaughter, Vera, who got married last summer is expecting."

"That's wonderful news," Armen replied. There was a soft knock on the door and Emin walked in. Behind him a young lady carried a tray with strong coffee and sweet little cakes. She placed the tray on the table rather nervously and then turned to walk out with Emin on her heels.

"I have a slight concern that I think you can help me with," Abel said, changing the subject to the business at hand.

"Tell me my friend what I can do for you," came the subservient reply which was not at all a reflection of true subservience but a just a way of speaking.

"Khimki," Abel said not beating around the bush. "Aerospace." Armen was not amused. After all, his presence on the board of Aerospace was an honour, for him and his fellow members of the Conseil. And no-one ever spoke about the intimate details of Aerospace and its inner workings. That was an unwritten law.

"I hear that the board of directors has passed a resolution not to oppose the city's and government's plans to build a new motorway to St. Petersburg," he said.

"That's correct," Armen replied. The fact was public knowledge. The mayor of Moscow had already held a press conference. It was an important feather in his cap.

"I need your help to find a way to block this project, not permanently, just long enough for me to ensure that this stupid private little war on alcohol companies comes to an end. We all have interests in beers, wines and spirits and it's important that there is no further interference, no unnecessary checks and companies losing their licenses for petty formal mistakes on their books," he said.

"And what exactly did you have in mind?" Armen asked. "The vote was unanimous."

"Yes, with your help and quite a bit of lobbying on your behalf," Abel added. Armen was furious. This really was nothing to do with Abel. He had overstepped the mark.

"Indeed," Armen said, trying to control his overwhelming urge to raise his voice. "Indeed! And I don't see what I can do now to back-peddle," he said. "The news is in the public domain. I have used my influence and cannot suddenly change my opinion. That would ruin my reputation. The mayor has held a press conference. What exactly do you expect me to do," he asked again, his voice now louder and his look much sterner.

From his position outside the oak door, Emin couldn't understand what was being said but he could tell that an argument was brewing. His boss rarely got angry but he could now hear the anger in his voice. And Armen was now loud, very loud. He didn't want to know what the disagreement was about. In his world it was sometimes better, indeed safer, not to know the details of what was going on. After twenty minutes the door suddenly opened and Armen stormed out.

"Tell Vanya to bring my car up to the front door," he barked at Emin.

"Certainly, Sir," he said and followed Armen to the entrance hall. A young concierge brought him his coat, hat and gloves and Armen pushed him away rather rudely. He didn't need any help. He put the coat around his shoulders, placed the hat on his head and without another word walked towards the door. The young concierge, somewhat intimidated, held the door open and kept his eyes firmly on the ground. Vanya held the car door open and Armen jumped in with an unusual youthfulness awoken by his anger. Vanya got behind the wheel and Armen growled: "Let's get out of here as fast as you can," and leant back in his seat fuming.

*

In Sydney it was six in the evening and Sam was sitting in his office at home. He put the last document into the envelope and sealed it. He had ordered a courier for a quarter past six and the company he used was always punctual. They used mainly motorbikes to avoid the frequent traffic jams in Sydney during the rush hour. He had already prepared the courier's address label and way bill. He stuck the originals to the envelope and filed the copy with the copies of the documents. The file was named "Tom Wyatt" and Sam put it back into his safe. At ten past six the doorbell rang.

"I'll go," Sam called to his wife who was reading some magazines on the deck, enjoying the last rays of sun. "It'll be the courier," he added.

He activated the video camera and saw a young man with "Orange Express" on his leather jacket. He had, as per his company instructions, already taken off his helmet so the customer could see his face. You just couldn't be too careful these days. Sam pressed the intercom and said "thirteenth floor, number one three zero three. The lifts are on your left," he added. The door buzzed and the young man walked into the hall and pressed the button to call the lift. He was used to going to houses and condos owned by the rich and the super-rich. This building didn't really look as if it were in this category from the outside, perhaps a little old-fashioned, but from the inside it just smelt of luxury. And what a superb location, in the middle of Sydney, he thought as the lift stopped at the thirteenth floor. I bet this guy has an awesome view from up here.

Sam was waiting in the doorway with the envelope. He had stamped and signed the flap of the envelope after he had closed it. After all, the documents were highly confidential. Accounts, balance sheets, ownership rights, bank records – it was all there.

The courier scanned the bar code and asked Sam to sign. He then printed out a receipt with the time the document had been picked up. It was exactly six fifteen. Sam thanked him and gave him two dollars. The young man smiled and returned his thanks. There weren't many people who tipped him. Most of his customers could afford it but it just didn't seem to cross their minds. Or maybe they had become rich by being mean, he thought. A couple of minutes later the envelope was speeding out of Sydney in the box on the back of the courier's bike and to Tom Wyatt's home.

*

It was six-thirty in the evening when Pete and Regan arrived at Archerfield. Regan was still very excited about everything she had seen and heard at her father's factory. The sun was going down and he knew Joe wanted to take off before sunset so they could enjoy the colours from the plane. It only took them twenty minutes to go through the formalities at the airfield and walk out to Pete's Cessna. Joe was sitting in the pilot's seat and going through a final check.

"Ready to go?" Pete asked as they both climbed in.

"Yep, no problems," Joe replied. "So madam, how was your trip?" Joe asked turning his head to Regan.

"Just awesome," she said and beamed at Joe and then her father. "I've learnt so much about trees and plants and homeopathic medicines. My mind is just in a whirl!" Regan replied.

"Well, let's get up in the air so you can enjoy the sunset as the last highlight on your trip," Joe said starting up the engines.

Regan and Pete chatted non-stop for the first half hour until the sky started turning a fiery orange with purple hues.

"Isn't this just beautiful," Regan exclaimed with her nose literally pressed against the window. "It's just so… perfect, absolutely perfect," she said. She turned to Pete and kissed him on the cheek. "Thanks, Dad, this has been such an exciting trip."

"I'm so pleased you came," he said. "And it hasn't made you change your mind?!

"No way," she laughed. "Once I'm finished and have a few years' experience under my belt in another company, there's no way you're going to stop me joining the company," she said with a laugh. "You'll just have to put up with me," she said.

"I'll manage," Pete said and put his arm round her.

Joe smiled too. It was so good to see his friend Pete so happy and obviously delighted with his daughter. He sighed. He wished that he could say the same for himself.

"It'll be dark in half an hour," Joe said. "If you guys want to get some rest when the light goes, don't worry about me. I'll be fine and I promise not to sing."

"Thanks," Pete said. "To be honest, I'm quite tired. What about you, Regan?" he said turning to his daughter. There was no answer. Regan had already fallen asleep, the purring of the engines lulling her into a deep sleep. It had been a long day, so many new things, so interesting, so exciting. Now, with the day over, she had suddenly felt exhausted, happy, relaxed and tired. And she was still asleep when they started their approach to Bankstown. Pete stroked her arm and she stirred.

"We've started our approach," he whispered. "We'll be landing in ten minutes," he said.

Regan rubbed her eyes. "How long have I been asleep?" she asked.

"About three hours or so," Pete answered. "You really must have been very tired."

Regan was now fully awake and turned to her father.

"I'll write up my notes tomorrow and probably have lots of questions," she said, the sparkle coming back into her voice.

"I'll be in the office all day," he said. "We can go through your notes after lunch if you like."

"Great. Are you going to phone Mum when we've landed?"

"Yes, I'll phone her from the car. She said she'd stay up until we get home and it'll probably be midnight."

The Cessna continued its descent and the lights on the runway grew larger and larger. She heard Joe pull the throttle back and there was a sudden thud as they hit the tarmac. The flaps went up and they braked quite hard. Joe taxied to his allocated spot and did his final check while Regan and Pete climbed down.

"You go ahead, Pete," he called. We'll catch up on Thursday over a beer," he said.

"Thanks, Joe. I really appreciate your flying us today."

"My pleasure. And I've got to keep my flying hours up to date," he said.

Pete and Regan grabbed their bags, waved to Joe and walked into the terminal building.

12

It was a snowy Sunday afternoon and the forest around Sheremetyevo was covered in white powder snow. The trees looked like miniature decorations on a Christmas cake as the Airbus gradually approached the airport. The March sun shone with an eerie glow through the thick clouds. Svetlana looked out of the plane window and smiled. She felt a slight pang looking at this familiar scene and one that brought back happy memories of her childhood and the days of innocence. She looked at her watch. Olesya would already be waiting for her. She could rely on her sister to be punctual – not like her brother Victor. Olesya would have left her mother's flat on Udalstova street at two o'clock even though there wasn't much traffic going in that direction on a Sunday afternoon and the weather was snowy but not stormy, quite calm, no wind and the temperature was around freezing. The flat that Svetlana and Thomas had bought for her mother in Moscow was in the south-west of the city around fourteen kilometres from the centre of Moscow. It was quite a good location, safe, not completely built up. The complex the flat was in wasn't what Russians called a post-Stalinist building but a modern building. Most of these buildings had suddenly emerged between 2004 and 2010, sprouting out of the ground like mushrooms on a manure heap. They were all built to Western standards on the whole, often with an underground car-park, usually twenty floors or so high, video security at each the entrance, air-conditioning and security personnel. And most of these modern buildings had one thing in common – a huge entrance hall which was elaborately decorated in a very neo-Russian style. The flats on the twelfth floor upwards had a great view of the surrounding area but Svetlana had persuaded Thomas to buy one on the third floor, just in case the lift was out of service and her mother needed to get downstairs to go out. From the balcony her mother had a nice view of a quiet private garden where children played in summer. The kitchen was quite spacious and the living room very large. There were three bedrooms and two bathrooms. Svetlana wanted one bathroom for her sister and herself or other visitors and one for her ailing mother. "Old people need their own bathroom and toilet," Svetlana had said to Thomas. "And it's better that the person living in has a separate one," she had added. Olesya kept her car in the underground car park and most of the time she used the Moscow underground, the Metro, to move around the city. The next station, Vernadskogo, was only five minutes' walk from the flat and she could be in the centre of the city in forty-five minutes and at work within an hour. Olesya transferred two thousand five hundred Euros every month to Svetlana's account in Germany for rent from the bank account she had set up to receive large amounts of money from Svetlana's business partner.

At the beginning Svetlana thought this was a huge amount of money and may be suspicious. However, the broker assured her that this was the going rate for a flat of this size in a prime position with all the amenities of a modern building. Svetlana had checked on the internet and indeed, the prices she saw there, usually in US dollars, proved that the broker was right. So she stopped worrying. It had been a big investment then but had really paid off. The flats in the building had doubled in price over the last five years.

The Airbus touched down and braked hard. All the snow ploughs were out and the runway was clear of snow. Thank goodness it's only light snow, Svetlana thought. She had chosen a Sunday to travel to avoid the traffic that was horrendous during the week. And her sister Olesya worked from ten till five at the Rostbank in the city as an investment analyst. The plane came to a halt at Terminal D which had only been finished just over a year ago. The jet bridge moved like a robot under the control of an invisible ghost and connected to the plane's front door. Svetlana stood up and put on her coat, scarf, gloves and hat and took her handbag and her cabin bag out of the overhead locker. She smiled and thanked the cabin crew as she stepped through the door and walked swiftly to passport control. In the old days she had needed more than an hour, maybe even two hours to get through passport control and customs. That was in 1993 when she was studying German in Mainz. Now it was just like arriving in any other country at an international airport. Twenty minutes later the glass exit doors to the arrivals hall wheezed open and she could feel the cooler air as the warm air mixed with the cold air coming in from the street. There was a crowd of people in overcoats, scarves and hats waiting for their friends and relatives. Some men had signs with names on – private taxi drivers picking up businessmen. And then as she moved away from the crowd a host of taxi drivers all wanting to know if she needed a taxi.

"Ne nado," she kept repeating over and over again, no, she didn't need a taxi. She had arranged to meet Olesya at the Costa coffee shop away from the crowd. She knew the coffee shop was not far from the rental car offices and she followed the sign, pulling her cases and holding her handbag tightly under her arm. Then she heard a shrill voice, almost a scream, as Olesya saw her and waved ferociously.

"Here I am, Sveta, here I am." she shouted using the short form of Svetlana's name. She ran over towards her sister and threw her arms around her. "Lesenka, Lesenka!" Svetlana exclaimed, tears welling in her eyes. She always had called her little sister Lesenka, even as a three-year old when Olesya was only a few weeks old. Svetlana let go of her luggage, hugged her sister and hoped that no-one would use the opportunity to snatch her suitcase! Olesya had tears in her eyes, too, and was obviously overjoyed to see Svetlana.

"Come on," Svetlana said. "Let's get out of here! I can't think straight with all this noise and all these people."

"Give me your suitcase," Olesya said grabbing the handle. "My car is quite a long way away in the car park. It was just impossible to get any nearer. A good job the weather isn't too bad."

Svetlana followed her sister and they negotiated their way to the exit. The doors opened and the cold air hit them as they walked on to the pavement.

They reached the car and put Svetlana's suitcase and hand luggage in the boot. Olesya had a new silver grey Ford Focus 1.6 L.

"Wow," Svetka whistled, "nice new car!"

"I wanted to surprise you," Lesenka replied with a smile. "Get in and I'll tell you all about it."

Lesenka started the engine and beamed at her sister. "It's new," she said. "They've just brought out the next generation so I managed to get this one, brand new, for just three hundred thousand. A bargain! And it has four doors and enough room for Mamochka to sit comfortably in the front."

Lesenka always spoke of her mother as Mamochka, the more endearing term for mother, whereas the others called her Mama. Svetka felt warm inside. It was good to hear Lesenka chatting. Her warmth was infectious. Lesenka stopped at the barrier and gave the man her ticket and five hundred roubles. He pushed a button and the barrier went up. Lesenka carried on her story.

"I would have preferred another colour but this one was ready to go. I found it on the car website at a dealer in Moscow, all taxes paid. So I bought it and just drove it back home. What a feeling! Thank goodness we have a garage at the flat. I was so nervous that something might happen to it the first time I drove it and I was a little bit worried about it being damaged if I parked it on the street. The good thing about the second generation is that the car thieves only take the third generation," she said and laughed. Svetka laughed out loud with her. Dear Lesenka, she thought. Always the optimist. Always finding the silver lining in every cloud.

They were on the M10 cruising along at 110 kilometres per hour. Since the new police reform had been announced, there were far more speed checks and document checks on the motorways and the outer ring road. So Lesenka kept to the speed limit. After about three quarters of an hour, still chatting away, they got off the ring road at Ozernaya street, drove along Michurinisky Prospekt for ten minutes and then turned right on to Udaltsova street.

Lesenka pressed the button on the aluminium post in front of the garage doors. This activated a video camera and an alarm light in the security office located on the ground floor of the building. The security guard looked at the picture from camera one and checked the number plate which he compared with his list of residents who paid for a parking space in the garage. Then he looked at the picture from camera two and saw Lesenka with another lady. Lesenka was chatting and smiling. Obviously everything was alright. He pressed the button which raised the garage door and Lesenka drove down to the second floor where her parking space was reserved.

Svetka couldn't wait to see her mother and her excitement increased as they stepped into the lift. The flat was only on the third floor but her suitcase was quite heavy. They reached apartment 302 and Lesenka, who was holding a bunch of keys, opened the door and let her sister in. They left the luggage in the hall and went into the large living room which was tastefully furnished. The parquet floor was made out of Russian wood and Svetka loved it. There were a few rugs here and there but not too many as Lesenka was frightened Mamochka might fall. The sofa was beige and had bright green cushions on it which matched the curtains. The sideboard was a modern, wooden sideboard with glass doors. Mamochka was sitting in her large light green high-backed armchair fast asleep with her feet up on a small footstool covered with a very Russian tapestry. Svetka sat down on the sofa next to the armchair and looked at her mother and then questioningly at her sister.

"She had a bad night," Lesenka whispered. "I'll go and make some tea in the kitchen and bring it through. Then we can wake her up."

It was just before seven in the evening and the sun had set. The blackbird in the garden had stopped singing and the darkness was growing outside. Lesenka, Svetka and their mother were drinking black tea with a slice of lemon.

"Tell me about your boys, Svetka. How is Misha? And Alex?" she asked.

Svetka sat and talked about her boys, about Thomas, their dog Blackie, her home and the weather. She took out a small album of pictures she had put together for her mother. She had brought her a small photo album every time she came so that her mother could imagine her in her home, cooking, eating, laughing and share her happiness. She had looked at all the pictures using the magnifying glass with a light that Lesenka had brought in on a tray. They had talked for an hour and now her eyelids were heavy. Her head fell back onto the cushion, her mouth opened a little and she fell fast asleep.

"Mamochka usually has a sleep around eight," Lesenka said seeing the look of concern on her sister's face. "She's sleeping a lot more these days but her waking moments are still very lucid."

"Is she in much pain?" Svetka asked, surprised how peaceful her mother looked.

"I manage to get all the medication she needs including painkillers," Lesenka said getting up. "I have a very good relationship with the pharmacist on Vernadskogo," she said and winked at her sister with a smile. Svetka got up, put her arm around Lesenka and they walked into the kitchen which had a tiled floor, fitted white cupboards and even a dishwasher.

"You're a marvel," Svetka said. "You can organise anything. Mama is so lucky to have you." She kissed her on her cheek.

"Aha, organising everyday needs is a true Russian characteristic," she said, smiling. "I think I inherited it from Mamochka. You go and take your poor clothes out of your suitcase and I'll get supper ready. She'll be awake in an hour or so and maybe she'll eat something."

Svetka picked up her cases and carried them into her bedroom. She certainly wasn't going to wheel them on her precious wooden floor and anyway it might wake mama. She put a blanket on the low wooden table and put the large case on to it gently. She opened the case, took out her clothes and laid them on the double bed which Lesenka had made up with a duvet in her favourite colour, green. There was a small vase of daffodils on the bedside table. Svetka smiled. In Moscow whatever the weather, whatever the season, you can always find some flowers to buy, she mused and opened the fitted wooden wardrobe. All the furniture in her bedroom was made out of pine from the vast forests in eastern Russia, in Siberia. Svetka ran her hand over the smooth wood and could still smell the pinewood resin in the wood after all this time. She hung all her clothes up and took a couple of blouses into the bathroom. The bathroom was bright with white tiles on the floor and white walls which had a red stripe around the walls at shoulder height. All the accessories were red and the fittings were expensive chrome fittings she had brought from Germany when she had first bought the flat. There were three mirrors which reflected the light and made the bathroom look bigger than it was. Svetka had explained to Thomas how important light is in a house and how to increase the light using chrome fittings and mirrors.

"When you're born in a country where there's not much light for six months of the year, Feng Shui is in your soul," she had told him. "You learn from your mother as a child to increase light in your home. You don't need to read a book about it," she had teased. Thomas read books on everything or surfed in the internet to learn about subjects which interested him. She turned the shower on and let the water run as hot as possible for a minute creating steam in the shower. She turned the water off and hung up the blouses on a washing line in the shower to get rid of the creases more quickly. Then she went back to the kitchen to help Lesenka with supper.

*

It was Monday evening and the restaurant was almost empty. All the same Armen had reserved a private dining room for his dinner with Svetlana. It was just a question of security. His bodyguard and chauffeur, Vanya, stood outside the door. Armen had ordered a bottle of Sassicaia 1998. The sommelier, Igor, had offered him this rare vintage and explained that it had been a warm year with little rain and the grapes were beautifully ripe. Due to the use of forty per cent new oak and almost two years of barrel ageing for this Cabernet Sauvignon with 15% of Cabernet Franc, Igor felt that the wine was now at its peak. Armen looked at the ruby red liquid in his glass and swirled it slowly. He looked at Svetlana, raised his glass to her in a toast:

"Welcome back to Moscow, dear Svetlana. "

"Thank you," she returned his smile and raised her glass, keeping her eyes firmly on his. They sipped the wine and she congratulated him on such a wonderful choice.

"This will really go well with our Wagyu beef," she said. "I find it difficult to get well-aged beef in Germany from a good breed that spends most of its life outside," she added knowing full well that this was Armen's favourite topic, food and wine. He smiled back at Svetlana:

"That's a pity. Then you'll have to come to Moscow more often! Or we'll meet in Düsseldorf. I know a steak house that has really good beef," he said.

"I'll be coming to Moscow quite often to see my mother. She isn't well. My trips will be purely for family reasons," she said to broach the subject of business.

"Does that mean that you won't be doing business with me in future?" Armen asked watching the reaction in her eyes.

"We can continue to supply you with decent entry-level French wine if you wish us to, but we are stopping the expensive luxury side of our business," she replied choosing her words carefully.

"I see," he said. "Is this decision definite or is it a question of money?"

"With a change of importer, the introduction of tax stamps and the increased police and customs activities, Thomas and I have decided to concentrate on our core business of making and selling estate German wine," she added. She had practised this speech several times in her head. "Thomas is going to stop importing wines to concentrate on the estate. The business has done well and we don't wish to be greedy," she said.

"That's a pity," he said. The door opened and the head waiter came in with a trolley. Dinner was served and Armen waited until the waiter had left the room.

"Then I'll have to look for another supplier," he said. "You're absolutely sure?" he repeated. There was a distinct tone of finality and a slight undercurrent of anger in his voice. Armen wasn't a man who liked being contradicted in any of his plans, however unimportant.

Svetlana looked at him and added: "I have my boys to think about, too, and Thomas and I both feel it's time for a change."

"Very well," he said. "Then the toast should be a different one." His usual charm returned and he raised his glass again:

"Thank you for all the wonderful wine you have supplied and for your company this evening." Svetlana raised her glass, looked him in the eyes and toasted:

"Za uspekh", to success!"

She knew that Armen was furious but trying not to show it. He never could totally hide his volatile moods, particularly not from Svetlana, and his fiery temperament was true to his Armenian roots. She knew he didn't understand her dilemma. As a Russian businessman he just could never earn enough money. And here she was saying she was going to do without his business which brought her around twenty million roubles a year. But as a Russian businessman, if he ever got caught doing something wrong he would either end up in the morgue or buy his way out of trouble. Russia was corrupt and money talked. If she and Thomas were ever caught by the German authorities smuggling wine, they could go to jail. She had trusted Armen and his company, Transmir, and she had known him for around fifteen years. She also knew about his past, how he had built up his huge fortune in the early nineties selling weapons, armoured vehicles, missiles, steel and anything that could be made into weapons to the Americans. It was rumoured that he had even dealt in plutonium. He had, as many others had, plundered his country, her country, stripped it and made it vulnerable. That was twenty years ago when Armen was in his early thirties. He had built up an empire and had a huge network of people who owed him favours. But he also had a long list of enemies. During the bank crisis in 1998 he had looked after his good customers and paid his suppliers. But he had also ruined other lives by insisting that debts be paid with huge interest rates. The late nineties were turbulent times and ritual mafia murders were a common occurrence. When she was a student at Moscow University studying the German language and German literature, the German papers always reported these horrible deeds. The offender would be brought to the cemetery, his hands tied with wire behind his back, petrol poured over his body and set alight. Thank goodness those days were in the past. Now the Government was combatting corruption and smuggling, or at least aiming to. The new police reform and severe customs checks were the order of the day. And Armen was losing his alcohol import licence. He would be forced to use another import company and that brought inherent dangers. Police and customs informants were everywhere. No-one was safe, except maybe the rich. And not always the rich were safe either. And women, who were no longer safe either. Svetlana had always told Thomas not to worry about her and her dealings with people who engaged in organised crime. When she first introduced Thomas to Armen in 2004 she had told him that women were of no consequence to such men. The matriarchal society of the former Soviet Union had created a cult barrier as far as women were concerned. Women, she had said, were never victims of violent crimes. That was true until Anna Politovskaya, the famous journalist who opposed and criticised President Putin and his government of Russia, was murdered. The shock sat deep and she, just as everyone in Russia, knew a dangerous line had been crossed.

*

It was eight thirty in Sydney on a Tuesday morning and the sun had only risen shortly before seven. Sam preferred the long daylight hours of summer. March wasn't his favourite month. It meant that winter was coming and the morning temperature was already below twenty. It looked as if it might rain and Sam put his raincoat over his arm. Karen was in the kitchen fixing some coffee. She found it even more difficult to get out of bed in the morning when the sun didn't rise so early. He walked into the kitchen, kissed her goodbye and she murmured:

"See you later."

He picked up his briefcase, opened the door, closed it quietly behind him and walked to the lift. He was feeling slightly nervous. Stupid of himself, he thought. Tom had already seen the accounts for the last five years and was still negotiating so he was definitely interested in a share of Sam's business. Now it was time to talk money and contracts. Sam would feel better, he decided, once the contract was signed and the money in the bank. Just a couple more months, he thought. Then we'll be out of trouble.

Sam drove his seven series BMW out of the garage and headed out towards the airport. He was meeting Tom at Macquarie Links at nine-thirty – a working breakfast in the private member's lounge with a spectacular view of the ocean. It probably wouldn't take him more than forty five minutes along the M1 and the M5 so he was in good time. He listened to the news on the car radio and to the usual early morning banter. It helped him to relax.

He drew up to the car park in front of the clubhouse at nine fifteen. The club's dress code was "casual attire in good taste" so Sam had put on a short-sleeved white shirt, a dark blue blazer and freshly pressed white linen trousers. Shorts and anything in denim was a no-go at this golf club. He headed towards the lounge and opened the door. The steward in an immaculate white jacket came towards him.

"Good morning, Sir," he said in a commanding way which meant he knew all the members and this person was not a member but obviously the type of person the club welcomed.

"Good morning," Sam replied with a smile. I'm looking for Tom Wyatt. He's expecting me."

"Tom will be out on the deck overlooking the tenth tee," he said with a smile, pointing to the open doors to the deck. Sam walked out and spotted Tom at a table set for breakfast with a copy of The Australian in his hand. The cane furniture was distinctly Australian. He was sitting watching the tenth tee but could observe the door to the deck at the same time. He saw Sam come in and stood up immediately. Sam acknowledged him and walked over. They shook hands and both sat down, took in the beautiful view and breathed the mild March air. Tom was wearing his "sailing togs" as he called them. The steward came over and they ordered breakfast with freshly squeezed orange juice and coffee.

"I'm famished," Tom said. "I was out on the driving range this morning at eight for an hour's warm-up. I'm playing with Frank Williams at eleven." Tom had politely and cleverly given Sam the deadline for the end of their breakfast meeting. Tom would need half an hour to change into his golf gear so Sam had an hour. He'd have to cut the small talk short and get down to business quickly.

"The course looks stunning," Sam said, not to look too eager to discuss his business.

"It is," he said, delighted to be able to talk about his favourite golf course. "It combines a fantastic links course with a feeling of being in the bush with native grasslands and mature gum trees. Some of the creeks and lakes are natural ones and the whole course ebbs and flows with the natural lie of the land. The tenth is a gentle par four to ease you back into the round but your drive has to be straight. If you hook it there are some deadly bunkers on the left," he said pointing down the fairway. "And if you're long with your approach shot to the green, it'll run off the back and there are some pretty deep bunkers on the right side of the green, too." He was living every minute of this narrative. A true golfing spirit, Sam thought. The steward brought coffee and orange juice and Tom suddenly changed the subject.

"Well, Sam, I like what I see in your business - a real Australian pioneering spirit, something different, something special. And the figures add up and the potential seems to be there. After talking to my advisors and due consideration, I'd like to come on board."

Sam's heart leapt in his breast.

"Let's shake on it," Tom said and held out his hand. "I'll leave it to my lawyers to work on the details of the partnership and investment. You've given me the figure you need for the investment and expansion you're planning and we have most of the information we need. They'll be in touch with you by the end of the month. There's no rush. The money won't become available until the end of April so we basically have eight weeks to get the contract done and dusted."

Eight weeks, Sam thought. He tried not to show his disappointment. He had enough cash to keep him going from his side-line with Pete Owen but he wasn't sure the bank would be so patient. He took a deep breath and said:

"Tom, I know that you're a very honourable person. I always take the view that business is business and there are a couple of investments I have to commit on in the next few weeks. Obviously I won't be talking to any other potential investors over the next eight weeks. Maybe we could both sign a letter of intent?"

Tom looked at him and pondered for a moment.

"I don't think that would be a problem," he said. "I'll get the legal boys to draw something up and send it over next week."

"Thank you, Tom," he said as a wave of relief went through his whole body. "I really appreciate your understanding."

Tom knew that Sam was short of cash. His business had potential but not the necessary cash flow for the kind of investment and expansion Sam was planning. Why would he be looking for an investor if he had the means himself? For Tom this was a pretty routine conversation but for Sam it was a matter of life and death.

"Ah, good," Tom said. "Breakfast!" he said as the steward put the plates on to the table. "Let's tuck in," Tom said and even Sam managed to rustle up an appetite. The conversation turned back to golf, wives, children and charities and the wonderful weekend Tom and Nancy had spent with them on Billy Jo. At ten thirty Tom looked at his watch and said with a hint of feigned surprise, "Goodness, it's ten thirty. I'd better go and get changed or I'll be late for my match."

Tom stood up and held out his hand.

"I look forward to having you on board, Tom. I hope you enjoy your round."

"Frank's a pretty consistent player, plays off nine, so I can't afford too many mistakes today," he smiled. They shook hands and walked down the steps of the deck together and parted on the path. Tom turned towards the clubhouse and Sam walked towards the car park unable to suppress a smile of satisfaction and relief.

13

It was just after five in the morning on Wednesday, 9th March. It was still dark on the HGV parking lot in the outskirts of Vilnius in Lithuania where Pavel had left the truck the night before when he arrived from Germany. He was headed for Podolsk, forty kilometres south of Moscow, not far from Domodedovo airport. He had picked up the load of wine near Bad Kreuznach on Monday, 7th March and had left Bad Kreuznach at nine in the morning. Tuesday was a public holiday in Russia, International Woman's Day, so he knew he couldn't cross the border into Russia until Wednesday. It had taken him thirty four hours to drive the sixteen hundred kilometres to Vilnius including the breaks and rest EU law prescribed. He always observed the legal breaks. It was far too expensive if you got caught driving longer hours and your tachograph couldn't lie. He would have to stop over in Moscow for twenty four hours to observe his weekly break but he didn't mind. Sonja, the canteen manager at Vodalko, would look after him. She knew he was arriving on Friday and she would, as always, arrange for a party on Friday night. Vodka would be flowing and she'd bring out the caviar that one of the other drivers gave her every couple of weeks and they'd eat it all with sour cream on small thick pancakes, blinis. Pavel rubbed his gloved hands together. It was around four degrees below freezing. He'd started the engine before he removed the ice from his windscreen. He climbed into his truck and arranged his things. He put his seat belt on, turned the radio to his favourite music station and released the brake. His brakes hissed. He looked at his watch. It would take him around six hours to get to the Russian border in the south of Latvia. On the radio they had reported only small queues of trucks waiting to cross the border so hopefully he'd be in Russia by early afternoon. He'd try and get to Velikiye Luki before he settled down for the night. There was a large petrol station near there with a huge HGV park at the back and a truckers' café with the best sausages he'd ever tasted. The weather report confirmed that the high pressure zone over Vilnius and Moscow would stay put for another few days at least. Temperatures were quite mild for this time of year and no snow was predicted. So his journey should be uneventful.

*

Svetlana cleared the breakfast table and put everything in the dishwasher. Misha and Alex had gone to school and Conrad had left for the workshop in Felsenhausen. It was a workshop for people with development disabilities and he just loved it. Thomas was in the cellar labelling some wine for a large customer. The sky was blue and the sun was shining although she could see some clouds coming in from the south-west. The morning had been cold but there had been no frost on the ground and now the temperature had risen to around 6°C although the wind was still a bit chilly. The kitchen stove was on and she relished the warmth it radiated in the kitchen. Such a comforting warmth. There were daffodils and tulips in a small white vase on the kitchen table and she looked around the kitchen with a sense of satisfaction. She loved her house, her home, her lifestyle, her family. She sat down in the chair in front of the picture window and put her cup of coffee on the small table next to the phone. She took the phone and pressed the speed dial for her mother in Moscow. A couple of rings later, Lesenka's voice said: "Alo"

"Hi, Lesenka, it's me, Svetka. How are you feeling?"

"Not too bad," came the reply but Svetka could hear in her voice that she wasn't feeling well. "I've drunk five cups of tea already and the sage tea you gave me with honey and lemon as well. I think I'll be OK by the weekend. Mamochka tells me I should boil fifteen black peppercorns in vodka and drink the whole lot before I go to bed!"

"Mama might be right," Svetka said. "It's an old Georgian method and I read not long ago that alcohol extracts the natural anti-biotic substances in peppercorns. So perhaps you should give it a try," she laughed a little to try and cheer her sister up. She always felt responsible for Lesenka despite the fact that Lesenka was a professional woman of thirty five with a good job and could really fend for herself. When they were children it was always Svetka who defended Lesenka, at school, in the street gang, playing board games with her father.

"And how is mama?" Svetka asked.

"To be honest, she's not too good." Lesenka's voice seemed to be a bit troubled. "I don't think it's anything in particular, she just seems to have become frailer and her mind wanders so much."

"The doctor did warn us that the painkillers she's taking would affect her memory and her mind. And that she would become less and less able to cope with daily tasks. Why don't you ask the doctor to come in?" Svetka said. It was OK for her to rationalise her mother's illness and symptoms but she wasn't confronted with them every day as Lesenka was.

"Yes, I may do that. Did you find the dress you wanted yesterday?" she asked, trying to change the subject.

"Oh, Lesenka, I found a really lovely outfit. It's in cream silk with quite a tight skirt and a jacket down to the hips. With some flowers in my hair and cream satin shoes I'll definitely look like a bride and I can wear the suit afterwards as a cocktail outfit."

"That's my sis," Lesenka said, her voice cheering up a bit. "Forever the practical one! It sounds perfect. I'd love to see it," she added.

"Well, the shop is shortening the skirt and the sleeves but as soon as I have it, I'll take a photo and send it to your phone."

"Great. I've applied for my visa to make sure I have it in good time. And Grishenka says he'll do it next week."

Grishenka, the more endearing diminutive for Grigory

was their elder brother. He was four years older than Svetlana and four years younger than Victor. Grishenka was an artist and the baby of the family even if he wasn't the youngest. Svetka and Lesenka mothered him but he didn't mind at all. Victor, the eldest of the four, would just shake his head at the way they all looked after him. Grishenka lived in St. Petersburg and worked as an assistant stage designer at the Mikhailovsky theatre. A lot of older people still called it the Maly theatre, literally "the small theatre", which was its famous name during the Soviet era. In 2007 it took on its former pre-revolutionary name of Mikhailovsky theatre.

"I'll ring him next week and remind him," Lesenka said. "You know how absent-minded he is." Svetka smiled. Absent-minded was a mild expression for her brother's forgetfulness!

"Good. Vic doesn't need one as his visa for Switzerland includes the Schengen area." Svetka didn't often call their eldest brother Vic. She liked his full name Victor, the victorious. It felt strong and protective. And that's how he was, strong and protective, just like his name.

"Grishenka and I are thinking of going to Rome after the wedding. We can catch a cheap flight from a small airport called Frankfurt Hahn, near Frankfurt I think."

Svetka laughed. "Yes, it's just an hour away but it's not that near Frankfurt! It takes longer to get to Frankfurt from Hahn than to our house. It's a small airport but very busy. That sounds like a good idea."

"Grishenka's already dreaming about the Coliseum and

can see himself designing a set for a stage version of "The Gladiator," she laughed. Typical Grishenka she thought.

*

Pavel had reached the border crossing before eleven. He'd had a clear run. Most of the trucks were now heading from Russia after the public holiday and he was lucky – he was a couple of days ahead of most of the drivers heading towards Russia. The queue at the customs office wasn't very long. He'd submitted his papers and had been told to come back in an hour or so. That would be great, he thought, if they managed to clear everything in an hour. Then he would get to Velikye Luki in time for supper with no problem. He went back to his truck and decided to have half an hour's rest. He climbed into his bunk behind the driver's seat and set the alarm on his iPhone for twelve noon.

The Latvian customs official looked at his screen in disbelief. It was this truck – the same driver, the same number plate, and the same destination and collection points. The warning on his screen meant that he couldn't continue the normal customs clearance process. He had a telephone number to ring if something like this ever happened. He was quite excited. Life was normally uneventful on the border. He called his superior over and showed him the warning. Both looked at each other in disbelief. This could be serious, very serious. The superior took all the truck's papers and rang the number that had appeared on the display. The conversation lasted five minutes or so. The other customs official went into the back office as soon as his superior had put the phone down.

"We've got instructions to check the weight of the truck and wait until an inspector arrives. He'll search the driver's cabin. They've had a tip off that this driver is smuggling toxic substances. They believe they're lethal substances and hidden somewhere in his cabin. So instruct the driver, when he comes in, to drive over to the weighing-in ramp and then we'll take him into the office for questioning. A detective from the organised crime squad will be with us within the hour. Until then, we have to detain the man on grounds of the truck's weight so as not to arouse his suspicion." They looked at each other in silence. There were often small problems, drivers smuggling cigarettes or whisky, they'd even found a small box of firearms. But this seemed a lot more serious. Lethal substances. Wait until an inspector arrives.

"Alex, go back to your desk and wait until the driver comes in," the superior in charge said.

At twenty past twelve Pavel walked into the office and stood in the queue. It took him ten minutes to get to the desk. The official took his papers from the pile and asked him to drive his truck into garage number 16 to be weighed. Pavel sighed. This would probably cost him another hour. Oh, well, there was nothing he could do about it.

"Garage number sixteen," he repeated.

"Yes," the official nodded and pointed outside to the right. "It's over there."

"Thank you," said Pavel. There was no point in getting cross with any of these guys. They were only doing their job. He was a bit surprised that the customs official didn't give him his paperwork.

"I'll give the paperwork to my colleague on the weighing machine," he said and shoved the wad of papers to one side. Pavel shrugged his shoulders and walked back to his truck.

Two rather surly customs officials walked up to Pavel as he got out of his truck which he had driven on to the weighing machine. He noticed they were armed which was unusual. One of them held his papers and said in a deep voice:

"Your papers say the truck should weigh 38 tons and it weighs 39 tons. We're having to do spot checks on weight today. So I'm afraid that we'll have to unload the pallets and then check the weight of the empty truck. That'll take half an hour or so."

"Jeez," sighed Pavel. "I wanted to make Velikye Luki before supper", he said.

"Shouldn't be a problem," the other official said. "Come on, I'll get you a cup of coffee while you're waiting," he added putting his arm on Pavel's shoulder in a friendly manner.

"Thanks," Pavel said. "I could do with a cup of coffee."

The official took him to the back office, picked up the phone and ordered two cups of coffee with four lumps of sugar each.

"I like my coffee sweet," he said, putting the receiver down. "Ah, I see you came from Germany. What was the weather like?"

"It was just below freezing when I left on Monday. I spent the night in Vilnius. My wife lives in Vilnius," he added.

The friendly customs official kept him talking for twenty five minutes – did he have any children, did his house have a garden, what did he grow in his garden. Just small talk as they sipped their coffee. Then two men in warm winter overcoats walked in and nodded at the customs official who stood up, said goodbye to Pavel and walked out. The men took off their coats and sat opposite Pavel at the table. He didn't like this at all. It was strange. And he had no idea what it was about.

"Good morning," the elder one said. "We have received information from an unnamed source that you are carrying toxic substances in your cabin."

Pavel turned white. Toxic substances? His mouth fell open and he stared at the man in the cheap grey suit.

"I've no idea what you're talking about," he said. "What kind of toxic substances?"

"The parcel must be small enough to fit into a hiding place in your cabin. We can take your cabin apart but it will take quite a while and we'll have to confiscate your truck. Or you can cooperate. You can tell us if you're carrying something for someone and where the parcel is. We will, of course, put in our report that you were cooperative and then the judge may well fine you instead of sending you to prison."

Pavel suddenly felt quite sick. He'd forgotten all about

the brown padded envelope he'd received from the warehouse manager when he picked up the load of wine. It was A4 size and felt as if there were a small box inside. He thought it was money or maybe even precious stones. He didn't ask what it was as the man had given him a second envelope and said: "For you, Pavel. Thanks for your help. Just put the envelope in a safe place where it won't get crushed or found and give it to the warehouse manager at Podolsk. There is a name on the envelope and he'll know how to deliver it." Pavel had gone to the men's, gone into a cubicle and looked inside the second envelope. He counted two hundred Euros in twenty Euro notes. Not bad for just putting an envelope under his seat and forgetting about it until he reached Podolsk.

Pavel looked down at the table and then up at the official. He knew there was no point in denying the envelope. They would no doubt find it and he would be looking at a prison sentence. The silence in the room was unbearable and he could hear the two officials breathing.

"I have an envelope that a man asked me to give to the warehouse manager at Podolsk. That's all. Just an envelope. It's under the driver's seat."

"Thank you," the man in grey answered. The other man got up and walked out the door. "So what's the name of the man who asked you to deliver the envelope and where does he work?"

Half an hour later the envelope was on its way to a forensic laboratory to be examined and Pavel was sitting in the back of a police car on his way to the police station to make an official statement and be charged.

The envelope had two letters in Russian on the front: AM. The police officer typing up the report and the charged man's statement wondered who AM was. The substance in the envelope had turned out to be strychnine, 30 g of strychnine, enough to kill a couple of hundred people if swallowed directly. What on earth was a harmless truck driver doing with such a lethal amount of strychnine? When he finished his report he saved it in their internal system and then rang his superior.

"Yes, sergeant," a voice at the other end enquired. "What's up?"

"I was just wondering, Sir, if I should post a report about the strychnine into Interpol's system," he said and waited a couple of seconds for a reply.

"Good thinking, Aleksey. Detective Inspector Lapsa will be on his way to Frankfurt in the next hour to follow the trail there."

Aleksey put the phone down and smiled. Good, he thought. A few more good ideas and maybe a promotion would be coming his way. He went into the Interpol system and typed in a summary of his report – just the details that would match any research done by an interested party. He looked at his watch. It was five past six in the evening and he logged off his computer and said goodbye to two colleagues still checking Pavel's tachometer.

*

Detective Kristaps Lapsa was waiting for his flight to be called at Riga airport. He was on an air Baltic flight to Berlin at a quarter past six in the evening and then from Berlin to Frankfurt where he would land just before ten. His friend and colleague, Max Baer, worked for the German Kripo, the criminal investigation department, which was based in Wiesbaden. He and Max were of the same age and had similar backgrounds. Kristaps spoke Latvian which he had learnt from his father, Russian and German. He was born in 1970 when Latvia was still a Baltic State within the Soviet Union. Thirty five per cent of the people in Latvia still spoke Russian as their mother tongue and almost all Latvians had learnt Russian at school and used the language in their daily lives. His mother had been born at the end of the Second World War in Danzig where her parents had been forced to move in 1939 under the Molotov-Ribbentrop-Act which regulated the Nazi-Soviet Population Transfer. His grandparents were ethnic Germans from the Baltics. They had been forced to leave their home, a beautiful farmhouse with over a hundred acres of fertile land which his grandfather's family had worked for over two hundred years. His grandparents had moved to the eastern part of Germany where farming was organised into collective cooperatives as a socialist principle and land was owned by the state. So his grandfather worked in a farming cooperative where his daughter met and married a Latvian in 1969. Kristaps Lapsa was their son. His father had always spoke Latvian to him and he had learnt Russian at school. When the Berlin Wall was opened in November 1989, Kristaps was 19 and had just finished his military service in East Berlin. He decided to work in Riga for a year or so to learn more about Latvian culture. When he returned to Germany, he applied to study for a Bachelor of Arts degree at the Police Academy in Hahn in the western part of the newly re-united Germany. That's where he met Max Baer.

Max's family was Jewish. His grandfather, Benjamin, was an ethnic German born in Novosibirsk in Siberia. In 1934, after the forced famine in the Ukraine in 1933 when thousands of people died every day at the hand of Stalin's policies, and with the mounting anti-Semitism in Nazi Germany, Benjamin's parents took the hardest decision in their lives, to send their son to America. They knew they would never be allowed to leave the Soviet Union as a family so they went on holiday to Vladivostok in the summer of 1935. They spent a whole week finding the right person to smuggle their son, Benjamin, on to a ship which was to trans-dock in Shanghai and then sail to San Francisco. They had pawned all the gold and diamonds which they and their parents had hidden in the lining of their furniture, in walls and cupboards, a lifetime's savings they had saved for a "rainy day". They kissed their beloved Benjamin goodbye for the last time. He looked back just once as he went aboard the cargo ship in a borrowed sailor's jacket and cap. Benjamin was 15 and didn't speak a word of English. He was smuggled from board in San Francisco and made his way to the nearest synagogue. He lived in two different foster families, one Russian-speaking family for two years and then in a German-speaking family. He learnt English in no time at all on the street and at work. He was given documents which friends had organized, real documents, not fake ones, which documented his birth as the oldest son of his German-speaking foster-parents. Benjamin worked hard for his foster father, a jeweller. In 1942 he married an attractive young lady he'd met at the synagogue. Her parents had had the foresight to leave Nazi Germany in 1935 before it was too late. Max's father was their first son and born in the USA. His mother was also Jewish and like his father was born in the USA in 1945. Her parents had left Germany in 1934 as teenagers with their families leaving everything behind them. Max's parents got married in 1968 and Max was born in 1970. He was brought up to speak German and English fluently and his father made sure that Russian still had a place in their family tradition. In 1989 Max was fascinated by the new opportunities that the re-unification of Germany would bring to Europe. He decided to go to Germany and come to terms with the culture that had had such an influence on his family's history. He lived in Frankfurt for a year and worked occasionally as a translator. Then he decided to apply for a German passport and to attend the Police Academy in Hahn where his language talents could be put to good use.

Kristaps smiled at the stewardess as he left the plane. It was quite a walk from the arrival gate to baggage reclaim in Terminal 1 at Frankfurt. He only had hand luggage but he knew Max would be waiting for him as he came out of baggage reclaim A. They shook hands and then gave each other a real bear hug.

"You look older," Kristaps said.

Max smiled. "So do you, old man! Let's get back to Wiesbaden so we can have a beer and catch up. Lottie is at her mother's and the kids go to bed around now so we'll have the place to ourselves."

After the first cool lager they had caught up the last five years' of their lives. They still phoned each other now and again but as the years went by, it seemed more difficult to keep up to date with all the changes in their lives. They had another beer and decided to leave the business at hand until the next day. However, they still talked about the USA and Russia and organised crime. They were both in organised crime units and they had some very valuable contacts and information which they could share. They really enjoyed each other's company and it was just like old times, at the Police Academy in Hahn. As Max said, the only difference was the time they went to bed! Up at six, he had said, so we'll hit the hay at midnight. It's going to be a long day tomorrow.

The next day Max and Kristaps arrived at the German CID headquarters in Wiesbaden around half past seven. Max signed Kristaps in and then showed him around the building and introduced him to some of his colleagues. They sat down with a cup of coffee and Kristaps took out his file.

"The driver of the truck is small fry, just paid to deliver the envelope with the strychnine in it to the warehouse manager in Podolsk. The envelope – here's a picture – was addressed to AM whoever that may be. He didn't know.

He had been told that the warehouse manager would know where to deliver the envelope and to whom. The person who gave him the envelope and two hundred Euros was the warehouse manager in Kelsterbach at Global Logistics' warehouse. He didn't have a name but here's the description and an EvoFIT picture" Kristaps said placing a reconstruction of the warehouse manager's face on to Max's desk.

"Which version of EvoFIT are you using," Max asked and Kristaps smiled. "The newest! With the amount of organised crime we have to deal with, we get enough funds to buy the best. What about you?"

"The same here. Well, we don't want to waste any time so let's go to Kelsterbach and interview the warehouse manager."

14

Sam and his wife Karen were sitting in the famous seafood restaurant almost under the Harbour Bridge and opposite the Sydney Opera House. They were waiting for Pete Owen and his wife Jean to arrive, just the four of them, for an informal dinner. Pete had rung him at the beginning of the week and suggested they go out for a meal. Sam suspected there was more to his request than just dinner among good friends.

"I never get tired of this beautiful view," Sam said and smiled at his wife. Karen was deep in thought. She turned her head and looked at her husband.

"I think Laura has a new boyfriend," she said with a look that showed her concern. Laura was their seventeen-year-old daughter who was currently on a year's exchange student scheme in the USA. She was just coming up to the end of her first term in Pittsburgh.

"Well, that's pretty normal isn't it for a young lady of seventeen?" he asked.

"Yes, only he isn't seventeen. He's twenty five," Karen replied. "His name is Steve and he works in his father's business."

"So where's the problem."

"I just hope the relationship doesn't get too serious. It's so difficult to talk to Laura about it on the phone. And now she wants to spend six weeks doing a tour of the USA when school ends on 15th June."

"Darling, let her do it. She's a sensible girl and if she doesn't do it now, she'll probably never find the time. Once she starts university she'll not have the freedom she does now." Sam waved his hand at Pete and Jean who had just arrived. "We can talk about it again tomorrow after breakfast," he said getting up to greet Pete and kiss Jean on her cheek. Sam moved a chair back so Jean could sit down.

"We certainly picked a nice evening," Pete said and they all nodded. It was still 24°C and they were enjoying the last rays of the sun.

The waiter came over and took their drinks order. The men ordered beer and the ladies went for a bottle of Chardonnay from the cool climate region of Orange.

Jean and Karen had already started talking about their daughters and Pete got up and said: "Excuse me, ladies, Sam and I have a short matter to attend to over at the bar. We'll be back in five minutes."

Pete asked the waiter to bring their beers to the bar and he moved with his arm on Sam's shoulder towards the back of the restaurant.

"Sam, I want to increase our quota of nux coming in," he said, "without it being on the books."

"How much more do you need?" Sam asked, wondering why Pete hadn't discussed it when they last met at his office.

"About 10% more. Can you do it?"

"Sure. Is there any particular reason? Not that it's any of my business but I was wondering why you didn't mention it when I last visited your office."

"The opportunity only arose a week ago. It's a new customer and I could do with the extra cash."

"Couldn't we all," Sam said. "I'll increase the amount not declared in the regular consignment by 10% starting from next week. I'll give Bill new instructions on Monday," he said.

"Great. Thanks Sam." Pete and Sam picked up their beer. "Cheers!" Pete said and raised his glass, "Cheers!" Sam replied, clinking his glass against Sam's. Pete looked back at their table and saw Jean raise her eyebrows.

"I think we'd better get back to the table," he said. "We don't want our wives getting nervous about what we may be planning!" he joked and moved away from the bar to walk back to their table. Karen and Jean were still chatting away about a new fashion shop which had just opened in Sydney.

"Phew!" Pete whistled. "This sounds like an expensive conversation!" They all laughed and took the menus from the waiter who had suddenly appeared from nowhere as if summoned by someone watching them on CCTV.

"Cheers!" Sam said, raised his glass and the others joined him. "I'm starving," he said opening the menu.

*

In Moscow it was lunchtime and Vanya had just showered and changed. He'd been training since six in the morning, driving manoeuvres, fitness, boxing and self-defence. He visited the training camp at Vodalko once a month to make sure that he was on top form for his job driving Armen and protecting him from unexpected situations. He would spend the afternoon on the shooting range but first he was to meet the boss, Abel, at one. Abel's assistant, Emin, stood up as Vanya walked through the door.

"Mr. Plemyannikov is expecting you," Emin said with as much of a smile as he ever managed. He wasn't the most charismatic of men but a good assistant and security manager. Emin knocked on the door softly and opened it for Vanya.

"Vanya, how are you?" Abel said walking towards him with an outstretched arm. They shook hands.

"I'm fine," he said, "thank you."

"I hear that you're on top form," he said. "You always were the best, Vanya."

They sat down on two leather arm-chairs in front of a low wooden table. Abel pressed a button and a couple of minutes later two ladies appeared in white aprons carrying two trays of healthy snacks. Vanya smiled.

"I also hear that you are most conscious about what you eat and drink, don't drink alcohol and don't touch drugs. It's about the latter, drugs, that I wanted to talk to you about."

Abel continued talking in a quiet voice and Vanya ate some of the snacks in front of him, listening intently. After twenty minutes Abel said: "Let's continue this conversation while we're walking to the shooting range."

Abel never discussed anything which may compromise him in his office. You really never could know who was listening. He had his offices swept for bugs regularly but he was a careful man. Men with power had to be careful, careful what they said, what they did and who knew what they thought. He trusted Vanya. He had known him as a youth and had recognised a will to succeed coupled with a judicious art of keeping himself to himself. Abel had taken him under his wing. Vanya's parents had died in a car crash when he was twelve during the Bank Crisis of 1998. He had been told that his parents had been killed in an accident but he knew it wasn't an accident at all. His father knew too much, had dealt with top leaders in organised crime, the so-called Russian mafia, for several years and had invested their money for them. Most of that had disappeared overnight in 1998 and had left a lot of unhappy investors. Vanya was suddenly alone and went to live with his aunt. He had decided that he needed to know everything there was to know about crime, criminals, self-defence, weapons and survival. He was good at school and after he had finished his homework he spent most evenings in a gym. His trainer had spotted his talents and talked to Abel. When he was fifteen he spent his Saturdays at the training camp in Vodalko and at the age of eighteen he started to learn to use weapons and drive cars at high-speed under difficult conditions. He spent the summer of 2004 at Vodalko training hard before he went into the army for five years. When he came out, he knew just about everything there was to know about warfare, explosives and survival. Abel had arranged for him to work for Armen. "He's the best I ever saw," Abel had told Armen. "Loyal, reliable, doesn't brag about his talents, I can highly recommend him." Armen had hired him and hadn't regretted it. Vanya was clever and he felt safe under his protection.

Abel had put on his overcoat, hat, scarf and gloves. The temperature had barely risen above freezing. They walked towards the shooting range, Vanya in his army jacket, beret and gloves. Abel talked as they walked, making right and left turns at every opportunity just in case someone was watching them or filming them. Abel was a cautious and clever man and knew from experience that many a secret had been read from the culprit's lips. Their conversation, said Abel, would "go with them to the grave". Before they got to the range, Abel turned round and hugged his protégé and as he did so he slipped an envelope into his pocket.

"It is sad," Abel said. "But we mustn't mix our emotions with business and necessity. "

Vanya nodded. They parted company. Abel went back to his office and Vanya opened the door to the changing room at the shooting range. He opened his locker and put the envelope inside. He took out a semi-automatic, a long distance rifle and a revolver. He turned the combination on the padlock and put the weapons into his holdall.

*

It was late morning in Kelsterbach near Frankfurt in Germany when Max and Kristaps parked in the car-park in front of the Global Logistics warehouse in an unmarked police car. They asked at the driver's desk if they could see the warehouse manager and Max showed his police ID card. The young operations clerk on the other side looked slightly alarmed and picked up the phone. A couple of minutes later Dirk Kramer came through the door in the drivers' section of the reception area and walked up to them.

"Good morning," he said with a congenial smile holding out his hand. "Kramer, Dirk Kramer. What can I do for you?"

"You loaded a Lithuanian truck here on 7th March destined for Moscow. It was carrying wine."

"If you say so," Dirk replied, his heart beating just a little faster. "If you give me the number of the truck's license plate I'll check for you."

Dirk walked out of the drivers' area and into reception behind the desk. He stood at one of the computer terminals and waited for Max to hand him the number of the truck's license plate. Max pushed a piece of paper across the desk and Dirk Kramer punched in the number. In just fifteen seconds the computer program had recovered the loading order and the road way bill which had been scanned in.

"Got it," he said. "The driver was a man called Pavel Etus," he said. "His truck arrived here at six forty-five a.m. on 7th March and he was loaded at ten fifteen with 29 pallets of wine."

"Can you give me a copy of the CMR," Max asked.

"And a copy of the invoice from the company sending the wine."

"Sure," Dirk said and printed out the documents. He walked over to the printer at the back of the office trying to calm himself down. He gave the documents to the detective with a forced smile.

"Is there somewhere we can talk?" Max asked.

"I'll open the door, then turn right and follow me," Dirk said, pushing a red button on the underside of the desk. Max and Kristaps followed him to a small office with glass windows all the way round and a glass door. As they sat down, Max introduced Kristaps:

"This is my colleague, Kristaps Lapsa from the Latvian Criminal Investigation Bureau," he said. The men shook hands. Dirk felt sick but was forcing himself to keep cool. Max continued: "The Latvian police are holding the truck driver, Pavel Etus, in custody for not declaring an envelope he was carrying in his cabin. Here's a photo of the envelope with a ruler next to it. You can see that it's A4 size and about five centimetres high. Do you recognise it?

Dirk's brain was working overtime. If they had the envelope and the driver, no doubt the stupid man had told them where he got the envelope from. Better to cooperate and play the innocent victim, he thought.

"Let me think. Monday. Yes, I had a brown envelope to deliver personally to the driver of a truck, could have been this one."

"What was inside the envelope?" Max asked.

"No idea," Dirk replied. "It could have been documents

that had gone missing. That happens all the time. These drivers leave them somewhere and they just disappear and then we have to supply duplicates so the truck can exit the EU."

"And who gave you the envelope?" Max asked.

"Let me see, now. I was in the office on Friday late afternoon handing over some paperwork to Hubert Walter, the head of logistics. He took the brown envelope from his safe and asked me to give it to the driver who was to pick up the wine from Becker's estate the following Monday."

"You're sure he said Becker's estate?" Max asked.

"Yes. We've been loading Becker's wines for some years now."

"I see from the invoice that Becker's estate is in Unterbach. Do you know where that is?"

"It's just south of Bad Kreuznach on the B48 in the Alsenz Valley," Dirk replied.

"So you've been there? Max asked, ever the enquiring policeman.

"Not directly. I belong to a motorcycle club and we go through the Alsenz Valley once a year. Pretty countryside and a winding road that's fun to ride! We go through Unterbach on that trip."

"Have you ever stopped at the winery or met the owner?"

"No, I don't know him. I don't even know his name. Sorry, I can't help you there."

"Thank you for your help, Mr. Kramer. We'll need you to come to the station to sign a statement."

"What now?" he exclaimed.

"I'm afraid so. If I could use your phone I'll order a car now."

"I can drive there if you want."

"Thank you for the offer but the rule book says we have to escort you," Max said. He certainly didn't want him to phone and warn Hubert Walter.

"Be my guest," Dirk said, handing the handset to Max.

Max punched in the number and spoke to the police officer on duty. When he finished he gave Dirk Kramer the handset and said: "The police car will be with us in five minutes so if you could grab your coat we'll wait with you out front until it's here.

"I'll be back in a minute," Dirk said.

"We'll have to accompany you, Mr. Kramer," Max said and got up to go towards the door with him.

"Another rule?" Dirk asked with just an edge of annoyance.

"I'm afraid so," Max said and they all walked out of the office, Dirk Kramer grabbing his coat from the hook on the wall as he went past.

Five minutes later Dirk Kramer was in the back of a police car on his way to Frankfurt having handed over operations to his second in command. Max had put his head through the window of the passenger side and said to the two officers in uniform. "Strictly no phoning. If necessary, you can read him his rights and arrest him," he said. The policemen nodded. This was just normal routine for them.

Max and Kristaps walked back to their black Audi.

"Well, it seems as if we're on the right trail," Kristaps said.

"Yep. Let's pay Mr. Hubert Walter a visit," Max said. He switched his satnav on and put in the address of Global Logistics offices which were about five minutes from the warehouse. "Their offices are literally just around the corner."

They drove into the spacious car park and parked on one of the "reserved for visitors" spots. The car park was covered by CCTV and so was the entrance to the office building. There was a sign on the door saying that the whole building was covered by CCTV for security reasons.

Max showed his ID card to the pretty lady at the reception desk and asked to see Hubert Walter.

"Do you have an appointment?" she asked.

"No," Max replied. "The matter is quite urgent," he added.

The young lady picked up the phone and spoke to Hubert Walter explaining that a detective from the Kripo was here to see him. There was a silence on the other end for a split second and then Hubert Walter cleared his throat and said he would come to reception in a couple of minutes.

"You can hang your coats up over there," she said, pointing to the row of coats on coat-hangers. "He'll be right with you."

Max thanked her. He and Kristaps hung their coats up and took a seat facing the large glass door which led to the offices. Hubert Walter came through the glass doors five minutes later. They all shook hands and introduced themselves before walking through the glass door and to the back of the room into Hubert Walter's office. Max and Kristaps eyed the safe behind the door. They all sat down at the small table.

"Mr. Walter, we're investigating a case of smuggling. The driver of this truck," Max placed the CMR in front of Hubert Walter's hands, "carrying 29 pallets of wine from this estate," and Max put the invoice down on top of the CMR. "The driver is in custody for trying to smuggle an A4 size brown envelope over the Latvian-Russian border." He laid the photo of the envelope on the top of the papers and it had the desired effect. Hubert Walter, already quite pale, turned white with fright and his pupils became quite delated. His heart was racing. Thoughts were dashing through his brain. The driver must have told him about Dirk and Dirk would have told them that he had the envelope from him. There was no way out. They knew. Oh, my God, they knew.

It only took a couple more questions and he decided it would be better to cooperate. Hubert Walter told them everything. Well, everything except for the money he had received to have the envelope smuggled into Russia. He told his version of the story as if he were doing a valued customer a favour. After all, Thomas Becker had been using their services for five or six years and sent around fifteen trucks a year to Russia and paid his bills promptly. Yes, he always paid on time. Why shouldn't he ask a favour? He needed the envelope to arrive within a week and the postal routes were disastrous. Even courier services had their limitations.

Max and Kristaps didn't believe a word of his story and asked him how much he had received for this favour. Hubert Walter insisted he hadn't received any money. This was purely a favour for a valued client.

Max explained that the envelope had contained toxic substances and he would most probably be charged with aiding and abetting a smuggling offence of a dangerous nature. Hubert Walter asked if he could contact his lawyer and Max said he could do so once they arrived at Wiesbaden for questioning.

"I hope there is no need for handcuffs?" he asked. "It's going to be difficult enough leaving the office in police custody in front of all my staff."

"No need for handcuffs," Max said. "At this point in time you are only helping us with our enquiries. Hubert Walter put his coat on and waited for the detectives to escort him. He switched his telephone on to the answering service and locked his safe and his desk. He looked around the room with a sinking feeling. Hopefully he'd be back in his office tomorrow.

The two officers drove back to Wiesbaden with a very unhappy Hubert Walter. It only took them twenty minutes to drive to the headquarters of the German criminal investigations department, the BKA, Bundeskriminalamt, and known to most Germans as the "Kripo" for short. The BKA building was in the Äppelallee, one of Wiesbaden's most attractive and expensive main boulevards. Hubert Walter looked at the four-storey grey and white building that looked more like a hospital from the outside than a CID headquarters. He remembered seeing the building being opened some three or four years ago and being described as one of the most modern buildings for criminalistics. He never dreamt that one day he'd see the building from the inside. They walked up the stairs to the second floor where the so-called SO department had their offices, the department for serious and organised crime. They only had around 30 of the 620 rooms in the building. More than fifty per cent of the rooms housed experts on criminalistics, technicians, computer experts, DNS laboratories and other faceless specialities. Hubert Walter was taken into a room with no windows and just bare walls and several CCTV cameras around the room. No need for one-sided mirrors these days, he thought. Each blink of an eye-lid was being recorded. He sat on a chair and the two detectives were replaced by an even younger colleague. He introduced himself as Detective Martin Feldmann, switched on the microphone and explained that everything they said would be recorded. Hubert Walter explained that he wanted to make a phone call to his wife so she could contact a lawyer. The young detective closed his file and waited. The telephone arrived. Hubert Walter typed in his wife's mobile phone number and prayed she would answer:

"Ina Walter," she said as she answered the phone. Hubert Walter sighed with relief.

"Ina, it's me. Hubert. Look, I'm helping the Kripo with some enquiries into a smuggling offence and am at their HQ in Wiesbaden. As the offence is a serious one and I'm a witness, I've been advised to wait until a lawyer is here before I make any statements."

There was a couple of seconds silence on the other end as Ina took in the full weight of this blow. She was an intelligent and quick-thinking lady who wasn't prone to panic.

"My goodness, Hubert," she said, trying to sound as calm as possible. "I'll get hold of Karl somehow and make sure someone gets down to Wiesbaden immediately."

"Thanks, darling, you're a gem. I wouldn't mention this to anyone else and try to keep off your mobile phone would you in case I need to get hold of you."

"Of course. Do you want me to come to Wiesbaden?"

"No, no need for you to come. Once Karl or one of his colleagues is here and I've made my statement, I'm sure they won't wish to detain me."

"I hope not," she said. The young detective coughed politely.

"Well, must go. Love you."

"I love you too," she said and the conversation was over.

"Well sir, if you don't mind, could I take all your personal details before your lawyer arrives?"

"No problem," Hubert Walter replied and forced a polite smile.

*

Max and Kristaps were driving down the A60 motorway on the left back of the river Rhine. It took them about an hour to reach the address on the invoice in Unterbach, a sleepy village that Max had no idea even existed a couple of hours before. They had phoned Thomas Becker just before they set off to make sure that he'd be available to speak to them. He seemed a little surprised but had the presence of mind not to ask why on the phone. It was early afternoon when they arrived. Max drove through the wrought iron gates into the well-kept courtyard and admired the sandstone farmhouse which was in impeccable condition although it looked as if it was well over a hundred years old.

"No doubt Thomas Becker is a successful wine grower," Max said and looked at Kristaps. "There aren't many wine growers in this region that make a good enough living to maintain a farmhouse like this in such good nick," he added.

They went up to the front door without putting on their coats and Thomas Becker opened it before they had a chance to ring the bell. He smiled and shook hands with the two detectives. "Come on in," he said. They followed him into a warm kitchen which had a romantic feel about it and a slight odour of wood smoke which made Kristaps think of his mother's house in Latvia. Only her house was about a third of the size and most of the furniture was old and in need of repair whereas everything in this kitchen was new and expensive. They sat down at the kitchen table and Thomas offered them coffee, tea or water. They both asked for water.

"We drink tap water here, not the bottled stuff," Thomas said, bringing a jug on a tray and three glasses. "The water is extremely good quality." They both nodded in agreement and then Max cleared his throat.

"Herr Becker, it's about the brown envelope you gave the logistics manager at Global Logistics to give to the driver of the truck of wine you loaded earlier this week," he said and watched Thomas' reaction. He looked completely bewildered. Either Thomas didn't know what Max was talking about or the man deserved an Oscar for the best performance Max had ever seen.

"Envelope? What kind of envelope? And I don't know the logistics manager at Global Logistics personally. We only ever speak on the phone."

"So you've never actually been to their warehouse or their offices?" Max enquired.

"I went to their warehouse when I first started selling wine to Russia to check the facilities first hand. That must have been, let me think, in the spring of 2004. I've been a couple of times since, just to check that nothing has changed. I think the last time I was there would have been 2009 when one of the fork lift trucks drove into a pallet of wine and I went to have a look, check the damage and take some pictures for my insurance company."

"And you haven't been there since?"

"No, no need. We do everything by email and their service is difficult to find fault with."

"And you've never been to their head office in Kelsterbach?"

"No, I don't even know what the building looks like," Thomas said with a smile. "What's all this about?"

"My colleague here from the Latvian CID is investigating a case of smuggling. The driver of the truck which was carrying your wine had a brown envelope under his seat which he was given by the warehouse manager of Global Logistics. The envelope contained toxic substances."

"Drugs?" Thomas said, quite alarmed.

"No, not drugs but certainly substances on the dangerous products list. I'm afraid I can't be more precise."

"I quite understand, inspector," Thomas said. "I really don't know why you think I can help you."

"The logistics manager at Global Logistics, Hubert Walter, claims he received the envelope from you personally and agreed to do you a favour."

"That's absurd," Thomas said. "I don't know what was inside the envelope and I've no idea who it was addressed to but I really don't know why he should claim I gave it to him. He doesn't even know what I look like."

Max and Kristaps looked at each other. They certainly weren't going to get very far with Thomas Becker.

"Would you mind coming to Wiesbaden for an identity parade. We'll have to organise it for tomorrow before Herr Walter is let out on bail and has a chance to check what you look like."

"Well, I had a couple of other things in my diary for tomorrow but if it will help you then sure, just let me know the time you need me."

"Thank you," Max said standing up. Kristaps stood up on cue and held out his hand. "Thank you, Herr Becker. We really appreciate your help."

In the car going back to Wiesbaden the two detectives

exchanged their ideas on what was going on.

"I think he was telling the truth," Max said. Kristaps nodded. "Then who gave Hubert Walter the envelope? Or is our friend Mr. Walter making up a tall story to give himself an alibi?"

"Why would he do that? He's not stupid. He must know that we'd find out sooner or later that his story wasn't true. What if someone did give him the envelope and claimed he was Thomas Becker. How would Hubert Walter know? He's never met him."

"Well, we'll see who he picks out tomorrow but before we get him in front of a line up, I think he should describe the man to us. I'll get Peter do an EvoFIT picture with him first. That could be interesting," Max said with a smile.

On Friday afternoon Kristaps put down the phone and put his head in his hands. He'd rung his boss to let him know how the case was progressing. This certainly was a strange case of smuggling. Hubert Walter had made a very detailed description of Thomas Becker which really was quite different in many aspects to the Thomas Becker Max and Kristaps had met apart from the hair and the blue eyes. Next morning in the line-up he hadn't been able to identify any of the men as Thomas Becker despite his very precise description. So far they had reached a dead end.

15

In Moscow the night owls were still up. In Armen's favourite discotheque, The Iron Man, he had spent most of the night with three other friends talking business and boasting about their success. The owner of the discotheque had brought three young women to their table. Introductions to selected prostitutes were all part of the service. Armen had ordered champagne for the ladies who sipped at their glasses and laughed with the men, even if their jokes weren't that funny. The music was loud and the women took turns dancing with one of Armen's friends. Armen liked dancing but he wasn't in the mood. At two in the morning Armen was ready to go and had arranged for the lovely young blonde with long legs and large breasts to leave with him. The owner of the discotheque rang for his driver Vanya and when the black Mercedes ML500 arrived, he went over to Armen, bent down and talked into his ear.

"Vanya is waiting for you when you're ready Armen," he said. Armen nodded, said goodnight to his two friends, ignored the women and grabbed the blonde's hand.

"Let's go," he said.

The blonde smiled a forced smile knowing pretty well what would be awaiting her when they got to a hotel or to this rich man's house. Most of the tricks she turned were in hotels because most of her johns were married. This one was not. He told his driver to drive home. This was breaking the rules and Vanya gave him a questioning look.

"I need a good glass of wine and one of my cocktails," he said. Vanya knew what that meant. He needed some speed to keep him going through the night.

In the car Armen kissed his new prize and felt her breasts. They really were exciting. He touched her whole body and then her legs bringing his hands up to her crutch. She moved around so he could feel her more easily in the car, a real professional. Twenty minutes later the black Mercedes drove through the large gates in the high security wall and stopped at the front door. The security man in the lobby was watching on CCTV as they tumbled out of the car laughing. He grinned. It wasn't often that his boss brought back a prostitute so maybe he had something on his mind. He rang the man-servant, Kolya, to make sure that he was ready for instructions.

In the lounge Armen's man-servant was standing to attention and greeted his boss politely.

"Get me two bottles of Chateau Malvaux" he said. "Then you can go to bed, Kolya. I won't be needing you any more tonight. Vanya will drive the lady home."

Vanya knew it was going to be a long night but it wasn't the first time he had kept awake to drive his boss home from a hotel or on a rare occasion drive a lady home.

The lady went to the bathroom to freshen up and Armen turned to Vanya.

"Get me a cocktail," he said.

Vanya went to the bar and took some soda water out of the fridge. He went to the drawer where Armen kept his speed and took out a small folded paper "envelope" and poured the contents into the soda water. The ground crystals dissolved in the glass and Vanya stirred them. He washed the stirrer carefully, dried it and put it back in the drawer using the drying up cloth. He then took Armen his cocktail. Armen was already enjoying his second glass of wine. He took the cocktail and swallowed it greedily. He really needed a lift-me-up tonight, he thought. Vanya walked back to the bar.

The young blonde returned to the lounge with her long blonde hair brushed and floating over her shoulders. She had carefully painted her lips and refreshed her eye and face make-up. She only used good make-up and lipsticks, Dior, Chanel and Estee Lauder. She needed to make the right impression to ensure that her john paid her price which was quite a large sum of money. After all, she was only doing it for the money. When she had enough money she'd find a foreigner with a handsome bank account who she would lead on until he married her. Then she would be able to live abroad. She would need her own money so she could buy her new passport and pay for her divorce once she had her passport. Two of her girlfriends had already managed it and this was her burning ambition. As she floated out of the bathroom back into the lounge her thoughts were on her future and this rich man would be able to contribute.

Armen seemed to be sleeping as she walked up to his

armchair. She didn't come from behind him. These sort of men got jumpy when you approached from behind. She had deliberately walked to the side to approach him at an angle. The music was playing quite loud and she could just about make out his driver behind the bar in the dimmed lighting. As she got nearer she could see that Armen's face was contorted with pain and he had dropped his glass of wine. His eyes were wide open and staring into space. My goodness, she thought. He isn't breathing. She let out a scream and Vanya came running from the bar with his Vektor SR-1 pistol drawn and at the ready. He looked at the young blonde who looked frightened to death and then at Armen. He went over to his boss and felt his pulse.

"He's dead," he said in a matter-of-fact tone. "He's been having heart problems. It looks like a heart attack," he said. "I'd better get you back to wherever you want before the police arrive."

The blonde head nodded and Vanya put his revolver back into its holster. He took her by the arm and half-pulled the petrified young woman to the door. The security guard on the CCTV had left for the night but the cameras were still on in the hallway. Vanya told the young woman to keep her face to the right as they left the hall through the main door. She did exactly what she was told. She knew that the police would give her a hard time if they discovered she had been there. She didn't need the hassle.

By the time she got in the car she was feeling a little better, relieved to be going home. Vanya turned round and gave her an envelope.

"That is what he would have given you plus another fifty thousand to keep quiet about tonight. It will be a nasty shock for some important people and I'm sure you won't want to be involved."

"No, I won't" she said, a little worried about her own safety. "I won't say a word," she added, putting the envelope in her bag. She didn't even count it. What she had, she had and she just needed to get home. She gave him a false address about two blocks from where she lived. Vanya drove off keeping an eye on her in the back. He was pretty sure that she would keep quiet. However, you never knew what these women would do for money. Blackmail was quite common among prostitutes.

It was eight in the morning when Katya, the housekeeper, arrived to tidy up and make Mr. M's usual breakfast of freshly squeezed orange juice, an omelette with ham and cheese and some tomato salad. The CCTV recorded her coming in and the time. It was two minutes past eight in the morning. She usually found the lounge in disarray and cleaned it up first before going into the kitchen. If it was very untidy, then she knew Mr. M had been entertaining some of his friends and wouldn't be up until after nine anyway. If it was fairly tidy, she'd make his breakfast straight away. She hated her job, working for a rich man with no manners and courtesy towards the people who worked for him. But such were the times. Better a job like this than what some women had to go through to earn money in these difficult times. Fortunately, she thought, she was no longer young and she had lost her figure after years of hard work and too much fatty food to keep her going. Fortunately, she thought, as it meant that Mr. M only saw in her someone who could cook and clean. He bought his sex from young women with a slim figure and painted fingernails. Even if she didn't approve of prostitution, she ignored it as she had ignored many things in her life in order to survive.

She opened the door to the lounge. It didn't look too bad. The lights were still on, dimmed, which was unusual. Perhaps Mr. M had forgotten to turn them off when he went to bed. She walked towards the kitchen and saw an arm hanging over the armchair. Goodness, she thought. Mr. M must have fallen asleep in his armchair. Not like him, she thought. She walked softly through the lounge. She didn't want to wake him. He would probably be in an extremely bad mood if she did. As she opened the kitchen door she looked back. Then she saw that Mr. M had spilt a glass of wine over his trousers. Strange, she thought. He must have been really drunk. And then she noticed his eyes and the expression on his face.

"Bozhe moy" she exclaimed, "Good God," and ran through the kitchen into the security room. It was ten past eight and she prayed that the security guard had arrived on time. She burst into the security office without knocking and the guard turned round reaching for his revolver at the same time.

"My goodness, Katya, you gave me a scare. Whatever's the matter?" he asked.

"It's Mr. M," she said. "I think he's dead."

"Where is he?"

"In the lounge, in his armchair."

The security guard dashed into the lounge leaving the shocked housekeeper behind. He went up to the lifeless body of his boss and checked his pulse. He was dead alright. As dead as a doornail. He walked back to the security office.

"You'd better stay here in this room, Katya, until the police arrive. We mustn't touch anything just in case."

"You mean he's been murdered?" she asked.

"I don't know," he said "but it's better not to touch anything until we know." He picked up the phone and rang his security office. He didn't want just any kind of policemen calling. It had better be the right kind, the kind who knew what they were doing.

Vanya arrived at nine in the black Mercedes and stopped at the wrought iron gate. He looked up into the video camera and the security guard opened the gates. He could see two police cars in the drive and as he drove up to the front door a detective walked out to greet him. Vanya parked the car in the driveway and got out. He walked towards the detective at his normal pace with long strides. As he reached the front door the detective said:

"Ivan Potemkin?" the detective questioned looking Vanya straight in the eyes.

"Yes, that's me," Vanya replied stretching out his right arm to shake hands. The detective took a quick look at Vanya's belt as his jacket opened. A trained eyed told him the man was carrying a weapon.

"I understand that you are Mr. Makaryan's driver and

bodyguard, is that correct?"

The two men walked up the steps to the front door.

"Yes, indeed," Vanya replied. "What's happened?" Vanya asked, turning to look at the detective with a questioning look.

"I'm sorry to tell you sir that Mr. Makaryan is dead."

"Dead?" Vanya exclaimed. ""But he was perfectly OK when I left him last night."

"Are you carrying a weapon?" the detective asked.

"Yes, I always carry a weapon when I'm on duty," Vanya replied.

"May I have a look at it?"

Vanya handed over his Vektor SR-1 and the detective said: "I presume you have a licence?"

Vanya smiled. "Of course," he replied.

"May I keep your weapon for a few days until we have completed our forensic enquiries," the detective asked.

"Was Mr. Makaryan shot?" Vanya asked, his eyebrows raised in sheer disbelief.

"No, but we need to cover all aspects of his death until we are certain whether he died of natural causes or was killed. Thank you for your cooperation," the detective added.

They walked through the hall and into the security office where the security guard was trying to comfort Katya, the housekeeper, who, once the shock had subsided, burst into tears and couldn't stop sobbing.

"The housekeeper found him just after eight when she arrived. We have her arrival on video. She rushed to the security office and the guard went to investigate, finding Mr. Makaryan slumped in a chair having spilt a glass of wine on his trousers. What time did you leave Mr. Makaryan last night?"

"It must have been around two thirty in the morning."

"Were you alone," the detective asked, having already seen the videos of the night before.

"No, Mr. Makaryan had asked me to take his guest home."

"A young lady, I presume?"

"Yes. He had been in the Iron Man disco until around two in the morning and then brought the young lady back with him."

"So she didn't stay very long?"

"No, there was some kind of disagreement and Mr. Makaryan told me to take her home at once."

"And where does the young lady live?"

"I don't know," Vanya said. "She asked me to take her to an address in the city but I'm pretty sure it wasn't her address. I have it in my satnav," he said.

"Good. And then where did you go?"

"I went home. It was then around three o'clock and I like to get five hours sleep if I can."

"And what time did you leave home this morning?" the detective asked.

"As always around eight fifteen. I had a quick shower and got dressed and left to come to work."

"No coffee, nothing?"

"No, Katya always makes sure there's hot coffee at nine

o'clock when I arrive and she always gives me an omelette with cheese and ham, the same as Mr. Makaryan."

"Were there any signs of a struggle?" Vanya asked.

"Our enquiries are still continuing and until we are pretty sure what has happened I'm not at liberty to say. My apologies for not introducing myself. My name is Inspector Vladimir Antipov from the URPO."

Vanya looked at him in surprise.

"The URPO? I thought you only dealt with organised crime and infiltrating criminal organisations," Vanya said.

"Exactly," Inspector Antipov said with a smile. "We have been observing Mr. Makaryan for some time as some of his activities were brought to our attention by other official departments," he said. "That's why we have been asked to investigate Mr. Makaryan's death."

The URPO was a specialist department within the Russian secret service, FSB, dealing with matters inside the country. It had been brought into existence in 1996 and had about 150 specialists fighting organised crime, some of them undercover agents within criminal organisations working under very dangerous conditions. Vanya was not surprised that Armen had attracted their attention. After all, he knew that his boss had made his fortune in the early nineties selling weapons, steel, plutonium and virtually anything that could be made into weapons, mainly to the Americans. Then he had used his money to build up a business empire, in particular buying companies that went bankrupt during the bank crisis of 1998 and re-building them with very aggressive and not very legal methods.

But he also knew that his boss had contacts in high places, particularly in the mayor's office. Inspector Antipov was walking on pretty stony ground.

"Mr. Makaryan was a well-respected businessman with extremely good political connections," Vanya added.

"Yes, yes," he mused, "I understand that he has a close relationship to the mayor of Moscow."

"Indeed," Vanya said.

"Then no doubt my phone will be ringing all morning," Inspector Antipov sighed. "I will need you to come to my office this afternoon to make a statement," he added giving Vanya his card.

"Of course," Vanya added. "Does that mean I can go now?"

"Indeed. We have already finished talking to the housekeeper. Perhaps you would like to drop her off somewhere. She's quite distressed."

"Yes, I can take her home. No problem."

"Very kind of you," Inspector Antipov added and wondered how such nicely mannered, handsome young men could be such ruthless killers.

Just two hours later Inspector Antipov received a phone-call from his colleague from the CID, Yuri Mamedov, who had woken up the owner of the Iron Man to try and identify the prostitute who had gone back to Armen Makaryan's house with him. They had a video picture but the woman had turned her head away from the camera. They had an address which the driver, Vanya, had given them but he was pretty sure when all the inhabitants had been interviewed which would take twenty-four hours that no-one would be able to identify her. His only hope was the owner of the Iron Man but it was a slim hope. None of the prostitutes working the clubs actually used their real names.

"Hi, Yuri, any news?"

"The owner doesn't keep files on his guests, he says. He can only say that Mr. Makaryan left just before two with a young blonde lady. He described her and what she was wearing. I passed it on to a colleague working on the organisers of Tochkas[1]. I know that the prostitution street markets are a different world to club prostitution but he promised to check the description. Well, you're not going to like the next bit. He didn't find anything in their records but he passed it on to homicide and they have an unidentified body found this morning. A young blonde woman that could fit the description. So I'm off to the mortuary to have a look and will let you know. She was shot once in the chest and once in the head. Looks like a professional killing possibly a gang killing."

Inspector Antipov sighed. "Let me have the calibre of the weapon as soon as you can, will you. And get the owner to identify the woman if you think she's the one we're looking for."

"Roger," Yuri said and hung up.

Inspector Antipov decided to wait for the post mortem on Mr. Armen Makaryan before proceeding any further. He should have a preliminary report by twelve thirty.

---

[1] *Tochka* is an organised street prostitution market in Russia.

Inspector Antipov swore loudly into his mobile.

"Well where the hell is the report?" he asked. "I need to know if we're talking of murder or natural causes," he added.

"I'm sorry sir," the polite voice on the other end said. "I have been ordered not to release the report yet. Apparently the order came from the authorities and I understand that the origin of the request came from the mayor's office."

"I don't care whose bloody office it came from," Antipov continued, red with rage. "We are fighting organized crime and the URPO has a special mandate within the FSB and I don't need to tell you how far up the political ladder that goes."

"No, indeed, but my hands are tied. I can only ask you to put in your complaint through the official channels." The man put the phone down and Inspector Antipov felt an overwhelming sense of frustration. How on earth was he supposed to investigate a crime if he didn't even have the forensic report. It stunk to high heaven and there was nothing he could do about it.

His phone rang. His assistant told him that Mr. Makaryan's driver was in the interview room. Inspector Antipov went down the corridor and walked in. Vanya stood up and both men shook hands politely.

"My assistant will take down your statement, Mr. Potemkin, and hand you back your firearm. Please don't leave Moscow without telling us until we have finished our enquiries."

"No problem," Vanya replied. "I shall be taking a few days off and looking for another job," he said. "I doubt whether anyone will be employing me until you know what Mr. Makaryan died of. It's not exactly a good recommendation in my line of business if your boss dies unexpectedly, whatever the circumstances."

"I understand," Inspector Antipov said. "I'll let you know as soon as we know more but it could take some weeks."

"Of course," Vanya replied. Antipov's assistant walked in with a laptop and sat opposite Vanya at the table. Antipov took his leave and walked back to his office.

*

It was early afternoon when Boris Makaryan was told that his brother had been found dead in his home early that morning. Boris couldn't believe it. His younger brother, Armen, dead! How on earth was he going to tell his ageing mother? The man who had brought him the bad news had worked for Boris for over ten years and knew both Boris and Armen better than anyone. Boris thumped his clenched fist against an antique cupboard and then almost fell into an armchair and put his head in his hands and sobbed liked a baby. Aram, the bearer of the bad news, didn't move. He was also Armenian and he knew how his family and friends showed their emotions. It was almost like a volcano erupting but he knew Boris would get over the shock quickly and take command of the situation as he always did. Several minutes later Boris got up and walked to the window. He wiped his eyes, sniffed and turned round to Aram.

"Was he murdered?"

"No-one knows," Aram said. "It's quite unusual. I can't get any information out of our usual informants."

"I want to see the body," Boris said.

"Of course. I'll make arrangements for later this afternoon. I understand there is no evidence of external force or bleeding."

"We need the post mortem report," Boris said in a determined, almost bitter tone. "Whoever has killed my brother will pay for it," he added.

"I'll get on to it straight away."

"No matter what it costs. I want that report."

Aram left Boris on his own with his sadness and his thoughts. He would need time to mourn for his brother. In the meantime he, Aram, would set all wheels in motion to get hold of the report on Armen Makaryan's death.

16

It was five thirty in the afternoon when Sam's mobile rang. He was on his way back to the condo after a tiring day at the office. It was Tom, his manager at the plantation in Queensland.

"Hi, Tom. What can I do for you?"

"Well, Sam, I don't usually ring you on such matters but I know that Pete Owen is waiting for a consignment urgently."

"Is there a problem?"

"Well, we made out the invoices as you instructed but now we have an unannounced tax inspection tomorrow and that means going through all of today's paperwork and checking batches etc. I just thought I might cancel the order and send it on Wednesday instead. Could you let Pete know?"

"I sure will," Sam said, not wanting to ask any more questions. He knew what Tom was telling him. The invoiced amount didn't tally with the amount sent and even a blind tax inspector would be able to see that he was selling around thirty per cent on the black market. Damn! This was the first time his business in Queensland had been inspected. He frowned and phoned Pete Owen.

"Hi, Pete, it's Sam."

"Hi, Sam, how're you doing?"

"We're going to have to delay the next shipment of nux vomica until Wednesday as everyone is tied up with some unannounced tax inspector's visit due for tomorrow. I hope that won't cause too much inconvenience?"

"Well, a bit difficult seeing as we have orders coming out of our ears at the moment but I'll see if we can't get some of the staff to come in on Saturday to catch up."

"Thanks, Pete. Talk soon." Sam pressed the red telephone button on his iPhone – still in deep thought.

In a small but extremely modern telecommunications centre of the New South Wales police headquarters in Charles Street, Parramatta, Sam's conversation with Tom and then with Pete Owen had been recorded. A delighted special agent listening in shouted "Bingo" and the other agents listening and observing different people and situations all turned round and smiled at him. Lucky b… one of them murmured. The special agent sent the transcript of the telephone conversations to his boss on their secure intranet system. Now they had what they wanted for a search warrant but it would have to be issued quickly. They would have to search late on Wednesday to be able to prove that Sam MacPherson was selling nux vomica on the black market to Pete Owen. They had already quite a lot of evidence against Pete Owen. The new customer he had was an undercover agent and he had ordered a large amount of strychnine on the black market. He knew they would catch him out. These people always got careless and greedy when they had dealt on the black market for a few years with no problems. Now we've got you, Mr. Owen. And you as well, Mr. MacPherson. Two fish biting on the same hook. Great!

*

It was ten in the morning in Moscow on Monday. Aram was sitting at the table in his boss' office with the original post mortem report on Armen Makaryan which confirmed the cause of death as a lethal dose of poison. The forensic report on the wine glass showed that the substance was strychnine. Boris' facial expression was motionless. His brother had been poisoned. The report hadn't been released straight away but Aram had managed to get it through an informant in the mortuary who had managed to bribe the right person in the forensic department. Poison. Strychnine. The wine glass. All these details were rushing through his brain at the speed of light.

"Aram, I need to know what wine he drank and where it came from. And I need to know why he didn't notice that it was laced."

Aram stood up and walked out to get all the information his boss wanted.

"Thank you," Aram said politely. "I appreciate your help. Mr. Makaryan will show his gratitude," Aram said and put down the receiver. He now knew that the bottle was a French wine, Chateau Malvaux, and the customs officer had checked but not found any importing company for such a wine. That meant only one thing. The wine had been smuggled into the country, not unusual for expensive Bordeaux as wine tax was based on the CIF price, not a fixed rate. He rang the security company that Armen had used and talked to the manager who also looked after Boris Makaryan's security. The man rang him back after half an hour with the name and address of Armen's housekeeper and his man-servant. The security guard had confirmed that the man-servant, Kolya, usually signed for all deliveries to the house. Aram ordered one of his boss' cars and ten minutes later he was being driven in a seven series BMW to the address he had been given. The driver, one of Boris' bodyguards, went into the building and found the apartment Kolya lived in. He went up the stairs and knocked on the door. Kolya answered the door. He was dressed but looked as if he had drunk too much the night before.

"Good morning. I work for Boris Makaryan, Armen Makaryan's brother. You have probably heard of Armen Makaryan's tragic death."

"Indeed," Kolya said. "It has saddened me greatly. What can I do for you?"

"We need you to come with us to Mr. Makaryan's house and go through some documents with us, perhaps even show us the wine cellar."

"But surely the police will have cordoned the whole place off?" Kolya enquired.

"Don't worry. We'll take care of that. Can you be ready in five minutes."

"Yes, of course," Kolya replied and opened the door

wide to let the man into his small but tidy apartment which had a corner for cooking and behind it a small room with a shower and a toilet. Kolya disappeared into the bedroom to finish dressing.

Aram had just made a couple of phone calls to ensure that they would be admitted to Armen's house. After all, it was the scene of a crime. He knew the police would have taken the most important documents and the computers but he hoped that the man-servant could tell him who delivered the wine. Ten minutes later the driver appeared with a correctly dressed man-servant in tow. The driver opened the car door and the man got into the back and sat next to Aram. Aram smiled and said:

"Thank you, Kolya, thank you for coming immediately to help us in our investigations. Mr. Boris Makaryan will be most grateful and I know, as always, he will show his gratitude."

"I was devastated by Mr. Armen's tragic passing," he said in a way that reminded Aram of the Tolstoy novels he had read at school when a serf talked about his master. The sense of subservience that came with the use of the master's Christian name with a title and no surname. He made no comment and instructed the driver to go to Armen Makaryan's house.

They reached the pompous mansion surrounded by a high brick wall topped with barbed wire and electric fencing in forty five minutes. The driver had avoided the notorious Garden Ring where the traffic was almost always bad whatever time of day. The entrance gate and the surrounding walls were being observed by CCTV. The driver announced the visitor on the intercom and the security guard in the security office took a good look at the passengers in the car on the monitor. He recognised the man-servant, Kolya, and the man sitting next to him. He looked at the detective who was on duty and said:

"This is the visitor you mentioned. The man works for Mr. Makaryan's brother and Kolya, the man-servant who works," he hesitated and repeated the last verb in the past tense, "worked for Mr. Armen Makaryan."

"Fine. Then let them in," the detective said a little disgruntled. He reported to Inspector Antipov but it had been Antipov's boss who had phoned him and ordered him to let the visitor in. He should be allowed to go through the house but not take anything away with him.

The two men were greeted in the hallway by the detective on duty who expressed his sincere condolences to Aram on the tragic death of Armen Makaryan. Aram mumbled a polite thank you and said that he'd like to start in the cellar and Kolya would accompany him.

"I have to go with you sir." the detective said, "As I'm sure you know nothing can be taken away from the house."

"Kaneshno, of course," Aram said not even looking at the inspector as he said it. "Let's get on with it," he added. They walked through the kitchen and down the steps which led to the cellar. There was a cool room for vegetables and fruit, three large freezers for meat and fish and then a whole cellar filled to the brim with wine. Aram looked at the well-kept wine cellar which even had a bottle displayed in front of the cubby-hole the stock was in. This man had taken his wine seriously. He wandered along the four walls until he came to a bottle of Chateau Malvaux. This was the wine. He hesitated and walked a few steps past the bottle to the detective.

"Would you mind just leaving us alone for a couple of minutes," he said amicably. "I promise we won't touch anything."

"I'll stand at the door out of earshot," the detective said.

"Thank you."

Aram put his hand on Kolya's arm and gently moved him towards the bottle of Chateau Malvaux.

"Kolya, I presume that you always counted the bottles before signing the receipt from the delivery truck?" Aram asked. He knew the answer to the question but he just wanted to get the man talking and at ease.

"Of course, sir. I always counted the cases and afterwards I would open all the cases and check that the right number of bottles were in each case."

"That must have taken some time to do that. What did the delivery man do while you were checking the bottles?"

"It was usually the same delivery man for most of the wine and he chatted to Katya in the kitchen and she gave him a cup of coffee."

"I see. And was it the same delivery man who brought these bottles," Aram said pointing at the bottle of Malvaux.

"Yes, they came about once a month, particularly if Mr. Armen was entertaining a lot."

"And which company delivered the wine?" Aram asked.

"It was delivered by Vodalko," Kolya said. "Most of the wine came from them. And some of the vodka, too."

"Are you absolutely sure," Aram checked.

"Oh yes, I took pride in making sure that the wine cellar was properly stocked and that all the deliveries were correct. I kept a cellar-book," he said moving over to a wooden table and opening a drawer. He took out a black leather-bound book and opened it. He scrutinized a few pages under the light on the table until he found what he was looking for. He showed it to Aram beaming with pride.

"Here you are sir," Kolya said. "The last delivery from Vodalko was in February, here." He pointed to the entry. Aram read the even old-fashioned scrawl and saw that indeed the wine had been delivered by Vodalko.

"Thank you, Kolya. You have been a great help."

The detective accompanied them to the front door and the driver opened the two rear doors of the car. Kolya and Aram got in and the black BMW drove off quietly through the gates and disappeared into the distance. The detective went back to the security room.

"What was all that about?" the security guard asked.

"No idea," the detective said. "It looks like the brother is more interested in checking that the wine cellar is intact than anything else," he said with a smile.

Aram arrived back to report to Boris Makaryan around six in the evening. The driver had taken him back to Mr. Makaryan's house first and then drove a smiling man-servant back to his flat. Kolya had received a small envelope from Aram and he had looked into it on the way back to his flat. There was more money in there than Kolya received for three month's work. Aram had said that Mr. Boris would be very grateful but he hadn't expected such a large sum. Tonight would be a night for celebrations.

*

It was late morning when Max Baer received an email tip-off. He had phoned his IT department to trace the mail but after an hour they phoned back to say whoever had sent the mail had covered his tracks completely. There was no way of finding out who had sent it or even an IP address. Max was intrigued. The mail was short but precise. It gave the name of a jeweller in Frankfurt, Norbert Mayer, on the Zeil and suggested the police check the parcels he received from Australia where most of the black market strychnine came from. It also said that Thomas Becker had visited the shop and he wasn't only buying jewellery.

Max arrived at Mayer & Mayer GmbH at two in the afternoon as the shop reopened after lunch. He introduced himself showed his ID card to the young lady behind the counter and asked to see Mr. Norbert Mayer. Her eyes opened wide with surprise and it took her a couple of seconds to compose herself before saying:

"I'll go and get him." She turned on her heels and walked into the back of the shop. There was a window between the back room where Norbert Mayer was working and the shop. Max could see him cowered over some papers. As the young lady announced that there was a detective to see him. Norbert Mayer looked equally shocked and cast a glance through the window. He turned back to his young assistant and said:

"Please show the detective through to my office."

Norbert Mayer stood up and walked into a small adjoining room that he used as an office. Max walked in, introduced himself and sat down opposite Norbert Mayer in front of his desk.

"What can I do for you?" Norbert Mayer asked rather sheepishly.

"I need some information on a customer of yours," Max said. "His name is Thomas Becker." Max watched the contours of Norbert Mayer's face and could see that he recognised the name.

"Thomas Becker, Thomas Becker," Norbert Mayer repeated in a low voice as if speaking his thoughts aloud. "Yes, I sold a Mr. Thomas Becker a diamond about four weeks ago, I think."

"Is he a regular customer?"

"No, I'd never seen him before."

"Did you ask where he got the name of your shop from?"

"No. I presumed he was just passing by," Norbert Mayer lied. He knew very well where he would have got his name from but he certainly wasn't going to tell the police.

"Could you describe the man?" Max asked.

"Yes, he was quite tall, medium build, that is slim but with broad shoulders. He looked very fit, probably a jogger or a body-builder," Norbert Mayer added with a touch of disdain in his voice. He hated the modern-day mania of "keeping fit". "What about his face?" Max asked.

"His face was sort of sculptured, quite high cheek bones and a long thin neck. He had quite remarkable blue eyes. I remember seeing them as he looked at me across the table while he was examining the diamond. And light brown hair."

"What kind of hair, straight, curly, long, short?" Max asked.

"Straight hair, not short-back-and sides but short and tidy. Probably used that gel stuff to keep it all in place," he added with a bit of a grin.

"While he was examining the diamond, did you notice his hands?"

"Oh yes, I always look at people's hands," he said with pride. "They were like musician's hands, long fingers, short finger-nails, clean and manicured, quite large and tanned. In fact, he looked as if he had just come back from a winter break in a warm country."

"And what was he wearing?"

"A grey suit and overcoat, not very flashy, quite run of the mill. And leather gloves which he left on the desk while we talked."

"That's quite a detailed description," Max said. "Do you take notice of all your customers in such detail?"

"Yes, I do," Norbert said, relaxing a little. "In my business you need to assess the means of a customer, what he does for a living, how much he earns. His clothes, shoes, hands and speech are all part of that."

"What about his shoes?"

"New, black leather, probably Italian, expensive," he said.

"And his speech?" Max prompted.

"He spoke pretty much High German but with a slight accent from the Pfalz."

"Are you sure?"

"Yes, I have quite a musical ear and a good memory for accents. It reminded me a little of a friend of mine from Mannheim, but only now and then."

"And where did Mr. Becker come from?"

"I didn't ask."

"Surely his address must be on the receipt you issued him for the diamond?"

"Of course," Norbert Mayer replied feeling a little flushed.

"Could I see the receipt?"

"I don't keep them here. I give them to my tax accountant every week."

"Could you ask your tax accountant to check?"

"Of course," he said with relief. As long as he didn't ask to see the receipt as there wasn't one!

"Thank you, Mr. Mayer," Max said handing him his card. "I'd appreciate you phoning me as soon as possible with Mr. Becker's address."

"Of course," he repeated standing up to show the detective the way out.

"Thank you for your help," Max said as he turned to walk out the shop glancing at the CCTV cameras.

In the car on the way back Max thought about Norbert

Mayer's description of Thomas Becker. It was very similar to Hubert Walter's description of him except for the hands and shoes. Hubert Walter couldn't remember his hands, only his hair, blue eyes, his build and his clothes. Norbert Mayer's description of his hands was very precise, like a musician, whereas Thomas Becker was a wine broker, winemaker and wine grower. His hands were large but a little rough from tending vines and working manually around the house and garden. His nails were clean but he certainly wouldn't have described them as manicured. And when Max saw him just two weeks ago he certainly didn't have the tanned face of someone recently returned from a warm country. The man called Thomas Becker who visited Norbert Mayer and Hubert Walter wasn't, in his opinion, the real Thomas Becker but an imposter. But it just didn't make any sense.

Back in the office he found the research on Norbert Mayer on his desk. Sandra had done a pretty thorough search. He lived in a very affluent part of Frankfurt, on the Nobelring in Lerchesberg on the south bank of the river. It wasn't uncommon for wealthy businessmen to live there and commute into the city. They could reach the city by car in less than twenty minutes. There weren't many international business centres around the world that could be reached by car in twenty minutes from an exclusive but still affordable town house. Sandra had researched the area and discovered that prices for houses on the Lerchesberg had dropped by about thirty per cent since the construction of the new runway at Frankfurt Airport was just months away from being completed. There were lots of wealthy citizens not wishing to live on the flight path of the intercontinental planes leaving or landing every five to six minutes and there were quite a few houses up for sale. Those who had decided to stay had lost thirty per cent of a valuable asset within just a few years. And Norbert Mayer, according to this piece of research, had a very high mortgage that was no longer covered by the value of his property. The researcher had also discovered one of Norbert Mayer's hobbies. Gambling. He had been photographed by a reporter at one of the exclusive poker matches held in Frankfurt, well-known for the celebrities from the film-world who took part. Norbert Mayer had been described by a follower of this scene as a wealthy man but who seemed to be addicted to the game and sometimes lost very considerable sums of money. That would explain the high mortgage despite a jeweller's shop in the best part of the city. Norbert Mayer was described as a man who lived above his means and was heavily in debt. Max sighed. Money usually was the compelling reason for a well-respected member of the community to start dealing illegally. They usually started with smaller, socially acceptable misdemeanours such as selling jewellery on the black market or just forgetting to put every sale through the books. Experience had taught him that when petty crimes worked and no-one noticed and if the debts were a real problem, the person would turn to larger crimes quite quickly. Could receiving and passing on strychnine be one of them?

17

Inspector Vladimir Antipov sat at his desk and scratched his head. He wasn't just an ordinary detective from the CID murder squad in Moscow. He was a high-ranking officer and specialist in organized crime in the URPO, a service set up in 1996 within the FSB secret service to infiltrate criminal organisations. The team wasn't huge, around one hundred and fifty specialists working in a highly dangerous area. He was reading a report from Interpol about strychnine. The autopsy report on Armen Makaryan that he had received had indicated a heart attack as the cause of death but on closer reading there were some substances found in his blood that could have been caused by a poison such as strychnine. It had taken him some time to get hold of the right person to confirm his thoughts. The only liquid that was near the body which could have been used to administer a fatal dose of strychnine was a red wine from France. There were traces of the same substance in the glass that his forensic colleagues had examined and fingerprints of the deceased all over the glass. He had rung the Customs Authorities and had asked for information on the importer. The wine wasn't registered with the Customs in Moscow or anywhere else for that matter. According to Customs it had never been imported. So he had sent his assistant to check if there was any more Chateau Malvaux in the wine cellar at the deceased's house, bring it in to be examined and check all the other bottles to see where Armin Makaryan had bought his other wines. He had just received a phone call from his assistant. Most of the wines in Armen Makaryan's private cellar came from Vodalko, a vodka producer and alcohol distributor in the south of Moscow on the outskirts of Podolsk. The company was owned by a right-wing politician and oligarch, Abel Plemyannikov, who also owned a training camp for bodyguards within the Vodalko complex.

Vladimir Antipov knew quite a lot about strychnine. You didn't need much of the poison to kill a person. A couple of grams would be enough to kill someone of Armen Makaryan's build. According to the autopsy report the deceased had a blood alcohol content of zero point one eight percent per volume. That was enough to make some people black out. Russian law didn't tolerate any blood alcohol if a person was driving but Armen Makaryan went everywhere with his chauffeur and bodyguard, Vanya, who had left him on the night of his death in the early hours of the morning to bring a prostitute back to the city centre. Not surprising. That amount of blood alcohol would make any man temporarily impotent. But was he so drunk that he didn't smell the strychnine in his wine? Still deep in thought, Vladimir Antipov phoned his assistant and told him to meet him at Vodalko at twelve thirty and then checked his records on the company. Vodalko had just lost its import licence for alcohol import and distribution due to irregularities in their accounts. This was nothing unusual in Russia in 2011. Lots of companies had lost their licence to import alcohol. Some had gone bankrupt and others had set up new companies which applied for new licences. President Medvedev was half way through his four year term of office and had put fighting corruption at the top of his political agenda. He introduced an Anti-Corruption Strategy in 2010 to coincide with the police reform. According to official records, the owner of the company was Abel Plemyannikov, a multi-millionaire with good political contacts. He had made his money in the early nineties with a series of successful import and export companies, mainly trading with the United States which in those days meant exporting weapons or any material needed to make weapons. He had invested in manufacturing companies in different branches, one of which was alcohol in general and vodka in particular. Antipov made a couple of notes on his pad and phoned the number in the company records.

"Good Morning, thank you for calling Vodalko." The automatic answering service was in Russian and English. "Please press one to talk to an operator, two for deliveries, three for sales and four for supply chain enquiries."

Antipov pressed one, heard the phone ring and waited. A polite female voice answered with:

"Good Morning, you are through to Vodalko's reception."

"Good Morning. My name is Inspector Vladimir Antipov from the URPO and I'd like to speak to Mr. Abel

Plemyannikov."

The voice gave him the standard reply. "I'll see if Mr. Plemyannikov is available," and put the caller through to Mr. Plemyannikov's assistant. After another round of introductions and a little more insistence which all took around three minutes, Antipov was put through.

"Good Morning, Inspector Antipov. What can I do for you," a very charming and authoritative voice said slowly and deliberately down the phone.

"Good Morning, Mr. Plemyannikov. Thank you for taking my call so quickly."

"It isn't every day we have a call from someone from the URPO," Abel replied with a slight smile in his voice.

"I would like to visit you this morning at twelve thirty to ask a few questions about a deceased businessman, Armen Makaryan."

"Oh, yes, poor Armen. It is such a tragedy. He was a very well respected member of the business community and we will miss him greatly."

Antipov rolled his eyes to the ceiling. He had heard similar things said before. He was convinced that hypocrisy came hand in hand with wealth and corruption!

"Will twelve thirty be convenient?" Antipov repeated.

"Yes, yes, of course. But why are the URPO involved?"

A rhetorical question, Antipov thought. This man has his fingers in every pie and a lot of spies in all sorts of organisations. He must know what kind of business Armen Makaryan was in and that organized crime was part of it. It was also an integral part of Plemyannikov's empire but they couldn't prove it yet. It would take time, a lot of time, but in the end they would produce enough evidence to put this man behind bars.

"I'll explain everything when I see you," he said politely but leaving no room for contradiction.

"Kaneshno. Fine," he said. "Then twelve thirty it is." Both men put the phone down simultaneously. Antipov picked the receiver up again and ordered his car.

*

In Queensland it was a warm autumn day and Tom was working on some plans for an extension to Sam's plantation as the three cars drove into the forecourt. He looked out the window and didn't recognise any of the visitors. Each driver had got out of the car and stood by his vehicle. Three of the men had gone into reception. The other men stood around waiting. Tom could see the tell-tale wire plugged into their ears. They were all connected to each other by walkie-talkie and he saw one of them speak without being near any of the others, presumably into a microphone on his lapel. Tom's heart missed a beat. This looks like more than a friendly call, he thought. He reached for the phone then decided it wasn't a good idea to phone Sam. The phone was probably tapped anyway. He tried to calm himself down and he sat down again in his office chair as the phone rang. It was Daisy from reception.

"Tom, there are some gentlemen here from the police with a search warrant. Could you please come to reception?"

"A search warrant!" Tom exclaimed. "I'll be right with you."

Tom walked the short distance to the reception area and looked at the three plain clothed policemen.

"How can I help you?" he asked.

One of them introduced himself as Inspector Sean Mallahan, showed Tom his ID and gave him a piece of paper.

"This is a copy of our search warrant, Sir. Please could you inform all the staff that they should leave their work stations and come to reception immediately without clearing their desks or shutting their computers down. They can just save whatever they're working on. I would then ask you to send everyone home except for yourself and any key staff who you may need to assist you."

"Assist me?" Tom asked.

"Yes. We may need to take some documents and IT equipment with us so maybe someone from IT and someone who knows where all the files are would be most useful."

Tom was genuinely shocked and a little bewildered.

"Yes, of course, but what's all this about?"

"I'm afraid I'm not able to comment," the police officer said. "Please would you ask all the staff not to make any phone calls until they have left the office and to bring their personal belongings to reception with them."

"Yes, of course." Tom went from office to office and to the lab and in a few minutes all of his members of staff were gathered in the reception area talking in low voices as if someone had just died.

"Thank you all." Tom said. "The police have a search warrant and will be searching our offices." Tom looked at his team who were speechless with shock. "While this is going on, we have to leave the offices but leave our computers on. Mary, please put the "offices closed" message on the switchboard. Please would you all leave the office now and go home. We have all your telephone numbers so we'll stay in contact and let you know when business can be resumed. Dave and Irene, could you please stay. I may need your help." Both nodded.

The rest of the staff looked at Tom in amazement. Peter was first to leave and then the others filed out the door in disbelief.

The policeman who had introduced himself as Sean Mallahan was obviously the one in charge. He turned to Tom and said:

"Could we talk to you, Dave and Irene somewhere more private, Sir?"

"Yes, of course. We have a meeting room down the corridor. Follow me, please."

The three policemen, Tom, Dave, Head of IT and Irene, the office manager, sat round the table in silence. Irene had put two bottles of water on the table and six glasses. They all helped themselves to water and then Tom said:

"Let me introduce Dave Collins and Irene Turner. Dave is head of IT and if you need them, he can give you a list of passwords for each member of staff. Irene is our office manager and will give me a list of all the staff with their addresses and telephone numbers. I presume she can use her terminal to do that?"

"Of course," Inspector Mallahan replied. "Thank you for your cooperation. Here's a list of the documents we need." He passed five copies of it around the table. "I suggest we use the meeting room to collate all the documents. My colleagues here will check the documents collated and if necessary take them with us for further examination. The other three policemen with us will go through each room one after the other and search the offices."

"What are you looking for?" Tom asked frowning as he said it.

"I'm afraid I'm not authorised to give you any details, Sir. The policemen are experienced in these matters and will only take what is absolutely necessary." He turned towards Dave. "I presume a lot of the information we have requested is stored electronically. Please would you transfer the documents and links we've asked for on to this external hard drive?" Dave looked at Tom who said yes with his eyes. Dave nodded and asked:

"How big is the hard drive?"

"Fifty gigabytes. I understand that most documents will not been downloaded but just links created so we can find them quickly. Our IT department says that twelve terra bites will be enough."

"Sure." Dave said. "This may take some hours by the look of the list."

"Not a problem," Inspector Mallahan said with a smile. "We probably won't be finished with the search until late afternoon so you have plenty of time."

"Well then," Tom said, putting on a brave face, "let's get on with it."

They all stood up in silence. Dave and Irene went out followed by the two policemen. Tom looked at Inspector Mallahan.

"I presume I can phone our CEO and let him know what's going on, and our legal counsel."

"Of course, you can make as many phone calls as you like." Inspector Mallahan gestured to Tom in a manner which said he could now leave the room.

"I'll get us all some coffee first," he said and walked out to the kitchen. He put the machine on and put twelve mugs on a tray with some milk and sugar. Then he walked to his office and rang Sam.

"Hi, Tom," Sam said as he picked up the call in his car.

"Hi, Sam. Sam, are you driving?"

"Yep, just on my way to Frenchs Forest."

"Sam, could you pull over please and call me back."

"What's wrong, Tom?"

"Just pull over first and then ring me on my mobile. OK?"

"OK, Tom. I'll be back to you in less than five minutes."

Tom sat at his desk waiting for his mobile to ring. He presumed that if the police had a search warrant not only the office phones would be tapped but probably his mobile and Sam's mobile as well. He looked out of the window and just hoped he'd wake up out of this nightmare. He jumped as his phone rang. The display just said "Sam".

"Hi, Sam."

"Hi, Tom. So what's the matter?"

"Sam, a search warrant has been issued for our offices and the police turned up this morning about half an hour ago. They've got a list of documents they want to see, accounts, invoices to certain customers. I'll send you the list by email. Dave is working on links to the files they want to look at. Irene is here as well. I sent the rest of the staff home. You know what Hawks Lift is like. This'll be the talk of the town after lunch and I expect we'll have a couple of reporters here this afternoon." Tom paused to let all of this sink in. "We'll obviously need some legal advice and I expect the police will want to speak to you either here or in Sydney. I'll email you the details of Inspector Sean Mallahan who is in charge of the investigation."

"Thanks, Tom," Sam replied in a quiet voice. He was obviously very shocked and wringing for composure. "I'll ring Frank straight away. Can you send Frank the details of this Inspector Mallahan as well and he can get in touch with them to see what's happening and when we can resume business again."

"OK. I'll stay here and deal with any press." Both men hung up and Sam rang Frank Moss his legal counsel. Sam was shocked and angry. This couldn't have come at a worse time. He was just weeks away from bringing a new investor on board and the publicity might scare him off. "Damn it!" he exclaimed. If it hit the press he'd have to ring Tom Wyatt and tell him about this "storm in a teacup" before he read about it. He'd do that from home this afternoon when he got back from Pete's.

Sam arrived at Frenchs Forest ten minutes later and drove into Pete Owen's beautiful azalea-lined drive. There were two large cars and a four-wheel drive parked in front of the house. Sam parked his car a little way behind them and walked up to the front door. Pete met him at the front door with Pebble his golden retriever wagging his tail.

Pete greeted him as he walked up to the door.

"Hi, Sam. I'm afraid we'll have to talk outside. The police have a search warrant for my house and are boxing up files and have taken my lap-top. They even confiscated my passport!"

"Goodness," Sam said genuinely shocked. "Let's walk round the garden."

"Come on Pebble. Walkies!" Pebble barked and followed them down to the swimming pool and into the garden.

"Pete, my plantation office was also searched this morning. That's too much of a coincidence."

Pete went pale and looked at Sam in amazement.

"My God," he said and looked back at the house. "I've rung Doug Parker, my legal guy. You remember Doug?"

"Yes, we saw each other at your New Year's drinks party. I've phoned Frank Moss. I'll give him another ring on the way home and get him to contact Doug. We've just got to ride out the storm, Pete. It's like looking for a needle in a haystack and they probably won't find it. We mustn't let a search warrant scare us to the point of confessing any irregularities," Sam added, choosing his words carefully.

"How's Jean taking it?"

"She's in the kitchen with Regan who's trying to calm her down. She was almost hysterical watching her house, her home, being searched. Regan will take her out for some lunch and then for a walk until all these people have left and things have calmed down."

"Good idea," he said. "Pete, I'd better get going. If there's anything I can do to help, let me know. Karen is out for the day shopping with a girlfriend and I'm beginning to ask myself what I'm going to find when I get home."

"OK, Sam. Let's meet up for a drink this evening at Murphy's. Let's say at seven? Then we can go for a walk along the harbour and have a chat."

"Fine. See you tomorrow evening."

Sam got back into Sydney just before noon. He drove slowly along the highway deep in thought. He parked his BMW in the underground garage and took the lift up to his penthouse on the thirteenth floor. He stepped out of the lift and saw the welcoming committee near his door. His heart sank. He had hoped that they weren't going to be there but no, they were there alright. He felt as if he was just watching from far away as the inspector introduced himself, showed him his ID and gave him a copy of the search warrant. Karen was obviously not at home otherwise they would have already started their search. He opened the door and let them in.

"You don't seem surprised," the police inspector said.

"No, I've already been told that the Queensland police searched my company offices this morning."

"I see," the inspector said and followed Sam into the beautiful lounge and admired the magnificent view of Sydney Harbour, the bridge and the opera house out of the large picture window.

"Please sit down," Sam said pointing to the cream leather sofa.

The police inspector cleared his throat. "I'd be grateful if you would open your safe, sir, and also give me your passport. Then we'll make a thorough search of your premises and do our best not to disturb too much. If there is anywhere you keep personal or business papers or any cupboards or drawers which are locked perhaps you could tell us now and open the locked drawers and cupboards?"

"Yes, of course," Sam said. He felt numb with shock. It had been bad enough hearing about the search of his offices in Hawk's Lift but here, in his home, his castle, his pride and joy, it was difficult to bear. The thought of these policemen combing through his papers, his belongings, his wife's underwear, damn it! He hadn't deserved this, He suddenly felt a wave of anger. And then he thought of Karen coming home to all this in a couple of hours.

"Yes, of course," Sam repeated. "How long do you expect this search to take you?" Sam asked, hoping they'd be gone before Karen got back.

"I should think three to four hours," the inspector said. "If it's alright with you, Sir, we'd like to get on with it. Could you please show me where all your papers are, open the safe and any other locked drawers or cupboards," he repeated. He could see that Sam was in a state of shock. He got up which prompted Sam to stand up too.

"Yes, of course. Follow me through here to my office."

It was four in the afternoon when the search was over, boxes carried out of the penthouse, his computer, the contents of his safe and all his personal papers. He had signed several receipts and watched the contents of his life be whisked away to a team of investigators who would paw through his private life with their grubby fingers. It was just horrible. He felt as if he'd been mentally raped. His strength had ebbed and he had an overwhelming desire to have a good cry.

"Don't be silly," he said out loud to himself as he jumped up off the cream leather sofa and walked into the white wood and marble kitchen. He made himself a freshly squeezed orange juice and went into the bedroom. After a shave and a shower he would feel better. "Keep calm, don't be weak, you'll ride the storm," he kept saying to himself and was now beginning to believe it.

Sam was sitting on the balcony looking out to sea when Tom Wyatt answered his mobile.

"Hi, Tom", Sam said in a cheery voice with all the courage he could muster.

"Hi, Sam," Tom replied. "What's up?"

"Tom, I just wanted to let you know that my offices in Queensland were the subject of a police search this morning and the police have just left my home with all my personal papers." He paused for a moment to let the news sink in.

"What's all this about?" Tom asked in a matter-of-fact

way. He didn't seem in the least bit shocked. What Sam didn't know is that one of Tom's informants at Sydney police HQ had already tipped him off about the search knowing that the two men were business friends.

"I've absolutely no idea," Sam said. "Frank Moss, my legal counsel, is trying get to the bottom of it as we speak. It must be some kind of misunderstanding, just a storm in a teacup that some bureaucrat has cooked up to enhance his image and further his career. I just wanted you to hear the news from me personally before you read it in the Sydney Herald."

"I appreciate that, Sam. No doubt the whole thing will have blown over in a couple of days."

"I'm sure it will," Sam replied, his stomach almost churning over.

"Just keep me abreast of any new developments, would you?" Tom added.

"Of course I will. Frank's arranged an appointment with the investigating officer at ten tomorrow morning."

"Perhaps we could meet up for lunch at the golf club. I should be in by twelve, latest twelve thirty."

"Fine. I'll see you tomorrow, then."

"Please give Karen my best and tell her not to worry. These things happen to the best of people."

"Indeed."

"Thanks for phoning, Sam." Tom hung up. Sam looked out to sea trying desperately to collect his thoughts.

At five-thirty Karen opened the door to their penthouse carrying two carrier bags. She shut the door with her elbow and walked into the lounge. She was wearing a cream designer suit by Armani which showed off her immaculate figure and a beige short-sleeved blouse. She couldn't see Sam but the door in the lounge out to the balcony was open. She put her bags down and went out on to the balcony. Sam was sitting in a recliner looking out to sea, watching the last rays of the sun.

"Hi, darling," she said kissing him on the cheek.

"Hi. Did you have a good day shopping?"

"Yes, a lovely day. Pauline was in good spirits and we stopped at that new salad bar on Patrick Street for lunch. I found some lovely shoes to go with this suit and a new blouse."

"That's great," Sam said trying to sound normal.

"Is everything OK?" Karen asked, reacting to Sam's rather subdued voice.

"No, not really. Sit down and I'll tell you about it."

Somewhat baffled, Karen sat down in one of the comfy wicker chairs and Sam sat next to her. He took hold of her hand.

"There isn't any way to say this without shocking you but our offices in Hawk's Lift were searched by the police this morning and our penthouse this afternoon." Sam paused to let the news sink in. Karen was literally flabbergasted. Her mouth fell open and her eyes were open wide.

"Whatever for?" she asked.

"I don't know," Sam said. "They wouldn't say. I've rung Frank Moss and we've got an appointment with the inspector in charge tomorrow morning at ten."

"What do you mean by search? Did they go through all our things?" Karen asked. It felt as if someone had just destroyed her feeling of security in her own home.

"Yes, my love. They were very discreet but basically they looked through every drawer, cupboard, nook and cranny. They even took my passport away, made me open the safe and my desk drawers. And Tom says that they have taken electronic files of all our accounts and have access to our emails."

"Oh my God!" she exclaimed, going white and not knowing what else to say.

"Why don't you put on your jeans and we can go for a walk along the harbour before the sun goes down. I really need some fresh air to clear my thoughts," he said.

Karen looked at her husband and saw that this wasn't a question but more of a command. She realized that he didn't want to talk in the penthouse and could understand why. After having your home searched, who would feel safe in their own four walls after that.

"That's a good idea," she replied trying to smile. "I'll be back in a jiffy."

Karen and Sam walked in silence until they approached the restaurants under the harbour bridge. Sam broke the silence.

"Karen, I can't be sure that our home isn't bugged. I don't think so but I believe our telephones have been tapped so we have to be extremely careful what we say to whom and how."

"What on earth have you done?" she asked, a wave of

anger suddenly coming to the surface.

"I wish I knew," Sam lied. "This is probably a storm in a tea-cup. I really don't know what they think they have. The only problem is that it'll probably be all over the newspapers and I'll be guilty before I've had a chance to prove I'm innocent."

"Oh my God! Have there been any reporters at home?" she asked. The alarm on her face was heart-breaking. Whatever Sam thought about Karen's lifestyle, she had been a loyal wife, a fantastic asset by his side in all walks of business life. The defamation, the shame, it would be a pain worse than death for her. He turned round and hugged her.

"No," he said. "No-one's been yet but Tom says reporters were out at Hawks Lift this afternoon so I think we can expect some tomorrow at our home." Karen burst into tears and sobbed. He stroked her back and whispered in her ear:

"We'll work out a plan, right now."

"A plan! A plan!" she shouted, almost hysterical now. "What good's a plan when my life is about to be ruined?"

He tried to comfort her, wiping the tears from her face, stroking her hair back.

"Darling, we need a plan and we need one now. We'll get through this and in a couple of weeks it'll all be over and forgotten."

He took her hand and walked on towards the bridge. They sat on a bank and Sam looked out to sea. He felt his strength coming back. He had to be strong for Karen's sake. And for Laura. She was bound to find out even though she was in the States. He knew she looked at the Sydney Herald most days on the internet just to keep up with what was going on in Australia. Sam turned to Karen and moved a little closer.

"We aren't going to be able to avoid reporters and whether we deny it or not won't make any difference to their reporting. So the best thing is to smile and say that we have absolutely no idea what this is all about, polite but firm. And before that happens tomorrow, phone your best friends and tell them what they're going to read and say that it's an absolute scandal how innocent people can be treated like criminals and their lives ruined just because some policeman has a hunch. And honey. Ring Laura. She'll read it sometime soon in the Sydney Herald and she'll be shocked seeing her parents' pictures and some made-up story about my business."

Karen stared at him and then back out over the bay to the Opera House. It was as if she had suddenly been thrown into somebody else's life. This wasn't her life. Her life was being a successful businessman's wife, buying the right clothes, belonging to the right clubs, having the right friends. All that may well disappear overnight. Sam was right. They had to take a proactive stance and be strong. She smiled at Sam and kissed him on the cheek.

"Yes, darling. You're absolutely right. We've done nothing wrong and we are being treated like criminals. I'll ring Mandy and Betty as soon as we get back. And I'll send Laura a text so she can let me know when I can ring her."

"That's my girl," he said, squeezing her hand. "You'll

see. Things will be rough for a time but we won't let them sink this ship."

"Have you rung Tom?" she asked.

"Yes, of course, for exactly the same reasons. I'm seeing him tomorrow after my appointment with the police."

"Then I'll ring Jean as well. Do you want me to ring Nancy?"

"Good idea, but not until I've seen Tom and told you what he said."

"OK," she said.

"Good. I'm seeing Pete this evening at Murphy's." he added.

"Pete?" She looked at him and frowned slightly as if to say this really wasn't the time to leave her alone at home and go for a drink with a friend.

"Yes, Pete Owen's office has been searched as well and we decided this morning to have a chat as there may be a connection."

"Good God!" Karen exclaimed. Then she recomposed her face, smoothed her dress and stood up. She took a deep breath and said "Then once more to the bridge, dear friends, once more to the bridge!"

Sam stood up and kissed her. Yes, that was his wife. Whatever anyone said about her, Karen was a fighter and she was a great actress. They walked back home hand in hand, their relationship suddenly strengthened by the troubles at hand.

*

The weather in Malta at the beginning of April was mild and the spring rains had disappeared. For someone arriving from the chill of Moscow with temperatures just above freezing, eighteen degrees centigrade seemed like summer. Boris had put his overcoat into his hand luggage before he left Rome while he was waiting in the transit lounge. He had arrived from Moscow but didn't spend a couple of nights in Rome as he usually did. He caught the next Air Malta flight for the short haul to Valletta. He smiled at the cabin crew as he walked out of the plane in a lightweight brown Corneliani suit and a short-sleeved beige silk shirt. He was wearing Santoni cognac leather loafers named after a famous Hollywood actor. He breathed in the warm air and looked at the cloudless blue sky. As he left the plane he put on his Gucci sunglasses and walked to the bus waiting to take him to passport control. At passport control he took off his sunglasses and handed his passport to the border control policeman and smiled. He had a two-year visa for the Schengen area of Europe which the Maltese immigration authorities had kindly granted him last year after he had finished building his luxurious mansion on Gozo, the smaller Maltese island to the north of the main island of Malta. The two men behind him also had visas. Boris had spent over two million Euros building his mansion which allowed him to sponsor several visas for his staff.

The border guard asked him in English how long he intended to stay.

"I'm here on business," Boris replied in good English but with a heavy Russian accent. "I'll be leaving for Germany next week but I'll be back home on Gozo after a few days." He smiled and the guard nodded. There were several businessmen and as many millionaires who used Malta as their first port of call. The border guard was a pragmatic man. He held no illusions that it wasn't only the wonderful summer climate that drew these people to Malta. As long as they employed people on the island, built houses and were no trouble to anyone else, why shouldn't they come. The border guard said thank you and handed Boris his passport back.

"Enjoy your stay," he said.

"I will," he answered as he picked up his cabin bag and walked up to the baggage carousel. He stood watching the tourists who had flocked off the plane. His luggage arrived first. The workers at the airport recognised the airline baggage tags, the expensive suitcases and the priority stickers. His luggage really was treated with priority. His bodyguards picked up the three suitcases, gave them to the porter who was standing by with a trolley and moved towards the exit about ten yards ahead of Boris. They scanned the crowd with their trained eyes as they moved through the electric glass doors. Nothing unusual, all clear. They carried on walking a little slower now so that Boris could catch up. He strutted behind them with his eyes watching every movement around him. He was now between the two bodyguards as they moved towards the exit where his Maltese driver was waiting. The man bowed his head slightly as the small group approached, turned and led them towards the VIP parking spot just a short walk away.

The two bodyguards looked at the windows and roof of the terminal building as they walked out. It was all a question of routine but a routine that may save their boss' life one day. The driver opened the rear nearside door for Mr. Boris, as he called him. He closed the car door as one of the bodyguards got into the front passenger seat, the other into the offside back seat. Then he walked round the back of the car where the porter was standing with the luggage. He opened the boot of the car and stowed the luggage in quickly and neatly. He got into the driver's seat, started the engine and off they went.

The large SUV drove slowly along the coastal road which was badly in need of repair. This was the quickest way to reach the ferry terminal at Cirkewwa and it took them just under an hour. At the terminal the driver drove straight to the line of cars waiting to board. He left space to manoeuvre at the front of the car just in case. No-one questioned him about it even if the ferry worker had signalled every other car to move up to the back of the next car. This car wasn't carrying a normal tourist. It had local number plates. The ferry workers carried on doing their job and ignored the car with the dark tinted bulletproof windows. In April there weren't many tourists going to and from Malta to Gozo. You didn't even have to pay to get to Gozo. You paid on the way back. Whoever went to the island had to use the ferry to get back so there was no point in having ticket collectors at both ends. Boris loved the pragmatic approach of the Maltese. The next ferry was due in twenty minutes. The driver kept the air-conditioning on. Boris stayed in the car with the bodyguard in the front. The bodyguard in the back and the driver got out for a cigarette, watching their surroundings like eagles. At last the ferry backed into the harbour, opening its huge jaws to disgorge trucks, vans and cars on to the quay which drove off at a slow pace forcing themselves into one lane and then disappeared over the slip road to the main road. The driver and the bodyguard both got back into the car. They followed the line of cars embarking and the ferry worker pointed to the right. His car would have a special spot, one for larger cars and also one near the stairs with room on both sides to get in and out. As they got out the car, the cars behind them had all parked and people were getting out with their belongings. Some of them were tourists with small rucksacks. Others were shoppers who had made one of their rare visits from their tranquil paradise Gozo to Malta's buzzing capital city, Valletta.

Gozo belonged to Malta but it was very different and even the mentality of its inhabitants set them apart from their fellow citizens on the main island of Malta. Gozo was much quieter than the main island of Malta, much easier for a Russian businessman like Boris to spend leisure time without being watched and more importantly without an army of bodyguards to protect him. Gozo could only be reached by ferry or fisher boat or by small plane or helicopter and he had observers on his payroll in all the right places who would warn him if they noticed anything at all of a suspicious nature. His mansion was in the north of the island in a little village not far from Ta Pinu, Malta's national shrine on high ground overlooking the plains for several miles. From the balcony of his mansion he had a similar view over the plain and could see the pilgrims arriving at Ta Pinu. There were hundreds of them every day. They arrived in coaches, cars and on foot to pay tribute to Maria who had appeared in a vision to one of the women from the village nearby centuries ago. The two bodyguards who travelled with him spent most of their time during the day on the balcony, tanning their well-trained bodies and watching through their binoculars to make sure that their boss was safe. At night they took shifts of four hours and slept four hours. They had all the necessary equipment to be able to observe the surrounding countryside day and night. The grounds were surrounded by a wrought iron fence with CCTV covering the grounds and each room of the house and trip wires in the garden. Inside the house they had quite a large arsenal and a helipad on the roof for emergencies. The cars in the garage were large four-wheel drive armoured vehicles. To the west of his mansion he could see the towers of Ta Pinu in the distance. To the north he looked over a landscape which had terraces of vegetables, clover and barley interspersed with rocky outcrops partly covered with gorse, fig cactus and Mediterranean shrubs. At the highest point there was an old lighthouse that was now used as a weather station. During the Second World War the lighthouse had been used as an anti-aircraft defence tower. He had a couple of cameras up there too which allowed his native security guard, Luca, to watch the land to the north and any movement along the shore. Luca was their main contact to all the local forces if there were any problems and spent most of his time in the security office in the cellar. In the evening his cousin, Jose, took over the monitors which were all around the room. Every room of the house could be observed, even the main bedroom. When Boris had a lady visitor, he was able to interrupt the CCTV in his private suite. When he pushed the button to cut the CCTV, the same button triggered off another alarm system inside the rooms of his private suite and at the entrance to each room. The mansion was a fortress with no expense spared. Boris had employed a team of local stone masons to build a replica of one of the noble mansions he had seen in an oil painting which an unknown artist had painted in the nineteenth century on Gozo. The local limestone wasn't the best stone to use but he wanted the building to be authentic and the locals to be proud of the work that went into this superb building. The whole village prospered from his presence, not just the tradesmen. He needed food, wine, housemaids, cooks and security. Every single family was involved in some way and benefitted from the presence of the Russian. He treated them all well and he knew that their dependence on him was his greatest asset as far as security was concerned.

To the south and east the plain stretched for at least three or four miles before reaching a hill or a village. It was a perfect spot. To the west the rocky limestone coastline with the famous azure window was a dangerous spot in winter. No boats would get too near to the coast or try and land. In summer fisher boats moved up and down the west coast and were under constant observation from the many hunters' hides that had been built out of local stone to shoot the migratory birds that used the island as a resting and feeding place in spring. Boris felt safe here. He was well looked after and had friends in the right places.

Boris sat at the stern of the ferry outside enjoying the warm breeze off the sea. He loved the Mediterranean and the countries bordering this majestic sea. His two bodyguards, Davit and Erik, were posted at each side of the stern watching the starboard and port decks. Most of the shoppers were inside in the lounge. Just a few tourists were sitting on the starboard deck waiting to get a glimpse of Comino, the smallest of the three Maltese islands with its famous Blue Lagoon. It was only a short ferry ride and after twenty minutes the two bodyguards nodded to their boss and they moved towards the entrance on the starboard deck and walked towards staircase D. All three Russians pushed their dark sunglasses on to their heads as they entered the stairwell. Davit walked up front, Erik in the rear, sandwiching Boris between them as they walked down the narrow staircase. Davit opened the door of the lower deck and looked around. He stepped out and walked towards the car with Boris and Erik in tow. The driver saw them coming and unlocked the car. Normally no-one was allowed to stay on the car deck when the ferry was in motion. An exception to the rule was always made to men like Boris. The driver didn't need to ask. He just shook hands with the man on the car deck and gave him a small gratuity. This was the reality of rich and poor, haves and have-nots.

And no-one questioned the natural order of things. Davit opened the nearside rear door and his boss got in. Twenty years ago he would have jumped in but over the last ten years he had put on a lot of weight and it had taken its toll. Boris sighed and thought of his brother, Armen. He had loved life as well, an Armenian trait that both brothers had inherited from their forefathers. They had been very similar in many ways, particularly in their ability to live on the edge. The main difference was that Armen untypically never married whereby Boris had a wife and family. Boris and Armen had both continually exceeded the normal limits in every way. Excess was part of their genes, whether it be drinking, eating, working or womanising. He had loved his brother and he was determined to revenge his death. The ferry worker signalled to the driver to leave the ferry first. They emerged from the gloom of the deck with its sickening smell of oil and exhaust fumes into the bright sunlight of Gozo's harbour Mġarr. The harbour had taken seven years to rebuild and had only been finished in 2008. They drove past the marina but Boris wasn't interested in yachts. He was more interested in the history and architecture of the island and he had turned to look back at Fort Chambray, an eighteenth century fort designed to defend this strategically important harbour. The driver turned to the left and Boris caught a glimpse of the Grand Hotel on the hill to his right. Then they were on their way driving northwest along the main road. There were no motorways on Gozo. The island was far too small to warrant a fast infrastructure. The road leading to and from the ferry had been financed by the European Union so it was a modern road, mainly single carriageway but in good condition. It would only take them twenty minutes to reach Boris' mansion and there was never much traffic. Boris leant back in his seat, relaxed and watched the landscape pass by. It was still fairly green, as green as a Mediterranean island with limestone outcrops can get in winter. Some of the barley had already been harvested as well as the clover the locals used as fodder. In two weeks the harvest would be finished and nothing more would grow until the rains started in late October. The grass would go yellow and only the huge fig cactus and the Mediterranean bushes of thyme, rosemary and similar shrubs would survive constant exposure to the sun for five whole months with no water. He loved this island and the way the farmers worked the land according to nature's calendar. They made something out of nothing. They planted tomatoes, beans, lettuce and other market garden produce anywhere they could find access to water which sometimes just sprung out of the bottom of a limestone hill or collected in winter in a small pond. He would give himself a few days to rest and think and then fly to Frankfurt.

18

Inspector Vladimir Antipov was puzzled. As his driver wound in and out of the heavy traffic on Moscow's infamous ring road, Antipov stared out of the window trying to reconstruct what could have happened to Armen Makaryan on the night he died. Why didn't he smell the strychnine in the wine? All of a sudden he hit his forehead with the palm of his hand and said:

"Durak, idiot. Why didn't I think of it before?" He grabbed his mobile phone and rang his assistant.

"Allo," a tired voice answered. Antipov didn't even bother about any answer. He was totally absorbed in his theory.

"Find out if there were any traces of crystal meth in Arman Makaryan's blood and find out if he used crystal meth. Talk to prostitutes, anyone you can find who knew him intimately. I want a report this afternoon."

"Yes sir," a distinctly sharper voice on the other end said.

You fool, Antipov kept saying to himself. If the man used crystal meth then it would be easy to replace the drug with strychnine. If both were pure, not cut, they would smell pretty similar, particularly to a drunken man. He picked up his mobile again and rang a friend at Interpol.

"Allo," a brisk, efficient voice replied.

"Andrey, it's me, Vladimir."

"Hi, Vladimir, what can I do for you? I presume this isn't just a social call?"

"No. I need a contact in Germany somewhere in middle ranks of their murder squad or organised crime department who speaks Russian."

"Well that's pretty easy," Andrey replied with a smile in his voice.

"Easy?" Antipov asked with surprise in his voice.

"Yes, we got a report in this morning about a case that the criminal investigation bureau in Wiesbaden is looking into. They had a couple of questions about a lorry coming from Germany with a load of wine and some strychnine under the driver's seat."

"Yes, yes, I know the case," Antipov replied gently. "And…?"

"Well, the detective on the case is Inspector Max Baer. He spent his early life in the USA. His grandparents emigrated to the USA in the nineteen thirties. His grandfather emigrated from the Soviet Union illegally, his grandmother from Germany legally. Both were Jewish. In nineteen ninety after the Berlin wall had collapsed, Max decided to live in Germany for a while. You may know that West Germany has a clause in its constitution that allows Jews to settle in Germany permanently as a small gesture to a religious minority persecuted during the Second World War. He then applied for a German passport and studied at the police academy in Hahn."

"How do you know all this?" Antipov asked, fascinated by his friend's attention to detail.

"Well, I met Baer once in the USA. We were both at the same conference on cyber terrorism and its links to organised crime. He's an expert on organised crime and he speaks fluent English, German and Russian. "

"Can you send me his mobile number?" Antipov asked, excited at the coincidence and having found the perfect contact man in the heart of Germany.

"Sure. You'll like Max. After his third beer he'll tell you that he's related to Max Baer the heavyweight boxer who beat Hitler's protégé Max Schmeling in 1933 and went on to win the world championship in 1934 to become the hero of all American Jews."

"Is it true?" Antipov asked and laughed.

"I'm not sure and I really don't want to know if it's not true. It's such a good story!" Andrey replied. They both laughed.

"OK, I'll give him a ring and use your name as an introduction. OK?" Antipov asked.

"Fine with me. Take care."

Inspector Antipov was still smiling when his mobile phone buzzed indicating a text message had arrived. He saved the number under the name of Max Baer which brought another smile to his lips. A really good story, he thought. He rang the number.

"Baer," a deep voice replied in a very German manner.

Antipov replied in Russian.

"My name is Inspector Vladimir Antipov, a friend of Andrey Pozdanin at Interpol. I don't speak German so I hope you don't mind me speaking Russian."

"Not at all," came the reply from the other end. "What can I do for you Inspector Antipov?"

"Please call me Volodya."

"And I'm Max," came a quick reply.

"Max, I'm interested in a case of strychnine smuggling in a truck full of wine that came from Germany."

"Aha," Max replied. "Then you have the right telephone number. I'm the chief investigator.

"Great. I think there may be a link to a death in Moscow that I'm investigating. I'm officially investigating as a member of the murder squad, not in my capacity as an officer in the Upravleniye Rasrabotki Prestupnytch Organisazi, URPO for short." Max Baer whistled. He knew what that meant. There were only one hundred and fifty people in this special unit combatting organised crime and all of them were specialists, top men in their field. He sat up straight, his brain working overtime.

"Wow, that is an interesting connection," Max replied having recovered his breath.

"I'm not one hundred percent sure about the connection yet but there are too many coincidences. Armen Makaryan died officially of a heart attack." Antipov could hear the clicking of Max Baer's keyboard. He was checking the man's name as they spoke. Antipov continued.

"The man was fifty, Armenian forefathers, Christian, overweight, liked good food, lots of alcohol and women.

He had nought point one eight percent blood alcohol content and the wine glass next to him was a red wine from Bordeaux without a tax stamp on it so smuggled into the country. I have no way of knowing where it came from. What I do know is that traces of a poisonous substance were found in his blood and that substance could well have been strychnine. I have a hunch that the man might have been taking crystal meth and someone may have given him a lethal dose of strychnine in his red wine. He was so drunk he probably wouldn't have been able to tell the difference between crystal meth and strychnine. His bodyguard left him alone while he took a prostitute back to the city. The prostitute was found murdered the next day. The bodyguard says his boss was still alive when he left. Armen Makaryan had a wine business called Trans Mir and had just lost his import licence which the authorities had refused to renew. He distributes through a company called Vodalko so I presume that the smuggled Bordeaux was coming in through them. I'm on my way there to meet Vodalko's owner, Abel Plemyannikov, a well-known right-wing oligarch and a great fan of Vladimir Zhirinovsky. He has a vodka factory in Podolsk, sixty kilometres to the south of Moscow, with a huge security wall around it, CCTV everywhere and at the back of the compound a training camp for "security personnel" that looks more like a paramilitary camp. Plemyannikov is the head of an elite council of businessmen who call themselves the "Conseil". One of the six members is Armen Makaryan. Shall I go on?"

"Please do," Max replied making short bullet points on

his lap top.

"Makaryan is the typical rich businessman who started his empire at the beginning of the nineties at the tender age of thirty, trading in steel, weapons and anything that could be made into weapons. The usual story. He had made a fortune by 1998 and had wisely invested in other companies, particularly abroad. When the bank crisis hit most Russian businessmen in 1998, this clever guy had most of his money in the Cayman Islands and in Cyprus. He took over several companies in 1998 and 1999 that were pleased to find a new owner to take on their debts and staff for just a symbolic sum of one thousand roubles. One of these companies was Trans Mir. He had extremely good political contacts including the ex-mayor of Moscow, Yury Luzhkow, who Medvedev fired in October 2010. The new mayor is one of Medvedev's protégés, Sergei Sobyanin. Armen Makaryan's political influence was beginning to wane but he did still have contacts in the mayor's office. Makaryan is on the board of AeroRusSpace in Khimki and according to my informant he used his influence with the board to swing a vote in favour of the new motorway from Moscow to St. Petersburg. The mayor's office has a vested interest in the motorway cutting through the forest that is owned by AeroRusSpace and is no doubt very grateful for his and the board's support. However, with the new police reforms, stricter customs controls, the much acclaimed fight against corruption, politicians can't be seen to be overtly supportive of anyone like Makaryan. His links to political and industrial contacts in Armenia are very strong and through the import of such products as Armenian brandy and the huge sums of money that are paid for these products, helps to launder money from dubious sources. I can't yet prove all this but the evidence is increasing from day to day."

"And someone was close enough to him and others to kill him without suffering any nasty consequences."

"Exactly! It's a real puzzle but gradually more and more pieces are fitting into place."

"OK, let me give you what I have on the wine guy – off the record of course."

"Of course."

"He appears to be clean. His name is Thomas Becker, a well-respected member of a small farming community in the Alsenz valley about a hundred kilometres south-west of Frankfurt. His mother took over the wine estate when his father suddenly died of a heart attack in 1989. He was still at school and then went to university to study oenology, living in a small flat during the week and in his parents' house on the weekend and during his summer vacation. He worked every free hour of the day on the wine estate while he was at university to keep everything going. His mother died in 2004 and since then he has looked after his handicapped brother who is a few years older than he is. He started a wine brokerage business in 1999 selling Bordeaux and other expensive wines to wine lovers. In 2004 he met his fiancée, or should I say re-met his student sweetheart, and she moved in with him. With his mother no longer alive, he obviously needed help, company and someone to share the huge responsibility of his business and looking after his elder handicapped brother. They're getting married this year. Now wait for this… Her name is Svetlana Shnaider, Russian born but of German origin. She was born in Novosibirsk in 1973, studied German in Moscow and spent a year at Mainz University from September 1991. She met Thomas in Geisenheim and they had a brief affair. She says that Thomas was too tied up with the family business then after the death of his father a couple of years earlier. They parted. She went back to Moscow but she returned to Mainz in June 1995 after she graduated. She ended up marrying a German, Klaus Schuhmacher in April 1996 and was carrying his child at the time. She has two sons and divorced in 2004 having re-met her student prince and moved in with him with her two sons. She had helped him sell a batch of expensive Bordeaux wine which Thomas had bought when the wine estate in Bordeaux went bankrupt. They couldn't remember what the name of the wine was and their company records for 2003 were destroyed in 2010. I have a list of wine estates that went bankrupt in 2003. If you can give me an email address I'll mail it to you."

"Max. Could you just check if Chateau Malvaux is on that list?"

"Chateau Malvaux… They're all called Chateau something, just give me a moment. Yes, here we are, Chateau Malvaux registered an application for insolvency in January 2003."

"Bingo!" Antipov exclaimed. "That, of course, doesn't explain how the deceased could buy bottles of Chateau Malvaux with more recent vintages."

"No, but believe me, the wine trade is only second to horse dealing when it comes to scandals! Quite honestly if someone bought good, inexpensive Bordeaux, re-corked it with original-looking corks and re-labelled it with fake labels, why not… And Thomas Becker has a re-corking business for expensive wines that wine-lovers lay down. And in the area he lives in, there are lots of printers, some of whom would print a label for him, cash, no questions asked."

"Max, that's really interesting. Anything else I should know? I'll be at Podolsk in five minutes or so?"

"Yes. For starters Svetlana Schuhmacher née Shnaider bought a flat in Moscow in 2004 for around 17 million Roubles and had it completely refurbished. Her mother and younger sister, Olesya, who works for a bank and cares for her mother, live in the flat. Svetlana visits them twice a year. She also visits her elder brother, Victor, who lives in Zurich. He works there half the year and then has to return to Moscow as the Swiss only give him a residence permit for six months. She visits him twice or even three times in that six month period. It could be, and here I'm only speculating, that she collects money at a Swiss bank. And in Russia from a Russian bank. Her sister transfers two thousand four hundred Euros a month for her rent. Obviously her job at the bank is very well paid!! Svetlana's sister, Olesya, has applied for a visa for Germany to attend her sister's wedding. I don't think there is any danger she won't come back, as long as her mother is alive."

"Max, thank you. I'll give you a ring to check my scribbled notes when I'm back in the office."

"No worries. And Volodya, the wine estate and brokerage business is booming. The farmhouse and out-buildings are in top condition. Looking at the cost of renovating sandstone buildings even if you do it on the cheap, I reckon this enigmatic personality has spent a million Euros on the buildings, interior and cellar. I bet we can't find all the sums in his accounts."

"Hmm, I wonder if you can check with Mr. Thomas Becker if there's any connection between him or his fiancée and the deceased Armen Makaryan."

"I'll do that straight away. In the meantime, here's another puzzle we can't solve. Apparently Thomas Becker handed the envelope with strychnine in it with a small gratuity to the logistics manager of the freight forwarder who hired the truck that was checked on the EU border to Russia. We had an anonymous email tip but couldn't trace the email back. Whoever sent it knew what he or she was doing. Now here's the strange bit. The logistics manager made a very detailed description of Thomas Becker and we had an EvoFit picture made up. Apart from the blue eyes and his hair colour, it really didn't look like Thomas Becker. The logistics manager had never seen this customer before although he had been working for several years with Global Logistics so he couldn't tell whether it was him or not and didn't ask for an ID. It appears that Thomas Becker sends sixteen truckloads of cheap table wine to Russia every year. I'll email you the paperwork of the last truck with the strychnine but I can see in the box for the addressee that the wine was destined for Podolsk on behalf of Trans Mir. Wasn't that the name of the deceased's company?"

"I can't believe it," Antipov said. "It looks as if we're working on the same case but for different reasons."

"Yes, indeed. In the email tip-off the informant mentioned a jeweller's shop in Frankfurt that was receiving strychnine from Australia and passing it on. We're currently in touch with the police in Brisbane and Sydney and I'll let you know if we come up with anything. The jeweller, Norbert Mayer, gave almost the same description of Thomas Becker that we received from the logistics manager. Only the jeweller is obsessed with people's hands and described Thomas Becker's hands as manicured, the hands of a musician. And he also said that he had a tan. When I met Thomas Becker he didn't look as if he'd just come back from a winter holiday and being a wine grower, his hands were a bit rough, not dirty but certainly not manicured. I'm certain that our Thomas Becker who bought strychnine in Frankfurt from a jeweller and gave it to the logistics manager was an imposter."

"Can you prove it?"

"No, not yet, but I'm working on it. But I just don't know why anyone would go to such lengths to frame him."

"I've just arrived at Podolsk," Antipov said. "I'll ring you again from the office and I'll send you my email address as soon as we hang up."

"It looks as if we'll be talking to each other a lot," Max said and then the line went dead.

The man at the gate in Podolsk knew that a high-ranking police officer from the URPO would be arriving so when the driver drew up at the gate the car was waived past. Vladimir Antipov jumped out the car at the main entrance and walked up the steps to reception. Abel Plemyannikov was waiting for him at the top of the steps – an unusually courteous gesture for a Russian oligarch. He held out his hand with a charismatic smile and welcomed the URPO officer to his domain. They turned round to survey the complex. As Abel pointed to the sports ground and shooting range, a good-looking man with a black holdall walked towards a car in the parking lot. Antipov's trained eye said thirty eight, one meter eighty, ninety-kilos and as fit as a fiddle. The man was Andrey Ivanov.

Abel pointed to the warehouses and then turned to Inspector Antipov.

"A dreadful thing, Armen's sudden death. Does your involvement mean you suspect he was murdered, Inspector?"

"We have to investigate every possibility," Antipov replied. "I understand that Armen's bodyguard and chauffeur, Vanya, was trained here at Podolsk."

"Indeed, one of the best. Very loyal and an excellent driver. He is a regular visitor to our shooting range," Abel added and gestured towards the main door. "Come inside to my office, Inspector. Would you like tea or coffee?"

It was quite late when Inspector Antipov left his office. The thirty minutes he had spent questioning Abel Plemyannikov, the owner of Vodalko, really didn't give him any more leads. The important leads had come from Max Baer in Germany. As soon as he got back to his office he made a draft report on his conversation with Max Baer and put in an official request to be able to pass information on to Max Baer on the death of Armen Makaryan. Up to now, everything had been strictly off the record so he just saved his draft. Max also put in a request to pass on information to the Moscow police and was granted permission within an hour and he emailed Antipov to let him know. Inspector Antipov was then able to turn his draft into an official report on the coincidences and findings which Max Baer had told him about. He kept back the EvoFit picture of Thomas Becker and didn't mention Max's theory about an imposter. He'd hold that back until he had a little more evidence. He made another report on the conversation he had had with Abel Plemyannikov, the owner of Vodalko, and had sent both to the archives, the URPO and his superior. It wasn't long after he had filed the report on the central server under the case number when an automatic copy was passed on to an external email address. It hadn't taken long for a clever hacker to plant an automatic diversion "send to" in the case file so that the deceased's brother received all the information as soon as it was in the system.

*

It was early evening in Gozo and the sun was sinking behind the cliffs to the west. Boris Makaryan was reading the police reports in the office of his mansion. The evidence so far was pointing in one direction only. For some reason this motherfucker of a German had sent strychnine with the truck taking his wine to Russia and someone had put the strychnine in the bottle of wine which his brother had drunk. But why? Armen always paid his debts and bills punctually. Had he discovered or suspected that the wine he was receiving couldn't be from Chateau Malvaux because the wine estate had gone bankrupt in 2003? And who was this German guy's accomplice? Boris re-read the report. The German, Thomas Becker, was engaged to a Russian woman called Svetlana Shnaider so he had the contacts and maybe a motive. Boris looked out of the window deep in thought. Then he rang his assistant in Moscow, Aram.

"Good evening," a composed voice replied.

"Good evening, Aram. I need some information."

"I'm all ears."

"I need all the information you can get on a German called Thomas Becker. He is a wine grower in Unterbach in Germany. And on his fiancé, Svetlana née Shnaider, married a German and divorced in 2004. Her married name was Schuhmacher. I'll send you the details in the next half hour. And I need the information quickly. The woman owns a flat in Moscow where her mother and sister live. Have them checked out as well. And find out if there's a connection between this woman and my brother. Did they know each other? She visited Moscow two or three times a year. She would have probably flown from Frankfurt."

Boris disconnected his mobile. It was a pay as you go Maltese mobile registered under the name of one of the villagers. No need to take unnecessary risks. Goodness only knew who was listening to whom these days. He pressed the intercom on his desk.

"Yes, boss" Davit replied.

"Come up to my office and leave Erik to check the monitors."

"Will do," he replied. In a couple of minutes Davit knocked on the door.

"Davit, this is a confidential police report and not to be emailed or given to anyone else. Aram is investigating the German, Thomas Becker, and his fiancé Svetlana Shnaider. The Russian woman has a flat in Moscow where her mother and sister live. He'll need the address to check up on them. All the information is in this report but send it in a disguised form. And use a secure email address. He needs the information within the next half hour."

"OK boss. I'll get on to it straight away."

Davit took the report and left the room. Boris was angry, angry at this German, angry at his Russian whore, angry at the mystery man who poisoned the wine. He picked up his Russian mobile phone and rang his mother. She had been devastated at the news of losing her younger son and since then he had phoned her every day instead of just twice a week. He knew she wouldn't rest until after the funeral but the body hadn't been released by the coroner yet. He took a deep breath and rang her number.

19

It was a warm autumn Saturday morning as Sam got out of his car in the car park next to the police force HQ, a large glass building. It had taken him half an hour to drive west on the A4/M4 to the New South Wales Police Force location in Parramatta. He walked through the front door to reception and saw Frank Moss sitting on one of the chairs watching the door. As soon as Sam walked in, Frank got up and greeted him without his usual smile.

"Hi, Sam. A Chief Inspector Green is waiting to see us in meeting room 303 on the third floor," he said, handing Sam a visitor's badge. "I've signed us both in. The lift is over there," he said and they walked past the security barrier, nodded to the policemen on duty and walked over to the lift. They got out at the third floor and looked for room 303. In the room they could see two men looking at a monitor and talking to each other. Frank knocked at the glass door and one of the men rose to let him in.

"Good morning," Frank said. "This is my client, Sam MacPherson and I'm his legal counsel, Frank Moss." Frank handed the man a visiting card. "We have an appointment with Chief Inspector Green."

"That's me," said the other man. "Please both take a

seat," he added gesturing to the two chairs on the other side of the table. "And this is Inspector David Clarkson whom you met yesterday."

"Indeed," Sam said and nodded politely at the inspector who had intruded into the peaceful environment of his home.

The Chief Inspector cleared his throat. "We have reason to believe that a business client of yours, Long Life, has been selling strychnine on the black market which, as I'm sure you know, is a serious offense. According to the records we have checked so far, you are the only supplier of nux vomica, the raw material for strychnine, to the said company. We are therefore checking your records against the records we have at Long Life. This may take a few days or just a few hours depending on what we find. We will keep you abreast of our findings."

"As my client is just here to help you with your enquiries, is there any information you would like him to provide."

"There is just one question I have which cropped up this morning. We have found an export route for strychnine which leads to Frankfurt in Germany and possibly to Russia. I don't suppose that you have any business connections in those two countries or have talked to someone in the last few months that was looking for strychnine?"

Sam's heart was racing. There was a man who had contacted him by phone. He spoke fluent English but there was something unusual about his voice which reminded Sam of a friend of his who had a German father. It must have been four or six weeks ago, he couldn't remember exactly. The man had got his name from a mutual friend down at the yacht club, he said. He was looking for someone who dealt in tropical trees, particularly the fruit of nux vomica. Sam had told him that his business was making anti-venom for snake poison and his trees were just a side-line. He couldn't remember the man's name, or was it Porter? Steve Porter? He had told him that he sold all his nux vomica to Long Life and didn't have any to sell. He hadn't thought anything of it at the time. Sam looked at Frank and Frank seemed to nod with his eyes. If there's something you know, tell them, son, is what his fatherly face was saying. So Sam told them about Steve Porter and the phone call. No, he hadn't met him. No, he didn't know what he looked like. No, he didn't have an Australian accent. His English was the kind of international traveller English where now and again a word, phrase or diphthong reminds you of another country or language. That was all he could tell them.

"Then if that's all, gentlemen, I have another appointment in town at eleven thirty," Frank said standing up. Chief Inspector Green gave both men his card.

"If you remember anything else, Mr. MacPherson, please give me or Inspector Clarkson a call."

"I will," Sam said, stood up, smiled and turned to go. He forced himself to walk slowly although his inner voice was saying "Just let me get out of here as quickly as I can." Frank was already at the door and held it open for his client. Frank nodded at the policemen and followed Sam to the lift.

"I'll buy you a coffee to go," Frank said. "There's a coffee shop just round the corner on Little Street. Then I'll show you one of my favourite buildings not far from here." They left the lift, nodded at the two policemen on security, walked to reception and handed in their visitor badges. They left the building and Sam breathed in the warm autumn air. He and Frank continued in silence. As they stood in line to grab a coffee to go the silence was deafening.

"Two Americanos," Frank said, "tall, to go." He didn't need to ask Sam what he wanted. He knew. They waited for the barista to give them their paper cups and walked out of the shop. Frank turned left and Sam followed. Frank turned to Sam as they were walking.

"Is there anything I should know, anything they could find?" he asked.

"If they compare all the weights of the nuts picked and the weight of the nuts sent, then we have quite a large amount of wastage, around ten to twelve per cent."

"Is that usual in your business? Do some get sorted out or thrown away?"

"We calculate on three per cent waste. I only have one customer. That's Pete Owen."

"Is he only interested in the fiscal aspects or is there more to it."

"There's more to it. I know he sells strychnine on the black market but I had no idea that he was exporting. I talked to him yesterday evening. He's pretty shaken up. He said that there's no trace of how the strychnine is distributed but his lab and storage records are all on computer. They need to be for his certification and licence. So theoretically they could prove that he is producing more than he is selling which is bad news."

"OK, then let's assume he talks or is found out. Then your line has to be you didn't know what he was doing with the extra amount, you were helping him out and it helped you too. You knew that he was financially in debt and so are you. Worst case would be charges for tax evasion and fraud but you would probably only get a suspended sentence."

"Only!" Sam said and rolled his eyes. "That would kill my deal with Tom Wyatt and ruin my chances of selling the business."

"How's Karen taking it and what does she know?" Frank asked.

"You know Karen. Quite hysterical to begin with but she's come back fighting. She's convinced that I'm a victim of some bureaucrat's crusade against the rich. The worst thing is the newspapers. She couldn't get her breakfast down after she read the small article in the Sydney Herald even if it was only on page three. And then Tom faxed me over a copy of the Hawk's Lift local. They obviously don't want to harm the company as we are an important employer for the town. But the editor in charge is the type that loves a bit of scandal if it'll sell more copies. And he had my picture on the title page and a headline that said: MacPherson's offices searched. I've faxed it to your office. We may have to sue them for libel."

They walked in silence to their cars and Frank shook

Sam's hand and put his left hand on Sam's arm and squeezed it gently.

"You'll find a way of surviving, Sam," Frank said quietly. "Just ride the storm and be careful.

"I will," Sam said. "Thanks Frank. I appreciate your support."

They got into their cars and drove off, Frank towards the highway and the city and Sam due south to Macquarie Golf Course. It would take him three quarters of an hour to get there so he'd be in time for lunch at twelve thirty with Tom Wyatt.

*

Inspector Antipov was looking hard at the EvoFit picture of Thomas Becker that Max Baer had sent him from Frankfurt. There was something familiar about the face staring back at him. Had he not seem someone similar walking in the grounds at Vodalko? Or was it just wishful thinking. Somehow he felt he had seen this man somewhere or at least a picture of him in Moscow. He called his assistant who came in within minutes. Antipov showed him the EvoFit picture.

"This is the description of the man confirmed by two eye witnesses that called himself Thomas Becker." He produced another picture which Max had sent him of the real Thomas Becker. "This is the real Thomas Becker. As you can see, there is quite a difference and apparently the possible imposter was sun-tanned and had manicured hands whereas Thomas Becker is a wine-grower and doesn't go on winter holidays." His assistant looked at him, pursed his lips and nodded.

"I see," he said. "Any reason to believe he's on our files?"

"The only connection is that Thomas Becker has a Russian girlfriend who lives with him and was selling wine to the deceased. It's a long shot but worth a try."

"OK, sir, I'll check with our criminal records and then other government bodies, the internet, newspapers and social media."

"I'll expect your preliminary report in three hours at two this afternoon," he said knowing that the computers would need at least two and a half hours to go through all the files they had on a preliminary search, "and the final analysis on Monday morning at ten sharp."

"Right sir." The assistant sighed. Working on a Saturday was pretty normal in his profession but he had hoped to get off at lunchtime so that he could meet his new girlfriend in the afternoon. Now he'd have to stay on until his preliminary report was finished and get in at seven on Monday to finish his final report. Inspector Antipov was a slave driver but a brilliant criminologist and knew just about everything there was to know about organised crime in Moscow. He was lucky to have a boss and mentor with such knowledge. After all, he was ambitious and this job would help further his career. Hopefully his new girlfriend would understand, maybe even be impressed that he was so important. Inspector Antipov picked up the phone and rang Max on his mobile phone.

"Baer," the voice on the other end said.

"Hi, Max. Volodya speaking. I've sent the EvoFit photo for a matching process, all accessible files plus public domain. I should know this afternoon if there are any preliminary matches and on Monday morning for sure."

"Good. I've sent a whole squad out to show the picture to hotels, restaurants, taxi-drivers, the usual routine. As you can imagine, I'm everybody's favourite person today! We've also sent it by email to public transport, airport security and so on. I should be able to give you any first indication of where this man stayed, how he travelled, what he did on Monday around lunchtime my time."

"OK. Then let's stay in touch."

*

Max Baer looked at the EvoFit picture again and shook his head. No, this man was definitely not Thomas Becker. He had interviewed Thomas Becker about the smuggling charge over three weeks ago but of course he didn't know then that his customer, Armen Makaryan, had been killed. The deceased was killed just a week ago. It was time he went back to Unterbach to see what Thomas Becker and his lovely Russian girlfriend had to say about it. He picked up his phone and ordered his car.

It only took him fifty minutes to reach Unterbach from Wiesbaden. Baer loved German motorways, particularly on a Saturday when they were virtually empty at this time of year. He had rung Thomas Becker to say that he'd be with him around twelve and had a couple of questions. When he got there, the large, ornate wrought iron gates were open and he parked his car in the yard which had been tastefully renovated with old cobblestones to match the style of the farmhouse. He looked at the outside of the house, the windows, the doors, particularly the heavy oak door leading to the cellar. Thomas had put his jacket on and walked out to greet Inspector Max Baer. He really had an affable smile and you couldn't help but like the man. Max shook his hand.

Thomas had seen that the inspector had been looking at the cellar door.

"Would you like me to show you around, Inspector?" he asked.

"If it's no trouble," Max replied.

"Then let's go down to the cellar." Thomas opened the heavy oak door and Max stroked the surface of the wood affectionately. Thomas smiled.

"Yes, beautiful wood. I love oak," Thomas said. "My father died in his early forties of a heart attack. I was still at school at the time. He never recovered from the glycol scandal in 1985, emotionally and financially. He used to sell most of his wine in bulk and not in bottle as I do. One of his wines was used by a local winery in a cuvee with some Austrian wine and he was suspected of having added glycol to the wine. He was innocent but he couldn't prove that the glycol had only come from the Austrian wine and not his wine. Normally you keep two bottles of each AP number but my father was unfortunately not as organised as he should have been and didn't have any library samples.

"What's an AP number?" Max asked.

"Quality wine in Germany has to be tested by the authorities and receives a special AP number. This is the current library," Thomas said and pointed to a vast area of shelves which were so high that they reached the old vaulted ceiling and were sixty centimetres deep. "I keep six bottles of each AP number in our library for ten years at least," he said. Each shelf had a number written on it for easy reference.

"Very impressive," Max said. "Why are they wrapped in cellophane?"

"This is the old, original barrel cellar of the wine estate and is made out of the local sandstone which is quite porous. So the humidity here is great for the barrels and the wine, but it destroys the labels within a couple of years."

"I see," Max said, fascinated by a whole new science he had no idea about.

"So when my father died in 1989," Thomas continued as they walked through the underground cellar "my mother inherited the winery but really couldn't cope with running it and looking after my elder brother, Conrad, who is autistic. I helped as much as I could and then took the wine estate over when I was twenty-one but, of course, I had very little experience. In the nineties I experimented with dry wines and secondary fermentation, hence the small barrique barrels which hold 225 litres. I still use them to mature some wines and also ferment some of the four hectares of Chardonnay in them which I planted in 1994. Before then it was a grape variety that you weren't allowed to plant in Germany. My first big project," he said and smiled. "I used some of the money from my father's life insurance to buy the young vines. I was just twenty two and it felt like a fortune. It cost me quite a few sleepless nights but it was worth it. These days I use half of the Chardonnay for sparkling wine. Most of our wines are white and the majority of the wines are made out of Riesling grapes. Traditionally wines were kept in old oak barrels which hold five hundred or a thousand litres. I kept a couple of them, just sentimental really. I realised in the nineties that there was a large market in Germany for imported wines and started importing as a broker even before I graduated in 1992. I studied to become a Master of Wine and developed a good nose for really good red wines which I bought young and laid down for five to ten years and sold to wine lovers through my brokerage."

"I've heard that can be quite lucrative," Max said.

"Yes. A good young red wine, if it develops the way you expect and wins a couple of gold medals, can sell for ten times the price you paid for it."

Max whistled!

"The largest cost is dead capital and storage cost. I had the capital from my father's insurance and plenty of storage space down here. The wines don't have labels on at that stage so I can keep them in the cool cellar and I label them before they're sold."

"Is that legal," Max asked.

"For estate bottled wines I buy the labels from the estate so that the wine is absolutely original. For other wines, everyday wines, I print the labels locally and have the bottles labelled at a small cooperative before they go into our sales warehouse in Gensingen. The expensive wines are labelled manually."

They walked past rows of pallet cages full of red wine bottles. Each cage had a metal plate with the details of the wine and the number of bottles. Thomas was most definitely more organised than his father was. At the end of the cellar there was a fire-proof door on the right which led into another part of the underground labyrinth.

"This is the new cellar," Thomas said with obvious pride. "When my father was alive, the cellar was full of large oak barrels and he sold the wine in bulk. When my brokerage really took off at the end of the nineties I replaced the oak barrels with stainless tanks which use computer controlled cool fermentation to increase the quality of our Riesling. I had already started marketing our wines in bottle when I left university and our customer base grew quite quickly."

"And where do you bottle the wines?" Max asked.

"We have a mobile bottler who comes and bottles at the estate. Above the cellar there's a bottling room which we use in February for bottling and for the rest of the year for storage. That was the only drawback to the underground cellar. We have to pump the wines up to be bottled instead of allow them to flow down to a bottling room using gravity and not a pump. Having said that, there are really good pumps these days which handle the wine in a gentle way."

Max followed Thomas up the concrete steps and into the bottling room. It was full of pallets, mainly wine bottles in cardboard boxes.

"In April the room is just a storage area. Follow me to my office."

They walked through a fire-proof door into an office with a large desk, some filing cabinets and no window although the room looked as if daylight was coming through a fake window in one of the walls.

"I'm out in the vineyards a lot of the time but I still find it difficult to work in an office with no natural light, no window to open. So I put in a fake window with a special light with around twenty thousand lux so it imitates indirect sunlight. The rest of the light comes from the indirect lighting just below the ceiling," he added pointing to a plastered frieze.

"Clever," Max said and smiled at Thomas.

"Have a seat, Inspector," Thomas said pointing to a chair opposite his desk. "You said you had a couple of questions."

"Yes, more a piece of information which I want to talk to you and your fiancée about."

"Should I call her and ask her to come down? She'll be in the kitchen getting lunch ready."

"I'd rather talk to you first and then go and talk to her afterwards, if that's alright with you."

"No problem, fire away."

"You have a large customer in Russia called Transmir,"

he said and paused. "Can you tell me a little more about the company?"

"Sure," Thomas said. "Transmir is based in Moscow and owned by a man called Armen Makaryan. He buys fifteen or sixteen trucks of cheap table wine a year. It's pretty straight forward business. I import the wine and have it bottled at a local bottler and stored at our freight forwarder's warehouse in Kelsterbach. The customer picks the wine up and the forwarder organises most of the paperwork. We just supply any analyses or copies of labels which may be required."

"Do you know Armen Makaryan personally?" Max asked.

"Yes, I've met him a couple of times in Moscow and we had dinner last year in March in Düsseldorf."

"You obviously have a very good memory," Max said. Thomas laughed.

"Not really. The biggest international wine fair is held in Düsseldorf every year in March and last year Armen came over to the fair. He doesn't usually bother."

"I see," Max said. "How would you describe Armen Makaryan?"

"He's Armenian and looks very Armenian. I should think he's around fifty years old. He's your typical Russian businessman. They like to show their success and wealth, wear nothing but big brands, heavy gold chains around their necks and usually a Rolex watch," Thomas said with a touch of disdain in his voice. It was obvious that his lifestyle was very different to his client's.

"How long have you been working with this client and where did you meet him?" Max asked.

"Svetlana met him when she was a student in Moscow. He bought Transmir as a bankrupt company after the bank crisis in Russia in 1998. Svetlana was then living in Germany with her husband Klaus and set up quite a few deals for him in Germany. I met him for the first time in 2004 in Moscow and he became a client the same year."

"And may I ask how long you have known Svetlana and where you met?"

"I first met Svetlana in 1993 while I was studying at Geisenheim." Max looked at him with a questioning look. "I was studying oenology and wine marketing. Svetlana had done two years of her German language and literature degree in Moscow and then decided to do a year in Germany, at Mainz University. She used to come over to Geisenheim for gigs and parties. That's where we met. I didn't have time for a steady girlfriend, with the wine estate and my degree course. We lost sight of each other. She married a German called Klaus Schuhmacher in 1996 because Misha was already on the way. Alex, her second son, was born in 1999. I love those boys," he said with a smile. "I treat them as if they were mine and most of the time I think they are mine," he added looking down to hide his eyes but his voice couldn't hide the emotion he felt. He and Svetlana had already spoken to Klaus about Thomas adopting the boys after the wedding. "In 2003 we met again and Svetlana had just separated from Klaus. She was working freelance acting as a broker for wine companies in Germany who wanted to work with Russia. It allowed her to work from home and look after the boys. She filed for a divorce in 2003 and when it came through in 2004 she moved in with me here with the boys. My mother died in a car accident in 2004 and that meant that my elder brother, Conrad, who is autistic, needed someone to look after him. Svetlana agreed to look after him to allow me more time to run my business. You know the rest. And this year we're getting married in May."

"Congratulations," Max said. "Do you know anything else about Armen Makaryan, his business contacts, anything?"

"Not really. I know that he's very well connected, in business and in politics. Svetlana told me that he made a fortune at the beginning of the nineties selling weapons and anything that was needed to make weapons to the Americans. That's all I know."

"Armen Makaryan was murdered three weeks ago," Max said looking straight at Thomas.

"Murdered!" Thomas exclaimed. His mouth fell open in surprise. "My God, I thought he was so closely guarded that no-one would have a chance of harming him. How was he killed?"

"He was poisoned, with strychnine."

"Strychnine?" Thomas stared at the inspector in sheer disbelief. "Does this have anything to do with the toxic substance which was found in one of the trucks carrying my wine?" he asked.

"We're not sure. We don't think so but we have to investigate every possibility."

"Of course," Thomas said.

"I'd like to inform your fiancée about the murder. Are her sons with her?"

"No, no, they're at a friend's house this morning in the next village and are staying there for lunch."

"Good. Then maybe we could go over to the house?" Max asked.

"Yes, of course." Thomas got up and walked in silence to the corridor and out of the main cellar door with Max in tow. They walked to the house and Thomas opened the door to let the inspector in. He took his own jacket off and helped the inspector out of his and hung both of them in the hall. He then walked towards the kitchen. Svetlana was at the kitchen table making pelmeni, a kind of Russian pasta filled with minced pork and beef.

"Oh, pelmeni!" Max exclaimed, a smile on his face.

"You know pelmeni?" Svetlana asked brushing the flour from her hands.

"Indeed. My mother used to make them quite often," he said and both Svetlana and Thomas just stared at him.

"Goodness," Svetlana said. "I thought you were German."

"I am now. When I was nineteen I emigrated to Germany. That was in 1990. Because I was Jewish I was able to settle in Germany thanks to paragraph 10b of the constitution and take German citizenship."

"And you speak Russian?" Svetlana asked in Russian.

"Yes. My parents still speak Russian at home but for me

German is now my second mother tongue."

"Then I must apologise for my remarks about Russian businessmen," Thomas said. "I didn't mean to offend."

Max smiled. "No offence taken," he said. "Frau Schneider, could I take ten minutes of your time?"

"Of course," she said, moving her baking tray from the table and wiping the excess flour from the table top. The inspector had used the German pronunciation of her name, Shnaider, not the Russian pronunciation. Very thoughtful of him, she thought.

Thomas sat down next to Svetlana and held her hand. He knew this was going to be a shock for her. Max looked at her and said: "Armen Makaryan was murdered three weeks ago in Moscow."

Svetlana gasped and covered her mouth with her hand. It took her several seconds to get her speech back.

"Murdered? But it hasn't been in the newspaper. And I only spoke to my sister in Moscow yesterday. She would have mentioned it if she had known."

"The Moscow police investigating his death have held back the information up till now but will be issuing a press statement on Monday. I felt I ought to tell you personally."

"Thank you, inspector. I know, I mean I knew Armen fairly well."

"When did you meet?"

"I met him just before I graduated from Moscow University in 1995. I came back to Germany then and I started working for Armen on a free-lance basis, helping him to do business with German suppliers. When I met Thomas in 2003, or rather when we saw each other again in 2003, I helped Thomas set up business with Transmir, Armen's importing company. How was he killed?" she asked.

"He was poisoned," Max said.

"How terrible. Did he suffer?" Max was quite touched by her question. She was obviously fond of this gangster boss despite everything.

"He died in a similar manner to a massive heart attack," Max said trying to soften the thought of a death through strychnine poisoning. "Did you know him well?"

"I suppose as well as anyone can know an Armenian businessman who had bodyguards and bullet-proof cars," she said.

"Were you aware of his business activities? His business contacts?"

"No, I didn't ask. I didn't want to know. Anyone who got rich in Russia in the nineties and survived probably made Al Capone look like a choir boy," she said with a sad kind of smile. Max nodded.

"Yes, probably very wise. How did he pay you for your services?"

"At the beginning I only received small amounts of money from him but as our business relationship grew he became extremely generous. I left the money in a Russian bank account. The rouble is very stable and interest rates in Russia are quite high. When I had enough money, I bought a flat in Moscow for my mother and sister. My mother is not well and my sister looks after her despite her job in the bank. Armen helped me find the flat and it was basically his money that paid for it." She flashed a look at Thomas. There was no point in hiding this information. The inspector spoke Russian and most probably had all the information he needed on her and her family anyway. "You know Russia, inspector, and most probably how things work in Moscow." Max nodded. "Without the right contacts it's impossible for most people to live a normal life. And Armen had not only good business contacts but also political contacts too."

"Yes, I understand he was quite close to the mayor's office," Max said and watched her face. Her expression hardened a little.

"Yes, I believe so. We didn't usually talk about politics, only business, business in Germany, and wine."

"When did you last see him?"

"It wasn't very long ago. I arrived in Moscow to visit my mother on 6th March. I remember the date because it was a Tuesday and the new police reform had just come into force. Everyone was talking about it and about nothing else. We met for dinner at Nostalgie."

"Nice restaurant," Max said, pursing his lips.

"Yes. As I'm sure you know, if you are rich and live in Moscow then Nostalgie is one of the restaurants you need to be seen at regularly." She smiled.

"Can you remember what you talked about?"

"Yes. It was an important meeting for me or should I say for us." She looked at Thomas and Max felt the tension in her voice. "Russia is going to introduce tax stamps for all imported wines at the beginning of next year and has already begun to intensify their customs checks in their fight against corruption and smuggling. As you know, Inspector, it's very difficult to fight the bureaucracy in Russia and having goods or trucks confiscated can be extremely costly."

"Why should you believe that your wine might be confiscated?" Max asked.

"Russian customs confiscate expensive products like wine on technicalities – the label may have a printing error, the name is similar to a Russian product, on just any grounds in the hope that the supplier or importer will give them a backhander to get the goods cleared. As President Medvedev has put fighting corruption high on his list of priorities, things are heating up as certain customs authorities have "a last fling" so to say. On top of this, Armen had informed us in February that he was about to lose his import licence. This is also part of the government's plan to reduce corruption. Small frauds or just mistakes in your accounts can mean you lose your licence. We have done good business in Russia over the last seven years and at the same time we have also built up other parts of our business. So at the beginning of this year we decided to stop selling to Russia."

"I see. And you told Armen Makaryan this when you went out for dinner in March?"

"Yes. He wasn't very happy about it. I promised to try and find him another supplier to replace us but our decision really was final. The truck that left in March will be the last of our export orders for Transmir." Svetlana's face suddenly went quite pale. "That truck, Inspector, was the one in which toxic substances were found. Is that not so?"

"Yes," Max said.

"Is there any connection between those substances and Armen's death?"

"We don't know yet but we are, of course, investigating all possibilities." Svetlana looked at Thomas and he squeezed her hand. She looked frightened, alarmed at something.

"Is there anything you wish to tell me, Frau Schneider?" Max asked.

"It may sound ridiculous and as you know, strange things happen everywhere, but they happen a lot in Russia. Even if it's only a coincidence that toxic substances were in a truck transporting our wine, not everyone will be aware of that."

"What do you mean," Max said. Thomas tilted his head and looked at her uncomprehendingly.

"I mean, if you are here talking to us, Inspector, then we are part of your investigation. On the face of it, we have a connection to a toxic substance, a connection to Armen and Armen was poisoned. This could mean that other people will be aware of our possible connections, people in Russia."

"Indeed," Max said. He didn't want to deny it and Svetlana was too clever to be fed lies.

"Because of your connections you would automatically be on our list of people to investigate. What motive do you think anyone could suppose you may have had to murder the man?"

"No idea," she said. "No idea at all. It was just a thought. In Russia it isn't healthy to be suspected of murdering an important businessman such as Armen."

"I understand," he said. "I wouldn't worry about it but if anything happens which you think I should know about, please give me a ring." He gave her his card. "You can reach me on my mobile phone day and night.

"Thank you, Inspector. I appreciate it." She looked at Thomas and added:

"Would you like to stay and have some pelmeni with us? I doubt I'll be eating much after such bad news."

"Thank you. That's very kind and certainly an offer I can't refuse. It's very rare for me to be able to eat homemade pelmeni!"

*

Boris was watching the sun go down over the Mediterranean Sea. He'd decided to go out for a walk above the Azure Window with Davit and Erik just five meters behind him. It was a great spot to see the sunset and the fantastic natural window on the west coast near Dwerja was a stunning picture in the beautiful orange sky. He was sat under a rocky outcrop on his fleece jacket. Davit was sitting on top of the rocky outcrop observing the surroundings and Erik was on the path at the fork which led to the sea. Boris looked over to the giant window. It was sad, he mused, that such a beautiful piece of nature would be gone within the next few years. The window had been created when two underwater caves collapsed. The local limestone was very porous and subject to massive erosion. The arch was disintegrating and the locals said that soon large pieces of rock would fall out of the underside of the arch destroying its perfect oval shape. At least the arch had been captured forever in several Hollywood films. He had watched the original version of The Clash of the Titans so that he could see the window on the screen. It was strange to think that he would probably outlive such a massive limestone construction. But then his younger brother Armen hadn't. His thoughts were interrupted by his mobile phone. He answered it knowing that it could only be Aram.

"Good evening," a polite voice said.

"Good evening, Aram," Boris replied. "What news do you have for me?"

"The woman, Svetlana, dined with Armen in Nostalgie about a month ago. The conversation was polite and intense; at one point a little tense. She had known your brother for about ten years and had done business with him for as long. Some suspect that she was an ex-girlfriend but no-one is sure. There were regular payments to her Russian account from Transmir and some from other accounts your brother held. She definitely received enough to buy her flat in Moscow. She seemed to be working for him officially but also receiving money for other invoices which probably didn't go through customs. I haven't found a motive yet."

"Then I'll have to pay Frau Shnaider a visit in Germany," Boris said. "I'll fly out on Tuesday to see what she and her boyfriend know."

Boris disconnected his phone.

"Davit," he called up to his bodyguard on the rocky outcrop.

"Yes, boss."

"When we get back to the house, book me on a flight to Frankfurt for Tuesday afternoon and hire a car."

"Yes, boss."

Boris continued looking out over the sea, the water afire with colour. He loved this spot. It was a symbolic meeting point for violence and the beauty of nature.

20

Sam arrived at the Macquarie links at twelve fifteen and parked his car in the spacious car park. He took his jacket off and pulled a sailing V-neck jumper over his head. Tom would be in golf gear so smart casual was the order of the day. A golf jumper may be a little too obvious. A sailing jumper would have a positive effect. He was wearing a casual dark blue pair of trousers and sneakers which he had put on this morning for the appointment at the police station with a white shirt, blue tie and blue jacket. He looked in the wing mirror to check his hair. He was as ready as he'd ever be. He walked in long sporty strides to the steps and sprinted up the steps two at a time. You never knew who could be watching. He walked through the front door and the steward smiled at him and said. "Welcome back, Sir. Tom is out on the deck."

"Thank you," Sam replied with a smile, impressed at the young man's memory. He walked out to the deck overlooking the tenth tee. Tom was relaxing in a cane chair reading the Sydney Herald. He saw Sam approaching and got up to shake hands. His smile wasn't as relaxed and all-embracing as usual. Sam smiled and said:

"Good to see you, Tom."

Both sat down and Tom looked at one of the waiters to summon him.

"What would you like to drink, Sam?" he asked. Sam looked at Tom's glass and saw he was drinking a beer.

"I'll have a beer, please," Sam told the waiter and tried to relax in his chair. Tom broke the silence.

"Nasty business about your plantation company," Tom said. How quickly is it going to settle down?"

"I wish I knew," Sam said honestly. "It's the bane of my life and a strain for Karen."

"How is Karen? How's she taking all this?"

"Karen's a fighter and a clever diplomat," he said. "She's a great asset in good and bad times."

"She rang Nancy and told her how unfair it was that you were being treated like criminals by the newspapers although you'd done nothing wrong." Sam nodded with a slight smile. Tom continued: "Good move, Sam. Nancy has told half of Sydney already!" Both men laughed.

"So what's the bottom line, Sam, strictly between you and me?"

"As you know, it's now two weeks since I was at the police station with Frank Moss helping the police with their inquiries. We only know that the main investigation is directed against one of my clients and that my company, as a supplier, has been drawn into it."

"You mean Long Life and Pete Owen, I suppose?" Tom looked at him. Sam was amazed at how quickly Tom seemed to gather facts. He must have a huge network with someone in every important place.

"Yes. I don't know enough about Pete's business to say whether there's any foundation to the allegations," Sam lied. "Worst case scenario, I lose a long-standing client and a good friend," Sam said trying to forget what Frank had said about fraud and tax evasion.

"Well, if that's all then the stormy waters will be a nightmare of the past in a couple of weeks' time."

"I daresay that you're right."

That was the answer Tom was waiting for.

"Then I suggest I put our little project on ice until the end of April and by then we should both know if it has had any effect on your business." Sam winced. He could now only hope that the investigators didn't find anything.

"Indeed," Sam said trying to affect a cool and calm demeanour. No chance in pushing Tom. He may jump ship completely.

"Let's order something to eat," Tom said. I'm starving.

The waiter came with Sam's beer and two menus.

"How was your round?" Sam asked him, eager to change the subject.

"Not bad," Tom said. "Not bad at all. A couple of birdies and an eagle to boot."

"Sounds pretty good to me," Sam said flicking over the pages of the menu, looking for something he felt he could stomach.

*

It was Sunday but Max Baer decided to go to his office to write his report. He put his weapon, wallet and keys into a tray and handed it to the security officer on duty. He swiped his card and went through the electronic barrier and the body scan. He collected his belongings and went up the stairs to his office. He only used lifts if he had to or the building had more than ten storeys. He needed to keep fit and used every opportunity, however small. He didn't smoke but he did like coffee. He stopped at the machine and pressed the button for an Americano. He took it to his office and looked through the windows of the other offices as he went, greeting the officers on duty and the others who were trying to catch up. He sat down at his desk and booted his computer. It took a couple of minutes before the window for his password popped up. He typed in his password and searched for the file on strychnine. He opened up a new file and typed in "Report Interview with Svetlana Shnaider and Thomas Becker, Unterbach, Saturday, 2nd April 2011." It took him an hour and a half to write the report. He finished with the following conclusion:

"There was no sign of any smuggling, no wines from Chateau Malvaux. The said persons have plausible reasons for stopping their exports to Transmir. There is no motive for smuggling dangerous substances, no financial necessity and no obvious threat to themselves or their family. Discarded from the list of suspects."

Max uploaded the file into the central register, sent an email to Volodya Antipov with the basics of his findings in Russian. He then wrote a request for Norbert Mayer, the jeweller in Frankfurt, to be asked to come to their offices on Thursday, seventh April at eleven to help the police with their enquiries. He wanted to confront him the EvoFit picture that he had sent Volodya on Friday. By then he should also have all the reports in from hotels, restaurants, airlines and the like. Who was this man? Had he been to Frankfurt? If so, why did he call himself Thomas Becker?

At exactly ten on Monday morning Inspector Antipov's assistant walked through to his office with the report he had finished off in the early hours of the morning. There were two matches for the EvoFit picture in the sources he had searched. Both looked very similar.

One of the matches was called Nikolay Kiryakov and had worked for the FSB until 2008. Then he just seemed to disappear into thin air. No mention of him killed but then there probably wouldn't be in a file he could access. They would have to request the full file to be sure. Kiryakov was born in 1976 in East Berlin where his father worked for the KGB. He was just 13 years old when the Berlin Wall came down in 1989 and attending an international school. He spoke fluent Russian and German and good English. His father sent him to boarding school in the north of England when it was clear that the family was going to be moved back to Moscow. When he was eighteen he moved to Paris where he spent a year learning the language. He went to the International Business School in Paris, the ESCE, where he did his Master's degree. In his fourth year he spent a semester abroad in the USA. Then he started working for John Deere, the American tractor manufacturer, in Mannheim to support their exports to Russia until 2002. He returned to Moscow at the age of twenty-six where he was officially recruited by the FSB. Presumably his whole education up to that point had been planned by the KGB and the FSK and then by the FSB. In 2008 a new director of the FSB was appointed and soon afterwards Nikolay Kiryakov quit the service, fluent in four languages and by the look of it a professional killer.

The second man was called Andrey Ivanov. Inspector Antipov frowned. That name must be one of the most common names in Russia! So checking his past was like finding a needle in a haystack. He was the owner of a sports shop in a wealthy district of Moscow where land wasn't cheap. And the items he sold weren't cheap either – luxury items for the rich. There didn't seem to be a sleeping partner and there was no note as to where he had the start-up capital. It probably wasn't worth checking as the person behind his company and his activities most probably knew how to cover his tracks. Apparently Andrey Ivanov travelled a lot, on business. He was quite discreet, didn't seek attention in the newspapers or on social media but couldn't always avoid going to social events, presumably organised by his clients, which meant that his photo appeared in some magazine or other. He looked like a more styled version of Nikolay Kiryakov; modern haircut, three-day beard, a handsome face, sun-tanned. Antipov couldn't help wondering if his hands were manicured. And then an interesting report on his last passport entries. He had spent a couple of weeks in Australia trying out new surfing equipment in January and flew to Frankfurt on Sunday, the sixth February. Bingo! He would have had a nice tan after two weeks in Australia at the end of the summer on the beach. In Frankfurt he attended a trade fair for sports equipment. His assistant was checking but no doubt there were hotel receipts, taxis to the fair, entrance tickets. Mr. Ivanov was probably a well-trained deceiver. He had an FSB training and was now active in the upper echelons of Moscow's elite. Vladimir Antipov decided he should meet Mr. Ivanov and told his assistant to make an appointment for Thursday. He wanted to wait for his German colleague's results before going to see this man with a perfect CV – or was it a legend?

*

Inspector Max Baer had just finished his third cup of coffee when his assistant, Paul, walked in with a smile on his face.

"We've got him," Paul said. "Your EvoFit picture was recognised by a young female receptionist at the Steigenberger Hotel. His name is Andrey Ivanov and he stayed over for one night. She described him as handsome, suntanned and very polite. He was also recognised by a concierge at the same hotel who heard the man tell the taxi driver to take him to the trade fair. According to the border police he arrived on Sunday, 6th February coming from Sydney and left the country for Moscow on Monday, 7th February. I've checked the trade fair visitors. Andrey Ivanov was at the fair on Monday, 7th February and his registration card gives the address of a Sports Shop in Moscow and he describes himself as the owner."

Paul handed over the report to Max.

"Any more details of his description?"

"Yes, the receptionist, second paragraph. She said he had lovely blue eyes and she usually guesses the profession of each guest upon arrival. Mr. Ivanov had put businessman on his guest form whereas she had thought he was a musician because he had lovely hands and perfectly manicured nails."

Max looked up and smiled back. "Welcome to our file, Andrey Ivanov." He looked at Paul and added: "I'll give Moscow a ring and see what they can tell us about our imposter."

Max picked up the phone and dialled Vladimir Antipov. After three rings Volodya picked up the phone with a spritely "Allo".

"Hi, Volodya, Max from Wiesbaden here," Max said in Russian. "I have some news for you."

"I'm all ears, Antipov said.

"Your man has been identified as a Mr. Andrey Ivanov, the owner of a Sports Shop in Moscow. I'll mail you the address."

"No need," came the reply. We have the same man at the top of our internet research list. Which hotel did he stay at and when?"

"He checked in to the Steigenberger in Frankfurt on Sunday, 6th February and visited a sports' trade fair on

Monday, 7th. He has blue eyes and manicured hands. He was tanned and had just arrived from Sydney. He left for Moscow the same afternoon."

"Perfect," Antipov exclaimed. "We have a notion about Mr. Andrey Ivanov. He has a perfect CV, is very discreet and travels a lot on business. He set up his business in 2008 and we have no idea where his money came from. At the same time a man called Nikolay Kiryakov who was a specialist at the FSB disappeared without trace." Max nodded as Antipov said specialist, a typical word used for a professional killer. "Mr. Kiryakov has an interesting past, speaks four languages fluently. Apart from Russian he can speak German, French and English, all pretty fluent. German is his second language. His father was a KGB officer in East Berlin when the wall came down. His son, Nikolay, was in Berlin at an international school. The father was ordered back to Moscow and he sent his son, then thirteen, to a boarding school in England. At eighteen the young man moved to Paris where he spent a year learning French and attended the ESCE International Business School there. He graduated from the ESCE with a Master's degree. In his fourth year he spent a semester abroad in the USA and then moved to Mannheim to work for John Deere heading up the export department for Russia. He moved back to Moscow in 2002 at the age of twenty-six where he was officially recruited by the FSB. By the look of his education he was obviously being primed for the KGB by his father or his father's employer. In 2008 he resigned and disappeared."

"When will you be seeing him," Max asked.

"On Thursday morning. We'll observe him for a couple of days and do some detailed research. It won't be easy. This man probably knows all the tricks in the trade and has friends in high places so we have to tread lightly until we know which hornet's nest we're treading on."

"OK," Max said. "I'll send you my report over and if I can have yours with a picture as soon as possible?" Max asked, excited at the prospect of seeing this man's face.

"Sure," Antipov replied. "I'll send you over the picture we have of Kiryakov but I'd appreciate it if you kept that one to yourself and didn't mention where you got it from."

"Will do," Max replied. "Poka!" he said which meant as much as "see you later" and put the phone down with a sigh of relief.

21

It was just before lunch on Tuesday in Sydney when Inspector Clarkson walked into Chief Inspector Green's office with a sizeable report in a folder with Sam MacPherson's name on the cover. Chief Inspector Green waved at the chair in front of his desk and leant back in his swivel chair.

"So what've you got," he said looking at Inspector Clarkson with a questioning look. He'd been in the force for a long time but he still got a buzz out of criminal investigations and Clarkson was one of his best detectives.

"A wasteful production of nux vomica fruit in Queensland," he said. "Our research shows that MacPherson's plantations produce around twelve per cent more nux vomica than they actually sell. The average industrial norm for wastage off plantations of this tree is two per cent. MacPherson only has one client for nux vomica, Long Life, so that would suggest that MacPherson is selling around ten percent on the black market to Long Life. We checked the sales of strychnine at Long Life and compared them to the amounts tested in their own laboratory. The figures don't stack up. There's a difference of nine point five percent which means that unless Pete Owen has a damned good explanation for the missing amounts of strychnine, then he will be charged with selling toxic substances without a valid licence. And Sam MacPherson will be charged with aiding and abetting. Both will be charged, of course, with tax evasion and fraud. These gentlemen are in for a rough time," he added with a smile.

"Next steps?" Chief Inspector Green asked.

"I've got applications in for a warrant. Both will be arrested this afternoon at three before anything leaks to the press. We know where both men will be at that time."

"Good. Let me know as soon as you've interviewed both men this afternoon and keep me posted on your progress. We have some influential on-lookers on this case and I don't want any pressure from above."

"Right you are, sir," Clarkson said, stood up and turned to go out.

"You'd better get a press conference set up for tomorrow morning at ten. When the shit hits the fan we need to be armed and sure of our facts."

"Yes sir," Clarkson said and walked out of the office. Chief Inspector Green looked out of the window. His thoughts were on the newspaper stories and another scandal in the business world of New South Wales which they could have done without.

*

Boris Makaryan looked out of the window on this sunny afternoon in Valletta. He had eaten an early lunch on the balcony before leaving for the ferry to Malta. Maria had made all his favourite dishes and a lemon cake with icing and "come back soon" written on top. He smiled. He loved the people here. They didn't worry about who he was, where he came from and how he earned so much money. They just saw the man who treated his employees well and employed someone in almost every family in the village to do something. And he felt at home here. He could actually get some rest and found as much peace of mind as he would ever find. The few days he had spent on Gozo with its clean, warm air without the hectic life he led in Moscow had given him renewed strength. He missed his family, he missed his wife, but he had to admit, the break had been worthwhile. The drive to Mġarr to the ferry terminal had been uneventful. He looked out onto the fields of barley, ready to be harvested. He knew the island would see no more rain until October and only the fig cactus plants and Mediterranean shrubs would survive the arid summer. A pity, he thought. With adequate water supplies you could probably produce crops twice a year. But then, he mused, that really wouldn't be in keeping with traditions and the island's mentality and who wants to work in that kind of heat anyway? When they reached the ferry terminal, their driver was told to go straight to the toll booth and then get the car parked in line for the one o'clock ferry. Boris liked the idea that you only paid on your way back to Malta for both journeys as there wasn't any other way you could get your car back to the main island. Simple and pragmatic. They parked the car in the third lane as indicated by the ferry worker. He would let them on first so that the driver could park in their normal spot and Davit and Erik could accompany Mr. Boris up the stairs before the rest of the passangers came on board. He felt a pang of sadness as he watched the island of Comino disappear to his left. The harbour at Cirkewwa didn't feel as welcoming. He was gradually being pulled back into his world of money, mafia and might, the three "m's" which Moscow stood for. It took them fifty minutes along the coast road to reach the airport of Valletta officially known as Malta International Airport. The high season for the millions of tourists who swamped Malta in summer wasn't yet in full swing so the airport was relatively quiet. He had said goodbye to his driver and given him a little present for his wife and some medication for his sick child. The driver had bowed his head slightly and thanked him profusely. Boris was deep in thought when Davit came over.

"We're boarding, boss," he said. Boris nodded. He took a last sip of his cool beer, grabbed his hand luggage and followed Davit to the gate. Erik came to join them and walked behind Boris. Once on board he settled into his seat and closed his eyes. He would try and rest for the short flight to Frankfurt.

*

Sam was working from home. It was three in the afternoon and he stood on the deck with a mug of tea in his hand looking out over the sea. The sun's rays were playing on the ocean. There was quite a gusty wind but it was still pleasantly warm for April, around twenty degrees. How he loved this view. He loved the sea even more. He could be out there on Billy Jo feeling the waves under her keel and the wind in his face. The wind would blow away his worries and the pure excitement of being at sea in rough weather would give him the adrenalin he needed to keep going. The doorbell rang and pulled him back out of his daydream into reality. Sam frowned. Karen had gone into the bedroom to change. He wasn't expecting anyone. The doorbell rang again. He went into the hall and peered through the peephole in the door. There were two uniformed policemen in the corridor. A wave of panic rose through his body and his breathing just stopped as shock took over. He closed his eyes and then took a deep breath. He opened the door with a smile and said:

"Good afternoon, gentlemen. What can I do for you?"

The taller of the two policemen asked if they could come in and Sam ushered them into the lounge. They didn't sit down. His heart was racing. Surely not, he thought. Surely they hadn't found the loophole in his company records and he had destroyed the handwritten evidence of his business on the side with Long Life which he kept in his safe in his home office. Surely not.

"Mr. MacPherson," the policemen said for the second time, this time raising his voice a little. Sam blinked and looked at him. "Mr. MacPherson, you are under arrest. You have the right to remain silent. Should you, however refuse this right, anything you say can and will be used against you in a court of law. You have the right to an attorney. If you cannot afford an attorney, one will be provided to you by the court.

Do you understand what I have just said to you?"

"Yes, yes," Sam mumbled. He felt as if the room was spinning and time had slowed down as if he were in space. Then a short female gasp made them all turn round to see Karen in the doorway. She dropped the pile of magazines she was carrying and just stared at Sam. Seeing Karen shook him out of his initial shock and he took a step towards his wife. One of the policemen moved to bar his way.

"I'm sorry, sir," he said implying that there was now to be no contact. "Your wife can accompany us if she wishes."

"No, no," Karen blurted out. "No thank you," came the more composed reply. I'll stay here and get hold of Frank for you Sam." Then the tears started rolling down her cheeks. She didn't want to kiss Sam goodbye. She wanted to hug him, tell him everything would be alright but she thought that her emotions might be interpreted as a sign of guilt. She turned to Sam.

"This must all be some kind of terrible mistake. I'm sure Frank will sort everything out." She forced a smile.

"Thanks honey. Just get hold of Frank as soon as you can." Karen nodded. The tall policeman moved towards the door followed by Sam and the second policeman who held Sam by the arm. The tall policeman turned round and said to his colleague: "No need for handcuffs." He nodded to Sam who nodded back. He wasn't about to run off. There was nowhere to run to. He bowed his head and walked out of the flat knowing in his heart that he wouldn't be enjoying the view from the balcony for a long time to come.

The police car drove up to Pete Owen's house just as Pete picked up his phone to dial one of his customers. The two uniformed policemen got out of the car and approached the front door. Pete's heart sank. He closed his eyes for a moment and put down his phone. The doorbell rang. He walked into the hall and opened the door.

"Mr. Owen, Mr. Peter Owen," the elder of the two policemen said.

"Yes, I'm Pete Owen," he said. "What can I do for you?"

"Mr. Owen, you are under arrest. You have the right to remain silent. Should you, however refuse this right, anything you say can and will be used against you in a court of law. You have the right to an attorney. If you cannot afford an attorney, one will be provided to you by the court.

Do you understand what I have just said to you?"

Pete nodded. He was dumbstruck. He was under arrest. The unthinkable had happened. This was it.

"May I call my attorney?" he asked. The policeman nodded and Pete let them both in. They followed him into his office and Pete picked up his phone. He rang Doug Parker. His secretary, Helen, answered the phone.

"Hi, Helen, it's Pete Owen."

"Hi, Pete. How're you doing?" came the friendly reply.

"Helen, I'm under arrest. Could you please get hold of Doug immediately and ask him to meet me at…" he turned to the policemen. One of them said "HQ in Parramatta:"

"Did you get that, Helen," Pete asked, "HQ in Parramatta."

"He's with a client but I'll pull him out of his meeting immediately, Pete."

"Thanks Helen."

Pete put the phone down and held out his arms expecting them to handcuff him.

"I don't think we need handcuffs, sir," the elder policeman said. "Bates here will accompany you."

The second policeman put his hand on Pete's arm and they all walked out of the front door to the police car. Pete forced himself to look back at the house. So this is what it feels like, he thought, when your whole life is suddenly ripped apart. He bent his head and got into the back seat of the car between the two policemen. What a good job Jean was out shopping, he thought. Then his mind went a complete blank and a feeling of, yes, almost relief mixed with fear seeped through his body. So this was it.

*

It was just after seven in the evening when the Air Malta plane landed at Frankfurt. Boris walked swiftly through the Schengen entrance towards the exit. He only had hand luggage which Erik was carrying. Davit was in front of him checking faces and hands as they walked up through the mass of people waiting at the exit for friends and relatives. They went up the escalator to the departures level. They reached the glass doors and walked out on to the street which ran past the terminal to set passengers down. Their car was waiting just outside A. Erik could see the car, a black Mercedes. When he reached the car he opened the rear nearside door to let his boss take his seat and got into the car in front of him in the passenger seat next to the driver. The driver turned and said in Russian:

"Dobriy Den, good afternoon, I hope you had a pleasant flight?"

"Yes, thank you," Davit replied. "Do you have a parcel for me?"

"Yes, there are two parcels in the glove compartment." Davit took out two envelopes and gave one to Erik.

Davit took the pistol out of the envelope and the ammunition. The pistol was a semi-automatic Grand Power K100, not his favourite, a little heavy for his liking. He felt the weight in his right hand, more than 700 g. He took out the box of 9 mm Parabellum cartridges and took the magazine out of the pistol and expertly loaded it with seventeen rounds. He checked the lock and put it into a universal holster which fitted most 9 mm guns and was attached to the belt on his trousers. It concealed the weapon and was quite comfortable to wear. He put the remaining cartridges into two Smith and Weston cowhide cartridge carriers and place one in each pocket of his suit jacket. He wasn't expecting trouble but he had learnt the hard way: *Amat victoria curam*, victory favours those who are prepared. Davit looked out of the window. They were on the main road leading to the city centre passing between Niederrad with its modern, high-rise office buildings and Sachsenhausen which was a bit like a village within a city. He admired the architecture of the modern buildings to his left, mainly housing computer firms and service companies. The houses on his right were mainly older buildings with three or four stories and flats where people lived. He could see plants and curtains at the windows, people on the streets with shopping baskets on their way home. The streets were clean, the rows of cars parked in an orderly fashion. He smiled. He liked coming to Germany and had been here often. He took the permit to carry a weapon out of the envelope and studied it carefully. It showed his photo, his name and the name and address of a security firm in Berlin. German gun legislation was probably the toughest in the world. He smiled – the permit was most probably forged but would allow him to get out of difficult situations and give him time to disappear. He put the permit into his wallet and turned to the driver.

"How long will it take us to reach the hotel?" he asked the driver.

"We'll be there in ten minutes," he said. Davit leant back in his seat. They crossed the river Main and the driver took a sharp right. It was almost eight in the evening and the rush hour traffic had died down. When they reached the hotel, Davit jumped out and opened the rear door to let his boss out, observing the hotel entrance and street as he did so. Erik got out and turned a complete circle surveying the whole area. Davit walked into the hotel with Boris behind him, Erik following at the rear. The porter grabbed the hand luggage and followed. There was a man sitting in a leather chair reading a newspaper. He didn't look up. They checked in and Boris turned to Davit:

"Book me that really good restaurant round the corner, the Villa Ilona, for eight thirty. I feel like a really good meal and then going out on the town."

"Will do," Davit said. He knew what that meant. They probably wouldn't get to bed until the early hours. Davit turned to the receptionist and she had already found the Michelin star restaurant on her screen when she heard its name but she didn't want to let on that she was listening in to a guest's conversation.

"Can you please book as a table for eight thirty at the Villa Ilona and give me the address."

"Of course, sir. Here is the address," she said giving him a print out from the website. "Weissadler Street number 23. It's about a five minute walk. Here's the post code for your navigation app," she added looking at his phone. Davit smiled.

"Thank you," he added and took the address.

The concierge led the way to the lift. The doors of the lift closed and the man with the newspaper watched the numbers of the floors light up. He then went to the desk and flashed his ID card.

"Kripo Wiesbaden," he said. "Could you print out the details of your new guests please?" The young receptionist studied his ID card and then printed out the details. There were three sheets, three names. When he saw the name of Boris Makaryan he thanked the receptionist, turned on his heels and went outside. He took out his mobile and rang the office.

"Paul here," he said. "You'll never guess who just checked into the Frankfurter Hof? Boris Makaryan, the deceased's brother." The voice on the other end told him to get back to base.

"Will do," the detective said and walked towards the car park. What a coincidence, he thought. The deceased's brother is staying at the same hotel as Andrey Ivanov.

*

Sam MacPherson and his legal counsel Frank Moss walked out of the judge's office at the back of the Sydney Courthouse at around six in the early evening. Sam breathed in the cool evening air. Free, he thought, or at least for a while. It had taken some time for his application for bail to be approved. The district attorney had asked for eight hundred thousand dollars but the judge had agreed to reduce this to five hundred thousand dollars which Sam didn't have either. Frank had arranged for an assistant to go to Sam's bank and pick up a bank guarantee. Fortunately he already had a standing guarantee covered by the deeds to his penthouse which wasn't mortgaged, thank goodness, and worth a fortune. His parents had left him their splendid home overlooking Sydney harbour in their will. They had both been killed in a plane crash when he was just a young man. He had inherited their fortune and their home. It hadn't taken him long to spend a lot of their money and turn some of the funds and shares into cash. But he had never had to mortgage the penthouse. It was probably worth a couple of million so it would certainly cover his bail. It was the only real asset he had and with a failing business, half of his herd of horses decimated by the floods just months ago, he may well need the deeds to cover a big loan from the bank to keep his business going. He had hoped to avoid having to go down that route but now, with charges against him which could put him in prison and at the very least earn him a suspended sentence , there was no way that Tom Wyatt was going to touch his business. Tom liked to be seen as the honest businessman, Mr. Clean, the one who made it and got to the top thanks to his own business acumen, hard work and cunning. He liked to be seen as a philanthropic top manager giving money, happiness and security through his wife's charities to people less fortunate than himself. There was no way that he would go near a company that was caught up in a scandal. And a scandal it was. Sam had had plenty of time to think about it while he was waiting to see the judge, locked up like a common criminal. He and Frank hadn't yet had an opportunity to draw up a plan but in the next few weeks he would have to decide how to play his part. And a lot depended on Pete Owen.

"Come on," Frank said. "I'll drive you home."

"Thanks. Do you know where Pete is?" Sam asked.

"Sam, I talked to Chief Inspector Green while we were waiting for bail. It seems that Pete has done a deal, a milder sentence for full information on the distribution channels for the strychnine on the black market."

Sam stopped in his tracks, his mouth half open and gasped. He looked at Frank.

"So they know I was selling him nux vomica on the side?" he asked. They started walking again to the car park, side by side. Sam looked straight ahead, the tension written in his face.

"Yes, Sam. They know everything. They found the discrepancies in weight between your production and your sales which gave them enough evidence to arrest you and Pete and put the fear of God into both of you. Then they found discrepancies in Pete's lab reports when compared to the sales of the same batch of strychnine. There was no way out for Pete and you are his only supplier of nux vomica. By confessing he has only confirmed what the district attorney knows anyway and maybe we can attain a milder sentence through cooperation."

They reached Sam's car. So this really was it. Everything he and Karen had, their whole life, was built on the money they had and the status that money and his business gave them in society. And now it was all going to disappear. He felt like running away but he had been forced to surrender his passport. He could probably get a false one and leave the country but he just couldn't do that to Karen and Laura. And he couldn't face the thought of looking over his shoulder for the rest of his life, panicking every time the door opened in case it was the police. No. He would have to stay and face the music, keep calm, a cool head. Remember. He was the born survivor.

"Yes, I'm sure you're right," Sam replied in an almost depressed voice and got into the passenger seat.

"Sam, give yourself a few days with Karen to sit down

and think things through. Let's meet on Saturday morning at my club. I'll get us a private room. We won't be disturbed and we can spend a few hours going through your defence. I'll need some financial figures to help your plea. We'll need to show that society has more from you being out of prison than inside. How many people do you employ, how many families are dependent on your business up at Hawkes Lift, what does your company mean to the town, the donations you made to the town after the floods, help you've given to local families, newspaper articles – I'll need the whole lot and we probably only have about three weeks before the case will be heard."

"I'll speak to Tom up at the plantation offices tomorrow. We have an employee, Jennifer White, who has made a hobby of keeping just about every single newspaper cutting about the company, about my father, about me, our family. I'm sure she'll lend us her scrap books."

"Good. And go through your financial affairs from both angles. What happens if you went to prison and what affect would it have on your family and your employees' families. Can you keep the business going if you were allowed to be there, even if you could no longer officially run the company? Could you sell the business? We need to prove that you being inside the company is of greater worth to everyone, you, your family, your employees' families, to business in Queensland and to the state who earns income tax."

"OK," said Sam. "I'll get it all down on paper, no-holds-barred, everything, however painful. " He looked at Frank.

"I want to survive this, Frank, with my wife and daughter. I want her to still be able to look up to me."

Frank turned round and squeezed his arm.

"That's the Sam MacPherson I know," he said and smiled.

*

Tuesday night in Frankfurt wasn't the busiest of nights but for a restaurant like Villa Ilona there never was a quiet evening. The restaurant was full of mirrors and Doric columns, green plants and finely granulated plaster on the walls with a touch of terracotta, just a hint of colour. The Italian and German waiters were dressed in white shirts, black waistcoats and trousers with long white aprons which almost touched the floor. The head waiter and sommelier wore black evening suits with bow ties. The restaurant manager was wearing the same black evening suit but with a discreet designer tie. When the hotel had asked for a table for some important Russian guests Giovanni, the restaurant manager, had asked his staff to set up an extra table for three. He showed them how to rearrange the tables so that the three gentlemen would be in an alcove, a little separate from the rest. His experience of wealthy Russian businessmen was such that he knew they needed to be a little bit apart, for the sake of his other international and German guests. He had welcomed Boris, Davit and Erik with a polished smile and a slight bow of the head which said "We are at your service". He showed them to their table. A waiter accompanied him and took the folded serviettes and placed them gently on each gentleman's lap.

"May we offer you a glass of champagne while you are looking at your menus?" Giovanni asked. All three nodded and Giovanni looked at the waiter and nodded almost imperceptibly with his head. He then walked away from the table to his station near the entrance. The menus were in German, English, Italian and Russian which said a lot about the wealthy tourists arriving in Frankfurt. Three glasses of champagne arrived and Boris raised his glass to speak.

"I owe this visit to my brother. Let's drink to his memory. To Armen," he said and took a large sip from his glass. The others repeated "To Armen!" and did the same. They closed their menus. The head waiter came to their table in a matter of seconds followed by the sommelier. They ordered their meals and one of the best Bordeaux wines in the restaurant. The sommelier didn't even blink an eyelid. He just said:

"A very good choice, sir." Boris looked at Davit and Davit translated the remark. Boris nodded at the sommelier. For a five digit price in Euros it had better be a good choice, he thought and turned his attention back to his champagne. All three were sitting with their backs to the wall facing the restaurant and the door. Davit looked at Erik and moved his head towards the bar. Erik knew what that meant. He was to check the bar, kitchen, fire exit and finally the restrooms. You couldn't be too careful. Erik put his serviette next to his plate, stood up and excused himself. Boris launched into a story about his brother and Davit listened intently, laughing in all the right places, but with his eyes peeled on the other tables and the front door.

It was a long meal and the wine was so good that Boris ordered a second bottle. Davit and Erik had sat with a small amount of wine in their glasses but didn't actually touch it. After all, they were on duty and had to keep alert. After an excellent desert Boris needed a shot of vodka. He only ordered one. He knew that his bodyguards wouldn't drink it. Davit had ordered a bullet-proof limousine from a security car service for eleven in the evening for the rest of the night. It would be waiting outside. He stood up, excused himself and went outside to check. The black Mercedes ML500 was waiting to the right of the restaurant. He looked at the car and realised it was the same model that Armen used to have. He hoped that his boss didn't mind. Still, it was a good car and it was easy to make it totally secure so probably not a bad idea after all. Boris was paying the bill when Davit got back to the table. He was paying cash and Davit felt several pairs of eyes watching this little scene. He left a very generous tip and the restaurant manager thanked him, wished him a pleasant stay in Frankfurt and hoped to see him again.

Frankfurt was just beginning to liven up as the black Mercedes ML500 drew up outside a night club called "The Fig Cactus" in Sachsenhausen. Davit and Erik got out and looked around. Davit went up to the man on the door and spoke Russian to him. He wasn't a doorman. He seemed to have been waiting for Davit, Boris thought. Maybe he's the manager. Davit gave the man at the door a wad of money and went back to the car. Boris got out and they walked into the night club with the Russian in front of them, followed by Davit, Erik bringing up the rear. The night club was crowded but as the Russian approached the guests moved back without being asked and let the new arrivals through. They were seated at the back of the night club near the fire exit. There was a table for six or eight people. The Russian spoke briefly to Boris, wished them a pleasant evening and went over to the bar where three young women were waiting. He told them to grab a bottle of Russian Standard vodka on ice, six glasses and make bloody well sure that Mr. Boris had the night of a lifetime. All three moved their well-shaped bodies off the bar stools and winked at the bar-keeper who had overhead their instructions and was already getting the glasses ready. They straightened their tight dresses and glanced in the mirror to see that their hair and make-up were immaculate. One of them grabbed the ice bucket, another one grabbed the bottle and the third one the silver tray with six glasses, all with an air of routine that betrayed their experience. They walked up to the table and put the ice-bucket on the table, the vodka bottle neck down in the ice and gently placed a glass in front of each of the guests.

"Good evening, gentlemen," the one with the ice-bucket said in Russian. "I'm Lilly. This is my friend Alesha and her friend Lara. Where would you like us to sit?"

Boris looked at Lilly and decided she should sit next to him. He told Lara to sit next to Erik and Alesha next to Davit. The ladies did what they were told. Davit moved his glass to the right for Alesha. Erik did the same for Lara and Boris took another glass from the silver tray for Lilly. The girls didn't say anything apart from thank you. They were used to rich Russian businessmen with their bodyguards and the latter never drank alcohol. Lilly summoned over the waiter and said to him in German. "Keep your eye on this table, Freddy. If there's anything the gentlemen want, you make sure it's done straight away. If you've got any questions, ask the boss." Freddy nodded. He knew the routine as well. Be attentive, be discreet, be pleasant whatever happened and he'd have a tip that was equivalent to half the amount most men of his age earnt in a month. And no tax to pay on it either. Freddy filled their glasses with vodka and waited nearby, watching the table out of the corner of his eye.

"So Lilly," said Boris, putting his hand on her knee. "Tell me what you like doing best."

Lilly moved her head closer to his and whispered something in his ear. Boris laughed, picked up his glass and held it up to toast the three ladies: "Na zdorovya!" They all replied with "Na zdorovya!" and drank the glass of vodka in one go. "Pey do dna" Alesha said and looked at Davit and smiled.

*

After spending a night in investigative custody Pete was brought to an interrogation room at ten in the morning where Doug Parker, his legal counsel, and Inspector Clarkson were waiting for him.

"Good morning," Pete said and sat down next to Doug. He looked drawn and obviously hadn't slept much. Inspector Clarkson opened a folder in front of him and cleared his throat.

"The customs in Lithuania and the police in Germany have found some strychnine that appears to have been imported into Germany by a jeweller. His name is Norbert Mayer. Does that name ring a bell, Mr. Owen?"

"Yes, he is one of my regular customers for relatively small amounts. I send it to him by DHL in jewellery boxes made in Australia." Inspector Clarkson showed him a picture of Norbert Mayer. Pete nodded.

"Yes, that's him. We met in Sydney when he was out here on holiday, or so he said."

"It would appear that someone bought strychnine from Mr. Mayer and intended to smuggle it into Russia underneath the driver's seat of a truck going to Moscow. It was found by the Lithuanian customs."

"Inspector, my client may have committed an offence by sending strychnine to Germany without declaring it but he cannot be held responsible for what happened to this toxic substance once it reached its destination."

"I just need some answers to questions which the Germans are investigating," he said. "The trouble is we're not talking about smuggling here but murder."

"Murder," Pete exclaimed. "What do you mean?"

"The strychnine that was sent to Russia didn't get there this time but it would appear that this may have been the second small consignment and the first was taken to Moscow by someone else who intended to use it to kill someone."

"Bloody hell," said Pete, "you're not serious, are you?"

"I'm afraid so, sir. The man in question, according to the German Kripo, responsible for criminal investigation, and the elite division of the Russian FSB investigating organised crime, have come up with the same person. And now the question is, have you ever met him?" Inspector Clarkson put a picture of Andrey Ivanov in front of Pete Owen. Pete was literally speechless and went quite pale.

"So you know the man," Inspector Clarkson pursued.

"I've seen him before. I met him in a bar in Sydney."

"When was that, sir?" Inspector Clarkson asked.

"My goodness, it would have been early February. Jeannie and I had had a row about an incident on Australia Day. I probably had drunk too much. I was angry and upset."

"Did you speak to the man first or did he approach you."

"Heavens, I was drunk. I think he approached me. He was interested in small planes and we chatted for quite some time. He asked me what I did which made me fly to Queensland so often. I explained the nature of my business and we got talking about strychnine. He said he had a friend in Germany who had an enormous mouse problem on his farm and it was impossible for him to get enough strychnine on the black market to kill them off."

"So you gave him the address of Norbert Mayer?"

"I told him that one of my dealers also had a jeweller's shop in Frankfurt on the Zeil. I probably mentioned his name, I don't remember. I was drunk. But I remembered the address because I've always thought it was a strange name."

"Did the man in the bar tell you his name?"

"Probably but I don't remember."

"And you're sure this is him?"

"Yes, he had a very memorable face, a bit like that French film star, the one who worked for the Russians. And I remember thinking that his hands and fingernails were those of a musician, not of a farmer, so I can't have been all that drunk. But that's all I remember."

"Was this man Australian?"

"No way. His English was very good but he wasn't a limey either. Nor a Yank. He could have been German or even Russian. I really don't know. I just remember his face and his hands."

"His name is Andrey Ivanov. Does that ring a bell?"

"No, can't say it does. And what does he do?"

"He owns a sports shop in Moscow. He may also be a mechanic."

Pete laughed. "With those hands, no way!"

"I mean a professional killer, Mr. Owen, as in the new film coming out this week. We don't use the term ourselves. It's just a movie."

Pete was silent.

"So I talked to a professional killer in a bar in Sydney and this man used my information to kill someone, is that what you're saying?"

"As I said, the case is currently under investigation and

you are an eye witness.

Doug Parker intervened.

"So why is the Russian FSB involved if they are organised crime specialists?"

Inspector Parker produced another photo, this time of a corpulent man with deep set eyes and a pronounced nose. "Do you know this man?" the inspector asked Pete.

"No, never seen him before."

"Sure?"

"Absolutely," Pete said. "Who is he?"

"His name is Armen Makaryan. He's dead," Inspector Clarkson said. "He was the head of an organisation in Moscow which deals in organised crime. Officially he was a businessman with interests in a whole range of companies and had very good political contacts."

"And how did he die?" Pete asked, suspecting the answer.

"He was murdered. It's believed that he was administered a lethal dose of strychnine in a glass of wine."

"Jesus," Pete said.

"Mr. Owen, you meeting this man, Andrey Ivanov, in a bar wasn't a coincidence. Nothing in this man's life is just coincidence. I'll need you to be at our disposition for further questioning if necessary." Pete nodded.

"Inspector, my client has been here since yesterday afternoon. He's cooperated in every way and the judge has granted bail on condition that he doesn't leave his house. It's time he was released and allowed to go home."

Pete was finally released at eleven thirty. He wasn't able

to walk out as if he were a free man like Sam had done the evening before. The judge wasn't prepared to go that far. After he had managed to get the bank to set up a bank guarantee, having transferred the deeds for his house, cars, life insurance and stocks to the bank, Pete was released into pre-trial custody at home. He could live at home but he couldn't leave his house. Better than living in a state prison, he thought as he walked to the police car with two policemen to accompany him. His passport had been taken and Doug Parker, his legal counsel, had done a deal with the district attorney to achieve a milder sentence for his client due to his cooperation with the police investigations concerning strychnine on the black market in Australia and apparently now in Europe too. He would be found guilty of offences he was being charged with but Doug was hopeful that the prison sentence would be suspended on probation. Doug was waiting for him near the police car. He took his arm and escorted him to the rear passenger door. He shook his hand and said:

"Try and get some sleep, Pete. The problems won't go away but we'll have a better chance if you're on your usual ingenuous form," he said with a smile.

"I'll do my best, Doug. I'm exhausted, absolutely drained."

"I'll come and see you tomorrow and we can talk everything through."

"OK," Pete said, "and Doug, thank you, thank you for everything." Pete got in the car between two policemen and the car drove off. Doug shook his head and walked to the car park. What a mess, he thought, what a mess!

*

Boris was having a late breakfast in his room. The trolley next to his table had just about everything you could wish to eat for breakfast. He had a hearty appetite and after the night's escapades he needed the right kind of foods to boost his energy. The girl had been good. She knew exactly how to press all the right buttons at the right time. He smiled and tucked into a large omelette with cheese and ham when Davit knocked on the door to his room. The suite had two bedrooms and Davit had slept in the second one. Erik was a little further down the hall. It was ten thirty and they planned to leave for Unterbach at eleven. Boris wanted to get to Svetlana's house at around noon when they would be home for lunch.

"It's ten thirty, boss. I've ordered the car for eleven."

"OK," Boris said with his mouth full and nodded.

Davit was carrying his holdall and put it next to the door. He packed the holdall next to the bed with Boris' clothes and most of the toiletries in the bathroom. He left the toothbrush and toothpaste on the shelf next to the washbasin. He knew his boss' habits and he knew how to keep him happy. Davit had been downstairs for breakfast with Erik. At five minutes to eleven Erik rang the bell to Boris' suite. Davit let him in. Erik had his holdall over this shoulder.

"Dobroye utro, good morning," Erik said politely and Boris looked at him through the mirror and replied "Dobroye utro." Erik closed the holdall and picked it up. Boris had thrown the rest of his toiletries into the holdall and was adjusting his tie in front of the mirror. The bell rang. "Get it, would you Erik," Davit said. "It should be the porter for the luggage."

Erik looked through the peephole and opened the door.

"Good morning, sir," the porter said. "How many pieces?"

"Just three," Erik replied and put them on the porter's trolley. The porter disappeared as silently as he had come, pushing the trolley to the service lift. Erik checked the corridor and nodded to Davit.

Davit helped his boss into his jacket. Boris turned and said "Poyem, let's go!"

Erik was waiting in the corridor. Davit walked out first and turned left towards the lift with Boris behind him. Erik shut the door and brought up the rear. They took the lift to the ground floor in silence. Davit had already paid the bill with two hundred Euro bills. A whole wad of them. The air was cool and it smelt of rain. The black Mercedes they had used yesterday had been cleaned and was waiting outside the main door. The three of them walked to the car, Davit and Erik keeping their eyes on their surroundings and the car. Davit opened the rear door and Boris got in. Davit shut the door and walked round to the front passenger seat. Erik was already sitting in the back next to Boris. The driver had been given the address they were going to and after a short exchange of "good mornings" they were on their way. They were silent during the journey. You could feel the tension mounting. Boris was thinking about his poor brother. He would soon know if this woman and her German lover had anything to do with his brother's death. There wasn't much traffic on the motorway and the car sped down the outside lane. This part of the A60 didn't have any speed restrictions. That's another thing Davit liked about Germany; their cars and motorways where you could actually drive at over two hundred kilometres an hour. Davit looked out of the window. He couldn't see the Rhine but he knew it was there. He could see the steep vineyards on the other side of the river and the curious statue on top of the hill. He thought it looked a bit like the statue of liberty. The driver slowed down at the junction to the A61. They drove down the A61 for just a few miles and then turned off towards Bad Kreuznach. They drove through the outskirts of the spa town and then drove towards Kusel. There were vineyards right and left. Then the vineyards disappeared as they reached the high plateau between the two valleys. There were arable crops on both sides of the road and a forest behind the fields. On the plateau there were windmills being built as far as the eye could see. The wind parks on the German hills and at sea would soon be generating electricity for Germany's industry and twenty million households. He was impressed at the amount of renewable energy this hi-tech country was planning to produce. In Russia renewable energy wasn't a topic at all and probably wouldn't be as long as they had reserves of gas and oil to sell. The car drove down the winding road into the Alsenz valley. It was a sleepy valley with vineyards on steep hills and a green forest with beech and oak trees. Some parts had been reforested with fir trees for quick growing wood, another form of renewable energy that Germany used. He loved the smell of wood fires. It reminded him of his grandmother's dacha out in the countryside. Signs warned them of wild animals crossing the road. Davit could imagine that the wild boar had plenty to eat in a forest with oak and beech trees. The road by-passed most of the villages and five minutes went by before the driver turned off the road towards Unterbach. They drove into the village observing the speed limit. The village was small, probably only a hundred houses or so. Most of them lined the main road. They reached the house with the cobble-stone yard and large iron gates. The gates were open and the driver drove into the yard and stopped behind a parked blue Ford Ranger. Erik and Davit got out and Davit opened the door for Boris. The house was made out of sandstone, probably a hundred and fifty years old or thereabouts, Boris thought. The windows were new. The doors were made out of expensive oak. Someone had spent a lot of money on this house and took a lot of care with its upkeep. Boris nodded to Davit and they walked up to the front door. As they approached the door it opened and Davit and Erik automatically moved their right hand towards the holster on their belt. The man in the doorway was unarmed and had a friendly smile on his face. He was holding a dog by his collar in his left hand. The dog barked twice, loudly. It looked like a mixture between a German shepherd and a Labrador. The man said "OK, boy," and the dog relaxed. Blackie, Thomas' dog, had heard the car drive into the yard and had barked. Thomas stopped chatting to Svetlana and looked out of the kitchen window. No-one in the village drove a Mercedes like this one and in fact no-one he knew drove one. It was an expensive car. When he saw Davit and Erik get out the car and look around, his instinct told him that this wasn't just a normal visit. The third man was dressed in an expensive suit and seemed to be important. Thomas grabbed his smartphone and activated the voice recorder. He put it in his pocket with the visiting card Inspector Baer had left. Svetlana had pinned it to the cork board in the kitchen just in case. Thomas looked at the dog and said, "Come on, Blackie." Svetlana looked out the window and stopped stirring the soup on the stove. She looked concerned, almost frightened when she saw the faces of the men outside. She waited and listened to what was being said at the door.

"Kann ich Ihnen helfen?" Thomas said with a smile. The man who had first got out the car spoke first: "In English, please." His accent was definitely Russian.

"Can I help you?" Thomas repeated in English.

"We want to see Svetlana Shnaider. Is she at home?" Davit asked.

"Yes. And who are you?" Thomas asked, looking in particular at the third gentleman in the expensive suit.

"This is Mister Boris Makaryan," Davit said. "He is the brother of Mister Armen Makaryan. You know Armen Makaryan?"

"Yes, he is a customer of ours."

"He is dead."

"Yes, I have heard," Thomas said. He looked at Boris and said "I am very sorry to hear about your brother. Armen was a trusted business partner." Davit translated his words into Russian.

"Spasibo, thank you," Boris said, his face expressionless. "May we come in?"

"Of course," Thomas said. "Follow me. Svetlana is in the kitchen." Erik took out a packet of cigarettes and indicated that he would stay outside to smoke.

Svetlana had turned the stove off and taken off her apron. She smoothed her blouse with both hands and took a deep breath.

Davit walked in first, then Boris. Yes, she thought. You can see the likeness. She automatically changed over to Russian.

"Welcome," she said. "Please sit down." She pointed to the chairs around the table. Her boys wouldn't be home until around half past one when the school bus brought them into the village. Thomas sat next to Svetlana. "I was very distressed to hear about Armen's death," she said and Boris nodded and got straight to the point.

"My brother was poisoned. He was poisoned with strychnine which was administered when he drunk some wine which you had sold him." Svetlana translated for Thomas into German.

"We only sold cheap wine to Armen's company. I can't believe he would drink that at home," she said.

"No, of course not. But you also sold him some Bordeaux wine. I saw the bottles in his cellar. They didn't have an address on them but they came from Vodalko. So I presume that you were sending this wine to Armen as a personal favour."

Svetlana turned to Thomas and translated. Thomas said: "Tell him we did many personal favours for Armen. He was a good client and a respected friend. Why does his brother think that we poisoned him?" Svetlana translated what Thomas had said. Boris continued.

"Not only was the wine bottle and glass found next to his dead body, I know that the police have investigated some smuggling of strychnine in one of your trucks and a man in Frankfurt says that you bought strychnine from him." Svetlana translated slowly to give Thomas time to think. How on earth does he know all this, Thomas thought. He must have access to the police files somewhere. This man is really dangerous. Thomas looked at him while he spoke to Svetlana in German. He asked her to translate each sentence so he could watch the reaction his answers gave.

"I have never ever bought any strychnine," he said. "I wouldn't know where to buy it. The police told me about the truck with strychnine. It was found under the driver's seat. I don't know the driver. I have never met him and I didn't give him any strychnine."

"But you did have a reason to kill my brother," Boris said, looking at Svetlana. She answered without translating into German.

"Why would I want to kill Armen? He was a good customer, he paid us everything he owed, he paid punctually."

"And he must have paid you a lot of money when I consider the apartment you have in Moscow," Boris said.

"I did quite a bit of work for Armen before I actually met Thomas. We were quite close then."

"I see," Boris said. Thomas looked at Svetlana who shook her head slightly as if to say "don't ask!"

"When did you last see him?" Boris asked.

"In March. We had dinner together at Nostalgie."

"Was it a nice evening?" Boris asked. "What did you talk about?"

"It was a little tense," Svetlana replied knowing that Boris had probably already asked the manager at the restaurant. His questions were far too pointed.

"I told Armen that Thomas and I had decided not to send any more wine to Russia. Armen was disappointed. The risks involved particularly with the introduction of tax stamps are now too great and our family responsibilities have to come first." Svetlana was clever. She knew that mentioning her family as the reason would be something no Armenian could argue with. She had learnt a lot from her dealings with Armen.

"I see," Boris said. "I will find out who is responsible for my brother's death and that person will pay. Anybody who has helped that person will pay. And I won't rest until my brother's murderers are in hell!" His expression was one of pure determination which would have put the fear of God into anyone listening. Svetlana translated for Thomas. She tried to calm her feelings by concentrating on the translation, as if it were a report and had nothing to do with her. Thomas got up.

"I am not used to being threatened, particularly not in my own house." Svetlana touched his arm.

"If you have done nothing, then there is no threat," Boris said and stood up.

"I will stay in Frankfurt for a few days until I know exactly who has done this dreadful deed." He nodded at both Svetlana and Thomas but didn't bother to say goodbye. He was in no mood for small talk. He walked to the door and let himself out. Thomas put his arm around Svetlana and they watched these men get into the car and drive away. Svetlana buried her head in Thomas' shoulder and he held her tightly, very tightly.

*

Sam and Karen were sitting in the lounge reading the Sydney Herald. There were three articles about Pete Owen and Sam and several pictures. The article on page two said that Pete had been charged with illegal distribution of toxic substances, fraud, tax evasion and quite a few other crimes. Sam's charges, the report said, were restricted to fraud and tax evasion. There was a picture of Pete getting into a police car with a couple of policeman. He was under house arrest. At least Sam had been let out on bail with no restrictions. Sam rubbed his eyes and went to get himself a glass of water. He needed something stronger but he didn't dare touch any alcohol, not at the moment. Karen followed him into the kitchen.

"Why don't you go and have a rest. You look really

tired, Sam. I'm sure it would do you good."

"Yes, I think I will," he said with a sigh. "I'm not sure I can sleep, though. I'm afraid my mind is in a whirl and it may be better to keep myself occupied rather than toss and turn in bed."

"I'll run you a bath and make you some verbena. That should help," she said,

"OK, I'll give it a try," he replied with a smile. "Thanks, Karen. I know this is just as hard for you as it is for me. I really don't know…"

"Shhh, shhh," she interrupted, her finger in front of her lips. "Just don't think about it. It'll all die down in a few days and we can talk about it in detail tomorrow. You've got to get some rest." She went to the bathroom and ran a bath. Sam's mobile rang. He looked at the number and his heart sank. It was Tom Wyatt.

"Hi, Tom," he said trying to muster up enough courage to put on a brave face.

"Hi, Sam. Look, I'm not going to beat around the bush. I guess you've got enough on your plate without worrying about our deal. It's off, Sam. No doubt you've seen the Sydney Herald? I really can't afford the connection. I'm sorry, Sam."

There was an awkward silence. Sam didn't know what to say.

"Let's have lunch at the club when all this has blown over," Tom said.

"Yes, let's do that," Sam said, knowing full well that Tom Wyatt wouldn't want to be seen again in his company.

"Give my best to Karen," Tom said.

"And to Nancy," Sam said and then the line went dead. It never rained but it poured.

"Who was that," Karen asked coming back into the lounge.

"No-one," he lied.

"I thought I heard your phone ring."

"Yes. It was a wrong number. I'll go and get in that bath while it's hot," he said and went to the bedroom to get undressed.

*

Thomas gradually moved Svetlana's head back and stroked her cheek gently. He held her hand and made her sit at the table. He got a bottle of Riesling out of the fridge and poured out two glasses. They sat at the table in silence for a minute. Then Thomas raised his glass and said "Nothing better to reset your electronics." He had a broad smile on his face that said "don't worry". She tried to smile back but she was too shocked and it showed. "Zum Wohl," he said, "Cheers" and she lifted her glass and took a sip. She looked at the wine and took another sip. She felt the wine tantalize her taste buds. After another couple of minutes she felt her mind slow down a little and her muscles started to relax. Thomas was right. She was beginning to feel life come back into her veins.

"I must ring Olesya," she said. "I must tell her what has happened, warn her in case she gets a visit like we did."

"Yes, but first we must ring Inspector Baer and let him listen to the conversation which I recorded."

"You recorded it!" Svetlana said in total disbelief.

"Yes. I hope you think it's alright for him to hear the whole recording."

"Let's play it back first so I can check. I'm not sure about his comments on the wine. He meant Chateau Malvaux."

"I think we have to at least let him hear the first bit and the threat at the end. I'll delete the comments about Chateau Malvaux."

Thomas played the conversation back and Svetlana said, "There, that bit. He checked the second hand of his watch until she said "Up to there." He rewound and found the bit again. He re-ran the recording for twenty-five seconds deleting what had been said. Then he went back to the beginning and played the tape again.

"Yes, the rest is fine," she said.

"Good. Then I'll ring Inspector Baer right away." Thomas took the landline handset and rang the number on the visiting card. Max Baer was at his desk and picked the phone up after just one ring.

"This is Thomas Becker, Inspector Baer. We've just had a rather frightening experience, a visit from the deceased's brother and what looked like two of his bodyguards to use a polite term."

"Is everything OK?" he asked, genuinely concerned for their safety.

"Yes. The boys aren't home from school yet and Svetlana is fairly shaken up but she'll be alright. I managed to record most of the conversation in Russian. I thought it might interest you."

"Wow, how right you are," he replied, excited at the prospect. "How the hell did you manage to record it."

"Well, I saw the car drive into the yard. No-one around here would drive a car like that unless they wanted to attract attention to their bank account or business methods." Inspector Baer smiled. This man really did have his head screwed on properly. "So I turned my phone on record and put it in my jacket pocket. The quality isn't great and I had a couple of problems in the middle, but Svetlana says it's understandable. Do you want to hear it?"

"I sure do. Do you mind if I record it?"

"Be my guest," Thomas said. "Here we go…"

Max pressed the play button on his phone and listened to the recording.

"Not very pleasant," he said when the recording was finished.

"How does he know all these details," Thomas asked. "He knew where we live, he knew that Svetlana had known Armen for quite a long time. He knew she had a flat in Moscow and…"

Max waited but Thomas had obviously decided not to continue with the rest of his sentence.

"In the world of organized crime, Mr. Becker, like in any business, information is the most precious asset you can have. It is sometimes quite unbelievable what sources these people have. However, the importance of information also means that disinformation can play an equally important role. But we must put your safety and the safety of your family first. Would it be OK with you if I sent a detective to your house this afternoon? He'll discuss a few different means of communication that should give you quick access to help if necessary and inspect your house to check your security and take appropriate measures if necessary."

"That would be quite a relief, Inspector. I don't want to worry our boys so I'll tell them that I've asked the police to check the house for our insurance company, if you don't mind."

"That's fine with me. I'll make sure the detective acts accordingly."

"Thank you. Svetlana is going to ring her sister as she is very concerned about her receiving a similar visit."

"Fine," he said. "Otherwise I think it best we keep this little episode to ourselves."

"Indeed," Thomas said. "Thank you for your help."

Thomas put the phone back on to its charging station and explained to Svetlana that a detective would be round after lunch but he would pretend that he was checking the security of the house for their insurance company. Svetlana nodded.

"I'll finish off making lunch," she said putting on her apron. "No doubt the boys will be starving when they get home."

Thomas kissed her. "I'll just go and lock the cellar and offices and then go and pick the boys up at the bus stop. Come on, Blackie. Let's go for a short walk."

He looked at Svetlana and smiled: "Not exactly your

classic guard dog but at least he barks at strangers!"

Svetlana smiled and continued stirring the soup on the stove.

*

Inspector Antipov was sitting at his desk when Max Baer rang him from Germany.

"How are things with you, Volodya," Max asked.

"Fine. And at your end?"

"It's a long story. I thought I'd tell you about it when I meet your for dinner. Could you give me a ring just before you get to the restaurant?"

Of course they weren't going to meet for dinner but Volodya realized that Max didn't want to talk through the official channels."

"Sure, I'll give you a buzz on your mobile just before I get there."

"OK, see you later," he said and put the phone down.

It was just before five in the afternoon in Wiesbaden when Max Baer's mobile phone rang. He told the caller he would ring him back in ten minutes. He got up, put his jacket on and walked out of the office, down the stairs and out into the fresh air. He walked down the street and turned left. It had been a sunny day and quite warm for early April. It took him seven minutes to reach the "Bauern Café". He went inside, ordered an Americano and rang the number in his phone from the last call. Volodya Antipov answered straight away.

"Hi, Volodya, thanks for ringing me. I need this conversation off the record."

"OK," he said. "What can I do for you?"

"Thomas Becker and his fiancé Svetlana Shnaider have just had a visit from the deceased's brother, Boris. A couple of heavies were with him. The conversation, or most of it, was recorded. The information given in that conversation means that the person speaking has access to FSB files."

"I see."

"He suspects the couple of poisoning his brother with strychnine. He knows about the smuggling affair but not that we both know about the imposter."

"OK. I'm seeing the imposter tomorrow. After that I'll file a report and see what happens."

"Thanks, Volodya. We'll see how quickly the brother gets on a plane for Moscow and hopefully before the couple have an accident of some sort."

"You can ring this number at five your time and if necessary I'll ring you back."

Max finished off his coffee and walked back to the office. He still had quite a lot of work to do.

*

Sam lay in the bath soaking in the warm water. Karen had added some herbal bath crystals to relax him. But his mind was racing. Thoughts were coming in and out of his brain like trains speeding through underground tunnels, pushing the air in front of them and sucking it back as they exited. He was ruined. He would have to sell Billy Jo, his yacht. He was so proud of his Azimut 62 but it would have to go. And he'd have to mortgage their apartment have enough money to replenish the herd of horses which he needed to increase his production of anti-venom. When the gods want to punish you, they sure know how, he thought. And even if his jail sentence was suspended, he wouldn't be allowed to run his own business. He'd have to hire someone and become a consultant to his own firm. And what would his employees say. Would they ever want to trust him again? Would they carry on working for him? It was all such a mess. And his friends, or so-called friends, how would they all react? Money attracted money and they would all know that he was a criminal, had lost his firm and probably most of his fortune. They would leave the nest like wasps in autumn. They'd drop him like a hot potato. That would be the worst bit for Karen. She would be ostracised. She'd be better off without him. And Laura? She wold never be able to look up to him again. She had always been proud of her father and he was so proud of her. But now there was nothing left to be proud of. The pain was almost too much to bear.

22

It was just before eleven in Moscow when Inspector Antipov arrived at the elegant sports shop. It was more than a shop. It was almost like a showroom, a trade fair for the rich. There was the most modern equipment for just about every kind of sport in the eight hundred square meters of steel and glass with marble tiles on the floor. There were mirrors everywhere. For these people sports were a question of how you looked and what equipment and sportswear you had, not how good you were at the sport. He went to the reception desk and showed a pretty young lady his ID. She was tall and slim. He wondered how long she needed in the morning to groom her hair and fix her make-up. Hours, probably. She picked up the phone and said "I will."

"Mr. Ivanov will see you now," she said and slipped off the high stool behind the desk. "Please follow me." She walked ahead of him through the show-room. She walked like a model in high heels. His sister had practised walking in those kind of shoes for hours. She said her feet hurt but she had to wear them for the job she was applying for. Unbelievable. To think that only twenty five years ago women were the mainstay of the working world, the head of the family, the backbone of society. And now here they were, reduced to a state which resembled a model in a shop window. It wasn't who you were, what you knew, what you did but what you looked like, how you walked. Was this what they had all wanted when Gorbachev came to power? What happened? How did it all go so wrong?

The young lady walked up the stairs with Inspector Antipov behind her. At the top of the stairs he could see Andrey Ivanov or was it Nikolay Kiryakov? The likeness was remarkable.

Andrey held out his hand in greeting.

"Good morning, Inspector. Thank you Larissa. Please follow me, Inspector."

Andrey Ivanov's office was like a picture out of Time Magazine, an office that had been designed for the rich, elegant and successful top managers of the world. Inspector Antipov waited until Andrey Ivanov offered him a seat at the glass table. Not a spot of dust to be seen. Not one fingerprint. Andrey sat opposite him and sat still in a chair waiting for the Inspector to start.

"Mr. Ivanov, I understand that you were in Australia recently."

"Indeed. Why do you ask?"

"Could you give me the exact dates, locations and the nature of your business? Or was it pleasure?"

"I'll ask my assistant to give you the dates and locations. I stayed mainly in Sydney. It was early February. I was officially on business but, of course, anyone who likes sport in that part of the world in late summer is going to swim, surf, go biking and enjoy himself," Andrey said with a smile that was affable but somehow cool, distant.

Antipov continued.

"And where did your journey take you after Sydney?"

"I flew to Frankfurt in Germany to attend a trade fair on sports. My assistant can no doubt give you my hotel and taxi bills, the ticket to the trade fair and so on if you wish."

Everything was perfect. He had an answer to everything.

"Did you meet up with anyone in Sydney or Frankfurt?"

"No. In Sydney I met a few sports enthusiasts. In Frankfurt a few suppliers who had stands at the fair."

"I understand you met a man called Peter Owen in Sydney."

"Who?"

"Peter Owen. He owns a company called Long Life which makes homeopathic medicines. You talked about Queensland, nux vomica and strychnine."

"Goodness, I can't remember a man called Owen. Or a discussion around his company."

"What about Frankfurt? I believe you met a jeweller called Norbert Mayer."

"Mayer, Norbert Mayer? No, it doesn't ring a bell. Why do you think I met this man and where?

Inspector Antipov didn't answer.

"In that case I have already taken up too much of your time. Just one more question. Have you ever met a man called Nikolay Kiryakov?"

He was sure that the man flinched. Only a little but his answer was just a second too late.

"Kiryakov? No, I don't think so. Is he a sportsman?"

"No, an ex FSB agent."

"Sorry, it doesn't ring any bells," Andrey Ivanov said. Inspector Antipov got up to go.

"Thank you for your time."

"My pleasure," he said. "I'll accompany you downstairs."

They walked in silence down the stairs and to the large glass doors at the front of the shop.

"Goodbye, Inspector."

"Goodbye," Antipov replied. Volodya walked out the shop his heart beating furiously. It was him. He is Kiryakov.

Andrey turned on his heels, smiled at Larissa who was perched on the high stool behind the reception desk and walked back through the shop and up the stairs. He went into his office and sat behind his desk and looked out the window. Damn, he thought. This ignorant Inspector knows who I am. He knows.

*

Karen had been watching a cookery programme on television while her husband was in the bath. She looked at her watch. Maybe he was fast asleep in bed. It was an hour since she ran the bath for him. She walked into the bedroom. Sam wasn't in bed. The bed was still made. She went to the bathroom. She tried to open the door but it was locked from inside. She called out but there was no answer. She grabbed the phone next to the bed and rang the concierge. He was on the ground floor but was up on the thirteenth within minutes.

"Thank you for coming up so quickly," Karen said. "My husband is in the bathroom and he's been in the bath for an hour. I went to check if everything is OK but the door is locked."

The concierge produced a bunch of keys. It took him a few minutes to find the right one but then he turned the key and the door opened. He walked in with Karen. Sam was lying lifeless in the bath. The water was red with blood. His wrists were slit and a razor lay on the tiles. Karen screamed. The concierge pulled her back from the bath but she wriggled free, fell to her knees in front of the bath and pulled her husband's head out of the water. The concierge went back into the bedroom and called the police and an ambulance. Sam MacPherson was most definitely dead.

*

In Moscow Inspector Antipov finished off his report. He explained his firm belief that the shop owner, Andrey Ivanov, had been an accomplice in the plot to murder Armen Makaryan. He had spoken to Pete Owen in a bar in Sydney and found out the name of the dealer in Frankfurt who was receiving Pete's strychnine. He had met Norbert Mayer and had claimed to be Thomas Becker. He had bought strychnine and given it to Hubert Walter, the head of logistics at Global Logistics, in a brown envelope along with a considerable bribe. Hubert Walter had passed the envelope to the warehouse manager who in turn passed it on to the driver of one of the trucks carrying Thomas Becker's wine to Moscow. The strychnine had been found by the customs in Lithuania and the trail led back to Frankfurt. Antipov clearly reported that this was a dead end and a trail meant to distract from the true identity of the person or people who had murdered Armen Makaryan. He sent off his report and emailed a copy to Inspector Max Baer and looked out of the window. Let's see when the hounds get wind and start to run, he thought.

*

On Friday Boris awoke quite early in the morning. He checked his messages. Aram had phoned a couple of times. He rang him back.

"It wasn't the German, and not the Russian woman either," Aram said without any form of introduction. "They were set up by an ex FSB man who is posing in Moscow as a sports shop owner called Andrey Ivanov. I don't know if he was directly involved or only set up a false trail."

"Then find out and find out who he's working for," Boris said and put the phone down.

Boris got up and showered. He called Davit and got him to order breakfast in his room and get them on a midday flight to Moscow. There was no reason any more to stay in Frankfurt. He needed to get back to Moscow. At eleven thirty they were on an Aeroflot flight to Moscow. Davit had arranged for their driver to meet them at Sheremetyevo and bring their coats to the arrivals area. It was Friday 8th April and the temperature was barely above zero. The air was humid but at least it wasn't raining or snowing. Davit walked out of the arrivals hall with Boris behind him. He could see the driver over at the ticket desk with their coats. Davit walked towards him. Erik was carrying their holdalls. Davit took his boss' coat and helped him into it. He gave him his hat, gloves and scarf. Davit took his coat and the driver took the holdalls from Erik and gave him his coat. They moved swiftly to the exit and walked over the road to the VIP parking spots. Davit longed for the sun in Gozo but duty called. They needed to be back in Moscow and his boss was angry. He hadn't said much since he had spoken to Aram but Davit knew. There was something going on and his boss was furious.

*

Max Baer rang Inspector Antipov on Friday at five in the afternoon German time on his mobile phone. Volodya answered after the first ring.

"The deceased's brother was booked on the Aeroflot flight which landed in Sheremetyevo at five your time this afternoon," Max said.

"The border police called me as soon as he arrived. It would appear that the news of my report was relayed pretty quickly," Volodya said. "I need to do some more digging in his affairs and it'll take me a few days. The man is a professional and his tracks will be hard to follow. I just hope he makes a mistake in the next week or has made one in the past couple of months."

"Good luck. It looks as if I can file my final report and pass the jeweller's file on to my colleagues who look after narcotics and toxic substances," Max mused.

"I'll let you know as soon as we have some results here."

"Thanks, Volodya. It was a pleasure to work with you."

"The same here," the Russian special agent said and pressed the disconnect button.

*

At around seven o'clock Andrey Ivanov left the sports shop and the all-night security man locked the door behind him. His car was just a few meters from the door. He heard a car and turned round to the right and then he heard one coming from the left. The two Mercedes C Class models had the typical blue stripes of the new Politsia who had taken over from the Militsia in March. He automatically put his hands up to show that he wasn't carrying a weapon. Two policemen got out of one car and asked him politely to get into the car. Andrey did so and asked where they were going. The policemen didn't answer but just drove. Then he felt a needle in the muscle of his right arm and he lost consciousness.

The fake police car pulled up at a Moscow warehouse on the banks of the Moskva River. The warehouse hadn't been used for a long time and the whole area belonged to a transport company that now operated from a modern warehouse near the airport. There was no one around. There were no lights and only the sound of distant traffic and trains on the other side of the river. The two policemen held Andrey Ivanov between them and dragged him into the warehouse. He was chained to a winch with handcuffs on his wrists and ankles. It would take a few hours for him to come round. One of the policemen opened one of the large wooden doors of the warehouse and the other drove the car under cover. They took off their uniforms and put them in an old steel barrel, poured some petrol over them and set them alight. They stripped the blue stripes off the car, the large initials DPS from the bonnet and the police insignia and the flag of the Russian Federation on the sides. The car was now just a white Mercedes like any other on the streets of Moscow. They jumped in the car leaving three men to deal with their prisoner. They had been instructed to bring him here. It wasn't their job to make him talk.

Andrey had been trained to withstand torture and pain. They knew that hurting him wasn't going to bring the results they wanted and they wanted them quickly. They had injected him with a truth serum. They hadn't used sodium thiopental. He would certainly have been trained to resist a simple concentration killer like that. They had much more effective truth serums which were only known to a few people within the FSB network. It took several hours before Andrey started to enter the twilight zone between consciousness and unconsciousness, the zone that made it difficult for a person to lie. At last he answered a simple question and they knew it was the truth. His name was Nikolay Kiryakov. He had worked for the FSB. It took another sixty minutes before they had the answers to the questions they had been given. The tall man in the middle who had been observing everything and writing down notes rang his boss. He relayed all the information and waited to be called back. Then he was given further instructions.

It was in the early hours of the morning when the body was found, male, between thirty and fifty, difficult to tell his exact age as he had fallen from the roof of a tall building and his face was a real mess. The ambulance took the body to the mortuary. The pathologist sighed. It was Saturday morning and Friday night had produced its usual list of deaths. He looked at the body and sighed again. He was due to leave work at eight. He'd sleep for a couple of hours and in the afternoon he wanted to take his grandchildren to the park. You needed to see the blue sky and watch the white clouds pass when you'd spent a busy night examining lifeless bodies to determine the cause of death. He looked at the body. His assistant was cutting off the man's clothes. The pathologist noted down that his clothes were smart and expensive, particularly the leather jacket. He was wearing Italian leather shoes. The assistant noted the size of each item of clothing and a short description before putting it in the plastic bag. He put the gold chain around his neck and Rolex watch into a separate bag. There was no wedding ring and his wedding finger didn't carry the tell-tale mark of a ring. His hands were manicured and soft, not a physical labourer. They didn't show any signs of age so probably around thirty to forty. His body was physically strong and trained. The pathologist examined the naked body and made notes: no tattoos, not circumcised, bruises on his chest, ankles and wrists. He examined the marks on his wrists more closely. They were the same as the marks on his ankles. The man's hands and feet had been tied with something stiff, maybe chains or handcuffs. He checked the report of the policemen who found the body in front of a ten-storey building. There was no mention of his limbs being tied, chained or handcuffed. Another murder, he thought, not an accidental death. He took blood samples and sent them to the lab. No doubt they would prove that the victim was pumped full of alcohol and supposedly fell accidentally to his death. He had seen many similar murders over the last twenty years and they were usually gang murders, the so-called mafia, organised crime. In the nineties the ruthless killers would take their naked victim to the cemetery, his hands and feet tied with wire, pour petrol over him and burn him alive. Yeltsin had once said that the methods of the Russian mafia were so brutal that the Sicilians would soon be flocking to Russia to study them. It was during the Yeltsin era that the so-called oligarchs had become rich overnight. During the Putin era their methods had become more subtle. Some of them even fell out of favour with the Kremlin, like Boris Berzovsky who moved to London in 2007 and preferred to live in exile. There were so many Russian oligarchs living in London now that some people called London Moscow on the Thames or Londongrad. They had bought fine houses in the wealthy parts of the city and in the surrounding countryside. But many of them also fell victim to their own cruel methods. The pathologist looked at the body again. Yes, it was definitely a new trend. No live burnings, no hail of bullets but a long drop from a high building. He would no doubt see more of these deaths in the months to come before he was able to retire at last and enjoy the more pleasant side of life. The man had no wallet, no identification on him. He would x-ray his jaws and see if his teeth revealed any more information on his possible identity. His fillings were gold, his teeth in very good shape. The deceased obviously had money. His assistant had filled in all the rest – height, weight, scars. There were a few unusual scars on this body, scars that he had mainly seen in war zones while he was serving in the army. He looked down at the body. A man of many secrets no doubt, he mused. Those who live by violence usually die by violence. After an hour the victim was taken to the cool room, labelled and put in a steel drawer. It was just another body to put on Russia's annual list of twenty five thousand murder victims.

23

On Saturday evening Abel Plemyannikov was giving a small celebration party for the rich and successful at Nostalgie. The papers were full of his photograph. He had been called a king of the new era. His financial and political power was second to none in Moscow and he revelled in the attention and fame. The papers were congratulating him on his appointment to the board of RusAeroSpace in Khimki. After the tragic death of Armen Makaryan, a close friend of Abel Plemyannikov, this mighty company had decided to appoint another oligarch to their ranks, another member of the Conseil. They needed the power and connections of such men. It was yet another feather in his cap and extended his influence into a world of high-technology. He owned several companies. He had made a fortune in the nineties selling oil and gas. Unlike some of his friends, he hadn't invested in the banking sector and hadn't lost his fortune in 1998 when the banks in Russia failed. No, he had been wise and stashed away his millions in foreign bank accounts like most of the rich Russians who survived the bank crisis. They were not interested in building Russia, in using their millions to help their homeland move from a communist era to a market-based economy. No. They were only intent on growing and keeping their own fortunes. Nevertheless they were important allies for more conservative businessmen and politicians with immense networks throughout the eighty regions of Russia, the biggest country in the world. They rubbed shoulders with some very influential people. Abel was telling the group how he was going to fly in a private jet to Warsaw the next day. He didn't own his own jet. He didn't particularly like flying. When he needed to fly he hired a small jet and used a pilot who was on his payroll. The following day would be the first anniversary of the tragic plane crash in Smolensk which cost the lives of ninety six people including the President of Poland, Lech Keczynski, and his wife. Several army officials and politicians were on board the plane including a very good friend of Abel. He had been invited by his friend's family to attend a memorial service in Warsaw, one of the many ceremonies to be held that day, in a divided Poland. In Warsaw's military cathedral the new President, Branislav Komorowski and Poland's Prime Minister, Donald Tusk, were to light candles in memory of those killed in the crash. Many were boycotting the official ceremonies including his friend's family. He would be leaving quite early on Sunday morning to be in Warsaw in good time for a short memorial service at his friend's grave. Then they would all be having lunch together. He was one of several businessmen and politicians who would be attending and the list of VIPs made the journey definitely worthwhile. Around ten in the evening Abel departed the restaurant. He needed a good night's rest before he left for Warsaw.

He shook everyone's hand and put on his coat. His driver was waiting for him near the door and accompanied him to his car which he had parked just outside the entrance to the restaurant. His driver opened the rear door of the car and closed the door. Then he got into the car and drove off quickly. There were security guards posted outside the restaurant and at the corner of the street but you could never be too careful.

"Drive me home as quickly as you can, Lev," he said.

Lev put his foot down and they sped through the streets of Moscow. It was a little bit risky. With the new police reforms, policemen earning thirty per cent more money and anti-corruption an important new topic, Lev couldn't be sure that the car wouldn't be stopped. He kept his eyes peeled for police patrol cars and knew where to slow down when he approached the fixed traffic police posts along the road. They reached Abel's house in thirty five minutes. Abel was dosing in the back. Lev drove through the gates and into the underground garage. He opened the rear door of the car and accompanied his boss up to the first floor of the mansion. Abel said goodnight and walked up the magnificent staircase to his bedroom. He was indeed tired and tomorrow would be an important day.

*

Karen was going through the arrangements for the funeral for the last time with the funeral director. It had only been three days since Sam had committed suicide. Sam had always said he wanted to be cremated and his ashes scattered at sea or buried in the bushland cemetery in Frenchs Forest. She was grateful to Tom for using his influence to have a slot created on Wednesday morning at the crematorium and for suggesting an undertaker who was a personal friend to make all the arrangements. He wouldn't be able to attend the service himself. He was conveniently out of the country in New Zealand that Wednesday. Quite a few people had prior commitments, or so they said. It was probably better that way. It would be more of a small family affair, probably easier for her and Laura to cope with their grief and for her to get used to going it alone without the support of most of her friends who would no longer seek her company. Pete and Jean Owen would be attending with their daughter Regan. Pete would have to be escorted but he had received permission to attend. He was quite devastated. There would probably only be about fifty guests and they would have a light lunch at the Yacht Club afterwards. They had kindly given her a separate room and entrance to keep away any prying eyes. She had organised a small wreath for the coffin but asked everyone else to make a donation to a lifeboat charity. Sam would have liked that, she thought. She had put everything else out of her mind until later in the week. She would have to make an appointment to have his will opened, talk to the bank and see the tax accountant. She wasn't even sure she could keep the apartment. But all that could wait. She had to cope first with her grief and her loneliness. Jean had been a great support which is more than she could say for most of her friends.

They had called to give their sincere condolences but when Karen asked if they had time for coffee next week, they all said their diaries were full or they were off for a rest or some other excuse. The article in the Sydney Herald had at least not been too scathing. She put her head in her hands and sobbed. It was all just too much to bear at the moment. Laura came over and hugged her mother. She had got the first plane from New York on Friday morning but it had taken her thirty hours to get home with the time difference. She had arrived on Sunday at eight in the morning. Karen had met her at the airport and they had come straight back to the apartment. Both were still in shock, their minds not wanting to believe that Sam was now gone forever. Their relationship was close and Laura's presence was a great comfort to her mother. Karen was so pleased she was there. They now just had to get through the next few days.

"I'll get you a cup of coffee," Laura said and went into the kitchen. Karen smiled at her. When she came back with a cup of steaming coffee in her hand, her mother was on the deck looking out to sea.

"Your father loved this view. He was a real sailor at heart." They walked back into the lounge.

"OK," Karen said. "Let's finish off the seating arrangements and then make some lunch."

*

Inspector Antipov cursed the Monday morning traffic in Moscow. It was still quite early for rush hour but the traffic on the Garden Ring was horrendous. He was tempted to use his blue light but resisted. He turned off at the next exit and went through the back roads to the office. It would take him longer but at least he was moving and didn't feel that he was standing still. It was seven in the morning and the news came on. A small report on the memorial services in Poland and Russia for the victims of the Smolensk air crash just a year ago and then the breaking news. A speaker for the Plemyannikov family had just confirmed that Abel Plemyannikov had been killed as his plane crashed shortly after take-off. It appears there had been an explosion and the two crew members and two passengers had been killed. Mr. Plemyannikov was on his way to Warsaw to take part in a private memorial service on the first anniversary of the Smolensk tragedy. And then the newsman reported that an unidentified body had been fished out of the Moskva River in the early hours of the morning, a man, thirty to forty years old, no details. Volodya parked his car in the underground car park and made his way as quickly as possible to his office. This was going to be a busy day. Abel Plemyannikov was on the top of his list and very much a part of the investigation into the death of Armen Makaryan. He took out his mobile phone and rang a number. The contact name "Akaky Akakyevich" came up on his display. The name was the main figure in a classic story by Nikolai Gogol about an impoverished clerk in St. Petersburg in 1842. The man had been described as a quiet, self-effacing man, a little like the man on the phone.

"I need to see you this evening if possible," Volodya

said.

"I'll be in the city on Wednesday morning. We could meet at the usual place to go shopping."

This meant they would be meeting at GUM, the old State Department Store which was now a shopping mall. There was a coffee shop where they met.

"Fine. I'll be there at ten." Volodya put the phone down. You never knew who may be listening.

Volodya checked his electronic in-box. There was a report on the plane crash that killed Abel Plemyannikov. The plane crashed in Russia which made the investigation a little easier. Most of the wreckage had been collated and was being transferred to the laboratory at RusAeroSpace. Ironic that this powerful oligarch had just been appointed to the RusAeroSpace board and now the same company was to examine the debris of the mangled plane he died in. It would take some weeks before any conclusive evidence would be released. Maybe a little sooner if they found evidence of explosives. Volodya presumed it wasn't an accident but in this particular case he would have to be patient until he had all the facts. And then there was a new file from the murder squad on the body which was fished out of the Moskva River on Sunday morning. It was murder but not just a common murder. It had been passed on to Inspector Vladimir Antipov because he was an expert in organised crimes and their victims. The man had a silk scarf around his neck which suggested that he had committed suicide and then been thrown into the river. However, the marks on his neck were horizontal which suggested he had been strangled. The marks on a person's neck if they had died by hanging were never horizontal but were angled steeply upwards at the back of the head. His fingerprints had been taken and there was a ninety per cent match with a man who had been arrested a couple of years ago on a charge of suspected murder. His name was Ivan Greshnev, born in Omsk on the twenty fifth of February 1975. He wore smart clothes, his body was well trained and his hands indicated that he hadn't done any physical work for some time. There wasn't enough evidence to uphold a charge of murder. The Inspector who had led the investigation was convinced that he wasn't just a bodyguard as he described himself but also a professional killer. Nevertheless, he had to let the man go and ever since Mr. Ivan Greshnev had been under observation. There were a list of his comings and goings and then a list of his employers. Volodya sat up with a start. There it was - the connection he was looking for. The man had worked for Abel Plemyannikov for two years as a driver and attended his training camp before he went into employment as a trained bodyguard working for Mr. Armen Makaryan. Vanya hadn't mentioned that when he interviewed him the day the body was found. And there was no mention of it on his last record. This was no coincidence. He was about to get up when another file arrived in his in-box. It had taken some time to identify the victim because the fingerprint check turned out to be classified. The clerk in charge of forwarding the file had waited until the classified information had been released. The name of the victim was Andrey Ivanov, an ex FSB agent under the name of Nikoly Kiryakov. Antipov whistled. All three on the same weekend. Too many coincidences. He looked out the window and then went to grab himself a coffee. This was going to be a busy day.

*

It was late Tuesday afternoon when Inspector Max Baer rang Thomas Becker and Svetlana Shnaider.

"What can I do for you, Inspector," Thomas replied.

"I just wanted to inform you that the person suspected of killing Armen Makaryan, the person the FSB suspects ordered him to be killed and an accomplice who posed as you and had the cyanide sent to Russia all died over the weekend, one in a plane crash and the other two evidently murdered."

Thomas was speechless. He felt as if his life was a film he was looking at and no longer something he could influence.

"Don't worry, Mr. Becker. This means that someone with a lot of power, money and information has taken revenge. It's quite common in Russia. It also means that Mr. Boris Makaryan no doubt knows that you had nothing to do with the death of his brother and probably knows who did."

"So this bad news is actually good news for us, is that what you mean?"

"Indeed. And the Russians are probably relieved that they don't have to take an oligarch to court and risk the lives of witnesses and investigators."

"I see. So someone has actually done the police a favour?"

"Officially, of course, I wouldn't be able to condone murder by a lynch mob as a solution to a police investigation but I do take your point," he said diplomatically.

Thomas smiled. "Then Inspector I think you should come over for lunch on Saturday. I remember that you like pelmeni. I'm sure that Svetlana will be delighted to make them for you. We'll open a bottle of one of my best Rieslings and have a private celebration. You'll have to put up with our boys and my brother," he added.

"It would be a pleasure. I look forward to it. And Mr. Becker, there won't be any further investigation of your affairs. The district attorney is satisfied that there are no grounds to suspect that the wine the deceased had drunk that evening really was laced with cyanide and that the wine originated in Germany."

Thomas sighed. Obviously their decision to stop smuggling Chateau Malvaux to Russia was the right one, in particular considering the untimely death of their client.

"I'm pleased to hear that. Then we'll be opening a bottle of our sparkling wine as well with a toast to a less turbulent future."

"Indeed," Max said. "I'll be with you just before noon." Thomas put the phone down and turned to Svetlana who was standing behind him. He repeated everything the inspector had said.

"What a relief," she said. "That's why Boris disappeared

so quickly. He must have been told who was responsible for his brother's death."

"I wonder who the man was who ordered the murder," Thomas said. "Probably the one who was killed in the plane crash."

"Thomas, it doesn't matter. What it means is that we won't be bothered any more, not by the German police, nor the Russians, be it police or mafia," Svetlana said with a huge sigh of relief. "We can start living a normal life again. I must ring Olesya and let her know."

"And I'll take Blackie for a walk before supper."

When Thomas Becker arrived back with Blackie, Svetlana was in the kitchen with the boys and Conrad. The table had been laid for supper. Svetlana went to greet him in the hall.

"It was Plemyannikov. Can you imagine it? Plemyannikov!"

"You've lost me. What was Plemyannikov and who is he?"

"He's one of the most famous oligarchs in Russia. He lives in Moscow and there's a rumour he has a training camp for professional killers. He was killed on the weekend in a plane crash according to Olesya."

"My goodness," Thomas said and looked at her in amazement. "I think the less we know about all this and the reasons for it the better."

"My dear Thomas, you're beginning to speak like a Russian," she said and laughed. She kissed him and went back into the kitchen.

*

It was a beautiful autumn morning in Sydney. The sun was shining and the heavens had held back their clouds and rain for another day. Karen sat in the crematorium with Laura by her side. Some distant cousins of Sam's had turned up for the cremation but otherwise his family was conspicuous for their absence. Pete arrived with Jean, Regan and two policemen wearing appropriate black suits. They were ushered into a seat in the third row. The funeral service was to start at ten and they only had fifteen minutes to take their seats and fifteen minutes to leave the chapel when the service was over. That was normal in a big city with a large population. Karen turned round. There were several rows full of people. Yes, probably about fifty or sixty people. She felt as if she had wept enough tears for the rest of eternity but when the music started, she couldn't hold back her tears any longer. Laura squeezed her hand. The coffin was at the front of the chapel with a wreath of white lilies on the top. The vicar walked in and went up to Karen. He took her hand in both of his and offered her some consoling words in a quiet voice. He then turned to Laura and talked to her in the same tone. The service was short. There was no eulogy. The vicar had agreed to say a few words. He talked about the burdens people had to bear. When those burdens were too heavy, he said, when someone was not able to overcome the hurdles on his stony path, then like Sam MacPherson they turned their back on life and chose to put their faith in God in the knowledge that God is great and forgives us our sins. He didn't talk about friends and family not being able to support Sam in these difficult times enough to make his life worth living. He omitted to mention the cruelness of newspapers and society who condemned him before he was found guilty. He kept it short and simple and Karen was grateful. The curtains closed around the coffin and as they sang "Eternal Father strong to save", the seaman's hymn, the coffin was transported automatically into the crematorium. After the hymn the vicar went over to Karen and Laura and escorted them out of the chapel. Sibelius's "Finlandia" accompanied them from the loudspeakers as they left by the front door. The congregation for the next funeral service was already gathering outside the back door. The vicar stood by her side in the glorious sunshine for five minutes until the first members of the congregation walked up to her and expressed their sympathy. She took a deep breath. This was going to be the hardest bit. The vicar waited for a short gap in the queue and expressed once again his sincere condolences and explained he had to leave to attend the sick bed of one of his congregation. Karen nodded and thanked him for his kind words. She turned to the next person. It was Pete, Jean and Regan Owen. Pete kissed her on both cheeks and had tears in his eyes as he said: "Karen, I'm so sorry, so very sorry for everything." Karen couldn't answer. There was a lump in her throat. She moved her head in a slight nod which expressed her feelings which had no words. Jean hugged her and they found a few moments of solace together in their embrace. There would be a time for talking but not now. Not right now.

*

Inspector Antipov had walked the short distance to Red Square. Spring was coming, the snow had melted but the daytime temperature was only just above freezing. Volodya wore a fur-lined raincoat against the cold and sleet. It was a typical April day in Moscow, cold and damp. He looked at the impressive nineteenth century façade which stretched along the east side of Red Square for more than two hundred meters. He had always liked the rounded windows and the symmetry of the building. It had a calming effect on him, almost peaceful. He walked into the building and was hit by a wall of warm air. He walked up to the upper trading rows, admiring the steel and glass roof which reminded him of the Victorian railway stations he had visited when he was on holiday once in London. He looked at his watch. It was a quarter to ten and he had deliberately left himself ten minutes to do a bit of window shopping and soak up the atmosphere of this busy shopping mall. Shortly before ten he wandered downstairs again. He was sure that he wasn't being followed. He walked into the Bosco Café on Red Square and a waiter came towards him.

"I booked a table for two. My name is Antipov," he said taking off his coat. The waiter took his coat and asked Mr. Antipov to follow him. The café was buzzing with customers' conversation. The walls seemed to throb. He liked the Italian flair in the café which was full of tourists in summer wanting to sit outside on the terrace and drink an Americano looking over Red Square. The waiter gave the coat to a concierge nearby who gave the waiter a wooden block with a number burnt on it. The green plants were a welcome contrast against the simple off-white walls. They walked through a couple of archways to a table near the back of the café.

"Your guest has already arrived," he said stretching his right arm out to indicate the table in the corner. Volodya walked to the table and his guest got up to shake his hand. The greeting was amicable but you could see the men weren't social friends. It looked more like a business meeting, but not quite that either. Volodya ordered an Americano and a piece of cake. His guest did the same.

"I hope you are well," Volodya said.

"Very well, thank you," the well-spoken gentleman said. "How is life treating you."

"Very well," he said, "in fact extremely well. At work one of my puzzles has just been resolved but I'm not sure I have understood why."

"Ah, yes, that's often the case," the voice across the table said and smiled. Their coffee and cake arrived. Both men took a sip of coffee and Volodya picked up his fork to eat a piece of cake, hoping his guest would continue talking which he did.

"You know, a friend of mine met a man on Friday night who actually held all the answers to one of my problems in his hand. He was quite talkative after a while. He had been in Australia and Germany and brought back some kind of extremely dangerous virus. When he came back he passed the virus on to a friend of his, a very rich man who unfortunately died from it over the weekend. The rich man gave it to a driver he knew, Vanya was his name, who then eventually infected his boss who also died. Vanya also died yesterday and the traveller apparently took his own life knowing that there was no cure for this virus. It has been a tragedy but now the virus has died with them all and for my friend it is a relief to see an end to this dreadful episode."

"I see. That is indeed tragic." Volodya had finished his cake. His guest was eating it slowly and looking at him.

"At least I will be able to file the puzzle which has been resolved and focus my attention on my next challenge." His guest looked at him with his dark, penetrating eyes which were sunk quite deeply into his skull beneath bushy black eyebrows. His skin was sallow, not sun-tanned, just naturally sallow. Volodya continued.

"I'm now part of the investigation into the plane crash that happened just outside Moscow. A private plane exploded just after take-off. The first question was whether the plane had a technical defect or was there an explosive device on board."

The man with the soft voice had finished his cake. He looked at his watch.

"Goodness," he said, "I must make a move. If I had to bet on the outcome of your investigations, I'd put my money on a technical defect," he said getting up smiling politely. "It was a pleasure to see you again, inspector. Our conversations are always helpful and interesting."

"The pleasure was all mine," Volodya said. The men shook hands. Volodya watched his guest walk towards a waiter. He gave him a little wooden block with a number on it and the waiter fetched his coat and hat. Aram turned to look at the inspector as he put his coat on. The inspector nodded and touched his forehead as if saluting. Aram nodded back, closing his eyes a little as he did so, and disappeared into the streets of Moscow.

Acknowledgements

My sincere thanks to John S for the cover design and preparing this book for publishing; to Thomas for his help with The Russian Boomerang website and all things technical. And last but not least to Werner for his patience, support and belief.

Jean Mills